MY
LOST
CUBA

MY

LOST

CUBA

— A NOVEL —

Celso Gonzalez-Falla

EAST
END
PRESS

BRIDGEHAMPTON • NEW YORK

MY LOST CUBA

Published by

EAST END PRESS

Bridgehampton, New York

Library of Congress Control Number: 2013945966

ISBN 978-0-9887673-2-4

Ebook ISBN 978-0-9887673-3-1

First Edition

10 9 8 7 6 5 4 3 2 1

Book design by Pauline Neuwirth, Neuwirth & Associates

Jacket Design by Oliver Munday

Manufactured in the United States of America

To my wife, Sondra,
who is responsible for this book,

To my mother, Isabelita, who taught me to love,

To my father, Celso, who showed me
how to love our land.

MORE THAN FIFTY years have passed since the events in this book occurred. This is a story about the Cuba I knew, the island I feel in my bones and in my heart. Some characters are people I knew, others were created by my imagination, crafted of bits and pieces of those who existed or should have existed. I lived through some of the experiences, others I wish I had. Some of the characters at the farm are real; their names may have been changed, but if I close my eyes I still see them, walking, riding, joking, and working. I loved the land. I still smell the cut grass in the pasture and the pungent odors coming from the stables. It was part of my life. My family worked to create an enterprise we shared, and now it is all gone, abandoned, and ruined.

I have not returned to Cuba, but I don't want to bore you with that. This is a long story. Sit down and enjoy it. Share my feelings, my memories, and my thoughts. One day, sooner than later, we may go and see our palm trees, the whiteness of our beaches, and smile at the jokes around a bar while we play a round of *Cubilete*. My children may visit the places where I grew up, where I loved, where I suffered. Cuba is there—waiting.

MY

LOST

CUBA

— I —

$\mathcal{B}ack$

DON MIGUEL WALKED on the paths of the garden early in the morning, wearing his red silk robe and favorite leather slippers. He had scarcely slept the night before, just turned over and over in bed. He was worried about everything and nothing. His mind was crowded with memories of people, images, thoughts, and anxieties. Just another night, as the ones he had had before and before that. He had turned around and stretched out his hand—and she was not next to him. At last he got up and decided to take a walk. No one else was awake in the big *bohío*. So many people lived, ate, and slept on the farm, but it did not matter. She was gone. Close to five years had passed, maybe six . . . who cares? Time did not matter. He could not bring her back, and he was alone without her. He heard the sounds of the *batey*, the windmill dumping the water from the well, and the voices of the *vaqueros*, bringing the cows to be milked. He did not want to talk to them—another day without her loomed ahead. He could return to his room and read a book, but he had read them all; he knew them all by heart.

He heard the crunching of gravel. Someone was walking behind him on the path. Who wants to bother me? He wondered querulously. I haven't bothered anyone.

"Don Miguel, how do you feel? Did you sleep well last night? Do you want me to bring you a cup of coffee?"

"No, thanks, Ricardo, don't bother. I'm a tired old man. Leave me alone for a while." He was trying not to sound curt, and he added, "Thanks for asking."

"I wanted to be sure."

"Thanks, I'm a little bit tired, that's all."

"I'll have Cuca bring you coffee. You'll feel better."

"Thanks, but not now."

Left alone, he toured the garden, looking at the roses and camellias she had planted, pulling weeds from flower bed after flower bed as tears came to his eyes.

THE DOORBELL TO his apartment rang, and he discovered a messenger with a telegram. Mike Rodriguez waited until he had closed the door to read it. His father's accountant had sent a short missive: "Your father needs you. Urgent. Come home. Call me. Pedro Lustre."

It was too late to call.

When he woke up the next morning, he called Mary, his best friend, and arranged to have her turn in his final paper of the semester. Then he called a travel agency and made reservations for Havana. The next step was to call Lustre at his father's office.

"Thank God you're coming," Lustre said.

"What's happened?"

"I don't like the way your father is acting and feeling. He's a different person."

"That's all?" Mike asked, slightly annoyed.

"No, that's not all. I was very worried. I hadn't heard from him, so I went to the farm."

"And—?"

"He raised hell, asking why I had made the trip. That I 'should take care of my own business, and not leave the office.'"

"That sounds like him."

"Yes, but I didn't like what I saw. He hadn't shaved in weeks. He spends most of the day in his red robe, walking around the garden, pulling weeds from the flower beds. He's not riding his horse. He's eating poorly."

"But what's the urgency?"

"Ricardo called me a few days after I left. Said that your father is getting more depressed, that he only talks about your mother and how he misses her. He hasn't been out of the *batey* in weeks. He doesn't even go to check the pastures!" He paused. "Your mother's anniversary is coming up."

"Yes, I know. In ten days it will have been six years."

"I thought that you should know how he's feeling. Ricardo is so worried about his health, and only you can bring him out of this depression."

"Do my sisters know?"

"No, I didn't want to tell them. Adelaida worries too much, and I don't have to tell you about your sister Lourdes."

"Are you sure that I have to make this trip? I have a lot of work here. I can still cancel my reservation."

"No, don't cancel. Trust me. He needs you."

Mike was still reluctant, but he gave in. "Well, I trust you. Thanks for worrying about my father. I'll call you after I see him."

"I'm having Fernando pick you up at the airport. Have a safe trip."

IT WAS LATE in the afternoon when Mike opened the door of his father's car and stepped out. Sweltering, damp air embraced him. His face was covered with the dust of the long, tedious trip across the island. He felt the weight of his woolen slacks and his blue oxford shirt, so wet with sweat they clung to his body. He stretched his back to ease the soreness from fourteen hours of travel. He took a deep breath and smelled the cut grass mixed with the pungent odor of the corrals and stables. The contours of the big house were softened by the setting sun that flooded the sky with pinks and reds, lurid against the deep green of the pastures. Fernando hoisted his bags out of the trunk.

Mike entered the house and proceeded to his father's room. He knocked on the door and waited. Not hearing a welcome, he slowly opened the door. His father was dozing, so he softly shut the door and left. In the back of the house, he opened the small iron gate leading to the formal garden that displayed a jumbled mixture of all the foreign influences on the island of Cuba. He sat down on a small bench—its stone was cold and damp to the touch—and eyed the gleaming pebbles on the path. How many times had he used one to hit a red-winged blackbird? How many times had he tried to hit a small lizard? He smiled. He felt like a bird that had flown from the North. He touched the left pocket of his shirt and pulled out a cigar, tested the degree of dryness of the wrapper, and then the dark outer leaf. He pulled out his grandfather Carlos' gold cigar cutter and cut the tip, then carefully lit it, and slowly inhaled the aroma. One big drag filled his mouth with blue smoke, and exhaling it, he watched it drift in the darkening sky. Before him were the rest of the buildings of the *batey*, the stables, the *bohíos* of the married employees, and the large warehouse where the unmarried men slept in rows of hammocks. All were painted in the farm colors of red and pure white. He heard the sound of the car being driven to the garage. Before long, the cigar had developed a delicate oval of ash. Mike took a last long puff and reentered the house.

The high living room ceiling had rough beams of mahogany that had been cut down by his grandfather from virgin forest to make way for the cane fields. A grand piano commanded a corner. The French doors on the opposite side of the living room opened into a large inner courtyard, filled with luxurious tropical plants. His father's room opened onto both that inner courtyard and to the outside of the house. Mike crossed the courtyard and knocked on the door again. His father still rested on the large bed with white sheets and big pillows. A white mosquito net blurred his face, and his strong body was partially covered by a white cotton sheet. An old German shepherd bitch slept under the bed and hearing Mike, lifted her head and started to growl, then recognizing him, she came out from under the bed and started to lick his hands. She was his father's favorite, and she followed him around like a dutiful Japanese wife, a few steps behind. Her name, Mitzi, was the first name of a movie star, and of an old family friend, both temperamental. His father, now almost awake, uttered irritably, "Why did you have to come?" and then coughed a deep tobacco cough.

"Lustre called. He was worried about you. I'm worried, too. When I arrived, you were dozing. I didn't want to wake you. Lustre told me that you're not feeling well, and I wanted to see you. Are you hungry? It's almost eight o'clock."

Mike stood close to his father's bed.

"I'm not hungry. Have Cuca make you something to eat. She should be in the kitchen. But before you go, tell me what's going on with you. I don't hear from you often."

"Of course you do. I write you all the time. I'm here now," Mike calmly answered.

"Bah, you only come to Cuba to party, and you seldom write to me. The only way I know you're still alive is when you cash checks that Lustre mails you."

"Father, please, that's not true. You know how much I love you. Lustre sent me a telegram, and I called him, and he insisted that I should come. I took the first plane. I'm worried about you."

"I'm fine, it's just a bad cough."

"That's not what he told me."

"You know I don't sleep well—I haven't since your mother died. Come closer, let me see you."

Mike moved closer to the bed and drew open the mosquito netting and extended his hand. His father clasped Mike's hands in his own, which were big and covered with sunspots. He coughed and motioned to a glass of water on the night table, topped by a saucer to keep out bugs. Mike gave him the water; he released Mike's hand and took a small sip.

"Pass me a candy." The honey-filled candies, wrapped in gold paper, filled a small bowl next to the glass. "They're good for me. The honey helps my cough. Dr. Paco says these are the best."

Mike tried to smile. Nothing had changed. He sank into his father's armchair, made of leather and mahogany—cattle and forest, tradition—and waited for his father to get out of bed.

FERNANDO HAD NOT liked the idea of driving all the way to Havana just to pick up Don Miguel's son. He had driven in a hot, muggy car for more than ten hours. Mike could have just taken the train or the bus. Fernando was tall, muscular, and had been working on the farm for many years. His skin was jet-black and when he smiled, which was often, the whiteness of his teeth contrasted with the color of his face.

Cuca had left food for him, and he sat at the dining table covered with a white-and-red checkered oilcloth, joining Ricardo for a simple and hearty meal of rice, red beans, beef jerky, fried plantains, and a dessert of rice pudding served with cinnamon and fresh milk from a big enamel jug. In the corner of the dining area, on a triangular wooden shelf, was a farm-made white farmer's cheese. The walls displayed five calendars, all showing blonde girls in bikinis advertising American-made products. An old RCA radio, powered by a car battery, blasted the news from Havana. Manuel, who took care of the farm's show string of cattle and horses, arrived and sat down at the table. Manuel was in his early forties, had a muscular build, more on the heavy side, and strong arms, and sported highly polished Texan boots. He wore Ray-Ban sunglasses inside the house and at night. He had strong opinions. All sat on red-painted *taburetes* covered with cowhides that bore the ubiquitous family cattle brand. Paulino wore a white Filipino coat over a pair of dark trousers. He did not wear socks, and his tennis shoes were worn out. He walked with a swagger as he was passing by to show that he was not another usual farm worker. Cuca brewed coffee in a charcoal-fired burner.

Manuel asked Fernando, "How's Mike?"

"He was asking constantly about Don Miguel. 'How is he? What's going on with him? How is he feeling?' I didn't tell him much. I didn't want to upset him."

"Do you know why he came?" Manuel asked.

"No, he said Lustre, the accountant, had called him. He was happy to see me. He asked about all of us. How we were doing. He tried to be nice, but he's worried about his father's health. The airport was full of soldiers and police, and he became very angry when the customs inspector stole a carton of his American cigarettes."

"He should have known. Why does he buy those when here we have the best tobacco here?" Manuel replied.

"The old man smokes them, too," Paulino said.

Cuca then asked, "Did you have time for lunch?"

"Yes, we stopped in Matanzas at Don Miguel's favorite restaurant. Mike insisted that I sit down with him, but I didn't want to. I was the only Negro in the restaurant. The old Spanish waiter wasn't happy when he saw me at the table."

"How was the service?" Paulino asked, curious about the waiter's reactions.

"It was slow," Fernando remarked with a grin. "After lunch, Mike took over the driving and drove fast. He started asking about the farm, if it had rained, the pastures, the show herd, and the horses."

Ricardo interrupted, "Mike should have never left—the old man isn't the same. He doesn't enjoy life anymore. He doesn't even go to the cattle and horse shows!"

"I have to take the animals by myself," Manuel said, shaking his head.

Paulino laughed, "You don't care if the old man goes or not. You like telling all the *guajiras*, 'These are *my* horses,' and then you invite them to see the silver tack and saddles in the saddle room. Hey, do I know you!"

Manuel smirked, "As if you never played games on them! You think they'll faint in your arms when you tell them that you're a doctor!"

Paulino, smiling, replied, "At least I went to the university."

Manuel said, "I am a graduate of the university of life." He got up, stretched, and reached for his big, dirty felt Texan cowboy hat. "I'm going to turn in. See you in the morning."

Everyone else soon left, except Paulino, who cleaned the table with a wet rag. He whistled an old tune:

> *Ausencia quiere decir olvido;*
>   Absence means forgetfulness;
> *Las aves quieren volver al nido.*
>   Birds want to return to their nest.

MIKE CAME IN a few minutes later and sat down to eat the meal that Cuca had prepared. He ate alone, since his father did not want to leave his room. After he finished, he walked around the *batey*, and lit a cigar that had the cattle brand of the farm on the ring. Mike walked slowly as he toured the manicured lawn, the rose garden, and the grove with coconut, mango, lime, orange, grapefruit, and avocado trees. He knew he couldn't express his frustration at what his father had said. He knew how to control himself; it had been part of his training. He was taught to measure everything—the way he spoke, drank, gambled, studied, and loved. As his father often reminded him, avoiding extremes—measure and prudence in all things—had made the family successful.

Ricardo saw him walking around and came to see him. "Hi, Mike, how was your trip?"

"Tiring. Say, I'm still worried about Father. What's going on, Ricardo?"

"You know I called Lustre. To be blunt, he's not the same. He doesn't laugh. He doesn't care. I wanted to take him to see Dr. Paco, but he won't leave the farm. Maybe with you here . . ."

"Thanks for calling, Lustre. I know how much you like to take care of him, but he seemed his old self with me tonight."

"That's a good sign. You know how much he loves you."

"Yes, I love him, too. Thanks, Ricardo. I really appreciate what you did."

"You know how I feel about the family."

"Yes, I do."

"Welcome back, Mike," Ricardo said as he left. "Let's see if he gets better."

Early the next morning, Paulino was making coffee in the kitchen. The water boiled in the beat-up enamel saucepan, and the coffee grounds rose to the surface. After he moved the pan to the side of the charcoal burner and let the coffee mixture rest for a few minutes, he poured it into a flannel funnel stained by previous infusions. He filled two small cups with the strong, bitter coffee.

He knocked at Don Miguel's door before he entered, put the cup on the small night table, and opened the windows. The sunlight filled the room, illuminating old photographs of family members at weddings, baptisms, on horseback, at black-tie parties at the Habana Yacht Club. In a few pictures, taken in the 1920s, the men wore English boots, ties, and Smith & Wesson .38 revolvers, and posed with lovely girls with short hair and shorter dresses. As Don Miguel stirred, Paulino said, "Good morning."

"Good morning, Paulino. We'll have breakfast in the dining room at seven."

"Yes, sir." He led Mitzi out of the room with her tail between her legs, cocking her head sideways up at him, ready to eat.

Mike's door was closed when Paulino knocked and opened it. Mike was already up, wearing an old Sulka silk robe, bought by his mother in Paris for his father when sugar prices were high and a bottle of champagne cost less than a dollar. The richness of its color and the sensuousness of its fabric contrasted with the masculine starkness of the room. The furniture was dark: a big mirror over the dresser, a massive mahogany rocking chair in the corner, and two night tables with brass lamps. An old Zenith Trans-Oceanic radio, its chrome gleaming against the black leather of its case, was placed in a bookcase filled with books in English and in Spanish, from the adventures of Tarzan to an illustrated Jules Verne story and bound volumes by Kant, Kafka, Papini, Maugham, and Marti. More family photos hung on the wall. One showed Mike at Varadero Beach with a goat, another with a big black rubber inner tube.

"Good morning, you look rested. I didn't want to bother you last night. I knew you had to be tired."

"Thanks, Paulino." His face changed as he signaled to Don Miguel's room. "Say, I'm still upset about Father. He looks well, but both Lustre and Ricardo are worried. What do you think?"

Paulino nodded in agreement. "He's not himself, but we can talk later. Remember, your father likes to have breakfast at seven in the dining room." Paulino placed Mike's coffee on the night table before turning to leave, whistling a tune from his repertoire of *décimas, sones, guarachas, boleros*—songs about birds, cages, and love, about hearts and men that depart, never to return.

Paulino considered his current job but a short detour in his life's journey. He was born in Cienfuegos, a southern city with a French park with elaborate lampposts and rococo cast-iron benches. The girls walked there in the afternoons, while the boys walked in the opposite direction so they could better enjoy the girls.

Paulino's father, Pablo, had immigrated to Cienfuegos from Asturias, Spain. As a young man he worked at a small *bodega* near the house where Dolores, Paulino's mother, worked as a maid and, later, as the cook. Pablo was first the delivery boy, and when he began to work behind the counter, Dolores stopped placing orders by phone and walked to the *bodega*. She told Luisa Abreu, her employer, that the *bodega's* phone was always busy and that she could choose the best products if she went there. Pablo liked the way she flirted with him, her eyes full of mischief every time she came to the *bodega* to order groceries. Dolores knew that the *Asturiano* liked her. The *bodega* was small, but it supplied the essentials for houses in the neighborhood: cans of condensed milk, rice from Siam, black and red beans from Mexico, Campbell's soup, and bars of soap with locks printed on the package—the brand that advertised on the radio novellas in the early afternoon. Dolores found reasons to make extra trips to the *bodega*, for the odd can of peanut oil, *petit pois*, or a slab of jerky.

Dolores loved to dance. She would have liked Pablo to take her to the dances at the Casino Español, but because she was half black and half Chinese, she was not welcome. She went to the other Saturday dances to drink beer, to dance, and to hear her favorite orchestra, which had numerous bongo drums and trumpets and a conductor who played a silver flute. Pablo liked a cheap date—a fried hamburger at the end of the day and maybe a Cuba Libre or two while the orchestra took a break.

Pablo liked Dolores's smile, her delicate form, and her feline movements. When they danced, he felt the rhythm of the music in her body. Her arms and all the rest of her moved smoothly as the music transformed her into a desirable beauty. One evening Pablo took her to a dance hall to hear a famous orchestra from Havana. They had a singer who had recorded many hits that they had heard on the radio. The band was famous for their slow *boleros* and for their new takes on classic songs. Dolores let Pablo kiss the lobes of her ears, but she objected when he tried to kiss her on the mouth. That night on the way back to her house, he asked her to sit on a park bench under a big laurel tree. Dolores, pulling at Pablo's hand, laughing, and teasing him gently, ran toward her house, but not too fast. Her simple dress was tight at her hips and showed the outline of her small breasts. She stopped at her garden gate, smiled again, and left the gate half open as she sauntered into the garden. It was long past midnight. Pablo followed, excited, as if he were in a Grecian mythical chase. Dolores laughed as Pablo kissed her and held her tightly. In that garden, under a luxuriant tree, Pablo lost his virginity.

After that, he was Dolores's nightly visitor. They tried every bench at the park, went to dances, took long walks, and glanced at the windows of furniture stores. When Pablo had extra money, they rented a room for a few hours at an inn. Within a few months, though, Dolores became nervous; she had missed two periods, and the smell of frying fish croquettes made her vomit. The other servants, with whom she shared a small bedroom, teased her. She took herbs as recommended by a *curandera*, but it was too late. Paulino was born. Dolores, like many *mulatas* before her, gave her son a Spanish name—Paulino Rodriguez. Pablo recognized him as his natural son at the Civil Registry, but he did not marry Dolores. It was fine to have a *mulata* as a mistress, but to marry her—that was different. As soon as Paulino was old enough to walk, Dolores sent him to live with her mother in Santa Clara. She visited him once or twice a month. Pablo forgot about his son, but his son never forgot him, and neither did the boy's grandmother, who reminded him that his father was a "businessman," building up his pride. Paulino's coloring was light brown, paler than his mother's. He inherited his father's square build and his mother's lithe movements and ability to dance and sing.

When Paulino was six years old, his grandmother died. Dolores received permission from Luisa, her employer, to move with him into a small room in the garage. Dolores cared for her child, cooked for Luisa's family, lost her figure, danced less, and drank more. Paulino, as soon as he was old enough, started to help around the house by running errands, and went to the nearby public school. The teachers liked him: He was bright, resourceful, and learned quickly. Dolores taught him to brew coffee, clean shoes, polish silver, and run to the drugstore for aspirin or cough medicine. He played baseball in the street with Luisa's children and their friends. A lamppost marked first base, a big laurel tree second, and third base and home were marked with chalk on the pavement. At first they played with discarded tennis balls, then later with the real thing—a hardball made of horsehide—until they broke a neighbor's window. When Luisa bought a new bike for her older son, she gave Paulino the old one, a red one with wide tires. Paulino soon was gazing at magazines he found in the boys' room with pictures of *vedettes* with scanty clothes, big cheeks, and bigger bosoms. At night in the kitchen, he sat with the servants at a rectangular marble table, eating leftovers from the main table with beans and rice. They listened to the soaps and news on the radio. When he grew older, he rode his bike to school, the Instituto de Segunda Enseñaza, in the center of town. In his group, he was the only one who owned a bike; the poorer kids had to walk or ride on the dilapidated buses. He wore Luisa's sons' old clothes. He went with them to the twenty-five cent matinees in the movie theater next to the park. The best families of Cienfuegos knew him by his first name. "Such a nice boy," they'd say to their children. "Please be as well mannered as Paulino." His schoolmates thought that he was stuck-up and called him *"mariconcito"* behind his back. Paulino read, and his books gave him other worlds to live in and belong to. After four years he finished his studies and became a *Bachiller*. At the age of eighteen, he had an education and dreams to improve himself. He went to see his father, now the sole owner of the *bodega*. Pablo stood squarely behind his ornate cash register. In back of him, bottles of beer and liquor from many different countries stood at attention and a dirty mirror reflected the cars and people passing in front.

"Good morning, Pablo," said Paulino.

"Good morning. How can I help you?"

"Don't you know me? Have you forgotten? I'm Paulino, Dolores's son. I'm your son," Paulino said indignantly. "I want to leave Cienfuegos and go to Havana to attend the university. I need you to help me."

Paulino was tall and muscular with short, straight black hair and his mother's feline mannerisms. Pablo recognized Dolores's almond-shaped eyes, blue in Paulino's face, the same blue as in Pablo's mother's eyes. Nearby, a customer nursed a beer. The radio played a *danzón*.

"Come," Pablo said, "let's go in the back. We can talk freely there."

They walked out onto a big open patio with empty wooden boxes and two large papaya trees.

"Do you want anything to drink?" Pablo asked.

"A beer," Paulino said.

Pablo went back and brought two bottles. A black cat moved lazily among the empty boxes. He gave one bottle to his son, took a gulp from his, and asked, "What do you want?"

Paulino answered, "I want to leave Cienfuegos. Here, I've learned everything I can."

"Does your mother know that you're meeting me?"

"No."

"Shouldn't you ask for her opinion?"

"No."

Pablo considered the request. What had he been working for, after all? To return to Spain and try to have another son, one he would never abandon? He was a practical man and went to the cash register and took out two hundred pesos.

"Here, this will give you a start," he said as he tossed the *bills* on the countertop.

"Thanks," Paulino replied happily as he took and held them in his fist.

"Good luck, but don't come back," Pablo said, and turned his back to his son to wait on a new customer.

Paulino promptly left, having sold his patrimony for two hundred silver coins, enough to pay the rent of a small room and feed him for a few months. He took detours on his way home, past the mansions near the water, where round glass globes hung like grapes from the lampposts. He gazed into small gardens with roses of different colors and palm trees planted in straight lines. He smelled the sea breeze and heard the waves beat against the piers. He arrived late at the house. His mother asked, "Where have you been?"

"I went to see my father at his *bodega*."

She was surprised. "Why?"

"I didn't want to tell you. I was afraid it might upset you. I asked him for money to go to the university in Havana."

Dolores sat down heavily and looked at the floor.

"I have excellent grades. My teacher told me I should. I can find a job. I saved a little bit of money and the *cabrón* gave me two hundred pesos. That will tide me over for several months. I was afraid that you would get mad."

Dolores, with her eyes full of tears, shuffled her feet. "When?"

"Maybe tomorrow, maybe Monday, I don't know, but very soon."

Paulino retreated to their room, sat on his cot, and glanced around before returning to the kitchen to fetch two cardboard boxes. In one, he packed his clothes, in the other, his few books: poems of Marti, a Neruda poetry collection given to him by a friend, and an old book, *Platero y Yo*, a collection of stories about a donkey and a boy, which he had earned as a prize in school.

The following day, he took a bus for Havana. He settled in the area near the university, and soon found a job as a busboy in a bustling café, where he slept in the back room. Paulino always kept a smile on his face, and earned tips so large they exceeded his meager salary. He quickly became friendly with the regulars, and soon knew all the political jokes. He laughed at the ones the customers told; then in his small room behind the café, he embellished them, adding new twists. He would then go from table to table, and as he poured the hot coffee and milk, recite his new version with gusto.

Paulino registered as a student and attended several classes during the day. He read Camus and Sartre on the recommendations of other students and of his customers in the café. He also read Kafka, discussed Nietzsche and Hegel, and learned the poems of Dario, Garcia Lorca, Neruda, Mistral, and Guillen. He started to go to nightly meetings to discuss books, theater, and music. He wrote articles for the university newspaper. Once, one of his letters was published in the communist newspaper, *Hoy*. He was an author. Paulino went to the political demonstrations on the broad steps of the university. The bronze statue of the alma mater opened her arms to all students: Some accepted her embrace and studied, others showed up because they wanted to change the government. The demonstrations were frequent and popular. The president sent the police to break up the demonstrations, and the police and students played cat and mouse games. The students barked speeches on loudspeakers, skipped classes, and finally went on strike, taking a symbolic page from the past, when rebellious students wielded true power, as in the thirties, when they had helped tumble the presidency of Gerardo Machado. Even the professors, not wanting to be called reactionaries and trying to support democracy, joined the strike. The formal educational process ground to a halt, but not the meetings, the committees, the banners, the speeches, the brandishing of guns, the letters to the newspapers, and the manifestos. Soon after, late one night, two men knocked at the door of the small room where Paulino slept, wearing only his shorts. The men carried him by force out into a tan Oldsmobile and drove to the west of town. They crossed the big bridge over the Almendares River, passed the Columbia army barracks, and stopped at the bucolic lake by the country club, where they made him drink a massive dose of castor oil. They tossed Paulino from the car and left him, sick from the castor oil to shit and pee in his shorts. Early the next morning, a taxi driver, who had decided to take a shortcut after dropping off customers at the *Playa*, saw Paulino's slumped body near the lake and took him to the university's hospital. Paulino was not the first, nor would he be the last. His stomach hurt. His ribs hurt. His pride was hurt. His ass hurt. He decided to put some distance between himself and his unwelcome new acquaintances at Batista's Army Intelligence Force, the feared G2.

Paulino had met Mike at a Sunday salon, where they had discussed the problems of the world until the early hours of the morning, and now he called him for help. Mike gave Paulino a letter of introduction to his father, and in short order, he became the manservant at the farm. He was removed from danger—but also from his dreams. Four years had passed since that day. Walking back to the kitchen, carrying the farm's big silver coffee service, Paulino thought bitterly, "I can still read, I still can write, I can still laugh, I can still walk, but I'm not free."

The Black Stallion

MIKE OPENED HIS armoire and smelled the musty odor that comes from clothes hanging too long in a humid climate. He chose an old pair of blue jeans, a long-sleeved *guayabera,* and paratrooper boots that a distant uncle had given him. He stuffed a few *Vuelta Arriba* cigars in his *guayabera,* and refilled his engraved Zippo lighter. Mike was not too tall, about five feet nine. He was muscular and had brown hair that he wore in a military-type haircut. His brown eyes were expressive. He briskly brushed his short hair and left the house. He headed toward the show barn with its guano-thatched roof and sides made of small timbers unsuitable for anything else: It looked like a stockade with a large straw hat.

As Mike slowly walked through the horse stalls, he remembered that one summer his father had made him work at the barn, insisting, over the strong objections of his mother, that Mike had to learn the business from the bottom up. He had cleaned the stalls, fed, and watered the horses. His hands bled from the rough pitchfork used to muck out the stalls. On the first day, an older worker ordered Mike to haul bucket after bucket of water to fill a large trough. When Mike had almost finished, the worker went to a nearby shed, and moments later, he walked out, holding a water hose. Laughing, he topped off the trough, his eyes full of disdain.

The work was hard, but Mike liked it, and he vowed on that first day to work harder than anyone else without complaint or expectation of special treatment. During that summer, Mike came to know the farm workers in a new way. They worked side by side, shared meals, and spoke of work, women, and their families. Mike came to appreciate and even take part in the workers' ritualistic taunts to each other. Yet that didn't stop him on some days, when he was tired of flies buzzing around his face and sweat clouding his vision, from dreaming of water-skiing behind a speed boat at Varadero and laughing with his friends.

Now Mike stopped at the stall of a dark bay horse, a son of the stable's black stallion. The colt had a small head; dark, intelligent eyes; a mane braided with small pieces of red cloth to protect it from the evil eye; and a long, braided tail. At horse shows, the tail was tied to a black leather and silver criollo saddle that had two pistol holders on each side of the pommel.

Manuel stood at the entrance of the barn, smoking a thick *Cohiba*, his eyes hidden by the dark Ray-Bans, as he oversaw the brushing of a nervous filly. He chewed his *Cohiba* one more time, spat out the tobacco juice, and turned around to greet Mike.

"It's about time you came to see the peons. How are the *Americanitas* treating you?"

Mike shook hands heartily with him. "Good morning, Manuel. Say, I think you need to work harder. You're getting soft," and lightly punched his stomach. "I see that everything here is in great shape." Mike nodded toward the tied filly. "Who's she by?"

"She's out of Butaca. She walks like a dream," Manuel answered as he inspected her. "You don't need to be a good rider to win on this one. Rancho Boyeros will be her first show."

"Do you have the key?" Mike asked.

Manuel fumbled with a key chain and picked out a large key. Going to the corner box stall, he opened its padlock and Mike entered alone. The stallion's back had started to sway, although he was still jet-black with no trace of white in his coat, mane, tail, or fetlocks. Mike spoke softly to the stallion.

"How you are doing, Lucumi? Do you still have a bad temper? How many mares have you jumped this season, old boy? Don't you ever get tired?" Mike touched his long neck, held his forelock, his fingers touching the stallion's withers and massaging him, slowly, with a gentle pressure, whispering. Memories flowed back: White linen suit, black tie, and a crowd roaring . . . the final competition for Criollo stallions at the national show in Rancho Boyeros. He was riding the Criollo stallion that had never lost. The one his father rode. On that day it was his turn: a rite of passage, an obligation. He followed the commands of the announcer: *"Paso," "Marcha,"* and *"Guatrapeo."* He sat erect on the unstable ornate criollo saddle, his hands in contact with the stallion's mouth. He was nervous; it would be unforgivable to be the first rider to lose a class on this horse. He had ridden Lucumi at the farm, but never in a show, and he did not want Lucumi to feel his apprehension. He had already ridden him for twenty minutes during the class, changing gaits at the announcer's cue. The announcer asked the contestants to line up in the middle of the ring. The three judges came by and checked his saddle, the bit; they examined Mike's short Cuban boots, their shine reflecting the powerful lights of the ring. The judges assessed the stallion's braided tail and the checkerboard combed on his rump. Mike knew the judges well. He had carried their briefcases and taken their notes and acted as their assistant at other shows. But he couldn't smile at them, and they did not show a single sign of recognition.

The crowd applauded and whistled each time the judges stopped in front of a horse. The judges, practical men, reconciled their knowledge of horseflesh with the taste of the crowd. The crowd went wild when the judges stopped in front of Lucumi. They took their time before giving their cards to a young girl dressed in a white cowgirl costume. Mike searched for his father in the crowd. He was sitting in the president's box with the president himself, the minister of agriculture, the minister of the treasury, and one of the owners of the big liquor company that had sponsored the competition. His father was laughing and having a good time; he always had a good time. The announcer called the name of the horse that won fourth place, then third place, second place. He paused, then requested silence from the crowd.

"Now ladies and gentlemen, the winner of this year's Bacardi Trophy, for the best Criollo horse is," he savored the tension his hesitation caused, "Lucumi!"

The president rose to his feet and applauded, and the crowd followed. Lucumi, though a veteran of twenty years, became nervous from the applause and began to prance. Mike pressed his legs on the horse's flanks and held him back with mild pressure on the bit. He walked the horse, still applying pressure slightly on the bit, to the front of the president's box. The girl in the cowboy outfit offered Mike the silver trophy and the red, white, and blue rosette. He tipped his hat, and took the heavy cup and the rosette in his right hand while his left held onto the reins. The other riders had left the ring, and now he circled it. The air was full of applause and cheers as the army band played a military march. Lucumi had won one more time. The announcer described all of Lucumi's triumphs, and mentioned Mike as the rider, but he called him "Miguelito," a diminutive that Mike, then eighteen years old, despised. He reached the end gate where the rodeo chutes were located, and met Manuel waiting with a farm employee. He handed the trophy and the rosette and the reins of the horse to them, dismounted, and went into a chute and pissed, not caring if anyone saw him. His legs trembled; he was exhilarated and drained.

When he returned, Manuel gave him back the big silver trophy and the rosette, and Mike went to find his father. The spectators were drinking Hatuey beer out of paper cups. Mike's starched white linen suit contrasted with the open shirts and the short-sleeved *guayaberas* of the crowd. He went to the boxes in the grandstand. The president, with his retinue of ministers and hangers-on, had left, but he found his mother and his sisters sitting in the family box. His family congratulated him when they saw him. A sister gave him an embrace. His mother said, "You looked so handsome," and gave him a kiss. Mike, slightly embarrassed, asked, "Where's Father?"

His mother replied with a resigned shrug, "You know how he is. He may be with the presidential group or with the minister. Why don't you look for him at the Patrons Club? I've hardly seen him all day."

Mike rushed through the crowd until he reached the club, and then entered a badly-lit bar filled with a dense fog of cigar and cigarette smoke. A multicolored Wurlitzer played a Benny More *guaracha*. The cocktail waitresses were dressed like Texan cowgirls with short culottes and tight blouses. The bartenders, imported from the Floridita restaurant in Havana, kept the blenders whirring with frozen daiquiris.

Mike found his father at a corner table, sitting with a mix of people, some of them important. At the next table were two army officers in tightly-fitted civilian jackets. Between them, drinking champagne, was a mulatto woman past middle age with gray hair and a nicely cut somber dress. She was Paulette, the famous madam who owned the Conga Club. Most of the patrons knew her, but they did not acknowledge her presence. Mike finally reached the table while his father talked, as always, with energy, laughter, and confidence.

"Papa," Mike said, trying to get his attention. "Papa, here's the trophy and the rosette."

His father stopped, noticing Mike, and nodded. "Let's have a drink, put it on the table." Calling one of the waiters, he asked for champagne. "The one of the Widow," he said, "let's enjoy the win."

Mike stood by the table with his white Panama in hand as his father resumed telling a story to his friends. Before he had finished, Mike left. He headed across the room as acquaintances congratulated him. He walked as fast as he could to his car. He did not want to go back to the house, to his mother and sisters. Instead, he drove to the old plaza in front of the cathedral. It was past midnight, and he had the plaza, its portals, its cobblestones, and colonial arches to himself. He lit a cigarette, and looked at the roughness of the cobblestones and the shadows cast by the streetlights. He sat on the steps of the cathedral. One of his friends had been married there. He laughed at the memory of how nervous his friend was before his marriage, and how he had fretted because he couldn't play around for a little while. "No more Conga Club," he had said. At last, Mike finished smoking his cigarette and went home.

A year later, Mike left everything behind. But now he was back, and as he stroked Lucumi's aging head, he whispered "You, old friend, you caused the problem. Father retired you after our win. Maybe he didn't like my riding you, but we won. Together, we did it."

Mike had to admit that he had missed his horses and life on the farm. He liked the smell of the barn, the heat caused by the animals, the camaraderie of the workers, and the sense of working together to create something, but he thought, why *now*? Lustre could have waited. He was so close to completing his last paper, so close to earning his master's degree, but he still had options. Mike stepped outside of the box and gazed out at the barns and pastures. He took a deep breath: He was home.

— 3 —

The Breakfast

THE TROPHIES WON by the farm animals were displayed on two walls of the dining room; on another, a large mirror encased in a mahogany frame seemed to increase the length of the room. The dining-room table, made of the cut halves of a giant mahogany tree, was flanked by *taburetes* covered with hides with the farm's brand burned into them. The setting for breakfast was sophisticated, but there were no flowers; the only nods to formality were provided by the colorful pattern of the Limoges china, a remnant of Mike's mother's taste, and by a Mexican silver breakfast set. The table was set with mangoes, grapefruit, and papaya, thick-crusted white toast, orange and strawberry marmalades, farm-made butter, freshly made orange juice, coffee, and milk.

"I'd like to tour the pastures in the back. You can drive the jeep. I haven't been there for a while," his father told Mike.

Mike was glad to see signs of interest in the farm. "Okay, when do you want to leave?"

"Half an hour. First I need to talk to Manuel and select which animals we're taking to Santi Spíritus. Have you seen them?"

"Yes, Papa, early this morning. Manuel gave me the tour. I liked Butaca's filly."

"She's one of the best that I've ever bred," he said proudly. "I'm giving her to Miguelito Quevedo, the publisher of *Bohemia*. He loves horses, and it's always good to have friends in the press."

"Why her? Lucumi is getting old. Shouldn't we keep our best?" Mike asked.

"Don't worry. Every year, mares have foals." He noticed the frown on his son's face. "Are you tired?"

"Not tired, confused. Lustre calls, says you are sick, depressed, not taking care of yourself, so I run back expecting to see you on your deathbed, and today, today you're up having breakfast with me, and you look *fine*, and you want to ride around, and then you ask if *I'm* tired!"

His father laughed. "I'm becoming an old man, old and sweet. That's what girls tell me."

"But, Father, you're not old. Look at you. You're quite strong. The last time we went riding to check the pastures, I was exhausted before you. And that was only last Christmas! Please . . ."

His father laughed, but quickly his laughter turned into a cough, a persistent hacking, and his face reddened. Paulino, who was hovering near the table, grabbed Don Miguel's arms and held them over his head. Angry, Don Miguel tried to whack Paulino, while Mike offered a glass of water.

"That's enough! I can take care of myself. Bring me some honey!"

Paulino, accustomed to such explosions, left the dining room whistling a tune. "Yes, Don Miguel, honey from the bees," and in a quieter voice, "Honey for a drone, coming, coming, coming, right away. You can have anything you want. You are my *Jefe*."

Mike glared at his father. "You haven't changed. Paulino was trying to help. He takes good care of you."

"Bah, he likes the food. He is getting lazier every day. Besides, his ideas and the things he says . . . I never should have hired him. He acts like he's a doctor of philosophy and letters—He only talks and disputes. He should have stayed in Havana. He doesn't belong here." Don Miguel took another piece of toast, covered it with butter, and dunked it into his cup. "How do you like our butter?" he asked in a milder tone. "Better than the ones you're having up north, or those sold in the small *tinajones*."

Mike ignored him and took another sip of his coffee and milk.

His father took another bite and said, "I'm getting older. Your mother is dead, God rest her soul. I have decisions to make about us, and the farm. Your duty is here, you know. Your sisters and their husbands can't handle the job of running this farm. The girls hate the countryside, but worst of all, the farm." He waved his toast slightly. "It's my fault. I've made it too rough for them. Their husbands, especially Julio . . . bah! He's a fake. When he comes here, he dresses like Tom Mix. But all he knows is how to play gin rummy, dominoes, golf, and go to the beach. He actually *likes* life behind a desk. Nine to five. He has no guts. Jose Maria is better, but he has his own family business to run." Don Miguel chewed on a bite before going on. "So, you're it. You have to continue what we started—my father, his father, and now me."

Mike had heard it all before. He tossed his napkin on the table.

"Give me time. I love you, I like the farm, but I have my own obligations," he said, pushing his taburete away. "I'm going to go check if the jeep is ready."

At the machinery shed, Mike ran into Fernando.

"Good morning, Mike!" Fernando greeted him with a wide smile and its full set of beautiful white teeth. "Did you sleep well?"

"Yes, I did. Oh, before I forget, I was too upset and worried to thank you yesterday for driving all the way to Havana to pick me up at the airport. You had to be tired. I wasn't good company."

Fernando was pleased by Mike's consideration. "Thanks, Mike. Your father will be okay with you back."

Mike asked, "Where's Ricardo? I haven't seen him this morning."

"He left about two hours ago. He went to the *Ceiba* pasture."

"Where's the jeep?"

Fernando motioned to the back of the shed.

"Thanks, I see it. See you later."

The jeep's new coat of red paint was already badly scratched from his father's excursions through the underbrush. His father treated the old jeep as if it were a tank. He had never liked new things—cars, tractors, or trucks—and was wary of trends. The shed was a museum of antique farm machinery: two Farmall Ms, one Farmall H, and a small Ford tractor with a gasoline engine. Mike checked the jeep's gas tank with a stick. The gas gauge had broken years before and was never fixed. Mike had walked many times to fetch gas when the jeep, driven by his father, had ran out of gas kilometers away from the *batey*. His father didn't take business risks, but he never checked the gas tank. Mike cleared the dust from the seat and turned the ignition key. Fernando had taught him to drive it, up and down the alleys, changing gears and playing with the clutch. Mike drove to the front of the house, where his father was already waiting. Don Miguel's boots had the deep glow of good leather meticulously cared for with saddle soap and countless polishings. In his *guayabera's* left pocket, he had tucked in a half dozen No. 3 H. Upmanns. Don Miguel smoked as he paced, arguing with Cuca.

"No, I can go. I feel very strong. You don't have to worry. If I can't smoke, I'll know it. The doctors don't know a thing about my lungs."

Cuca was upset. "Don Miguel, you haven't felt well. It's a hot day, and it's a long trip to the end of the farm."

Don Miguel drew on his cigar, opened the left door of the jeep, and motioned Mike to move to the other side. "Let's go, Son, let's go. I'll drive, you'll open the gates." Paulino waved good-bye and Cuca made the sign of the cross.

"We started too late," his father complained, "We should have started at six o'clock, and it's eight already. We aren't going to have enough time to check on everything I wanted to see today."

"Papa, it doesn't matter," Mike calmly responded. "It will only take us half an hour to reach the *Ceiba* pasture. We have nothing else to do."

It was a slow start. They had pastures on each side of the alleys that crisscrossed the whole farm. Each alley was one hundred feet wide; three *vaqueros* could move thirty to fifty head of cattle through any of them from a pasture to the corrals at the *batey*.

Don Miguel sped down the dirt alleys while Mike eyed the cattle. His father talked and gesticulated with his cigar, "Here we'll plant another pangola pasture. There, we'll drill another water well. Do you see those white rocks? It is a sign that there's water, good water at sixty meters deep." He sighed. "The farm isn't finished. It will never be finished. We need better grasses to fatten more bulls per *caballería*. We need water wells in the back pastures. Without water, pastures can't be subdivided. It's cheaper to fertilize than to plant."

Mike nodded idly. He had worked the numbers and had even discussed them with his father, but he knew how much the old man loved to talk about the farm, and so he didn't interrupt.

"The *manigua* always wants to come back. It is a never-ending fight," Don Miguel grumbled. "People don't want to work anymore. They like to dance, play, screw, go to the *valla*, play baseball, but to work and save money—no, they'd rather eat mangoes and cornmeal." He waved a dismissive hand. "This is ours, and it will be here for your children and your children's children. It is not, and will never be, solely mine. God just gave it to us to improve. You have to continue to improve it. You do it for your children, and your children will improve it for their children, if they don't lose it from gambling and screwing around."

Mike pulled a cigar from his father's *guayabera* pocket and lit it.

"Hey, you're old enough to buy your own."

"Yes, but the ones you borrow taste better. In the States they're more expensive. Remember, I'm just a college student."

"Yes, but you have expensive tastes," his father laughed.

That inevitably led to coughing his hard, violent cough. "I know I shouldn't smoke. Your mother always said so."

Mike waited out the latest spasms. He knew his father had too much pride to say, "Mike, I'm quitting the farm." *Quitting* wasn't in his father's vocabulary. He would never say, "Mike, come back." No, that would be too direct, too open and clear.

Mike's chain of thought was interrupted by the sight of a clump of gnarled fruit trees next to a windmill. A sugar farmer who dreamt of being a sugar king had planted them more than thirty years ago. He and his dreams did not survive the drop in sugar prices after the big crash of the late twenties. The big sugar companies wouldn't finance small sugar plantations; they didn't have enough money to take care of their own. There was too much sugarcane planted. The economic rotation of land on the island continued: forest, sugar, pasture; and then sugar again, if the prices were excellent. When small sugar farms went under in the 1930s, Don Miguel had bought farms adjoining his own from the banks that had foreclosed on them. He had cash and was creditworthy, and the banks wanted out of the sugar business. The times when the bankers of the house of J. P. Morgan visited the island were gone. The young bankers, graduates of Ivy League schools, had to work in a foreign land to complete their training until they returned to the more civilized north. They never walked the land that served as collateral for a loan. A flurry of bank lending was followed by a flurry of foreclosures, and then by more sales. Don Miguel bought farm after farm. The banks seemed to operate on the principle: "Lend to the big companies and to the ones who speak our language and drink our drinks." Later, laws were passed to protect the small plantation owner, but for many, the legislation was too late. Each farm Don Miguel bought had a small *batey* and a house on it, but he always said, "Burn them down."

The Guardia Rural, riding their Kentucky-bred horses, in their McClellan saddles with their machetes out, would aid new owners to take possession of the land. A land empty of *guajiros* could not cause problems down the line. "Burn, do not leave a house unburned, do not leave a *bohío* standing, burn, burn, burn. A *bohío* left standing will bring squatters. Squatters will plant crops, and then you have to wait for them to harvest their crop. No squatters, no crops, no *bohíos*." The Guardia Rural escorted the old owners and tenants out of their homes to the Central Highway. They left behind their mango trees, with their red and yellow fruits; orange trees, sweet and bitter ones, those whose fruit was used to make *mojo*; lime trees, with small green fruits; and the grapefruit trees. Turning their backs to their lost *bateyes*, they headed toward the city on foot to try to create a new life. Always thinking of his business, Don Miguel befriended the Guardia Rural, especially the captain of the garrison: A case of liquor, a box of the best cigars, and a wad of money in a paper sack contributed to peace and understanding. The guardia represented authority, peace, and stability on an island where stability was as unknown as the future price of sugar in the London market, or the landing place of the next hurricane, or the results of a numbers game. Now the guardia never came unless it was invited, and Don Miguel never invited them. He owned the land.

Don Miguel and Mike reached a five-strand wire fence that enclosed a pasture with short natural grasses growing out of red dirt. At the top of a low hill sat a *bohío*, its wooden planks painted white, now faded. Tied to a post, an old mule slumped under a much-abused McClellan saddle, stirrups attached to its tree with ropes. Mike opened the pasture gate, and his father honked as he lit his second cigar. Slowly the door of the *bohío* opened. An elderly black man appeared, wearing baggy khaki trousers, mended and mended again, and a blue work shirt washed so many times it was almost white. Recognizing the jeep, Alfred walked as fast as his deformed feet would allow. He held his frayed hat in his hands as a sign of respect, and greeted them.

"Don Miguel, Mike, welcome. Mike, it's so good to see you again. You've been gone a long, long time. If your father allows me, I shall bring to the *batey* a young lamb, so you may have good meat."

Alfred's English was perfect, clipped, all sentences finished with a pause.

"Alfred, how are you doing?" Mike asked. "How is your girlfriend?"

Alfred laughed while he patted the old mule's rump. "She is fine." He turned his attention to Don Miguel. "How are you doing, sir? Do you feel any better?"

Don Miguel got out of the jeep and shook Alfred's proffered hand.

"How is everything? Do you still have problems with stray dogs?"

"No, the strays have left your sheep alone. None were recently killed. I placed poison last month, there, near the forest. I think it killed a bitch that was going to have puppies. I have not seen her anymore. I do not think the *batey* dogs are coming up here. It's been a long time since I've seen Mitzi or the black dogs. I'm sorry, Don Miguel, would you like some coffee?"

There was only one possible answer. If he did not accept, he would have hurt Alfred's pride.

Alfred brought out clean, thick porcelain cups with double bottoms. The amount of coffee in them couldn't fill a thimble, but the coffee was strong and freshly brewed. They sat in the small living room. The floor was gray cement and spotless. A hen ventured in, but Alfred shooed it away. They drank coffee and Don Miguel asked questions about sheep, weather, fences, and corrals. After ten minutes, he got up, thanked Alfred, and headed to the jeep. He had wasted enough time. Mike remained, talking with Alfred, until he heard honking from the jeep.

"Good-bye, Alfred, thanks for the coffee. I'll see you at the *batey*."

Alfred followed Mike to the car. "Good-bye, Don Miguel. Good-bye, Mike," Alfred said, as he shut the passenger door behind Mike. "It was so nice to see you."

As Don Miguel drove the jeep away, Mike turned and waved back.

Ricardo and the Bulldozer

SWEAT POURED DOWN his chest under Ricardo's thick cotton work shirt. He had tied a red handkerchief over his nose and mouth; dark aviator glasses protected his eyes from the dust. He sat on the old bulldozer, surplus equipment from World War II, when the *Americanos* had built Air Force bases on the island. A base near his home was supposed to be secret, but there were no secrets on an island. As a child, he dreamt of driving of one of those gigantic machines they used to build the runways on the base.

Ricardo's father had once worked for Angelin, Don Miguel's uncle. Angelin had a small farm near Havana. He had grown up in a period when certain gentlemen thought that gentlemen did not have to work. They dressed to go to the office, drank coffee, read the newspapers, walked on the streets to look at the pretty girls, went to lunch, took a *siesta*, dressed again with a new shirt, went to the club to play cards or dominoes, returned home, and dressed in different attire for dinner. Angelin dressed well. He was tall and loved life. No, he devoured life. If he had been born in France, he would have been a *boulevardier* or a *flâneur*. He showed off a magnetic smile. He knew how to court a lady and be chivalrous. Sometimes he had money, other times he did not. If he had it, he gave his mistress orchids; if he did not, he wrote her poems. He married early in life, and he loved his wife and everyone else's.

One night at the opera—when Havana had formal-dress opera nights—he was with his mistress in the box reserved for the mayor of Havana, a cohort in his escapades. The mistress sat in the front seat. She had that rare combination in the tropics of red hair and fair, almost milky, skin. Angelin, resplendent in his tails, stood behind her. The box was full of unusual orchids, grown in Angelin's hothouse. The only problem was that a close friend of Angelin's wife recognized them, and the next morning promptly called her. When Angelin returned from his fictitious long visit to his farm, his wife confronted him.

"You were at the opera!"

Angelin replied smoothly, "You know I don't like opera."

Years later, his wife told a friend she never learned for sure if Angelin had been at the opera with a woman that night.

As a child, Ricardo helped his father with those small chores that country children do. One day, while picking pineapples in a field, a pointed stalk struck his left eye, piercing the cornea. Ricardo lost his vision in that eye. The children at school called him *Tuerto*—one-eyed—and made fun of him and picked fights just to hit him on his blind side, but Ricardo grew stronger. One day, in a fight which he had not started, he knocked another child out cold. They never bothered him again.

Angelin admired Ricardo's spunk. He started to use him for small errands around the farm. Ricardo got tired of school, but not before he had learned how to read, write, multiply, divide, and figure percentages. When Ricardo was old enough to drive, Angelin made him his driver, and when he partied, Ricardo took him there. When he got drunk, Ricardo carried him home. In the 1930s, Angelin lost his farm to a bank, though not his craving for life.

While Ricardo was acting the playboy—*El Habanero*, the boy-man who drove a car and acted sophisticated—Cuca was the girl next door. When she was just sixteen, a small, well-proportioned young woman, she wrote in her little diary: "I like Ricardo." One day, Ricardo parked Angelin's Buick in front of his house to clean and wax it. On its polished hood he saw a reflection: the face of a beautiful woman. He smiled and the face smiled back at him. Their courtship lasted two years. Ricardo wanted to be alone with Cuca, but her mother, aware of Angelin's and Ricardo's fame as womanizers, chaperoned them on every date. Ricardo had thought Cuca was going to be an easy conquest: a country girl, just a teenager. He took her on trips to Havana, to Varadero, and to see the sponges in Batabanó. Cuca's mother accompanied them in the car, at the movies, always next to her daughter. After two years, Ricardo gave Cuca an ultimatum: "Tonight we are going to be alone. I am tired of paying for your mother. I am tired of stealing kisses. I am tired of sitting on the porch of your house, hearing the rocking chairs squeak. I want you."

Cuca smiled, but she trusted her mother's advice: "Of the forest, not a twig." "Ricardo, Ricardito," she said, "I love you. You have to respect me. What happens to me if you don't come back? If you get tired of me? I lose everything. I'm a virgin and will be a virgin the day we marry. No, I won't do it. You will not respect me if I do. You may think that I am like other girls, but I'm not. I don't fool around."

Ricardo talked to Cuca's father that night, but before she would accept Ricardo's proposal, Cuca set one condition: "You can't work for Angelin."

Ricardo then found work as a chauffeur for Don Miguel. Cuca was happy about that, since the new boss was a serious and stable man. Cuca and Ricardo married and moved to Don Miguel's farm in the center of the island and far away from their families. Whereas Angelin, an excellent equestrian trained in France, had taught Ricardo how to ride, Don Miguel taught him how to break horses. When Ricardo did not drive, he broke the bigger ones.

Ricardo liked to use a *bozal*, and after the horse's nose was soft and tender, he changed to a snaffle bit. Don Miguel did not allow Ricardo to break his best show horses. He left those for Manuel, but Ricardo trained the four-year-old farm horses, which made excellent riding horses. They were gentle, never spooked, but had fire and stamina. He broke four horses at a time. He saddled up early in the morning. The first day, Ricardo took a saddle blanket and placed it in front of the horse's nostrils, so the horse could smell and feel it with his whiskers. Then he played with the blanket, and waved it in front and back of the horse. Some horses spooked and bolted. Ricardo would talk softly to them, as if telling them a bedtime story. When the horse accepted the sight and smell of the blanket, it was placed carefully on its back, and Ricardo slowly moved, using the same tone of voice and the same cadence. The horse's muscles quivered, he was frightened, and he knew he could not free himself from the *bozal*. Ricardo then held the saddle in his right hand, while his left hand held the *bozal*. He lifted the saddle and let it fall gently on the horse's back. Ricardo took the horse to the middle of the corral and tied him with a slipknot to the center post. If the horse fought the tether, the *bozal* cut into his nose and put pressure on the top of his head. Ricardo stayed next to the horse, and using a smooth voice, calmed it down, and then released him with a rope tied to his halter. Holding the rope, Ricardo made the horse move in circles, always forward, forward, and forward. Some bucked, others crow-hopped, and others were more rebellious and tried to get rid of the saddle by throwing themselves against the sides of the corral. He did this for several days until the horse accepted the weight of the saddle. When he thought a horse was ready to ride, Ricardo moved him against the side of the corral, placed his foot into the stirrup, and grabbed the horse's mane. In a single fluid motion, he mounted the saddle, and then coaxed the animal forward with pressure from his legs. After a few hours of riding in the corral, he rested. Then, after a few days, he took the horse to an open pasture and rode it for hours. After returning, the horse would be tired, but not defeated. Then Ricardo took the horse for a long easy walk to cool off, removed the saddle, and hosed it down with cold water to remove sweat and dirt. The next day, he would feel the horse's back to see if it was sore. At the end of a horse's fourth month of training, Ricardo would use him to rope calves in the corrals, and at the end of six months, to rope bulls in the pastures.

He soon took on an additional duty. In the late forties, the land at the rear of the farm was not good enough to grow sugarcane or corn. It had native grasses, and in the dry season, its pale yellow color resembled wheat fields. Yet the weeds and brush affected the growth of the native grasses, and the land had to be improved.

Don Miguel knew that the International Harvester dealer in the city of Camagüey had acquired some US Army surplus bulldozers, and after some serious haggling with the dealer, Don Miguel purchased one. When it arrived, Ricardo felt as if he were the most important man on the farm. He sat in the driver's seat and started the engine. The San Joaquin group was there: Nandito, Martinito, and Mando the *curandero*. They gasped at the big red bulldozer, and touched it all over. They took in the smell of the diesel fumes, heard the sounds of the machine's engine, and marveled at the size of its blade as it moved up and down with a touch of a lever. Ricardo put the machine in reverse and slowly lowered it to the ground from the flatbed trailer. Two years later, he was an efficient bulldozer operator. He was the only one at the farm who could drive it.

BY NOON, HE had cleared part of a tract in the savanna, and was eating the sandwich Cuca had packed for him. That's when he noticed the jeep with Don Miguel and Mike. Ricardo did not like *El Viejo* to show up and check on his work. Ricardo was proud of his work and did not mind the long hours, but he also liked his fighting cocks, which he kept hidden in the forest at the edge of the savanna.

Don Miguel hated cockfights. He did not care about the cruelty of one animal killing another one for sport. He believed that if people gambled, and thought they could make a lot of money with their gambling, they would care less about how badly they lived, and accept their poverty, believing that gambling was their key for a better life, and never work to improve their lot.

Every Sunday, Ricardo went to a nearby *valla* to fight his roosters. It was a small one with a roof of zinc, sides of salvaged wood, and round grandstand seating made of rickety boards. The fights started at one o'clock, and they lasted until the last pair of roosters had fought. The crowd, a mixture of Haitians, Jamaicans, mulattos, and whites, typified the island's population.

Each rooster had his own handler who cared for it from infancy and trained it to fight. Referees checked the roosters' spurs—some were natural and others were made of steel and attached—and then the feathers, to be sure that no foreign substance had been used on them. Two cocks were set face to face and then released. The fight always began with a crescendo of shouting and betting: "Five to the *Colorado*, ten to the *Jerezano*," until one of the roosters quit the fight. In some cases, it ended because a rooster had received, in a flurry of flying, a fatal cut in his neck. The crowd tossed back more beer and rum, and another fight would begin.

Ricardo's father had brought hens from the south of Spain. He bred them with roosters from Mexico, and the result was a group of heavy and fast-fighting birds. Ricardo fought the roosters and kept them in square wooden cages. On his day off, he went early to the forest and selected the ones to fight at the *valla* that afternoon.

For his part, Mike enjoyed going to the cockfights. He loved the speed and color, the animation of the people, their shouts in patois, and the ardent way they gambled their scarce pesos. Mike also enjoyed having a beer or two.

Don Miguel stopped the jeep to listen to the sounds: the swish of the trees falling, the crescendo of the motor when the blade had to push, the noise of the big blade scraping the earth to remove roots. Ricardo jumped from the cabin and approached them as he cleaned the specks of dirt from his face.

"Good afternoon, Don Miguel. I'm glad that you feel better and decided to see how much I've cleared. Are you showing Mike how much the farm has changed?"

Ricardo knew *El Viejo* always liked company: someone to open gates, to listen to his ideas, to allow him to vent his anger about the government, about the stupid way politicians controlled the prices of cattle on the hoof, and the way they still allowed the stockyards to be controlled by a few. The topics seldom changed. Don Miguel had the same discussions with Paulino, the minister of agriculture, his friends at the Club Hipico, and the president, if given the opportunity. Now it was different. *El Viejo* still had passion, but he preferred to stay at the *batey*, walk around the house in a robe, pull weeds, smoke his cigar, and look at the show string animals. Even though Ricardo knew it was time for someone else to take charge, he loved the old bastard.

"Yes, it's time for my son to see what we're doing here. He has to learn firsthand, Ricardo. How is everything working? Did you grease the bulldozer this morning, and check the oil?"

"Of course, Don Miguel, you know I always check it. You taught me well."

No detail eluded Don Miguel, at least not until recent months. Don Miguel was lumbering back to the jeep when he suddenly pointed to a small tree about fifty yards away and instructed Ricardo, "You have to eliminate that little tree over there. It isn't big enough to provide shade." *El Viejo* climbed back into the jeep, where he sat slumped and breathless, exhausted by the oppressive heat. Before turning the ignition, he said to Ricardo, " I want to talk to you tonight."

Don Miguel turned to Mike, "Let's go, Son. We have other chores to do."

Mike shook Ricardo's hand, "Good-bye, Ricardo. I'll see you later. It looks great. Good job."

Once the jeep left, Ricardo climbed into his protected seat. He maneuvered the blade of the bulldozer next to the trunk of the small tree. He powered the engine, released the clutch, and moved the lever. The tree was sliced away.

— 5 —

Chirra

CHIRRA WOKE TO the crow of a distant rooster and stumbled out of his scruffy cot. He searched the small room for his army boots. He was afraid of scorpions and hated burrs, so he never left his *bohío* barefooted. Chirra had slept in his clothes, and his shirt smelled of cheap *Aguardiente*. He remembered dancing. He was not that young anymore, but he really could dance and drink. His mouth was dry. Droplets of dew covered the short grass, the early fog was lifting, and a line of royal palms stood like Tropicana chorus girls waiting for a cue. It was another hot day. He walked to end of his yard, held himself up with one hand on a tree, and urinated. He felt better, but he was still thirsty and stumbled back inside.

Chirra's daughter, Consuelo, slept in her bed. Her delicate features reminded Chirra of the girl's mother. One night when he had been too drunk to make love to Consuelo's mother, she laughed at him. He slapped her with his open hand and then hit her with his machete, as he used to hit *guajiros* when he was with the Guardia Rural. He was boss; women must respect men. Consuelo's mother cried and cursed him, and in the end, she left.

Chirra looked around. There was not much to eat, and he had no credit left at the *bodega*. He had coffee and cornmeal. In his backyard, he had mango and papaya trees full of ripe fruit, but he was tired of eating fruit all day. He swore that his guts must be yellow from all the mangoes, papayas, and cornmeal he ate. Consuelo had to have milk. Girls always need milk to help them grow stronger and have better bones—at least this is what he had always been told. It didn't make any difference that she was seventeen years old. She was still his baby. That meant he had to find work.

He scratched his chest and smelled his underarms; he stank. He took a small bar of soap and walked to the stream to clean up. He could have looked for work at the farm, but it was too late now. The sun had long come up, and the *batey* was a half-an-hour walk away. He had to see Manuel, who always needed a body to brush horses and rake manure. If he got the job, he would ask for an advance from the farm; with it, he could go to the *bodega* and reestablish his credit. He knew that he could talk to Cuca about food "for Consuelo," as he would say. He might borrow the old gray mule from the *batey*. He was soon going to have money, milk for Consuelo, transportation, and maybe, with the advance, he could get a small bottle of *Pati Cruzao* from the *bodeguero*. He felt better already.

NANDITO OWNED AN old truck and worked sporadically for Don Miguel. He walked to the stream in good spirits. His team was going to play a baseball game against the Vertientes, the number one team in their league. It would be played in San Joaquin's field, and he was optimistic. The girls and ladies were going to see him pitch. Now he had to borrow a tractor from the farm to mow the field that was used to play baseball. His speech was ready: "Don Miguel, you may know that we have the Vertientes team coming to play in our field. You know we are good and that we can win, but we need to see the ball so we can catch it. The grass and the weeds have grown too high. Yes, I know, we could have cut it with our machetes, but you know we have to be fresh and rested to play good ball. Cutting grass by hand takes time, and with a machete your arm gets tired and sore. I need a fresh arm. I'm the only good pitcher my team has. Yes, I will grease it well. I will put gas in the tank. No, no, I don't have a girl right now. I'm married. I'm a serious man. No, no, I know you heard the drums last night, but I didn't dance. I wasn't at that party. I was resting. You see, I'm in training. I told you. I'm the pitcher." It was a good speech. He felt confident.

MARTINITO, WHO WORKED at the farm as a tractor operator, had not slept well. His baby girl had a horrible colicky night. He had spent the previous day in the seat of the blue Ford tractor mowing grass and weeds on the pasture next to the house. He didn't mind the work, but it was a hot day, and the worst part was that Don Miguel watched him all the time, so he couldn't stop mowing. It was easier when he was working in the rear pastures. There he could take a long lunch break, take a walk, wash his face, and refresh his body in a water tank and talk to the *vaqueros* as they checked the fences. It was a lot easier, with no hassles. Yesterday, it was rough: up and down the pasture, around and around, no stopping. The old bastard was even timing him! Now he wouldn't have an excuse anymore if he spent more time mowing another pasture. He was running late. He couldn't find a ride to the *batey*, and he still had to check his tractor, fill it with fuel, grease it, and check the tires for air and the radiator for water.

THE THREE MET on the bank of the stream. Chirra was naked in a deep pool of water. Nandito watched Chirra with scorn. Martinito yelled to Chirra, "Hey, you got so drunk last night. Juanita said you tried to take her behind a tree and she laughed at you. She said when you're drunk, you can't get it up."

"Bah, she was just jealous because she couldn't have this sweet thing," Chirra said, thrusting his hips and grabbing his penis.

Nandito laughed, "What? How can you call that anything! It looks like a worm. You have to be kidding, man."

The three finished bathing and headed down a red dirt road to the *batey*. Nandito was tall. Chirra was small, but not as small as Martinito, who was tiny. Near the *batey*, they heard the sounds of the milking shed, which was now full of cows, calves, and *vaqueros*. Arturo, the head *vaquero*, sour as always, was doing the milking with three other men. The old black stallion paced in his paddock, and in the employees' dining room, Cuca had prepared breakfast—bread, butter, and coffee—for all the hands. Manuel and Paulino waited for the first bucket of milk to have their *café con leche*. Under a big *Ceiba* tree next to the show barn, the job seekers congregated, smoking their cigarettes, hats in their hands, sitting on their haunches, waiting to see if Manuel had work for them.

MIKE HAD NOT slept well. He was not accustomed to the farm's early morning sounds, the croaking frogs and the barking dogs. During the quiet darkness he had heard his father cough throughout the night. He needed to take his father to see a new doctor. Mike had tossed and turned in his bed, got up, and then walked around on the porch until he finally felt sleepy again. That morning, Mike dressed slowly in old work clothes. He had heard that Manolo, the *mayoral*, was going to brand, vaccinate, and dehorn. Mike looked like a broke *vaquero*, his straw hat no better than his threadbare shirt. He went to the employees' dining room.

"Good morning, Mike. How did you sleep?" Manuel asked.

"Not too well. It's so quiet around here."

Paulino, who enjoyed jumping into every conversation, said, "Yes, you're a big city man now. You need big lights, the sound of buses, the clinking of the glasses, and *mucho* mambo. We are monks here on the farm. We pray for rain. We have had enough of skinny cows. We pray for fertile cows and strong semen for bulls, diseases and hurricanes in every cane area except ours, and a world war or two. We need *Libertad*! You want coffee, sir?"

Mike nodded absently as he caught sight of Nandito, Chirra, and Martinito as they walked to the show barn. What a trio, he thought. Manuel, having finished his coffee and milk, got up from his taburete, picked up his crumpled hat, and left. Paulino and Mike followed to meet the group.

"Good morning, Mike, it's been a long time!" Chirra called out with a wide artificial grin. He held his hat in his hands like a supplicant. "Mike, I had a good dream about you last night. I'll throw the shells for you. I know they'll tell me good things!" And when he saw Manuel, he turned to him, "Good morning, sir, I'm ready to work."

Manuel relished the power of his position. "Maybe. Let me see what we have to do today."

Mike greeted Nandito, "It's rather early for you. I thought you'd still be asleep. I heard the drums last night. Did you dance all night?"

"No, I didn't. I'm in training," Nandito replied. "Hey, Mike, we have a game next Saturday. Do you want to play? Ricardo may. I want to talk to your father about the game."

Mike laughed and shook his head. "Nandito, you haven't changed a bit," he said, and patted his back.

"What?" Nandito said, feigning shock, though he knew what Mike meant. "I really need to talk to your father. It's important!"

"Okay. I'll tell him you're here," Mike said, and left with a half grin on his face. He walked past Chirra, who, with quivering hands, trailed Manuel, laughing nervously at everything Manuel said. Mike knocked on his father's bedroom door.

"Father, are you awake? May I come in?" He heard a noise on the other side of the door.

"Yes, I'm very awake," Don Miguel, answered gruffly. "You know I haven't been sleeping well lately. Well, come in!"

Mike opened the door and stepped into the bedroom. Don Miguel stood shirtless before the lavatory, rinsing his mouth. The father spat, patted his mouth with a plush white cotton towel, and then reached for his red silk robe. His father had not lost all of his muscular build. He was the same size as Mike, but his belly had begun to show the lack of exercise. He still looked younger than his age, which was fifty-five.

"What were you doing last night walking all over the house?" Don Miguel snapped.

"It seemed almost too quiet for me, at least until the dogs started barking early this morning," Mike answered.

"You *know* it's very quiet around here. What? Do you miss the city lights and women? I don't want you to go with Ricardo to the whorehouses."

Mike sighed and sank into his father's oversized leather chair. "Father, you know I don't go visit whores." Mike glanced around the room. "Paulino hasn't brought your coffee yet? I'll check with him about that. But first, I want to know how you're feeling this morning. Are you okay?"

"I've never felt better! . . . Paulino? Ha! He's getting too big for his breeches. He thinks that because you're here and because you're his friend that he doesn't have to be a servant. It's ridiculous! That's what happens when we help these guys. They forget everything."

Mike, accustomed to his father's dramatic pontifications, calmly sat with his left temple resting on two fingers. A smile slowly appeared on his face. Mike knew full well how much his father liked Paulino, especially for his independence and cockiness.

Diverting from the topic, Mike said, "They just brought milk from the shed. Arturo looks old and tired. I didn't see him yesterday. How are his children?"

His father replied, "You would look old, too, if you had to milk cows every day, had five children, and a wife who complains. Did you get up on time for the milking?"

"No, not today. I heard the *vaqueros* singing when they brought in the cows. I want to help Manolo in the corrals. I'm riding La Nina. Do you plan to ride?" Mike said.

"No, I have to inspect the show herd. If I don't, we'll be late with the registrations." He groaned as he added, "Manuel wants to take too many animals—it's not his money. He thinks he knows more than I do."

Mike headed toward the door. "Oh, and Nandito wants to talk to you. He's waiting outside."

Don Miguel bristled. "I know what that character wants! I heard they're going to play next Saturday. He wants the tractor because they're too lazy to cut the field by hand. Mike, *mi hijo*, please tell Paulino to bring me my coffee, then I'll deal with Nandito. Later, I need to call Havana. We'll go to the *pueblo* and make phone calls. Cuca wants to order more food for you, anyway. You eat more than I do. I also need Scotch. Dr. Castillo said I should have at least two drinks before each meal to help my circulation."

Don Miguel left his room wearing his comfortable slippers, holding a cigar in his mouth, and a gold lighter in his left hand. The silk robe flowed gently behind him as he walked down the hallway. Paulino rushed toward him with his demitasse of coffee.

"Don Miguel, Arturo was a little late today. I didn't want to use the milk from the refrigerator. It smelled sour. You want your breakfast in the dining room or on the porch?"

"Paulino, I'll have breakfast later. Now I just need coffee."

Don Miguel stood on the porch and had taken his first sip when Nandito approached with his red baseball cap in his hands. "Nandito, what do you want?"

"You know, Don Miguel—" Nandito began.

"Yes, I know. You're the pitcher. You're playing the Vertientes, the best team in the league. Your playing field is a mess. Your arm is your weapon, and you can't afford it to be tired. You need a tractor to cut the field you lazy people should have cut and cleaned a week ago. You come to me because you like me? No, because I have the tractor, the mower, the gas, and I'm a fool. Yes?"

Nandito gaped at him with an open mouth, nervously touching his cap.

Don Miguel continued, "Who's paying for the gas? Who's going to fix the machines if they break?"

"Don Miguel, we are responsible people. I know how to take care of your equipment. You can trust me. I—"

"Yes, if my grandmother had wheels, she would be a bicycle. You forget, you're talking to me. You think I'm just an old man. I may be, but I'm not a fool. This is what we're going to do."

Don Miguel motioned to Martinito and said, "Come here."

Martinito approached the men, puzzled, and started to babble. "Don Miguel, I tried to clean the tractor. I needed to talk to Ricardo, so I had to ask Cuca where Ricardo is, and I had coffee because—"

Don Miguel tried in vain to contain his laughter. "Hold it," he ordered as he held out his right palm. "I was very happy to see you working the way you worked yesterday. Now, this is what you're going to do. Martinito, you check the tractor—the old gas Ford—and see that everything is okay. You give it to Nandito with the mower. He'll mow his own field. He'll bring back the tractor to the shed. Clean. Nothing broken. You will report to me—not to Ricardo, to me—that the tractor and the mower are in the same shape as when they left. Nandito and his team will help clean around the house and the *batey*. They'll weed the flower beds, cut the grass and weeds with their machetes, especially around the fences and the garden, the week after the game. Okay, Nandito?"

"Yes, sir. I'll be here the day after the game. I'll bring my team with me. Thank you, sir."

"Nandito, you better win!" Don Miguel finished his coffee. Paulino took the empty cup and saucer, and left for the kitchen, singing his latest song.

Nandito and Martinito left for the tractor shed. Martinito mumbled, "*El Viejo* made a fool of me. What does he know about working? He's never worked a day in his life. Walking around in slippers and a red robe, he looks like a *maricon!*"

Nandito thought, "He won. I'll still have to work Monday. He's a tough old bird."

. . .

MIKE AND HIS father walked to the show barn. Chirra tried his best smile as they approached. "Good morning, Don Miguel. You're looking very well. I'll throw the shells for you tonight. Everything looks great. The horses look excellent."

Don Miguel looked at Chirra and smiled. He turned to Manuel and asked, "Manuel, is Chirra in trouble again? I expect he's out of credit at *la bodega*. Can you use him?"

"I always need to have stalls cleaned, and I could use more help preparing the animals for the next show."

Don Miguel continued, "Find out if Chirra owes any money to the farm. If he does, please pay him half the wages and withhold the other half until he repays everything he owes us."

"Yes, sir," Manuel replied.

"And, Manuel, no advances to Chirra, just let Cuca give him enough milk for that daughter of his. No money advances until he has earned some. He's much too fond of the Pati Cruzao. Be sure he does not drink liniment as well."

And turning to Chirra, "Do you understand? Do we have an agreement?"

"Yes, sir. You know I work well. Thank you, sir." Chirra's mind was still clouded by the bad *Aguardiente*, but he knew that it was better than nothing, and he needed money. "I'll take good care of the stables. You'll be able to eat off the ground."

Manuel said to Chirra, "Start with Lucumi's stall, and bring him in from the paddock. It's time for him to be out of the sun. I don't want his coat to be sunburned. I'll talk to you later."

"Yes, sir. Yes, sir. Thanks, Don Miguel."

Don Miguel led Manuel to the stables. "Manuel, let's see what we have."

"Father," Mike interrupted him, "I'm going to saddle up. I'll see you at lunch. When do you want to leave to make the telephone call?"

"Let's do it at one-thirty, during siesta time. It's going to be too hot for them to work in the corrals. You can drive."

Mike left to catch and saddle his cutting mare. La Nina was a good size, fifteen hands or better, a product of one of the Kentucky cavalry mares he had bought from the army and Don Miguel's Arabian stallion. She had an expressive face, a wide-dished forehead, small ears, good solid leg, and a short-cut cow-pony mane. The fierce sun had dulled her chestnut coat. Ricardo had trained her, and Monito, Manolo's oldest son, wanted to ride her, but Don Miguel had ruled that only he or Mike rode her, so she grazed fat and lazy in a pasture next to the *batey*.

Mike brought a halter and a rope. He knew that when La Nina saw him, she would move to the foremost end of the pasture to wait for him, and then sidle away as soon as he drew near. Instead, Mike held out a bucket of oats, shook it, and when she ate a small amount, he placed a halter rope around her neck, rubbed her mane, and put on the halter. He led her back inside. The saddle room was small and crowded with trunks and show equipment, criollo saddles with silver ornaments, three English hunt saddles used by Mike's mother and sisters, one old sidesaddle owned by a niece, and a few "Texan" saddles, all with the patina of old leather that was often cleaned with saddle soap. A few faded pictures hung above the tack hooks: his father stadium jumping, Mike riding his first pony, and Adelaida, his mother, riding a white horse. Mike selected a black Texan saddle with a comfortable seat, and by the time he left the room, he found Chirra busy cleaning up his mare.

"Chirra, I can do it. You have other things to do."

"No, Mike. I'm happy to help you. She was very dirty. You wouldn't want a beautiful girl to be filthy when she goes with you to a party, would you?" He continued his currying, then asked, "How is life up north? You know, I have only been to Havana once. I've never crossed the sea. I don't believe in moving around. Me? I like it here, yes, sir."

Mike watched Chirra with disbelief. He was a bundle of energy. He finished brushing the mare, and then raised each hoof and cleaned its frog with his small knife.

"Mike, the hooves are dry. Should I put some black stuff on her hooves? You have some in the tack room, and it helps the pastern. You see, when you were gone, nobody took care of your horse. You should hire me to keep her in shape. You know I'm the best."

"Thanks, Chirra, but Manuel has taken good care of her. See how fat she is?"

"I can do it better," Chirra offered. As he went on, his voice took on a doleful tone. "Mike, I know you've been gone for a while, but things aren't good. My daughter, Consuelo, you know her. She's grown so much, she's almost a young lady, but she's very, very sick. She needs medicine badly! I haven't been able to take her to see a doctor. I'm out of money. Manuel is angry with me. I couldn't work again here until right now, and that's only because your father told him so. Can you lend me a little bit of money? I'll pay you on Friday. I need to get medicine for her badly. I'm desperate. You know I work hard."

Mike knew he was lying, but he wanted to help Consuelo.

"How much do you need?" Mike asked. " I'm going to help you, but only for medicine."

Chirra tried to act nonchalant. "I don't need that much, five pesos. I'll repay you. I knew I could count on you! Here, let me saddle your horse."

Chirra joyously shook Mike's hand as Mike slipped Chirra a five-peso bill, while from a distance Don Miguel watched the transaction.

He turned his attention back to the cattle. Monito was at the head of the herd. They had started at five o'clock in the morning. The cattle were kept in a pasture near the outer limits of the farm. It took four hours to reach their destination, round them up, and bring them to the *batey*. Monito was at the front of the herd pacing it, while Manolo and the others pushed the herd from the rear. The maneuver required a delicate balance between the lead man and the back. If the lead man rode too fast, the herd would disperse, and if the back men pushed too hard, the lead man would not be able to contain it. The voices of the *vaqueros* and the thumping of the hooves on the hard ground composed the music for a dance between the nimble horses and the riders who coaxed the cattle into a long, not-too-wide column.

MIKE JOINED THE *vaqueros* at the main gate of the corrals. He sat on La Nina with a big smile on his face, hat in his hand, his spurs shining in the sun as he soaked up a rare, powerful moment. He was riding his favorite mare out in the open. He enjoyed the sun as it warmed his body. The moment brought on an inexplicable bliss. Mike knew that life rarely allowed pleasures this great, and already at twenty-four, he had lived long enough to know that such moments in time left as suddenly as they appeared, and that such times would help sustain him until his last breath. La Nina, who until that moment had been lethargic, became alive, her ears pointing backward, her eyes and body following the movement of the cattle in the corral, ready to bolt at the slightest transfer of Mike's weight. The bawling of the calves, Manolo's shouting, and the *vaqueros'* curses created a chorus of exciting sounds.

It was hard work, but for Mike, it was like a sport, requiring the same skills as the ones needed to anticipate the next jab of a boxing opponent or the block of a rider on the opposite Polo team. Mike had a great time. The *vaqueros* joked with him. He laughed as he cut a calf away from his mother to force him to the gate held open by Monito. Time passed fast as they sorted the cows, calves, and bulls into different corrals until it was well past noon. Manolo then decided to break for lunch and a siesta. They all tied their mounts to the hitching post. The horses were hot and sweaty, not watered yet, but the riders loosened their cinches, took the bits from their mouths, and hung them from the horn of the saddles. Cuca had prepared lunch for all the *vaqueros*. Mike sat with them as he drank his first glass of water, and they chatted about their horses and their work. The *vaqueros* ate their rice, beans, jerky, fried eggs, and fried ripe plantains, while Mike ate plantains from the big tray in the middle of the dining table.

Paulino came into the employees' dining room. "Mike, your father is waiting for you to have lunch. It'll be served soon."

Mike got up slowly from his *taburete*. He was sore and stiff already. The riding in the corrals had strained the muscles of his legs and back. The *vaqueros* noticed Mike's stiffness and hooted.

"Man, you're getting soft! Those books don't help you much out here, do they?" Monito said.

The *vaqueros* broke out in laughter. Mike smiled as he felt the soreness in his muscles and touched his back, "Don't worry, I'll be back riding with you in the morning," and left to meet his father.

Don Miguel was on the porch. He had his first Scotch and water, and now he was nibbling on saltine crackers and Gouda. "I wish you wouldn't ride in the corrals. Any *vaquero* can do that. I didn't send you to college to be a peon," he said critically. "And what were you doing with Chirra? You're too soft. The man's a drunkard. You should know by now that drunks will play you like a fiddle, and that's exactly what Chirra did to you!" His voice rose as Mike ignored him, and poured himself a stiff drink. "Do you really think that Consuelo will see a dime of that money? Do you think she's sick? He's probably laughing at you right now."

Mike took a sip, tasted it, added a splash of water, took another sip, and stretched his legs in front of the white rocking chair.

"Dad, I know what I'm doing. Chirra will be okay. He'll pay me back. He has too much to lose. Look, if I'm coming back, I need to know these people again. I'd like to find a way to help the people that need help, like Consuelo. I want to know, *really know*, all the workers, what they need. See how I can help them. Come on. Let's have lunch. Paulino said it's served."

His father sighed. "Okay, you may work in the corrals, but only this time. We're branding purebreds tomorrow."

Their lunch was simple with beef tenderloin, mixed canned vegetables, one baked yam each, and fruit for dessert.

Paulino brought the coffee and the cigars. "Don Miguel, the jeep is outside. Fernando just brought it over, and he said it's full of gas."

"Okay, it's time to go to *El Pueblo*."

Paulino added, "Don Miguel, Cuca wants you to buy these groceries from the warehouse. Plus, you need more Scotch whisky. We're running low." He took the list, finished drinking his coffee, and grumbled about the poor quality and manners of the help.

Mike went to ask Monito to put La Nina away.

His father waited in the driver's seat only a few moments before he honked impatiently "Let's go, Mike. If we don't call soon, we'll miss the people in Havana. They may have left their office. They don't work like we do."

The red dirt road was dry, and the dust caused by the car contrasted with the blue sky. The pastures on each side had the best animals on the farm. Don Miguel honked when he saw Nandito mowing the San Joaquin baseball field. Nandito waved back with his red cap.

"He's a good boy, but he doesn't have guts. He's afraid of throwing the right ball when it really counts," Don Miguel commented. "He has speed and that's good, here in the boondocks. But he'll never pitch for the Almendares team. If I thought he could, I would have talked to July Sanguily to give him a try."

Mike was surprised. "I knew you liked baseball, but I never thought you followed the players down here."

He laughed. "I need to know about them, too."

6

The Family

DON MIGUEL HAD worked at the family bank for five years, but he never wanted to be a banker. He loved the land, horses, cattle, and the outdoors. He was born into a large family that honored loyalty and had traditions. Among the many unspoken rules and expectations, it was acceptable for a family member to become an attorney, a banker, and a dry-goods salesman, to sell paint by the bucket, refrigerators by the gross, or machinery by the ton. The family approved of a career planting or harvesting sugar, rice, or sisal. They gave a nod to work in the cattle industry. A Rodriguez was never to be a politician, a judge, or a member of the armed forces. The family, like many in their position, offered bribes, but did not accept them. Mike had been raised hearing family stories about the land, who bought it and when, who worked, who played, who lost, who was good, who was bad, and who kept his word.

Don Miguel drove the jeep over a small bridge that spanned a crystal clear stream. The water moved slowly towards the south. Big trees shaded the stream, and on its way through the pasture, the road curved gently. Don Miguel slowed down, since he nearly always stopped to enjoy a view of the water before it flowed into the blue sea. He looked toward the small beach, which was lined with dark sand and crowded with children at play. He honked. The children looked up and happily waved back, unashamed of their nakedness, which was as common as the midday heat. They drove a few hundred meters past the bridge, where Don Miguel and Mike reached the main gate to the highway. The *pueblo* was due east, a short drive away. Don Miguel liked to check on the cattle in the neighbors' pastures, and look at their cane fields to see how tall and green their sugarcane had gotten. He did not talk as he smoked his perennial cigar, and to Mike's annoyance, he kept the radio volume low. Mike was starved for Cuban music. He wanted to hear everything: *guarachas*, *boleros*, and *mambos*, even *décima* contests.

The highway was a straight line from the gate to the *pueblo*, no curves to break the monotony, no interesting hills or beautiful mountains. Mike took over the wheel in front of the telephone office and drove to the warehouse. The telephone exchange was a small utilitarian building. Four telephone operators sat in cane-backed swivel chairs in front of the telephone equipment. A dark wooden counter separated them from the public. There was no magazine rack, and the only reading material was the phone books from other cities. Their only way to pass the time was to talk to the operators. They welcomed Don Miguel's visits. He had spent hour after hour waiting to talk to his family, a buyer for his purebred stock, a friend, or his banker, and he enjoyed flirting with the girls. They, in turn, enjoyed his encouragement, advice, and tantalizing stories about places he had visited around the world. When he placed an international call to Houston or McAllen, Caracas or El Salvador, San Jose or Miami, they asked him to describe the foreign cities. He obliged with a storytelling prowess that briefly transported them to those faraway places.

"Don Miguel, we haven't seen you in a long time. Are you feeling better? We know that Mike just returned from the United States. How is he?" It wasn't a single voice; it was like a quartet of acolytes singing High Mass. The voices changed and came from different directions, mixed with laughter, promises, innuendoes, gossip, and expectancy.

"Oh, he's okay. You'll have the chance to see him, and I feel great! Now, how about some service, and then we can talk." Turning to Carmencita, he said, "How's your new boyfriend? Is he still bringing roses, and are you still telling him perhaps, perhaps, perhaps?"

"Don Miguel, please! That's between him and me. He's been traveling a lot, but he's coming next week."

Adela laughed. "Yes, he travels. He's never here. Maybe that's the way to keep a romance going—never close, never near, always waiting."

Carmencita responded, "No, Adelita, that's not the way it is."

Don Miguel noticed the strain in Carmencita's voice. "We need to have a long talk," he told her. "Let me get these calls out of the way first."

She gave a slight nod.

"First, I need to talk to this number in Havana, B-3779. Then, I'd like to talk to my office at F-2081."

In the meantime, Mike headed to the warehouse. The sugar harvest was getting started. No matter how much work there was to do, the street corners had idlers, who would rather watch the girls, talk baseball, and discuss sugar prices than work. He found a parking place next to the warehouse, and swept into the spot with a quick turn, unwittingly cutting off a battered army jeep. The military vehicle screeched to a halt. A portly army sergeant fumbled out of the driver's seat.

"Halt!" he shouted. "Who do you think you are? Didn't you see that I was parking here?"

Mike had just turned off the ignition, and he turned around, unsure whether the aging military officer was addressing him. "I'm sorry, officer. Are you talking to me? I didn't see you."

The sergeant's eyes grew wider and his breathing more rapid. He stepped toward Mike and boomed, "How dare you question me! Are you calling me a liar?"

"Certainly not," Mike firmly answered as he exited the jeep, and slamming the driver's door, stepped in front of the officer standing squarely before him.

Passersby noticed the confrontation and gathered.

"So, how can I help you?" Mike asked, looking directly into the sergeant's eyes.

The army officer smiled, and with eyes fixed on Mike, suddenly fetched his machete from the front seat of his jeep and flung it up over his shoulder. Grabbing Mike's hair, he forced him to double over. He lashed the machete, flat side down, across Mike's back with all his strength. The men gasped, and the women looked away.

Mike grimaced from the force of the blow. He felt its stiffness against his spine. Images jerked before him: the pavement, the machete's glint, and the sergeant's arm waving back the horrified onlookers.

"You better have more respect for authority!" he shouted as he put down the weapon. "Who do you think you are?"

Mike managed to break away, taking three steps back, red-faced and angry, while he tried to take a steady view of his attacker.

"My name is Mike Rodriguez Fernandez," Mike said in a firm voice. "I live at Las Guásimas farm. Who do you think *you* are? I've done nothing to deserve this." He pulled himself up tall and took a deep breath. "You don't have the right to hit people. I demand an apology from you. Now!" Mike roared.

The sergeant's countenance slowly shifted from rage to fear when he realized he had struck a member of a powerful family. He knew this mistake made him an excellent candidate to join the forces now deployed against the Castro guerrillas in the Oriente province. Mike was dressed in his old ratty clothes, but he realized his mistake now. Yes, it was Mike, the son of Don Miguel. The crowd became silent. The officer did not want to lose authority by apologizing to Mike in front of the lookers.

"Miguelito, sure, I know your father very well," he mumbled. "I haven't seen you since your mother died. You've changed so much, and your clothes—" With a half-smile, the sergeant looked around at the crowd, then leaned in toward Mike and suggested in a hushed voice, "Do you have time for a beer?"

Mike glared back. "No, thanks," and turned his back and walked toward the warehouse. The sergeant looked at the gathered crowd. "Keep moving!" he ordered with the sweep of an arm. Quietly, the people went back to their business. The sergeant, panting and sweating, waddled back to the jeep, threw his machete on the front seat, and roared away.

Mike walked slowly, and gingerly touched his stinging back as he entered the warehouse. The floor was made of rough wooden planks. In the corners, wooden barrels stood open, full of rice, red and black beans, chickpeas, and lentils. Slabs of jerky hung from the ceiling, and rectangular boxes of imported dried codfish were piled on the floor. Behind a wooden counter at the rear, canned goods were stacked high: albacore tuna, soups, tomato purees, sardines, olive oil from Spain, and peanut oil from the island.

Mulato, the clerk that serviced the farm's account, saw Mike and approached him with a smile and an open hand. "Mike, you're lucky, it could have been worse. Welcome to the new era. It certainly wasn't a nice welcoming party. When did you return from the States? What do you need?"

"It's nice to see you. I'll be here for a few days," Mike replied, trying to mask his anger with a smile as he gave him Cuca's list.

Mulato whistled. "Boy, Cuca really wants to take care of you. I haven't seen a list like this since your mother visited the farm. All your father wants these days is blue cheese, whiskey, and corn flakes." He looked up from the list. "I'll have the order finished in half an hour. You want me to put it in the jeep?"

Mike nodded as he reached his arm around again to rub his sore back. Mulato leaned slightly toward him and said in a hushed tone, "Yes, he thinks he's hot stuff. His time will come. Things are changing. Soon he'll be gone."

"I know, but I hope he doesn't hurt anyone else."

He shook hands with Mulato and left to wander the streets. Mike stopped at a street stall close by to buy fruits. The farm had limes, avocadoes, mangoes, and papayas, but his father liked mameys, sapodillas, and custard fruit as well. The fruits had been arranged, as if by a painter, to show their contrasts. The rough texture of a brown mamey was next to a Philippine mango, its pendulous phallic form accentuated by its yellow color. The green and black apple custard fruit, looking like small hand grenades, were piled next to the brown sapodilla, and the large pineapples were surrounded by the vibrant green of the small criollo limes. A mamey that the fruit seller had sliced open displayed its red-pink color, contrasting in texture with the large watermelons and in color with the large green and gold plantains in different stages of ripeness.

"Here, young man, what do you need? Look at these papayas. They're so sweet, they beg to be eaten. These mangoes are from El Caney. I have honeyberries, and if you buy one of the mameys, see how good and ready to eat they are, I'll give you the honeyberries for free."

Mike smiled as he remembered the fruit stands near his college in the little Italian neighborhood—apples, grapes, pears, oranges, grapefruits—but the color, the variety, the textures of the tropical fruits! Each one brought back memories of his grandmother arguing with the fruit vendor about the price of a mango, and how she tested the ripeness of a pineapple by pulling on its leaves. The honeyberries brought memories of swimming pools, girls, and laughter as he pressed the fruit with his fingers, seeing the green skin break, sucking the juice with his puckered lips from the small, hairy pit.

"Yes, I want some mameys and sapodillas. I want a good, large pineapple, ready to eat. I like that Hayden's mango, the big red one. Yes, yes, I want the honeyberries and the melons."

The vendor was happy to find such a willing buyer. "Yes, *Doctor*. I have specials for you. How would you like some real apples from New Jersey? You want red grapes? I just picked them up at the railroad station. They're from California."

Mike smiled. "No, no, I have enough already. Just give me what I asked for. I appreciate it."

Mike paid and walked back to the jeep, both hands weighed down with paper bags. Then he remembered that his father loved grapes and returned to buy some. Mike got into the jeep, and dropped the fruit-filled bags on the front seat. He stopped in front of the telephone exchange and honked the horn. The heat in the cab had become oppressive. His back ached, and his dirty clothes made him even more uncomfortable. He grew irritated waiting for his father and wondered, once again, why they didn't have a phone at the farm. Why drive to the *pueblo* every time they had to call Havana? Wasn't their time worth something? He parked the jeep and entered the exchange, where he had previously spent hours waiting for telephone lines to be free to call his father at an agreed-upon time, only not to find him. He remembered those calls to the United States to find out how his mother was doing, the hesitancy in his father's voice and the softness of his mother's.

"Don't worry, everything will be fine. The doctors are great. New York is very pretty in the winter, all this snow. I'm seeing a very good doctor at Sloan-Kettering. He's the best. Don't worry. Take care of your sisters. We'll be back soon. I'm going to see a musical tonight. I found another horse print for your collection. I love you."

The next time he saw his mother, she was gaunt and lifeless. Her hair was gone, reduced to stubble, and she wore a wig.

He entered the small front room, trying to veil the pain he felt on his back as his father shouted on the phone.

"That's stupid. That's not the way to handle the problem. I have to call the minister. There's a difference. Meat is so cheap it's not even fashionable. A steak on every table, meat is cheaper than chicken. No. No. Don't they understand? I can't help it if some idiot doesn't know how to write a law! That's why we should write it ourselves!"

"Vintage Father," Mike thought with a smile. Perhaps the company of the young beautiful women lifted his spirits, if only for a while. Rita, the youngest operator, was the first to notice that Mike had entered the exchange.

"Mike, what's happened to you? You look so serious! Come here, you know I don't bite. I bet you all those *Americanitas* can't leave you alone."

Mike smiled. He had always liked Rita's sassy style. "Rita, you look great!" Mike said, admiring her beauty, from her long, slender legs and lean build to her flowing blonde hair. "What have you been eating that makes you look so good?"

"Flattery from men like you! I heard that you only have time for your studies. No fun, eh? It's about time you return to this hot land of passion."

"Hey, you little doves, it's not time to flirt. We have a business to run." His father said, holding his hand over the receiver. "I know he's good looking—like his father!" He turned back to Mike, "Mike, son, come here. I need to know if you can find where Dr. Andres Comillas is right now. You can use that station. Here's my little black book. Call his office. You remember the doctor. He's the mercantile notary, and has all those exotic chickens and rabbits. I need to talk to him and set up a meeting with the minister. I may have to go back to Havana. The politicians are destroying everything."

He nudged Mike toward the unoccupied telephone booth. Mike asked, "Rita, please see if you can connect me to F-6162 in Havana. No, I know he was joking. We can talk later."

Dr. Comillas's secretary answered the phone. It was three o'clock. The doctor might be at the Floridita, she said, but she wasn't sure. She didn't know if he would come back to the office that afternoon. Yes, he might have gone to his farm. Yes, she would give him the message. Maybe, he could be at the American Club. No, she didn't know where his chauffeur was. Yes, she would tell him. Mike left the booth and tapped his father's shoulder as Don Miguel flirted with Rita. Mike's touch surprised Don Miguel. Rita looked up and winked. She knew she was part of a game.

"You couldn't find him?" he asked Mike.

"No, sir. I spoke with his secretary. She didn't help much."

"I may have to go back to Havana. I need to talk to all of them. It was a bad time to call him. Do you have everything we need?" his father asked.

Mike nodded "Yes, I'm ready to go. Good-bye, Rita. It's nice to see you. Good-bye, girls."

Father and son left the office. Seeing that Mike had left the bag full of grapes on the middle of the seat, Don Miguel promptly took a handful and started to eat them.

"These are good. I haven't had grapes in a long time. You know, I think Eve gave Adam grapes instead of an apple. They're more inviting. They always paint Bacchus with grapes in his mouth," his father said as he savored the fruit. "My Son—a word of advice. Don't play with the merchandise unless you plan to buy it. Rita is charming, but she's not for you."

Mike was upset by his father's suggestion. "Dad, why did you tell the girls that I'm staying at the farm? You know I have to get back to the States. I have to finish my master's. What are you thinking? And why do we waste time taking these trips to the *pueblo* to make phone calls? It's such a waste of time. You should get a phone at the farm."

"Yes, sir. These grapes are good." His father drove, all the while ravishing the grapes as he kept one hand on the steering wheel. With the other, he made forays into the paper sack, searching for more of the plump grapes.

7

Martinito and Havana

AFTER MIKE AND his father left, Manolo continued to work the cattle in the corrals. He was the foreman, the *mayoral*. He had taught all of his sons, including Monito, to be *vaqueros*. He did not know about tractors, but he knew about bulls and cows, horses and saddles, pastures and fences. Manolo munched on the last of his *Cohibas* while he worked among the cattle of three pastures, vaccinating and branding more than ninety calves, dehorning and vaccinating one hundred ten cows and nine bulls. Finally, it was time to leave for his *bohío*. He would have been home if he lived at the *batey*, but he did not like to have to answer to Don Miguel's questions every night, like Ricardo and Manuel. He liked to drink his rum in peace.

Monito followed his father to their house. He was thinking about La Nina and Mike. She was the best mare at the farm and she could cut cattle. But she was out of shape. He had watched her, lathered with white sweat, breathing hard. Mike shouldn't have ridden her so hard. He wasn't in good shape, either. He laughed when Mike dismounted, because he was so sore he could hardly walk. Plus, his skin was so pale that the morning sun had colored his face a glowing red. Was that why people went north? To get pale and soft and to hurt when they rode a good horse?

For his part, Chirra was happy. He had finished the day without a major fight with Manuel. He did not like to muck stalls and carry the wet, smelly hay to the compost pile. It was tough work and his muscles were sore. He wanted Manuel to hire someone else to do his job, so he could supervise the other guy. "Is that not the way the *El Viejo* does it?" Chirra put a blanket on the gray mule as he said to Manuel, "I want to be here very early in the morning. The walk of this mule is faster than my trot. I don't trot well, as you know. And the only time I run is away from husbands."

Manuel laughed and let him use the mule.

Chirra, with a smile on his face and thirst in his throat, left the *batey*. "I have *cinco* pesos in my pocket and a mule for transportation. Now, let's see how I do at the *bodega*."

After he left, Martinito went to talk with Cuca. His baby girl had diarrhea and his wife knew very little about those things.

Paulino was cleaning Don Miguel's boots, polishing them while the radio played. He was whistling along to the tune, a conga.

> *Si te vas al Cobre,*
>   If you go to the Sanctuary of the Cobre,
> *Quiero que me traigas*
>   I want you to bring me
> *Una Virgencita de la Caridad . . .*
>   A small Virgin of Charity

Martinito approached Paulino and asked, "Is Cuca in? I need to talk to her."

Paulino shouted, "Cuca, Cuca! Martinito is here to pay his respects to you. He forgot his visiting card, though. He didn't bring flowers, either."

Cuca, with her white apron snug around her body, came out. "Paulino, I'm not deaf. Yes, I'll see the gentleman. Madame is receiving today, Martinito, what do you want?"

"My Anita was very sick last night. She has the runs and she cried all night. This morning she finally went to sleep. Ana doesn't know what to do. My baby had the runs so many times that she has to be hungry and weak. I don't know what to do. I'm pretty nervous. Can I borrow milk from you?"

"No, not milk, she needs to be hydrated. Have you given her water?" Seeing how dumbfounded he looked, she went on, "Please borrow the car and bring her over here. Don Miguel and Mike should be coming shortly, and I don't want to leave. Paulino, why don't you give Martinito the keys to the Ford? I know Don Miguel wouldn't mind."

Cuca went back inside the house to see what medicines she had in the medicine chest.

CHIRRA RODE THE old gray mule to the front of the *bodega*. He tied the mule to the hitching post, and strutted inside the dimly lit store. When Carlos the *bodeguero* saw him, he was not pleased. He knew that Chirra was not working.

"Hey, *bodeguero*, you have a customer who is very thirsty. I have money." With a flourish Chirra threw his five-peso bill on the counter. "Now, let's see what type of rum you have that I may wish to drink. Matusalen? Bacardi? Or maybe I should start with a cold beer? Hatuey? Polar? Cristal? Or maybe a soft drink like a Materva, a Coca Cola, or an Orange Crush? Oh, how many decisions when you have money!"

Carlos, who hated Chirra, had to smile. The man had style. He had not been able to buy food in weeks, and now he just appeared with cash in his pocket, acting like he owned the place. "Yes, Chirra, how can I help you?"

"Well, Carlos, let me see. I have this list of things I may need, but I would also like to celebrate being back in the world of high finance and employment as the newest and most experienced member of Don Miguel's team. Let us start with a small glass of *Aguardiente*—a good brand, not a Pati Cruzao—and then I can reflect on what I should have next."

Carlos pulled a shot glass, filled it to the brim, and put it in front of Chirra. He smelled it, caressed it as if it contained a thirty-year-old cognac, and with a rapid motion, gulped it. "That feels good. Now, let's see, I owe you ten cents for this elixir. It's lonely, so let's have another to celebrate the start of a great relationship. I'm employed, you see. I can afford to buy goods from you. Let's see, I need coffee, black beans, and rice, and do you have some cornmeal? No, no cornmeal, I don't want to buy anything that's yellow. But while you look for those things, how about another drink? My body feels tired, and it really could use a lift."

Carlos poured, then took the five-peso note from the counter, and started to weigh the beans in a paper sack.

MARTINITO CAREFULLY DROVE the Ford home. He stopped the car on the dirt road, crawled under the fence, and ran to his *bohío*. His wife was holding the baby. "Hurry, let's go. I have Don Miguel's car outside. Cuca will treat the baby. Leave the others behind. You don't have time to dress them. Hurry, Cuca is waiting!"

"Should we call a neighbor?"

"Yes, do it in a hurry."

Don Miguel was driving on the road to the *batey* when he saw his Ford parked at the roadside and stopped. Mike got out of the jeep. He saw a small procession with Martinito in front, his wife, Ana, right behind, holding a small child in her arms, and the rest of her brothers and sisters, some of them naked, others with only shirts, accompanied by a woman neighbor.

"Martinito, what's happening?" Mike asked.

"My baby is sick. I'm taking her to Cuca to see what medicine she may need."

Don Miguel crooked his finger, "Let me see the baby." The mother offered the foul-smelling baby to him, and Don Miguel touched her skin. It was dry and lifeless. "Don't take her to Cuca. You'd better go to see a doctor right away. This baby is dehydrated. Mike, you take them to Dr. Paco. He'll know what do to."

Ana climbed into the backseat with the little baby, while Martinito sat up front. Mike took off, driving quickly. The Ciego de Ávila clinic was half an hour away.

Don Miguel asked himself bitterly, "When are they going to learn?"

Mike wanted to sound hopeful for Ana, but he was afraid that his voice would betray his concern. Martinito sat twisted around, facing the backseat. "She'll be fine. Don't worry. We'll be there soon." Ana held the baby tightly to her bosom.

The clinic was located in the middle of the town, on the south side of the highway. There was no emergency entry. Mike pushed open the door for Ana, and said, "Martinito, go and ask for Dr. Paco. I'll meet you there."

Martinito, bewildered and nervous, took the lead and entered a crowded reception room. A nurse sat at a small desk. Small benches were filled with patients waiting to be called.

Martinito exclaimed, "I need to see Dr. Paco. My baby is very sick. Where can I find him?"

The nurse told him sit down and wait, but seeing Ana and her small bundle, realized that it was an emergency.

She called another nurse, "Come, come here. Take them inside."

They were taken in a hurry to a room as a pediatric nurse came and took the baby and held her in her arms. She touched her dry skin and asked how many hours she'd had diarrhea.

Ana replied, "Six to seven."

"What have you done? What have you given her?"

"I tried to give her some milk. She didn't take it well. Is she sick?"

"Yes, she's very sick. We have to give her fluids right away."

She went to fetch the IV equipment and electrolytes. She was an older woman who had seen so many of these babies, malnourished, sick, with their tummies distended, full of parasites. Their mothers didn't know any better. They were afraid to ask questions, unable to read instructions, and were unfamiliar with the basic tenets of health and prevention.

"Are you the father?" she asked Martinito. "Hold her down, against the table. We have to find a vein. Near her foot is the best place." And talking to Ana, "Hold this bottle high so the liquid can go into her veins until we can set it right. We don't have time to waste."

Ana started to cry. "Is she going to die?"

The nurse didn't answer. She was busy finding the vein.

Out in the waiting room, Mike asked about his group and found them. Dr. Paco had just entered and went directly to touch the baby's skin.

"Your baby girl is going to be okay. She'll have to spend the night here, though. I want to be sure she's well-hydrated." To Ana specifically, he added, "You and I have to have a long and serious talk. You can't wait this long to come here. This was a close call—another hour and your baby would have been dead."

He turned to Martinito. "I don't know how many children you have, but you better stop, unless you want to be a widower and have orphans. This child has to eat better, and you have to fuck less. Do you understand?" Martinito nervously nodded. "Okay, now you keep holding her, and we'll see if she needs another bottle of electrolytes." As he continued to examine the baby, he broke into a smile. "What a pretty little girl. What's her name?"

Her mother answered with a half-smile, "Anita, doctor, Anita."

Dr. Paco left the room to speak to Mike privately. "Mike, I'm glad you came. That baby could have died."

"Yes, it was close."

The doctor relaxed, knowing a patient had been saved. Smiling fondly at Mike, he changed the subject. "Boy, I haven't seen you since your mother died. I know how well you're doing by the stories your father tells me. He's really proud of you. Do you know that I see him at least twice a month?"

"No, I wasn't aware. I thought he didn't like doctors."

The doctor didn't acknowledge the remark. "I'm a bit worried about his depression and his breathing. I told him not to smoke another cigar, and then he comes and brings me a box of Larrañagas. Now he wants me to give him some Swiss injections of B-12. He thinks this will keep him young and help him with the way he feels, but he doesn't take care of himself. He can't relax." The doctor reflected, then frowned. "He misses your mother very much. It's hard to believe that more than five years have gone by since she died."

Mike seized his cue, saying, "I'd like to speak with you for a few minutes about how he's doing."

Dr. Paco nodded. "Let's go to my office, where we can talk privately."

He guided Mike through a maze of hallways. Every few steps he stopped to say hello to a patient or a family member. His office was small, cluttered, and full of medical periodicals published in the United States and France. The pictures of his family were the only nonmedical intrusions. Among the photos, Mike recognized Rosarito, Dr. Paco's oldest daughter, whom Mike had briefly dated when they both were attending *bachillerato* in Havana. He offered Mike a seat, and then he sat behind his cluttered desk. Dr. Paco looked tired. He took off his eyeglasses and rubbed his face.

"I was afraid it would be too late," Mike said, shaking his head. "That poor baby looked so fragile. How often does this kind of thing happen?"

"Too often. They don't take precautions, they don't use clean water, and they usually come too late. We don't educate them, and they surely aren't educating themselves. Your father tries, but most people? They don't care. Yes, they breed, party, drink, fuck, and have babies, and their babies have babies."

"Yes, then once the kids get strong and old enough to work, their parents want them to leave school to help them. We don't allow that at the farm."

Dr. Paco nodded. "Many of the children who come here actually get hurt on the job, but many don't come in because they don't have medical insurance."

Mike answered, "We carry it."

"Yes, your father does. It's the law, but few farms carry it, and the law isn't enforced. Most workers hardly know how to read. They're too afraid or nervous to come see us, and they listen to that lousy singer on the radio who sings *décimas* telling them they'll be cured if they put their hands over a glass of water next to the radio. They drink the water and believe their ailment has miraculously disappeared. It's ridiculous! Or, they go to a *curandero* for a *despojo*, a cleansing."

"Ha!" Mike laughed. "Yes, Mando, our *curandero*, is very good at that. He's always asking Father what new medications may be available to mix in his potions." Mike continued, "He's a good man, though. Some workers are just afraid of coming to you. They know that at least this *curandero* is not going to hurt them."

Dr. Paco shook his head. "I don't know why I'm here. I should quit and go to Havana to be with my daughter, who's growing up without me at her side. Her mother and aunt are with her, but I hardly see them." He left off his complaining, turning to a related subject. "Say, you're friendly with Rosarito. She says she wants to get married. I think the boy is one of your school friends."

"Yes, I know Manolo very well. We played basketball together."

Dr. Paco continued, "She's still too young. They're always too young. I wanted them to be educated, and that's why I sent them away. Our educational system is a mess. Everything is Havana, Havana, and Havana. Here, we are at the asshole of the world."

Mike had known Dr. Paco as far back as he could recall. He had diagnosed his mother's cancer before the Havana doctors understood what was wrong with her. Yet he would grouse, unless someone got him on the topic of medicine.

"Doctor, Father has changed. He coughs a lot and smokes at least five cigars a day, not counting the cigarettes he pilfers from the help. He has this crazy diet of meat and potatoes at lunch, one or two Scotch highballs before each meal, and pound cake, cheese, and ice cream for dinner. He tells me that you recommended he have two drinks before each meal. 'Dr. Paco, who went to the Sorbonne, says I should have my Scotch.' Then he tells me he's going to die, that he needs me here. What's happening with him?"

Dr. Paco stood up and looked down at him. "Mike, we grow old. The first time I saw you, you couldn't have been older than five or six. You had eaten some green bananas and had a bellyache—your mother thought you were dying. She didn't trust me. She thought I was a country bumpkin. She would have taken you to Havana if she thought you could survive the trip." Dr. Paco was wandering, but not too far off the subject. "And I've known your father since our childhood. Yes, your father isn't well. He worries too much, smokes too much, and misses your mother terribly. I've told him to have a drink or two. It's good for his heart, and at least he comes to me when he doesn't feel well. If I always said no, you can't do this, you can't do that, I'd never see my patients until it's too late."

Mike scratched the back of his head and smiled. "Well, that drinking prescription he follows well."

"I told him to find a young girl and have a ball. He needs to rev his engine once in a while. You know an old man and a younger woman can make a good combination—if the old man knows what the young woman wants. Sometimes it gets screwed up. He thinks that he's in love, that he's young again, that she loves him for his looks, not his money or his position. Then you have a problem. I don't think your father will follow my advice, though—he's too conservative. Are you surprised by what I'm telling you?"

"Yes, in a way. I've never thought about it, well, at least not where my father is concerned," Mike laughed.

"Look, he needs you right now. Maybe you can help at the farm, so that your father can be free to do things he's passionate about, that make him want to get up in the morning. Maybe he'll find someone to help him recover his zest for life. He would trust you with the farm. He's not going to take care of himself until he knows the farm is secure, but we both know he isn't going to ask you for help, even though he badly needs it right now."

Mike thought for a moment. "Father really isn't old. He's in his early fifties. I don't know why he hasn't started seeing other women."

"He doesn't think he could possibly enjoy life with them as he did with your mother," Dr. Paco answered. "He's too young to think that way. If he took care of himself and quit smoking, he'd be okay."

"Is anything really wrong with him?" Mike asked.

"No, not really. He should exercise as he did before, lose weight, and eat better than he does now. His blood pressure is good, a little on the high side, but that's normal for a man like your father."

Dr. Paco got up and moved to the door, "Now, let's see how that baby girl is doing. I hope I haven't scared you. It's always difficult to be sincere with a patient's family. They rarely want to hear the truth."

Mike stood up and shook Dr. Paco's hand. "Thank you. I really appreciate it." He followed Dr. Paco back to Anita's room.

Martinito sat on his haunches outside the room, fingering his dirty old cap in his hands. Ana was in the room with Anita. Dr. Paco knocked at the door and entered. The baby was asleep while her mother dozed off on a chair next to the bed. She lifted her head as Dr. Paco closed the door behind him. Dr. Paco smiled as he read the chart. "Your daughter is fine. You have to be cautious with her. You need to watch her very carefully for the next few days. Lydia, the nurse, will tell you what to do. We may need to give her more liquids. Good night, and please remember—don't leave without seeing me in the morning."

Mike assured Ana, "Martinito will pick you and Anita up tomorrow. I've got to go back to the farm." He gave her ten pesos. "If you need more money, I'll give it to Martinito. I hope you feel better. Anita will be fine. She's a beautiful girl."

"Thanks, Mike. Thank your father. I appreciate it."

"Don't worry. Anita will be fine. Rest a little."

Mike and Dr. Paco left the room and found Martinito waiting at the door. Dr. Paco said, "You can stay if you want, but you're not needed."

Martinito nodded, slightly baffled. Everything had happened so quickly: the trip, the clinic, and the IVs.

"Do you want to stay?" Mike asked.

"No, I have to go see about my children."

"Come, let's go. I know Father is worried about Anita. You know she's in good hands. She'll be okay. You'll come and pick her up tomorrow. I'll lend you the jeep. Don't worry."

"Thanks, Mike."

Mike drove back to the ranch, and as they arrived at the main gate, Martinito opened it. They heard someone shouting behind them. They weren't surprised to see Chirra riding the old gray mule. He was drunk.

AT SIX O'CLOCK the next morning, Paulino knocked at Don Miguel's door. "Buenos días, Don Miguel, your coffee. Do you want it on your night table?"

Don Miguel was half asleep. "Thanks, Paulino. Please tell Ricardo I want to see him."

"Yes, sir, with pleasure. I'll convey your message right away."

Ricardo had finished his first cup of coffee when Paulino came up, whistling a new tune. "Hey, *El Viejo* is in great shape this morning. He wants to see you right away."

Ricardo knocked on the door as Don Miguel was putting on his robe. "Come in, Ricardo. I want you to finish the last pasture. Root plow, burn it, and scatter Guinea grass seed. Mike will stay at the farm while I'm in Havana. He's in charge, be sure you take care of him."

Ricardo nodded. He knew Don Miguel and how to carry out his orders.

Mike woke up sore, but he wanted to ride La Nina again. He came upon his father sitting at the dining room table. Don Miguel had his usual breakfast as the radio broadcast the self-censored morning news.

"Good morning, Son. I hope you slept well. You know, you have to start earlier. You're not in your college now. You're on a farm."

"Father—" but before he could utter another word, his father interrupted.

"I've already met with Ricardo. Now I'll see Manuel, and then go to the *pueblo*, and depending on whom I can talk to, I'll stay or go to Havana."

"Dad, I think —"

"Oh, and yes, it may be a good idea for you to stay for a few days. I want to be sure that Ricardo gets what he needs to finish that pasture. I don't trust Manolo. He thinks that Ricardo is too close to us, and he'll do everything to make him look bad."

"Yes, Father."

"I don't want you to advance money to the employees. You'll be tested."

"Yes, I understand," Mike said, then quietly drank his freshly squeezed orange juice.

"You're now in charge, but no hiring, no big decisions. See how it works. You'll call me once a week. At night after six; it's cheaper."

"How long you will be gone? I do need to get back to the university, you know."

His father's face remained blank. "I don't know. It depends."

Mike knew how pointless it was to talk to his father when he erected his infamous soundproof wall.

Without adding a single word, Don Miguel stood up and left the dining room, his red silk robe billowing out behind him.

Mike gulped his coffee. He was disturbed and disappointed. He took the last swallow, and trailed his father out of the house for another day as his dutiful son.

Manuel had lined up a group of heifers in front of the stalls to dry off after they'd been washed. Chirra had already cleaned out the barn, and was not visibly hungover. Don Miguel fished a cigar out of Mike's *guayabera* pocket.

"I forgot mine. You can afford to lend it to your father."

Manuel, munching his own, lit Don Miguel's cigar and said, "We're going to need two or three more young calves. All the ones we have are white. I'd like a few reds. Reds are selling well. The de la Torres are having good luck with theirs, and new breeders like to have color and Indú-Brazil ears for their show string. I know ears don't weigh on the scale, but they sure sell."

Don Miguel, staring at the young heifers, turned his cigar in his hand. He was visualizing the future shape of one. "Is she out of Manso by the 256/12 cow? She has that look. You should increase her feed. She could use additional weight."

The *vaqueros* had brought in another purebred herd to the corrals. This time, Mayajigua, the oldest cowboy on the ranch, was the lead *vaquero*, and he sang in his fine, clear voice. Don Miguel had inherited him; he came with the property. When Mayajigua saw Mike, he gave a loud yell and threw his hat in the air.

"Mike! Welcome. You're back."

Mike smiled. "You, old man, you haven't changed a bit. Are you teaching the other *vaqueros* how to ride?"

Mayajigua laughed and replied, "Yes, I am, and you haven't changed a bit, either!"

Don Miguel went back to the house. He always ran late in the morning. There was much to pay attention to. Also, he often slowed his pace to take pleasure in the silence of the morning and the gradual waking up of the *batey* with its voices, the clatter of tubs and pails being filled, the rhythmic sound of windmills pumping water into holding tanks. A world full of sound and activity followed, surrounding him. It was his: He had created it, formed it, and made it happen.

He went into his bathroom to shave. He loved to feel the soft bristle brush against his face, the hot lather, the clean smell of the English shaving soap, and then, little by little, to see his face appear in the mirror, clean and smooth around his thick mustache, which had started to show a few gray hairs. His father had worn one, smaller, clipped, and Germanic. His grandfather also had one, but his had handlebars, florid, fuller—and his great-grandfather? He didn't remember, but now it wasn't important. He had to live for today. Somehow that had become impossible to do since Adelaida's death. Memories, only memories, filled the space. Their images filled his library in Havana: old photos, small paintings on ivory medallions, hand-colored photos in small silver frames, their colors mellowed with the passage of time. No one left to pray for their souls. His mind needed room for new ideas, new things—and maybe new loves? He smiled. Is that why I am shaving so closely? He examined his body in the dressing mirror. It wasn't what it once was. He was heavier and his muscles had relaxed. He had strong legs, but he could not keep his gut in. Adelaida was no longer with him to enjoy the small pleasures of life, mornings in the parks of Rome, afternoons on a white beach, looking over the blue sea waiting for what she called the *green ray* that appeared for a brief second as the sun's orange sphere dipped into the blue sea. When she saw it, she smiled, because her wish would come true.

He dressed simply, since it was a hot day. He selected a white linen *guayabera* and a pair of linen slacks, a small gold stud on his collar, to show he could both afford one and that, if he wanted, he could close the collar and wear a bow tie, and a pair of jodhpur brown boots. He felt old and stiff as he bent over to pull up his boots. Who would take better care of him than Cuca and Paulino? Oh, yes, they did not want him to smoke cigars. Paulino and Cuca smoked, but they didn't want him to smoke. Young people believed they were immortal. Dr. Paco wanted him to quit smoking. What's the difference? I'm going to die. He splashed Bay Rhum on his face. Now he was ready to go to the *pueblo* to talk to those idiots in Havana who were mishandling everything.

Paulino, in the dining room, stopped his make-believe cleaning. "Don Miguel, are you going to a funeral or a wedding? You're all dressed up. You look like a new man. What has Dr. Paco given you lately? Another B-12 shot?"

Don Miguel ignored the bantering. "Paulino, see if Fernando has the car ready. I may come back before lunch, but if I'm not here at one, I'll eat in the *pueblo*. Mike and I will have dinner together. I would like to eat at seven-thirty. Be sure Cuca knows."

Paulino noticed the harsh edge in his voice. His boss had not liked Paulino making fun of him. "Yes, sir, I'll tell Cuca. Do you want to eat a leg of lamb? I heard that Alfred told Mike he was bringing a small lamb."

"Ask Mike," he said brusquely. "He's going to be in charge. He can order whatever he wants to eat from Cuca. Anything is fine with me."

"Don Miguel," asked Paulino, "would you please check the post office box? I'm expecting letters."

"Letters, or checks for articles you're writing under your nom de plume?"

Paulino shrugged his shoulders. "Hemingway wasn't published on his first draft. I'm going to be famous one day."

"Bah, see if Fernando is outside waiting for me. I'm running late."

Don Miguel went to his office to raid his humidor, but it wasn't there. He strode back to the kitchen, "Cuca, what the hell is going on? Where are my cigars? Paulino, by God, what is happening in this house? I leave for a few minutes and I can't find a thing. Where are my cigars?"

Cuca came hurrying out of the kitchen. "Don Miguel, Dr. Paco told Mike that you shouldn't smoke. Mike told me he was going to hide your cigars, so I gave him your humidor and your cigar boxes. I don't know what he did with them."

"So that he could smoke and share them with Ricardo and Manuel!" he cried. "Well, you better find out. I'm still paying you, not this juvenile Americanized twit. If he thinks he's going to control me, he has a rough job ahead of him. I feel perfectly fine. Find out where he hid my cigars!" His face was red, and his voice had reached a high pitch. The exertion of the confrontation fueled his cough. "Cuca, Cuca, get me some water. I need water. Please."

"Here's the water. Don't worry. Mike is trying to take care of you. He's a good boy, he loves you."

"With so much love, I may die of suffocation," Don Miguel muttered and finished his glass of water.

Outside, Fernando opened the door to the Ford, and Don Miguel sat next to him and fidgeted. "Fernando, do you have a cigar?"

He laughed. "Don Miguel, with what you pay me I can hardly buy a bad cigar like the ones Manuel smokes. So I quit buying. I have to save my money. I just borrow."

"Stop at the *bodega* then. Let's see Carlos. He has the good cigars hidden in the back. If I'm going to die, I want to die smoking a good cigar!"

"Yes, sir. Whatever you say."

After their stop at the *bodega*, they went to the telephone exchange. Don Miguel instructed Fernando, "I'll be here less than an hour. Fill the tank with gas, check the oil and tires, and come back and wait for me. It might be earlier, but I doubt it."

The operators gaily greeted Don Miguel, who replied with aplomb, "It's a great day! How are you doing? I'm doing fine, thank you! Who's the lucky girl who's going to take care of me? I may surprise her!"

Adela answered with a smile, "I'll take care of you."

He pulled out his black phone book from his briefcase and gave the numbers to her. "Remember, nothing is worth anything until you try it, and sometimes you have to try it many times." He laughed at his own stab at philosophy, a watered-down Dale Carnegie, while he waited on the uncomfortable bench smoking his cigar.

Adela's first call was to Dr. Comillas's office. "Please, this is a long-distance call, *pueblo* wants to speak with Dr. Andres Comillas, is he available?"

A few minutes passed and he heard a ring in the next booth. He picked up the phone and heard Andres' warm voice: "Only one person could be calling from the asshole of the world. What do you need? I know that you're living the quiet, monastic life. No women, no brandy, nothing to excite or disturb you, while I'm here, in this cesspool of corruption and intrigue, trying to keep our great country together, using Band-Aids and iodine."

"I have to work for a living," Don Miguel answered.

"When am I going to see you? People are forgetting you're alive. If you're not seen, you may be dead," Andres replied.

"You know I work," Don Miguel said with a laugh. "I don't have a sinecure for life, like you, and not everyone is doing my job for me, but I talked to Pepe, yes Pepe, our friend. This time he knows what he's talking about. He told me that our good friend the minister doesn't want to sponsor our prepared decree. How can he do that? We, at the Cattlemen's Association, have always backed him. We're not asking anything for ourselves. It's for the country! What do you think?"

Comillas remained silent for a few seconds.

"Hello, hello, are you there? I can't hear you."

Dr. Comillas's voice came back. "No, the line is okay. I heard an echo in your voice and I didn't like it. Yes, I also heard that from Pepe. It's difficult to talk on the phone these days. You should come back here. We'll play dominoes, have a drink or two, see the minister, or better yet, invite him to my penthouse. He likes and needs to hear from people like you to know what's happening in the interior of the country—in the provinces. Too many rumors are floating around. Yes, you should come back." Suddenly Don Miguel was left with a hum on the line.

Adela spoke to him. "The communication was cut. Don Miguel, do you want to place another call?"

"Yes, Adelita, please call my office. After that, please call my son-in-law, Jose Maria."

The conversation with his office was peremptory. He talked to Lustre, who gave him the balances in his bank accounts and updated him on the farm receivables. Jose Maria was happy about Mike's returning to Cuba. He didn't try to reach his other son-in-law, Julio. He was probably playing gin rummy at the yacht club on the fifth floor, where the men's bedrooms and lockers were, or playing golf at the country club. At least he was well dressed and had a low handicap, but there was no point discussing farm business with him. Maybe I should send Mike to Europe. Do what my father did to me. Let him have fun, get fluent in French, dance a little, drink a little. After I tasted all of those nice things and knew how to enjoy them, he called me back and put me to work. I had to be married—right away! At least I loved her. Yes, I loved her.

Rita called him over. "Don Miguel, I'm sorry that I couldn't be of much help today. Adela told me you had many calls to make. Did Mike come with you? He looks so much like you."

He smiled. If only he were younger, he could teach that blond tease a thing or two. "No, Rita, but his father is here, and he has experience." Rita played along, laughing at what he said as he continued, "Mike is at the farm. I may have to go to Havana, maybe tomorrow. Maybe you want to come to the farm and see our new horses?" The string had been played out long enough, and he turned serious. "Can you dial my house, please?"

Rita connected him and said, "I have your house on the line. Give my regards to Mike, but please don't tell him I asked about him."

"Don't worry. It's a secret I'll carry to my grave." He started shouting on the phone, "*Alo, alo*, Estrella, yes, it's me. I'll be at the house tomorrow night, late. I'm bringing Fernando, be sure that the garage room is ready. Yes, I have the key. Bye."

He left the booth, thanked the operators, and handed each of them a small bottle of French perfume from his briefcase. "I found these little things. People sound better when they smell sweet. I'll be calling you from Havana. Have fun. Don't do anything I wouldn't do. I'll tell Mike to come here and make his calls, so you be sure you take good care of him."

They left the *pueblo* and returned to the farm. In a few minutes, Don Miguel was packed. He carried a small leather valise with his shaving kit, a box of cigars, clean underwear, and an extra white *guayabera*. Adelaida had never left any house without a large suitcase or trunk in tow, so he had learned to pack light in rebellious behavior. The sun was low on the horizon. Don Miguel knew the road by heart, and Fernando came as company. A long boring trip was an ideal time to catch up on the farm gossip and the state of their universe.

They entered Havana from the north side. The new tunnel under the bay still had its French-built freshness, the sculpture of its heroic horses standing at its exit. The Morro Castle lighthouse moved its useless stream of light over the bay. The steel bridge over the Almendares still needed paint, and Quinta Avenida boasted of its richness with its clock tower and cultivated gardens. His house was nearby on a hill on the other side of the polluted river. On still nights he smelled the decayed matter that floated through its waters to the sea. It was two o'clock in the morning when they arrived. Fernando stepped out in front of the garage and opened the door for the car.

"Don Miguel, do you want me to ring?"

"No, I have the key. Estrella is probably asleep."

The house was not large by wealthy Cuban standards. He had built it in the late thirties, and it had a modern French influence with wide windows, glass bricks, curves, clean lines, and white paint. It was a bridge between a sophisticated modern European sensibility and the demands of a tropical climate. The foyer was of marble and the downstairs floor was of terrazzo. A large Oriental rug partially covered the formal living room's floor; Chinese porcelain figurines adorned the room's mirrored wall. A carved wooden image of the Sacred Heart of Jesus above the front door was the only sign of the Catholic faith in the public rooms of the house. Don Miguel's library on the first floor was the only room with air-conditioning. Next to the library and the formal living room was a large covered porch onto which the dining room opened. A large pantry and laundry room adjoined the kitchen. Despite the modern convenience of the washing machine, Estrella, believing such an abhorrence was the best way to destroy good clothes, did all the washing by hand. She had left a note for Don Miguel on the foyer table, written with carefully formed small block letters: "Dr. Comillas called you. Please call him in the morning. Key to the garage room is in the envelope. Goodnight. Estrella." He crumpled the note, gave the key to Fernando, double-locked the front door, and went up to his bedroom.

He was spent, and yet not sleepy. He thought, "Years ago I would have still had enough energy to go to Montmartre to catch the last show. Now all I want is a hot chamomile tea and a bath." For most of his life, he had believed that aging was all in your mind. Now he wasn't so sure. He entered his bathroom, not changed since his wife's death. It was one of her shrines: The perfume in the bottles slowly evaporated, and her silver toilette set, combs and brushes with engraved initials, was still on her makeup table. His red toothbrush and her golden toothbrush leaned against each other in the same Lucite holder.

He threw his *guayabera*, socks, and underwear in the wicker hamper and put on a pair of short-legged pajamas. He opened the windows to let the night breeze in along with the sounds of the night, recited three Hail Marys and made the sign of the Cross, put the lights out, and tried to go to sleep.

He always felt her presence, but more in this room than anywhere else in the house. Adelaida had designed it, picked out the furniture, feminine and practical. Her face was in every photo. Their daughters had given her clothes to the nuns, and he had given her jewels to the girls with the exception of her favorite diamond ring. "You should buy only perfect stones," his father had always told him, and this one was perfect. He had found it during the war in a small jewelry shop in Havana. It had belonged to a lady who had left Europe with the stone hidden in a small pouch in her brassiere. He had been casual about it when he gave it to Adelaida. The price of sugar was high. "This is for having our son," he had said. At the end, when it was the only piece she wore on her now-thinner finger, she told him to keep it for Mike, for when he got married. "You gave it to me. I want it for him, so that he can make another woman as happy as you've made me."

FERNANDO OPENED THE door to his simple utilitarian room. Estrella had placed a clean towel on the bed. A small window with bars offered the only ventilation. Fernando hung his shirt and pants on wire hangers and went to sleep nude.

Estrella heard the opening of the garage door and made the sign of the cross. "Thank my Lord, they arrived safely." She could now sleep in peace. Estrella had grown up on a small farm in the interior of the island, playing barefoot in the mud, running in the fields, and riding horses bareback. Eventually she tired of taking care of her screaming brothers and sisters, so she left them, her mother, father, aunts, and uncles to come to Havana. She brought a letter of recommendation to Adelaida's mother, Lola, who hired her to work in the kitchen, washing and cleaning dishes and pots, plucking chickens, peeling potatoes. She liked the work. She followed Otilio, the cook, and learned how he prepared the traditional dishes. Lola believed that a family was kept together by eating together. Every other day, she had her children and their spouses for a traditional Spanish lunch, and one night weekly for her grandchildren. Lunch was served at twelve-thirty sharp and coffee at two o'clock; after that, you could leave. Two servants waited on the table, formal style. Everyone talked at the same time. When Otilio retired, a casualty of old age and a taste for cooking sherry, Estrella became Lola's cook, and when Lola died, Adelaida kept Estrella as a connection to her childhood. Estrella wore a simple blue uniform with her dyed jet-black hair worn in a tight bun. The color of her hair and cooking the best custard, a recipe she had stolen from Otilio and improved upon, were her vanities. Estrella was up early, as usual. Fernando stood outside the kitchen door.

"Good morning, Estrella. Coffee? This man is tired and needs to perk up."

She was accustomed to Fernando's mockery and had seen him try to seduce, sometimes with success, each girl employed in the household. At this point, she was surprised that Fernando had never tried his advances with her.

"Come in, you bad boy. You know I always take care of you. We have a lovely new young girl. Her name is Georgina. Don't mess with her." She said this half in jest and half with the concern of a mother for her virgin child at her first all-night party.

Fernando laughed, "I only have eyes for you," and sat at the white marble kitchen table.

"What did you bring from the farm?" Estrella asked, "Fresh fruits? The ones in the market are too green."

Fernando smiled at her questions, but before he could answer, they heard Don Miguel: "Estrella, what the hell is happening here? I'm gone for a while and you forget that I like to have my coffee and juice in the morning. Do I have to travel now with Paulino and Cuca to get service? Have you forgotten who pays you every month?"

"Coming, coming," she called. "I was brewing good strong coffee for you. You have the newspapers in the library. Remember to call Dr. Andres. He called again."

Everything was normal. Now the house had voices, the kitchen had people, and she had something to do. The young maid came down the service stairs wearing a tight white uniform. She mumbled a short hello, and then tried to look busy in the corner of the kitchen. Fernando followed her with his eyes, as a cat follows a mouse.

"Fernando, this is Georgina," Estrella said. "Remember what I told you."

"Yes, ma'am," Fernando replied, "I have enough at home."

"So, then, 'do not touch.' She is from my *pueblo*."

Fernando drank his cup of coffee and glanced one more time at the young girl.

"Breakfast is ready. Thanks to God, it's ready," Estrella announced.

DON MIGUEL KNEW he had to see his girls and his sons-in-law and finish the phone calls. He reminded himself that it's always hard to do the things you hate; best to do them first.

He called Dr. Comillas, who played the role of an English country gentleman, owning a small farm on the outskirts of Havana where he kept a few Jersey cows, exotic poultry, rabbits, and beautiful Doberman pinschers. His law office was in Old Havana, but he never arrived before eleven in the morning. He worked late, and his reputation as a draftsman of complicated commercial contracts was well-deserved. He had inherited a small fortune from his parents, so he worked more for the principle of working than for pecuniary need. Comillas was not married, but maintained mistresses in different apartments, never asking for exclusive rights to their well-paid favors. He was well known in the *demimonde* of the *poulet de luxe* and commended for his generosity. He lived for the good food, better wines, and great cheeses of France, but felt that in the tropics, wine loses aroma and bouquet, so in Cuba he only drank cognac, Scotch, and rum. He kept his wine tasting and guzzling for Europe.

Comillas answered on the third ring and instantly suggested lunch. After he agreed, Don Miguel crossed out the first name on his list. After hanging up, he wondered why his friend was so reserved about talking on the phone. He placed a short call to Lustre to set a ten-thirty meeting. The minister was not in his office, so he spoke to his private secretary and requested a short audience, hopefully later that afternoon. Pepe was next. His wife answered. They spoke about her health, his health, how their two daughters were doing, what was happening to Pepito, their son, who had left for the States, and finally he found out that Pepe was not at home but at the Rancho Boyeros airport, waiting for a shipment of electronic equipment for one of his cargo planes.

Adelaida, his oldest daughter, was at home, but Lourdes was at some religious retreat and gone for the next two days. Jose Maria, Adelaida's husband, was at his office; Julio, Lourdes' husband, was out of his office, "visiting a client." Don Miguel suspected he was actually playing golf at the country club.

His banker was happy to hear from him, but did not invite him to lunch (he didn't owe him money). He said mildly, "Please, drop by."

Don Miguel answered, "I'd like to talk to you. I have a lot of questions about the States," and they set a date for next week. He wanted to talk to Mike as well. He missed him. He was angry with himself for feeling this way. "Why? He's back and when I leave him, I worry about him."

FERNANDO WAS RESTING on the fender of the freshly washed car talking to Georgina, who, when she saw Don Miguel, rapidly returned to the kitchen.

"Let's go. Today we have a lot to do," he said to Fernando.

Don Miguel's office was located in the financial center of town, which was being replaced by the new office buildings in the La Rampa section of El Vedado. The office buildings were tall, and built in the early twenties during one of the *vacas gordas*. Their styles differed: Some had the austere simplicity of an Italian Renaissance palace, and others the influence of the Art Deco movement, which, combined with tropical influences, ended up as a Cuban version of the elegant style. His building was a clear example of the latter: The lobby was ornate, and uniformed attendants in gray suits guarded the elevators; commoners were kept outside this lobby. The streets around his office were narrow, crowded, and full of cars and pushcarts.

Everyone honked their horns, as if the noise would help them advance faster. The *guaguas*, with a painted route number, sputtered along as they carried their masses of humanity. Small coffee stands rang bells to announce the brewing of fresh coffee. Street urchins waited for parking spaces to open up so they could get a tip from the next *Doctor* who tried to avoid the parking lots that had replaced the old colonial structures, razed to create new apartments and office buildings.

Fernando stopped at the main entrance, and Don Miguel jumped out of the car and entered without acknowledging the welcome of an elevator operator, who, in his gaudy uniform, resembled an impoverished Austrian prince from a badly produced operetta. His office was on the tenth floor. Each business suite had a wooden door with a glass pane, the names displayed on it in black block letters. He did not believe in advertising his presence, so the sign on his office door was simple: *Ganadera Lucumi S.A.* In the small reception room, pictures of his horses and bulls provided the decor on the walls. Copies of *Cuba Ganadera, Bohemia, Carteles, Time,* and *U.S. News & World Report* were piled in a disorganized way on a small coffee table located in front of the plain Bank of Boston chairs.

Clara, the receptionist, an older lady who knew how to type and file, was surprised at his appearance. "Don Miguel, I didn't expect you so soon."

"Clara, how are you doing?"

"Well, but not as well as you. I heard Mike is back."

"Yes, Mike is fine. I left him at the farm."

Don Miguel went to Lustre's office and found him at his desk. A large ten-key adding machine was posted on his left, next to a black telephone, and ledger books and ten-column green analysis pads were neatly stacked on a worktable behind his chair. He was inputting figures in the adding machine, and its clatter prevented him from hearing Don Miguel's entrance until the latter abruptly dropped his briefcase in an empty chair. Lustre, surprised by the sound, raised his head from the book and quickly rose to greet him.

"Good morning, Don Miguel. Did you have a good trip?"

"Good morning, yes I did. How are you doing?" He clapped his hands on his knees. "Well, are you happy with your success in luring Mike back to the farm? What did you tell him?"

Lustre took his glasses and carefully cleaned them with his black silk tie. "That I thought he should be with you."

"I'm not sure it's the right decision. He seems irritated to be at the farm, but now it's too late. He's there. Well, we'll make the best of it. Maybe he'll learn something. What are you doing now?"

Lustre's face showed his disbelief that Don Miguel minded having his son around. "I'm just finishing the monthly reports. You're making good money in your export sales to Central America and Venezuela. You're spending too much money on the maintenance of the show herd. The fat cattle profits are steady. Hope it rains, but you're making money. Your living expenses are down. You haven't spent any time in Havana. The rental properties need paint. The cash going to your children will have to be cut back if we paint them. The tenants don't pay much. You know how old the buildings are; they're all rent controlled."

"So nothing changes," Don Miguel said. "My father said the same things. I know you're going to tell me that I should have some money invested in the States; that I shouldn't spend cash in improving the pastures; that the price of beef is too low; employ fewer people at the *batey*, and buy the cattle from other farms for fattening, instead of my own mother cows. I know. That's why I pay you. To tell me what you think. You count and advise. I decide."

Lustre smiled. He had started working for Don Miguel's father as an errand boy, then as clerk, after that as bookkeeper. Don Miguel's father liked the way he worked, the neatness of his penmanship, the conservative way he dressed. He was never late and never showed up with a hangover. The family was there for him, and paid for his books at the university while he was going to night school. He was employed even during the Depression. Don Miguel was different from his father. He liked to take risks, was flamboyant, had a stronger personality, but was not as good an administrator as his father was. Lustre knew he could help. This was his time to help. If Don Miguel would at least listen!

"I need money," Don Miguel said. "I didn't bring enough cash with me. I left the farm in too much of a hurry."

"How much will you need?" Lustre asked

"Two hundred pesos. I have to give money to Fernando. I brought him with me."

Lustre went to the office safe, opened it, and gave him the cash, after making him sign a chit.

"You never change," Don Miguel said.

"No, you pay me not to change."

Now that he had the money in hand, he was ready to go. "I have to run. I'm meeting Dr. Comillas for lunch. I need to speak to the minister. I want to spend time with you tomorrow, though. I have to decide how much I'll pay Mike. I'll call you in the morning." Don Miguel got up to leave. Lustre escorted him to the door. He said good-bye to Clara and left.

The old Centro Vasco was the meeting place for Basques who loved to eat, drink, and play jai alai. Games of *pelota* before and after meals were as common as the large portions of *Bacalao al Pil Pil, Merluza con Salsa Verde,* and *Gambas al Ajillo.* The restaurant, with its *frontón* court, its large portions, its special dishes, its nationalistic Basque priests, businessmen, and *pelotaris,* was always crowded, and years later it moved to a new building next to the sea in the Vedado. To address the patrons' yearnings, a Basque painter had used garish colors for murals of the motherland around the bar and dining room. The larger restaurant continued to be crowded; you had to know the right retired pelotari maître d' to get a table. Don Miguel was greeted effusively by the maître d' as he accepted Don Miguel's generous tip without acknowledging it.

"Welcome back, Don Miguel. Dr. Comillas just arrived and is waiting for you at the bar. I have a nice quiet table for you. It'll be ready in a few minutes. Please come, come."

Don Miguel made it to the bar after a series of hellos and handshakes, while others, busy in their own worlds, acknowledged his presence only with a nod of their heads as if saying: "Yes, I know who you may be, but, you see, I'm busy."

Dr. Comillas was holding a Dunhill cigarette holder with its permanently lit Pall Mall. Upon seeing his friend, he stopped a casual conversation with the bartender. Comillas went to his friend and gave him two strong embraces.

"Nice to see you. You finally came. What would you like to drink? Pinch? I've been here for almost an hour! I was worried about you. I have a lot to tell you, but not here, not now. Let's sit down and enjoy our meal. I don't know why you want to come here. It's so crowded! The food in the old place was better."

They sat, and Don Miguel, tired of Cuca's plain codfish, ordered his cooked *al Pil Pil,* and Dr. Comillas, a believer in healthier foods, ordered a broiled red snapper. They did not order wine or beer, just plain water.

Dr. Comillas was nervous. "Miguelito, you have no idea what has been happening. Our best friends are leaving the country. There are rebels in the Escambray and in the Sierra Maestra. My phone is tapped. I know they follow me." Without pause, he dove into his story. "Yes, I was a revolution-ary in the *Machadato,* and I was exiled to Brazil. I was young then. Now, look at me. Do I look as if I belong in the hills? No, you know better." He waved his hands distractedly. "Everyone is leaving the country. You re-member Antonio? 'Seven-sugar-mills Antonio'? Some of his mills were near the area taken over by the rebels. He was helping them with lots of cash, but apparently got tired of spending the money." Don Miguel looked mystified, and Dr. Comillas noticed. "Yes, that friend, who says he's always broke, and yet has more money than all of us combined. Well, he sold all his sugar mills and moved to Florida." The doctor snorted with laughter. "I heard from a very good source that he's having a rough time. He doesn't know where to spend his nights—with his mistress or his wife. He no longer has the excuse of telling the wife he's going to be at a sugar mill. All three of them are staying at the Everglades in Miami! You know what I did? I sent a message with a very close friend: 'Leave Miami. Everyone knows what you do and where you go. Go to the islands. You have enough money to buy one. Fewer taxes and no one gives a damn about the color of your mistress.'" His eyes twinkled as he gave the punch line. "You know what the bastard did? He sent me a postcard that said: 'Amigo, I don't pay taxes. Thanks for the advice. See you at Lyford Cay.' The son of a bitch hasn't changed a bit!"

The conversation made Don Miguel uneasy. "That was a bad move. I know the price he got for the mills and his sugar plantations. It was a fire sale! Yes, the price of sugar isn't very high, but with our American sugar quota and the London agreement, we're making money. Look at all the new hotels. They sprout up like weeds in a badly kept garden. He wanted to leave and be called 'Mr. So-and-So.'" He shook his head at the idea. "Those *Americanos* laugh at you the moment you leave the room. He thinks he's respected, but they just want his money. I know. I've worked with them."

"Miguelito, it's good to be laughed at by someone when you own him. Come and relax. I know how you feel, but you don't have one bull, you have several, and you're diversified. Man, you're an empire. Cattle, sugar, houses, savings accounts, stocks with your son-in-law, and you still drive that old dilapidated car, and I bet that your chauffeur today is that black man from your farm."

"I don't like to throw money away," Don Miguel grumbled. "My car takes me to the same places as your Mercedes."

"But you don't travel anymore, and since Adelaidita died, you don't have any fun. Hey, I have a good idea. Let me call two good friends of mine, and we can have a pleasant *tête-à-tête* with them. They have an inviting apartment, very nice girls. They only need help with their rent. I know you're going to say no, but what else can we do this afternoon while we wait for the minister to receive us?"

Don Miguel shook his head. "No, no. You know we have to work. I want you to read my last draft of the decree. You're the only one who can help me. The minister respects your legal mind."

Don Miguel started to recite all the ills endemic to the regulated Cuban cattle industry. Dr. Comillas, who had heard this speech many times before, lit a cigarette, and started to scan the room in search of a candidate for his next romantic escapade. He did not like the Centro Vasco because, with the exception of a few women who admired the pelotaris, hardly any were unattached.

"Miguelito, you know I believe in you," he said after a while. "All that you have said is true and is very interesting. But I have to go to the bathroom. Please excuse me. If the waiter comes, let him know that I want coffee."

Don Miguel nodded as he selected a cigar from a pocketful of them.

When they left the restaurant, Dr. Comillas guided his friend to a small apartment where the girls lived. After the usual introductions and drinks, the younger of the two picked up Don Miguel's hand and took him to her bedroom. After a time, he came out of the bedroom to find Andres sitting in the living room with a lit cigarette and an ingratiating smile.

"Miguelito, things are fine in Havana, aren't they? You're only as old as you think. Don't you feel better? I'm a very good doctor, you know.

Sometimes you need to forget what you've lost and try something new." He pointed toward the bedroom Don Miguel had just vacated. "They're nice girls, kind of crazy. This? They do it just for fun. I pay their rent. At this rate, I could have bought them an apartment at the FOCSA."

Don Miguel nodded, but he felt conflicted. He had enjoyed the encounter, but the girl, Maria, had been so young and slight that he had felt as if he were in bed with a daughter's friend. She knew and could talk about nothing. Then again, maybe at his age that wasn't important. Did he feel any better? He didn't know the answer. He was hesitant at the beginning and not fully engaged with her all the way through, and she noticed it.

"What is wrong, *Papito*? Don't you like me?"

"Yes, yes, I like you, but it's been so long."

Don Miguel told his friend, "Maria is a very sweet girl."

"She likes you, too. I'll give you her number." With that mission accomplished, Dr. Comillas turned to the next order of the day. "Now it's time to go and see the minister."

When they arrived at six o'clock, most of the civil servants had left. However, the parking lot, shared with a popular bar, was full of cars. The chauffeur opened the door for Dr. Comillas, and they walked past the ministry guards without stopping. The guards saluted them as they headed to the private elevator to the minister's office. Upstairs, the main reception room had stiff leather chairs and tables with ashtrays brimming with butts of cigars and cigarettes, giving the room the ambiance of a decadent nightspot. The room was full; some people had been waiting all day, while others waited for days on end.

Dr. Comillas picked up the black chunky phone from the receptionist's desk and dialed the private number of the minister's secretary. "Roberto, I'm outside." Dr. Comillas was in the habit of regularly plying Roberto with bottles of Scotch. "I'm with Don Miguel. Is he available in the next few minutes? We just want to say hello. I also need to make private phone calls. You know I don't want to use this phone."

The door opened with a smiling and efficient Roberto waving them into his small domain. "Don Miguel, I'm so happy to see you. Dr. Andres, welcome. Don Miguel, the minister has been very busy with the coffee crop in the Oriente province and in the Escambray Mountains. We want to show the people that the hills are safe, and everything is normal. The other day he asked me to call you back, but you had left the telephone exchange. He'll be happy to see you today. Please, please come in."

Roberto ordered freshly brewed coffee, and they sat on a comfortable leather sofa to wait for their audience. Don Miguel pulled out the marked draft of a decree that reflected the wear and tear of many readings, changes, and underlines. He was reading it with so much concentration that he didn't notice that the door to the minister's office had opened until Roberto touched him on his shoulder and asked him to enter the inner sanctum. He stuffed the draft in his briefcase and followed him. The minister was laughing at one of Dr. Comillas's jokes. He sat behind a large desk that had an accumulation of reports, files, and sealed cigar boxes. Seeing Don Miguel, he got up to give him a big old-fashioned hug.

"Miguelito, I've missed you. You never come to Havana! We're overdue for a game of dominoes. I hope you haven't lost your touch! Your hiding in the bushes may make you a little rusty, but I have full confidence in you. Let's get together this weekend and play." He jabbed his thumb toward the doctor. "Maybe we can play against Andres and steal his money."

Don Miguel, however, wanted to conduct his business. "I just came back from the farm in Camagüey. I was planning—" but before he had finished, he changed his mind. "Yes, I'm planning to be here. Sure, I'd like to play, when and at what time?"

"How about Saturday?" the minister answered. "We can all have lunch, and after we play, we'll visit my farm at Guanabo. I've imported a few Holstein cows that I know you'll like. Your friend, the vet from Wisconsin, brokered them for me. They're producing a lot of milk. Now, what's your hurry?"

Don Miguel knew that he had his attention for only a few minutes and wanted to make the most of it. "We have to create a price differential for the cattle sold for beef. You know we have a problem. There's no difference in the price you receive for your fat cattle on hoof. You get paid the same for an old bull as you do for a steer bred to give a tremendous yield. It doesn't make any difference how or what we feed our cattle. I can give you a steer that will provide excellent cuts, but I get paid as if I were selling you an old ox that's too feeble to pull a cart."

The minister interrupted. "I know the facts. But the most important rule of politics is to give the people cheap food. The Romans knew it. In Cuba, beef has to be cheap. Plus, I don't control the price. The minister of commerce does that, as you know."

Don Miguel countered, "All beef?"

The minister went on, "Yes, the construction worker likes to eat meat three times a day. We would have riots in Havana if meat prices were to go up. How do you think you can sell your idea to the president and expect commerce not to oppose it?" His voice was sympathetic, but he was as smooth as any politician. "I'm supposed to go again to Oriente province to pick coffee beans to show we have a good coffee crop this year, and that for five cents, the *Habaneros* will still be able to slurp coffee. I've survived in this job because I hear all sides. The president doesn't agree with everything I say. He has other people that bend his ear, maybe better than I. Who in the press is going to be in favor of your plan? You give me the facts, I promise to give it serious thought."

"Thank you," Don Miguel said as graciously as he could manage.

The minister was elated to avoid any sort of commitment. "Okay, let's firm up our domino game. I want to win against this Dr. Andres Comillas. You and I are unbeatable." When Don Miguel nodded, he changed the subject briskly. "Now excuse me, I have other people that I must see. I still don't know why the president wants me to go to the mountains and pick coffee beans. I know sugar. I'm a sugar man," he protested. "Politics, that's what it is all about. My wife wants me to resign, you know. She says I'm too old to be going up and down a mountain." The minister shook his head ruefully, got up, and gave his friends strong embraces as they left.

8

The Visitor

DON MIGUEL'S FORD trailed a red dust cloud down the dirt road. "Playtime is over, my friend," Mike muttered as he headed to the corral where Manolo, the *mayoral,* had a new herd ready for calf branding. Branding was always a battle of wits and speed between the calves and the *vaqueros.* Each calf was brought into the corral, where one *vaquero* would lasso it while another twisted its head and pushed it to the ground, immobilizing it. A third *vaquero,* with a single sweeping motion, branded the calf. With good team play, the branding of a calf took less than five minutes.

Manolo felt too old to fight animals in the corral. He sat on his horse and munched on his big cigar, directing the action. To make a clear impression on a hide, a branding iron had to be red hot, so more than one branding iron was always in the fire. If the hide was wet, the iron might not burn deeply enough or slip, and the brand would be poorly defined. But that morning the weather was dry and hot, perfect for branding. An intense log fire was set up next to the branding chute. Mayajigua fanned the fire with his hat and kept the irons ready. He did not know how to read or write, but he knew his numbers well enough to distribute the irons as they were called for. Cuca sat on a taburete with a tablet in her hand. Monito called out the name of the sire and the dam to Cuca, who then gave the number to Mayajigua and Monito. They were so involved in their work that they didn't notice Mike's arrival. Only Mayajigua and Cuca looked up, surprised, when Mike jokingly said, "*Buenos días y adiós.*"

MANUEL HAD MENTIONED that Arturo, who was in charge of the milking herd, was unhappy with one of the new *vaqueros.* Arturo was a short, husky, powerful man, who was cleaning pails, filters, and tubs at the milking shed. He was the only *vaquero* who wore lace-up boots, and when he took off his hat to clean his brow, he revealed a stripe of white forehead against his sunburned face.

"Arturo, good morning. How are you doing?" asked Mike.

"Good morning, sir. I missed you yesterday. I heard from Paulino that you're staying for a while. Welcome back," Arturo said flatly, his eyes still on his work.

"How are Neraide and the boys?"

"Fine, they're just fine. The boys are going to school."

"I'm sorry I haven't been able to visit with you before. Yesterday was a tough day. It seems that everything has happened in the last two days." Mike rested his foot on a board of the milking corral.

"Yes," Arturo answered, "Cuca told me about Anita. She was lucky that you took her to the clinic. I don't understand them! They should know better." He shrugged his shoulders while continuing to scrub a stainless steel pail.

"I'm here to help my father. I know he's very happy with your work. I'd like to have a good idea of what you're doing, so we can work better together." It was difficult for Mike to utter the words. They sounded scripted, even to him.

Arturo, if surprised by the overture, acted as if they were having a conversation about the weather. "Sure, you know I've worked well for your father. I'll work for you, too."

Mike shook Arturo's hands. "Thanks, I know I can count on you. I'll see you early tomorrow morning, after you finish the milking."

As Mike went to the machinery shed to find the jeep, Arturo finished cleaning the pails and buckets, and started to work on other chores. He had a fence to fix, a cow needed medicine for her udder, and he wanted to see what his boys were up to. They could easily get into trouble, especially if he didn't keep a close watch.

Mike drove the red jeep down the alleys, checked the new pastures created by clearing, seeding, and fencing the savanna, and visited Pedro, the *vaquero* who lived farthest from the *batey* on the south side of the Central Highway next to the railroad tracks.

When he returned to the *batey*, Chirra approached Mike.

"Mike, do you know how you feel when you become truly thirsty? It's a powerful force. It's like a woman. You want to be next to her. You know that she's no good for you. You go, she talks pretty, you touch her skin with your eyes, and then you caress her. Slowly, she smiles, and you get hot and before you know it, you're gone. You're not thinking. You just want that woman. Even if you know she's bad for you, you are hard, and you know she is bad, bad, and bad for you, but you don't care. You think you need her. You only think of her."

"Chirra, what are you getting at?"

"Pati Cruzao is my woman," Chirra went on. "She never fails me. I know she always waits for me, and then I get into trouble. Mike, you can help me. Don't give me money. Just please tell Carlos to sell me only food, but no Pati Cruzao. I don't need more women. Mike, my daughter needs food. I promise you, I'll try. I swear. I'm a good worker. I'll try." Chirra looked at Mike like he was a newly canonized saint, nervously holding his hat, his two-day beard showing white.

Mike felt sorry for him, but not enough to forget that Chirra had played him before. "Okay, Chirra, remember you owe me five from the last time."

"No problem, Mike, deduct it. I promise, I'll try."

All in a day at the farm, Mike thought. He led a simple life at the *batey*, eating his meals alone on the long table in the dining room, and then dropping by the employees' dining room to talk with them as they watched the news on the television Cuca had forced Ricardo to buy. He went to bed early, muscles tired at the end of the day, his energy sapped by the heat. At night, he read from his father's collection of genetic and animal husbandry management books, while Mitzi slept under his bed.

That Friday morning, Paulino was walking briskly, singing in a loud voice, smiling and joking when he brought Mike his coffee and a cigar. Mike, accustomed to Paulino's cool banter, was surprised by this change.

"What's happening?"

Paulino, whistling, answered, "It's Friday, and Nandito and your devoted server are going to the *pueblo*." He sang:

Me voy p'al pueblo,
   I am going to the village,
Hoy es mi dia,
   Today is my day,
Voy a gozar
   I am going to enjoy
El alma mia.
   My own soul.

"I'm getting Coca-Colas, beers, soft drinks, and potato chips, and sell-ing them at a stand at San Joaquin's Saturday baseball game. They're play-ing against the undefeated Vertientes sugar-mill baseball team. Do you plan to go? A large crowd will come from the *pueblo*. It's going to be great!"

Mike knew that Paulino dreamed of owning a *bodega*, as his father had. "You have to start someplace," Paulino always said. It might be bred in his veins to make money by selling things to other people.

"I don't know. I may want to stay at the *batey*. I have a lot of work."

Mike planned to stay all day at the *batey* to study the show string. He wanted to better understand the animals' conformations, as his father did: Analyze their legs, the rectangular shape of their body, the shape of their head and horns, and assess their similarities and differences. Memorize their sire and dam. This was his time to learn, to prepare a sales pitch, to recall the trophies the sire had won, and tell a story about the wins of each bull and cow in the farm's show string.

Mike wandered to the black stallion's box. He felt better there, alone as he rubbed the horse's silky coat, combed his fingers through the black, lustrous mane, looked into his eyes, and talked to him. He believed, as the Bedouin Arabs did, that a horse communicates with his master. "Are we not one when we ride?" Horse and rider, one entity, one feeling, one coor-dinated movement. He had begun to miss those long nights of discussions in college, of reading poetry or essays or short stories, and going to his apartment with the first rays of the sun to fall on his bed, tired, but not sleepy, his mind racing with thoughts, unleashed feelings, new concepts, and plans. Now, at the farm, where Paulino was the only person with whom he could have a decent conversation, he could understand his father's need to go to Havana to talk, argue, and communicate with more people who talked as he talked.

Mike's thoughts were broken by the sounds of an automobile horn, loud voices, and laughter. A taxicab from Fernando's stand had stopped at the main house. Cuca was talking to a woman in a colorful cotton print dress with long sleeves, holding a white parasol to shield her face from the sun's hot rays. The cabdriver smiled as Cuca called out, "Mike, you have a visitor."

His curiosity aroused, he hurried toward the parasol lady. It was Rita.

"Mike, I had the day off. Your father always talks about the things in the *batey*, and he said recently that you had some new horses in the show string, so I came to look. Do you mind?"

He was shocked. He had never experienced a woman taking the lead. "Not at all, Rita, it'll be a pleasure. Why don't you stay for lunch? Cuca will be more than happy to prepare it."

Mike nodded to Cuca. "You don't have to keep the driver waiting. I'll drive you back, if you wish. Anyway, I have to go into town to call Father. It'll be a pleasure to drive you."

Cuca, who knew the driver, offered to brew coffee for him.

Mike took Rita to the main house and led her to one of the white rocking chairs on the porch. "Would you like a drink?"

"Yes. It's so hot. I'd like to have a glass of cold water with a little bit of lime. That would be lovely."

Mike excused himself and went to kitchen. He found Cuca smoking a cigarette, waiting for the water to boil.

"Mike, what would you like?"

"Don't worry, Cuca. I'll take care of it. Where are the limes?"

Rita wasn't sure if Mike was delighted to see her. She had dressed carefully. Afraid that the sun would damage her peachy white skin, she wore a long-sleeved but tightly-cut dress. She was not sure about her perfume. It was a hot day, so she had chosen a jasmine-based scent. But was she was too dressed up?

Mike returned with the water. "I'm sorry it took a while. I've been away for so long that I don't know where anything is. Cuca will prepare sandwiches for us. I'm sorry it's not more, but I always have a light lunch."

"Oh, Mike, I didn't mean to put you through so much trouble."

"It's no trouble. I wasn't expecting such pleasant company. Please, please sit down. I have some time and I'll show you around. There's a bench in the garden near the fountain, but it's still too hot. The nights are cooler." Mike grinned as he eyed her svelte figure. "Maybe that's why the siesta was invented. So that one can be relaxed and be ready for the night."

Rita smiled and began to slowly rock her chair. "What is it that you want to show me?" she asked, slowly sipping her water.

"Here, let me show you the trophies our animals have won at the shows. Some are silver and others are made of precious woods—the man who makes them lives in Santi Spiritus. He is a real artist."

Mike led her through the house like a museum guide. He had to control the tone of his voice, because once or twice he used an apathetic singsong, the same tone as the *cicerones* he had encountered in the old museums in Spain. The fact was, he hated to talk about the trophies, but he felt that he had to do something. Really, he was more interested in being with her. He looked over at Rita, and she met his gaze. She was more interested in looking at him than in hearing his recital. Drawn to her, he touched her arm. Yet he felt a jolt in his conscience: "Be careful. You know how your father feels about this. You know she didn't come to look at horses, cows, or old pictures."

Wanting more privacy, Mike took her to the office to show her more photographs. This time she moved close to him, and he touched her back as he steered her to another spot. He caught the scent of her perfume.

"I'm boring you," he said. "This is the past. Would you like to look at the future, or better, the present?"

"Sure, I came here so that you can show me. Please do."

Mike went to get her parasol and selected a wide-brimmed Panama hat for himself, and then led her to the show barn.

"Well, this is the show string. This is where everything starts—our dreams, our frustrations. So many years of thinking, planning, and breeding in our heads to create a perfect animal, one that will reproduce itself, a genotype that is a phenotype. The ultimate goal of a breeder is to produce an animal that's beautiful and breeds true. It seldom works, though. That's why you can't breed by formula. Breeding is an art, but truth be told, it's mostly luck." He was startled to hear his father's words coming out of his own mouth.

Rita murmured sounds of agreement. She knew that one way to a man's heart was to assent, assent, and assent. Make believe you understand what he says, no matter what, and be sure you don't allow your mind to wander during his monologues. Mike held Rita's hand as they walked through the barn. He enjoyed the soft feel of her skin as they went over rough cobblestones. They ended up at Lucumi's box, where Mike spoke softly to the stallion as Rita stroked the horse's mane. She laughed.

"You talk to that old horse as if he could understand your feelings. You're crazy!" She looked closely at the stallion. "It's almost as if he wants to talk to you, too. He doesn't snort or bite you, yet when I touch him, his ears go back. Now, explain that to me!"

Mike continued the tour, answering questions and enjoying the scent and feel of the woman at his side. They went to the house and sat again on the rocking chairs. Cuca first showed up with a plate full of different cheeses and crackers, and then a bottle of Scotch, a silver ice bucket, two tall glasses, and a small pitcher of water on a silver tray.

"Mike do you want anything else? I'm preparing a few sandwiches, and you'll have fruit on the table. Lunch will be ready soon."

"We're fine. Thank you, Cuca."

Rita stood up. "Cuca," she asked, "do you want me to help you in the kitchen? I'm sorry to cause so much trouble."

"No, no, enjoy your stay. You're our guest," Cuca replied, and with a pleasant half-smile, she left.

Rita and Mike drank their Scotch and water in silence. Mike slowly rocked, suddenly unable to figure out what to say next. He had explored the cattle market, the breaking of the horses, the help, the lack of a telephone at the *batey*, and the mugginess of the weather. He didn't want to discuss politics or religion.

Rita, wanting to appear sophisticated, gazed at the show barn and the garden. "This is so beautiful, so peaceful," she said to Mike, while wondering why the garden seemed neglected. The contrast was severe. Weeds grew in the flower beds, yet the home was immaculately kept. That showed the absence of a woman's touch, Rita surmised. When Mike remained silent, she became nervous and fretted: Why was he suddenly so serious? He was talking up a storm and now . . .

They ate quickly and did not talk too much. Rita took little bites from her sandwich and ate her banana with fastidious grace. Mike drank his second Scotch and ate two small sandwiches. He played at carving a mango, but was uneasy about sucking it.

"Do you want coffee?" he asked.

"Yes, I drink mine with lots of sugar. You should know that I'm very sweet," Rita said with a cautious smile.

"Yes, you sure are. Sorry, I have to leave you for a few seconds. I need to see Cuca. Don't run away."

"Don't worry. I'll be waiting."

Mike went to make sure that Cuca had started brewing the coffee. In the meantime, Rita stood up and looked at the silver trophies. When Mike returned, he said, "Let's go to that small bench in the garden. It's my favorite place to sit. It's peaceful and it's in the shade. Cuca will bring the coffee in a few minutes."

The marble bench faced a dry fountain with a lonely Greek statue. Mike brushed off the seat with his handkerchief. He sat nervously on the bench, not knowing what to do next. He wanted to be closer to her, but did not know how to do it, and was afraid of going too far, too soon. He idly took a pebble and threw it against a tree, while Rita nervously shifted on the hard marble bench. Cuca called, "The coffee is ready."

Rita got up. "Let me do it. I love to play house."

They sat again and drank their coffee, watching the blackbirds return to their perches in the *Ceiba* tree. A mockingbird sang, marking its territory.

"I have an idea," Mike said, "let me show you the small stream, the old way. I'll get the gig and the gray mule will pull it. It's fun. It'll take me a little while to harness her. I'll come back to pick you up. Make yourself at home."

When Mike drove the gig to the front of the house a half hour later, Cuca, who was in the kitchen, had to contain her laughter. "This is getting serious," she thought.

Mike found Rita dozing in a chaise lounge in the living room. Her face was tranquil, and her blonde hair fell softly over her eyes. Mike carefully pulled her hair away from her face. She twitched, as if to avoid a bothersome insect. Mike picked up a lock of her hair and kissed it. At last Rita woke up, and Mike had to wonder if she had really been sleeping as he helped her up.

"Let's go, the gig is waiting. We have a lot to see."

Mike took his Panama hat and Rita her parasol. Together in the gig they resembled a vision from the past, a time before jeeps, trucks, and autos polluted the tranquility of a lazy afternoon. Mike drove toward the pasture next to the stream. Rita sat straight, angling her parasol to protect her from the sunlight. She pretended to admire the view, as if it were her first contact with a well-kept pasture. Mike kept the mule walking at a quick pace, which took his full attention, since the mule was not interested in moving at all.

The bank of the stream was inviting. Large trees gave abundant shade, and the dark sand at the stream's bottom could be seen through the clear running water. The early afternoon light reflected dancing shimmers onto the tree trunks. Mike stopped the gig and invited Rita to sit at the water's edge. When she hesitated, worried that the grass would stain her cotton dress, Mike removed the gig's small cushioned seat and placed it on the ground for her. Mike looked at the water and threw pebbles into the stream as he watched for trout. Rita, disconcerted by his silence, asked, "What are you thinking?"

Mike was still feeling awkward. "I enjoy being with you, but maybe we should go back. It will take us another hour or so to reach the *batey*. It's such a pleasure to have you here."

"You want to talk?" she asked. "I know only a little about you, and you know less about me."

He was relieved she had opened a way forward. "What do you want to know? I don't have secrets. I'm a university student. I like to work and study. I've been in the States for six years. It's cold there. I miss the sunlight, the trees, the sea, the sand, and the beach. I want to hear my music. There, I feel alien. If I thought I had to be there the rest of my life, I would be miserable. I love my country. And you?"

"I like my work, it's the best I can find right now. I wanted to go to Havana and study there, but I'm the only child and my mother is alone.

She knows how to pull my heartstrings, 'Are you leaving your poor mother?,' and so on, and on, so I stayed." She noticed him watching her intently, and she went on. "I'm the youngest of the operators, so I have the least seniority. They give me the worst slots. I want to get out of this job, but there's so little opportunity. I want to learn more, travel, and see the world." She gestured all around them. "Your father always talks about places he's gone to. I feel so jealous of him, of the things he has, the places he's visited. I would love to do that."

They talked, though each held a little back. They were hesitant, cautious. Mike slowly reached for Rita's hand. She gave it to him and looked into his eyes, and Mike said, "I'm a little nervous. You never can tell where you'll find what you're looking for. Sometimes it just appears."

Rita appreciated his honesty. "You're very nice."

After a while they slowly went back to the gig holding hands. The sun was still high as they rode along, and Rita thought of her parasol, but she no longer cared about her complexion. She leaned against Mike, who would have stopped the gig and made love to her then and there, on top of the green pasture grass under the clean blue sky. But he could not. That was not proper.

It was six o'clock when they returned to the *batey*. As they rounded the driveway, Rita snapped open her parasol and sat upright in her seat. Mike slid as far apart from Rita as the small seat would allow. Cuca came out when she heard the rolling wheels of the gig.

"Rita, did you like the ride?"

"It was lovely."

"Do you want something to drink?"

"No, thanks, Cuca, I think I have to leave."

"Rita, I'll uncouple the mule. It will only take a minute or two."

Ricardo was standing behind Cuca as curious as she was, and he offered, "Mike, don't worry. I'll do it."

The trip to the *pueblo* went too fast. Rita's house was modest and built near the street. The outside was blue painted clapboard, faded to a soft pastel. Mike opened the door and escorted her to her door. Rita asked, "Would you like to have a drink?"

Mike answered, "No, thanks. I have to call my father."

They formally shook hands, Mike thanked Rita for her company, and left. Feeling lighter than air, he went to the telephone company. His father was out, so he left a message with Estrella, and then slowly drove back to the *batey*. He was still surprised at Rita's visit. He had had a good time even though he had not accomplished his objective for that day. What will the employees think of his taking Rita for a ride in the gig down to the river? Did it matter? Maybe the farm wasn't such a lonely place.

9

The Baseball Game

NANDITO DROVE A rusted metal heap with worn-out tires that had once been a farm's proud International Harvester truck. Its original red paint had faded, and the truck had acquired a patina similar to that of a bronze sculpture. The license plate was tied to the front bumper with baling wire. In the two-person cabin, three men huddled. In the middle was Ernesto, Nandito's catcher and cousin. Paulino, experienced in personal comfort, sat next to the right window, talking nonstop.

"I'm buying at least ten cases of beer. Do you think that'll be enough?"

Nandito was focused on avoiding the highway police since he carried incomplete truck papers. "I don't know," he curtly replied.

Paulino continued, "I need to buy Coca-Colas. I should get four cases. Do you think it will be better to make lemonade? We have all of those limes at the *batey*. I couldn't even use them all if Mike drank one hundred daiquiris a day. I make more money with the lemonade. Maybe I should also buy rum."

"No, no, I don't like idea of you selling rum. We had problems at the last game when Chirra got drunk and pissed on the leg of the home-plate umpire. The umpire was ready to leave the game." Nandito bristled at the memory and pointed out another problem. "People get violent when they drink. I especially don't like the look of drunken Haitians on cheap rum. They're really scary. I hate violence when I pitch. The Haitians may bet on the game, but I'm not a fighting rooster."

"We better win this one," Ernesto uttered, leaning away from Nandito's hand as he changed into fourth gear. "I'm tired of losing. Ricardo has to play," he said hopefully. "Don Miguel hurt us when he took Fernando to Havana. He's our best hitter."

"Those are negative thoughts. You can't harbor negative thoughts. Negative thoughts affect your performance," Paulino said, with an air of expertise. "You need to think you're going to win. It's the only way. We're going to win. Repeat. We're going to win. Nandito, you're going to pitch a no-hitter. You're going to hit that ball every time you're at the bat. You, Ernesto, are going to catch every strike and every foul ball, and you're not going to allow anyone to steal a base. As for me, I'm going to sell every bottle of beer, every glass of lemonade, and every Coca-Cola that I have, hot or cold. We're going to win this game, without Fernando, or for that matter, the apostle Santiago, even if he rides down from heaven on his fucking white horse," Paulino assured them.

Nandito continued to drive slowly. As Ernesto leaned closer to Paulino, he was suddenly overcome with the intense reek of Ernesto's body odor. Paulino suddenly jolted back as if he'd just been sucker punched.

"Hey, Ernesto!" Paulino protested, "You smell so foul! When we stop at the warehouse, I'm giving you a special gift. It's called soap. Have you heard of soap? Do you know how to use it? Or is your body odor your special weapon?"

Ernesto cast a brief sideways glance at Paulino, and fixed his eyes back on the road. The three fell silent, bumping along quietly inside the creaking old truck.

After another minute, Paulino resumed his chatter. "I don't think we should stop at the warehouse after all. Let's go to Camagüey. I can get a better deal there. It's only an hour away."

Nandito, who was having a difficult time figuring the batting lineup because of Fernando's absence, revolted at this suggestion. "Hey, you're not paying for the gas. I am, and we don't have much left." He peered across the cab at Paulino. "You have all these great ideas, but no money. Where can you find the dough to buy all the beers and Coca-Colas? I don't think you have enough cash in your pocket to buy one bottle of anything!"

Paulino took umbrage at this accusation. "No, you don't understand how business works," he fired back. "That's why you're driving me."

"Yes, in *my* truck," Nandito reminded Paulino.

"No, you still don't understand. You see, I'm a born businessman. I love and understand business. Business is based on credit. You borrow money.

With it you buy goods. You add a profit to the goods for sale, then you sell them, and you get money from the sale. You pay back what you owe, and borrow more. The more credit you have, the more you can buy and sell, and the more profit you make. If you played a game every day, I would make lots of money, because I would sell lots of beers, Coca-Colas, soft drinks, fried hamburgers, and fried potatoes. It's simple—the more I sell, the more money I make." Paulino felt content with the tutelage on capitalism just provided to his unsophisticated friends.

"But what happens if you don't pay it back? If you don't sell beers, soft drinks, and lemonade?" Ernesto asked.

"Ha! You just don't understand. You only buy what you can sell. You have to know your customer and your market. I'm not going to sell Tri-Maltas, because only nursing women drink them, and we don't see too many of those at our games. I buy Hatuey—people in Camagüey like Hatuey. If I were in Havana, I would be buying Polar and Cristal, but have you seen anyone here drinking a Polar? No, that's why I don't sell Polar. I simply don't buy what I can't sell."

Ernesto was not convinced. "You don't know if it's going to rain. If it rains, we don't play. If we don't play, you won't have customers. You won't sell anything and you're fucked."

Paulino sniffed. "You have to think positively."

They reached the warehouse. Nandito couldn't find a parking place, so he gave the wheel to Ernesto while he and Paulino went inside. The warehouse was busy. Paulino shook hands and greeted people as if he were running for political office. Nandito, cap askew on his head, followed him. Paulino found the clerk who handled the farm's account and raised his voice to a near shout, "Hey, Mulato, come here! I need to place an order."

The clerk rushed over. "Paulino, I saw Mike a few days ago. He was angry! Did he tell you what happened?"

"No. What are you talking about? Look, Mulato, I'm in a big hurry today. I don't have time to socialize with you. This is a business visit. I have to order something fast. I'm needed at the *batey*." Paulino handed the clerk a list.

"Oh, I see," the clerk replied, looking over the list. "Ten cases of Hatuey, ten cases of Coca-Colas, two of Matervas, one of Gaseosa Salutaris, five pounds of sugar, one sack of potatoes, one gallon of peanut oil, and lard. Charge it on which account? The farm's?"

Paulino hesitated. "No, you don't understand. I'm buying it on my own account. San Joaquin plays Vertientes this Saturday. There'll be a crowd, hungry and thirsty. I'm selling real cold drinks, fried potatoes, and *fritas*. This is a great opportunity to make real money. If you come to see the game, I'll give you a free drink."

The clerk's face had changed considerably while Paulino was talking. "Well, how much money do you have? I don't remember you having an account with us."

Nandito smirked, looked to the floor, and cleared his throat.

Paulino had a bout of anxiety. "Well, you know I'm good for it. Look, I buy every week from you. You always get paid."

"Oh yes, but we're not selling to you. We're selling to Don Miguel. He has excellent credit. You don't have credit with us."

Paulino faced the first obstacle in his new career.

"Mulato, let's start again. Please understand, Mike is at the farm, alone. He's throwing a big party. I work for Mike. He needs beers, Coca-Colas, Matervas, peanut oil, potatoes, and yes, rum. I'll sign the chit. You'll deliver it to me. I'm the one who is responsible. I'll come back on Monday and pay you. I'll take care of you. If not, the farm will pay you, and I'll be dead. What do you think?"

Mulato was inclined to agree. He knew how much Don Miguel liked Paulino. "Wait, let me think about it. First, I have to find out how many cases of beer I have in the back. Why don't you come back in a few minutes? But before I do that, I need to talk to the boss."

Paulino turned to Nandito. "Let's get ice. When we return, we'll load the truck. Think positively."

NANDITO HAD NOT gotten enough sleep because one of his boys had cried all night. To make matters worse, he was suffering from a bad case of pregame jitters. Nandito's nerves were especially jarred because he was going to pitch against their league's undefeated team. As he lay awake, he glanced over at his bed, a collection of arms, legs, and heads. His wife, Rosita, and all three of their children were in bed with him, and he needed more room. Yes, he wanted more room in his bed, more space in his house, more money in his pocket. Nandito had fallen in love with his wife when she was twelve years old; she had been the prettiest mulatta around. Now, at twenty-two, she looked spent, even in her sleep.

He slid into his worn work shoes, found his pants, and picked a shirt from the row of nails on the wall. He would have to return to change into his baseball uniform, which Rosita had washed and dried on the clothesline. Nandito was proud of his white and red uniform. Don Miguel had ordered it from the Casa Vasallo in Havana, the same store that made the uniforms for the professional teams that played baseball in the winter in El Cerro stadium. He had never seen a baseball game in Havana, but regularly listened to the games on the radio. Everyone did, even Don Miguel. Nandito walked to the clearing where they had created their baseball field.

Paulino was supervising the setting up of his concession stand. He was building it with Martinito and Chirra. "The board will separate the customers from the drinks," Paulino said, even though he was more worried about how to separate Chirra from the alcohol.

Ernesto watched the scene with interest. "I don't think you're going to have enough cold beers. I know you're going to run out of ice. A hot beer is a bad beer."

"Hey man, leave me alone. Ernesto, you catch. I sell drinks. First, you tell me I won't sell even one bottle. Now you tell me I don't have enough. Look, there's Nandito, go pester him. You make a great team."

Nandito said good morning to Paulino. "Have you seen Ricardo? I wasn't able to speak to him yesterday. I hope you told him that we need him."

"Yes, yes. I saw him before he left. He'll be here. You still have four hours before the game." Paulino shooed him away. "Please, go do something else. Go and screw your wife, I don't care. Don't you see how busy I am? Let me take care of my business. I have to confer with my helpers." Paulino left to talk to Chirra and Martinito, who were having a heated argument over the best way to position a board.

Nandito knew he had to stretch and warm up, but it was too early. All of his players were there except Ricardo, and they didn't have anything to do. They wore uniforms, and some had washed them. Those who had not had uniforms tinged by the savanna soil from the last field they played. Today's soil was dark black, bottomland dirt. Good land for crops, better for baseball players.

Around twelve o'clock, friends and relatives of the San Joaquin players began to show up. The small children were barefoot and the younger ones wore only shirts. Some Joaquineros had brought their *taburetes* to watch the game, and a few ladies wore long-sleeved shirts and shielded their faces from the sun with large straw hats tied with colorful bandannas. The girls paraded in their tight dresses, but the young men ignored them. Today they only had eyes for the players on the field. At the moment, they were busy finding, fetching, and throwing the balls back to Ernesto. Later they would be with the girls. For now, they proved their manhood by ignoring them.

Ricardo showed up in Fernando's taxicab, to Nandito's relief. Then he addressed the group of players and fans, "Gentlemen, we have to decide on the lineup. I'm the pitcher. Ernesto will be the catcher."

A voice was heard in the background: "He has to be the catcher. He's the only one who has a catcher's mitt."

Nandito looked with impatience at the wiseacre. "Ricardo will play with us today in center field. Mando, Carlos, and Enrique will play first, second, and third base. Mariano will play shortstop. Gumersindo will play left field, and we have to pick one more player to play right field."

The young fans raised their hands, anxious for a chance to play with the team. It would be their initiation into adulthood. All were good to excellent players, for they had caught, thrown balls, batted, and played baseball as soon as they could walk. Nandito's eyes stopped on a young black man, six feet tall with well-developed muscles showing under his work shirt. Nandito was afraid to make the decision alone. He summoned Ernesto. "Let's talk in private," Nandito whispered to him.

Ernesto relished his newly assigned power. He played with the ball, holding it in one hand and then another, throwing it in his mitt as fast as he could, to make believe that he was concentrating, or perhaps to distract from his uncertainty about who to choose. The group waited silently for their decision.

"Yes, he could be a good player," Ernesto finally proclaimed. "Which uniform can he use?"

Nandito answered. "I have to run to my house and change. I can pick up Fernando's uniform on the way." The hangers-on congratulated the new pick, Julio, on his induction into the team.

Shortly after, two open trucks arrived, followed by a group of cars and taxis, all honking their horns. The Vertientes team had arrived with their fans. To Paulino's dismay, they had brought a copious supply of beer and rum. They cheered and raised their team banner, even before all the players were out of the trucks. Their uniforms were as immaculate as if just purchased. The team had, besides their captain, a coach, an assistant coach, and a uniformed umpire. They even had a uniformed batboy! Nandito approached the rowdy group, welcomed their team captain, and motioned the opponents toward their dugout. The Vertientes captain and his coaches walked around the playing field to examine its condition. Nandito started to join them but abruptly left. He was ashamed by the way his freshly mowed baseball diamond and field looked, and he ran home to dress.

The first innings were played without incident. Nandito made some wild pitches in the first inning without serious consequences. The Vertientes' pitcher did not have Nandito's fastball, but had consistency on his side. By the fourth inning, Nandito's arm was tired when the Vertientes' center fielder came to bat. The count ran to three balls and two strikes. Ernesto did not want Nandito to pitch to him. He wanted to give the batter the base, but Nandito insisted on pitching a hard curve. Nandito delivered the ball near the chest. The batter hit a home run, and after that Nandito lost control of his pitches. Three runs later, a strong line drive to the San Joaquin's shortstop became a double play, and the inning ended.

On the way to the dugout, Ernesto unleashed his anger at Nandito. "Don't you know to follow your catcher's advice? Look what happened!"

Nandito could only complain about his tired arm. Mariano, the *curandero*, gave Nandito words of encouragement as he massaged his pitching arm with a strong potion made of alcohol, basil, mint, and Absorbine.

Ernesto was the first batter up for the San Joaquin team. He had a two-base hit, and Gumersindo followed with a single. Carlos, a powerful hitter, bunted, and the pitcher, undecided where to throw the ball, allowed him to reach first base safely. The bases were loaded. It was Julio's turn to bat. He had done poorly up to that point. All of the San Joaquin fans chanted and shouted: "Home run, home run, *dale palo, dale palo.*" The first ball pitched was high. Julio tried to kill it and drew a strike. The pitcher smugly sent another high fastball, but Julio hit the hell out of it for a triple. The inning ended with three runs for the San Joaquin team.

The next two innings were a bore with wild pitches on both sides and no errors on the field. In the bottom of the eighth, Nandito was the first batter up. The Vertientes pitcher threw a hard ball too close to Nandito's right shoulder and hit his pitching arm. The San Joaquineros jumped into the field and tried to hit and kick the Vertientes pitcher for his unsportsmanlike behavior. The fight had to be broken up by the umpires and the calmer members of the San Joaquin team. Nandito held his arm in pain, and, complaining all the while, was sent to first base. The top of the batting order came up again. Ricardo had not batted well. He felt out of place, playing with such a bunch of young fellows with his hangover. He had partied all night, and when he came back home, he fought with Cuca. He was insulted when one of the Vertientes fans called him grandfather— *abuelito!* He let the first ball go. The second ball was a clean strike. Ricardo heard Mike's voice: "Ricardo, prove you can bat!" The pitcher gave him an opportunity and Ricardo struck the ball with a powerful crack that sounded like a rifle shot. The ball traveled like a bullet over center field, past the barbed wire fence that separated the San Joaquin playing field from the farm, and ended up in the breeding pasture next to the stream for a home run.

The Joaquineros joyfully invaded the field to show their euphoria over having scored so many runs against the best team in the league. Chirra, who had behaved rather well, forgot his job and gave beers away. Paulino, caught in the excitement of the game, didn't notice Chirra's generosity until a crowd formed in front of his small stand for free beers. His reaction was swift.

"Chirra, you're fired! I don't believe what you've done! How can you do this to me?"

Chirra, who by then had drunk more than enough, laughed. "Paulino, you only live once. Isn't this wonderful?" he said grandly as he swept his arms over his head, while gripping a bottle of Hatuey by its long neck. Chirra threw back one more gulp, then disappeared into the throng of fans.

The top of the ninth inning was the Vertientes' last chance. They had their best batters coming up. Nandito felt good. The first batter, their center fielder, lined a single between shortstop and third base. The second batter struck out. The third batter hit a deep fly to center field that was easily caught, but it was so deep that the Vertientes player was able to take a base.

Needing only one more out, Nandito was nauseated, his skin drenched with a cold, nervous sweat. He pulled out his dirty handkerchief and mopped his brow. He heard the voices of his teammates urging him to pitch a fastball and Chirra's laughter and cheers as he danced in front of their bench. His first pitch was wild. His second pitch was high. Yet he came back with two strikes. With the count two and two, Ernesto asked for a low ball, but Nandito didn't know if he could control the ball, so he shook his head. Ernesto then gave a signal for an inside pitch. Nandito did not like that one either, and Ernesto asked for a time-out. The umpire told Ernesto to make it quick. The fans of the Vertientes team, knowing that this was their last chance to win the game, chanted:

> *Pin Pon, que se vaya el cabrón*
> *Pin Pon que se vaya el cabrón*
> *Vertientes para acá,*
> *Vertientes para allá,*
> *Dale,*
> *Dale,*
> *Hasta que se acabe*
> *Cachin, cachan, cachunga*
> *El Vertientes le zumba*

Ernesto asked for a curve ball. Nandito, with all his remaining strength, looped a ball that ended up sailing across the outside corner. The umpire, to his annoyance, was forced to call it a strike. The game was over. San Joaquin had won.

Nandito could not believe it. They had won a game against the best team in the league. His teammates lifted him up and carried him for a triumphal lap around the field. Amid the celebrations, Paulino stood by his stand and swatted off the kids who tried to cadge free drinks.

The Vertientes group sullenly walked off the field. Many boarded their trucks, cars, and taxis deeply stung by their unanticipated defeat. Paulino had run out of cold beer, and was selling the remaining warm ones.

Ernesto appeared in front of the makeshift stand. "Hey, my friend, how about a drink? It's time to celebrate."

Paulino handed him a beer. "Hey, this one is on the house. I told you we were going to win. See, you have to think positive," he said with an exuberant smile. "This is my last one. I ran out of beers!"

Ernesto took a swig and said, "Yes, but it's hot."

Nandito was dropped at last by his teammates, who congratulated each other on their win, embracing, laughing, clapping, and shouting, "We won, we won! We're going to win the league championship!" They drank hot beer and threw their baseball caps into the air as the children ran around the field, sliding into home plate, hitting imaginary home runs, and making difficult double plays.

A group of well-wishers followed the team from the playing field to the *bohíos* in San Joaquin. Beer was abandoned for rum, drums played, and young girls danced, shuffling their feet on the black dirt, hips moving to the sound of the bongo and the conga drums as claves set the rhythm with their syncopation. The men joined, aloof, unconcerned, and in control, but then the music, the energy of the dancers, the heat, the sight of the girls moving their hips and arms, and the rum circulating in their blood brought out their passion.

A tired Nandito rested his lanky body against the trunk of a mango tree. Rosita placed her hands on his shoulders and gave him a kiss. "You were great, my man. You were great."

The tiredness drained from his bones with her words, and he took her by the waist, led her to the middle of the crowded dance floor, and danced with his Rosita to show that this pretty mulatta was his. He felt her legs rubbing his legs. He was excited, young, and proud. Their eyes locked as they danced with each other, for each other. The other dancers noticed and like a dance troop, following the precise instructions of a choreographer, formed a circle around them and encouraged them to do what they knew best, moving their bodies to the beat of the drums. Then a trumpeter joined and his trumpet whooped with joy. Rosita, seeing she was the center of attention, increased her swaying, and the drummers, watching her hips, increased the speed of their beat. Nandito felt the urge to be only with her, outside of this crowd, and held her tightly by her thin waist. Still dancing, they crossed out of the circle amidst thrown kisses and friendly slaps. Nandito took her hand and slowly walked his young wife to the quiet of their *bohío*.

Chirra, watching Rosita and Nandito, felt happy for them, for himself, and for the whole world. Everything was so easy, so free, and so pure. He was thirsty and searched for a stronger drink. He saw Paulino looking for bottles in the bushes. "We won, the girls are dancing. I need one more drink," he convinced himself. "And then I'll be complete again. I'll talk nice and pretty to the girls, and they'll laugh at my jokes. I'll take them to the beach at the bank of the stream, and they'll feel the softness of the sand on their naked backs while I make love to them. They'll moan, and swear that I'm their man, and I'll laugh and make love again. Now, where is a bottle of rum?"

He searched around the perimeter of the dance area for abandoned bottles. He took a sip from one and a sip from another. He felt the heat of the rum and staggered close to the dance floor. He saw his daughter Consuelo dancing with Ernesto, who had abandoned his dour sense of humor and now tightly held his partner, a large smile stretched across his face. "But Consuelo is so young!" Chirra thought, outraged.

Chirra broke into the group of dancers, grabbed Ernesto roughly by the shoulder, and said, "Who do you think you are? Just because you have a glove and play catcher, you can't dance like that with my daughter. She's not a *puta*. You better behave! I have my saber and I know how to use it on scum like you."

Ernesto merely laughed at him.

"You have to respect me. I won't permit it," Chirra blurted.

Ernesto put his arm firmly around Consuelo's shoulders and led her away. He did not want to confront a drunken old man.

Chirra shouted one more time, "I'm her father. Stop!"

Ernesto and Consuelo ran instead. Chirra stumbled a few steps and fell down amid the laughter of the dancers.

PAULINO WAS PICKING up the returnable beer bottles. His recalcitrant helpers had vanished, so he used children young enough to think that finding the amber bottles with their Indian head logo was a fun game. Paulino wanted to finish loading the boxes of empties on Nandito's truck so he could go back to his room and count his money. He had to keep it in a safe place. He didn't believe in banks. They had crashed before, and he remembered the stories of businessmen firing revolvers in their mouths or jumping from tall buildings.

Paulino had always kept his money in his socks, but now that he had more, he reconsidered. Maybe he would open an account at a bank for the first time. He surrendered to the sound of music—drums pulsating, trumpet blaring, the claves clicking. He sat next to a tree to get a better view, sipping his first hot beer. He never relaxed at a *quateque,* and did not feel at ease with the uneducated girls and women of San Joaquin, pretty as they were. Their fathers and brothers also knew him, so he had to behave. Marriage and living in this area did not fit into his life plans.

He noticed three attractive women in their late twenties or early thirties, sitting on *taburetes* as they watched the crowd. Paulino had seen them around. They were sisters who owned a sugar plantation near the farm. They rode and trained their own horses, managed their land, and had a reputation as tough businesspeople. Perhaps because of their self reliance, they had not accepted local suitors. Carlos, the *bodeguero,* had approached the oldest, but she was not interested in a *bodeguero.* The three sisters wore long sleeves and large soft straw hats with bandanas covering part of their faces and their necks. Their bodies betrayed the slight movements of those who want to dance, but can't because of the rules dictated by society. The sisters were not free to mingle with the Joaquineros, young sugar cutters, and *vaqueros.*

Paulino, emboldened by the beer, approached the sisters. He had always preferred to read about romance rather than to practice it, but today would be different. He had planned his speech. First, the weather, second, the game. But when he stood in front of the sisters, he mumbled his words and his voice trailed away. He just stood there with a half-empty amber bottle of Hatuey in his hand, unable to move or talk.

Elena, the youngest sister, got up from her taburete,

"I would like to dance this number. Thank you for asking me." Taking Paulino by his hand, she led the speechless man to the dance floor.

10

The Park

DON MIGUEL WAS sitting on the terrace reading the *Diario de la Marina* when Estrella came with his breakfast. He had been at the house for a week, and Estrella was frustrated, as she hadn't cooked a meal for him yet.

"Don Miguel, when are we going to have the girls for dinner? I don't know why you have me here! I'm not a charity case. The wives of your friends constantly call me to find out when I'll be ready to leave your service. Yet once you show up, you only eat out."

She well remembered the family meals at Lola's house: The whole family had gathered at the table. The *Señora* at one end, presiding over her children, cousins, aunts, married, and unmarried; and then, after her death, Adelaida, as her oldest daughter, continued the tradition. Don Miguel remembered, too, but such memories haunted him. Why recreate the past and give life to thoughts that tormented him? Why bring them back?

"No," he said. "Soon, I'll call the girls. *Punto y acabado.* Tonight, soup and ice cream in the dining room at seven-thirty. You can serve."

Out in the garage, Fernando absentmindedly passed a dry chamois over the headlights of the car. He was bored, and walked to the kitchen to see if Estrella had leftover meat loaf for a sandwich.

"Fernando, what do you want? Take a walk or go somewhere," Estrella snapped as Georgina came into the kitchen. Georgina had prepared Don Miguel's room for the night, placing his pajamas and night-robe on the bed. She glanced at Fernando and slowly stretched her short skirt, making it tight on her ass as she walked past him.

"Hi, Fernando!" she said with a hint of seduction in her voice. "How do you like *La Capital?*" She didn't wait for his reply, but added, "I love it myself, but to truly enjoy Havana you need companionship. It's so big. Maybe if—"

Estrella cut in, "Georgina, you have to clean the table, and then I'll find you something else to do. I told Fernando that he has better things to do than stay here and be a drone."

Fernando knew that it wasn't his day and disappeared. Besides, he was finished with Georgina and the sexual frustration she caused. Three blocks from the house was a French-designed park. It occupied a square block; four sidewalks met at a big round fountain with thick concrete sides, a gigantic wafer inside a concrete cross. Benches were scattered around the park. Large ficus trees, whose massive roots broke their way up through the sidewalks, shaded them. The abandoned fountain had debris, abandoned beer bottles and dirt, at its bottom. The air near it was putrid with the smell of decomposing leaves as puddles of rainwater waited to evaporate.

Fernando had used that park to charm the maids who had preceded Georgina. He knew exactly what to say and do to them to make them breathless, pining, in virtual physical pain, full of desire, and then take them to a nearby inn that rented rooms by the hour, where they would surrender in his arms. Fernando chose a bench that had a good view of the sidewalks, hoping, perhaps, that a new romance might appear.

A car stopped at the corner, and a young man, who wore a tight white *guayabera*, dropped a package behind a large ficus tree, then jumped back into the car, which sped away. A moment later, the small explosion startled Fernando. His first reaction was to run from the park, but he was afraid that it would call attention to him, so he started to walk, as fast as he could, back to the house.

He was half a block away when a tan Oldsmobile screeched to a halt in front of him. Two men jumped out and threw him against the hood, roughly patted down his body, and then shoved him into the backseat.

"You're under arrest. What are you doing here?" one of the men said, closing the door as the car sped towards the G2 station next to the entrance of the bridge on 23rd Street on the Vedado side of the Almendares River.

Once they arrived, Fernando was thrown in an empty cell.

"Hey, you have the wrong guy. Let me call my boss. He lives nearby. He'll tell you. Hey, this is a big mistake. Please let me call him."

"Shut up. We know what to do."

The cell door clanged, leaving Fernando in the loneliness of the room. He sat there for an hour and nothing happened. He started to pace, and out of frustration shouted, "Hey, I have to make a call. Let me out. I haven't done a thing. I don't live around here. This is a mistake. A big mistake."

Two agents swiftly came for him. Letting him out, they shoved him into a small office and pushed him into a steel chair. They took his wallet, his driver's license, the few pesos that he had in his pocket, his lighter and cigarettes, belt and shoelaces.

"Your name"

"Fernando Gomez."

"Where do you live?"

"Finca San Joaquin, Piedrecitas, Camagüey."

Before he answered any other questions, he was lifted from the chair and thrown into another cell. He heard screams from a nearby room, followed by periods of silence. He nervously paced around his cell. Paulino had told him of young men who were against the government who had disappeared, but he never thought it could happen to him. Another hour passed and the door of his cell opened, and a mulatto, younger than Fernando, holding up his slacks with his hands and wearing a *guayabera* that had seen better times, was thrown in. After he recovered from being pushed, he pressed up against the bars of the cell and screamed, "You can't do this to me! I want out. I haven't done a thing. I want out! Let me go, let me go."

"Hey, you'd better calm down," Fernando said, "It's just a matter of waiting. If you haven't done anything, they'll let you out. Just calm down and sit. Relax, it'll be fine." Fernando tried to be reassuring with the young man, although he was getting more anxious every minute.

The young man looked at Fernando with disbelief. "Do you know where you are?"

"Of course," Fernando answered. "I'm at the G2 prison, but I'm not the person they want. I was just sitting in a park when a bomb exploded. I walked off, and they came after me. But I didn't do anything."

The young man smiled wryly. "You don't know a damn thing about the G2. They'll torture you, maim you, and even kill you. Yeah, sure, you just walked by. They couldn't care less who you are. This is the G2! Are you crazy! They're going to beat us up badly, very badly, or even worse," he said, as a look of terror swept over his face.

They sat silently on the floor of their cell and stared blankly at the dingy hallway beyond the iron bars. Each one was afraid to confide in the other. They were nervous the other could be a G2 informer. Sporadically, men were forced to walk in the hallway, subjugated, with fear in their eyes. At the end of the hallway, a door opened into an office where Fernando could hear the laughter of the jailors. A radio played at its highest volume to conceal the shouting and howling coming from the room.

Suddenly, the younger prisoner leaned his head back against the wall and stared up at the ceiling. "I can't believe I'm here. Who is taking away my freedom? When did we give them that power? God help me. Help me understand. Help me be free again." He turned to Fernando and said flatly, "They don't know who I am, and I'm not going to tell them."

"I would tell them with pleasure who I am, but they haven't even tried to find out. I work for this man who owns a large farm in Camagüey. I don't even live here. If they ask the right questions, they'll let me go."

The young man smirked. "Man, are you a fool! Do you *guajiros* know anything about what is happening in Havana? They may not ask any questions, or they may ask you the wrong one."

Just then, two guards appeared and opened the cell door. They jerked Fernando to his feet, led him to the same small office, and sat him on the metal chair.

"What are you doing in Havana?" a tall agent asked him.

"Why were you near the park?" a second agent, smaller, almost rodent-like, asked.

"Do you come from Oriente province?"

"Who are you?"

"Fernando Gomez, I told you so."

"Where were you tonight at six-thirty?"

"Walking near the park close to my boss's home."

"Do you drive a blue car?"

"No."

"Do you drive a Chevrolet?"

"No."

"Do you know Enrique Perez?"

"No."

"Romualdo Rodriguez?"

"Romualdo, no"

Fernando answered most of the questions without hesitation, but if he hesitated even briefly, the rodent slapped Fernando on the mouth.

"You can not think. You answer!" he commanded.

Fernando controlled himself, though he was angry. He wanted to stand up and hit the rodent with his fist. He tasted the blood in his mouth.

They asked questions for two hours, and they didn't believe any of his replies. Fernando's back hurt from sitting in the uncomfortable steel chair. Still, they wanted to know more. He was groggy and tired. He wanted it to end.

"Do you have friends at the university?" the agent asked.

"I don't know anyone there. I'm poor man. I'm a worker at a farm."

The rodent slapped him again. "I don't care who and what you are!"

"Do you travel to Trinidad?" he then asked.

"Never," Fernando replied.

"Have you been recently at Bayamo?"

"I have, with my boss's farm cattle and horse show string," Fernando answered, hoping the agent would ask about his boss, and learn that he was a well-known man. They ignored his reply.

"Can you read and write?"

"Yes, I know how to."

"Are you writing slogans on the walls against the president?"

"I'm not a painter." Another slap in the face and at the end, the interrogators, tired of abusing Fernando, concluded that he was too dumb to play with bombs and threw him back into the cell.

The young man was now smoking a cigarette. He looked up at Fernando and asked, "How do you feel? Are they taking you back?"

Fernando muttered, "Leave me alone. I'm tired. I'm in pain," and sat down on the floor of the cell.

The prisoner held out his cigarette. "Do you want to share a smoke? They gave it to me."

Fernando shook his head, "No thanks, I don't feel like it. You can keep it." He leaned his shoulders against the wall, closing his eyes.

The prisoner took a deep drag and shrugged. "I know I'll get out of this place. Batista is a dictator, but he won't last. The people are against him. Just wait. Don't you agree with me? We have to be together."

Fernando muttered, "Leave me alone. I'm exhausted." He looked down at the floor of the cell and closed his eyes.

A few minutes later, the cell door opened. The guards came for his cell mate. The young man held onto the bars and started shouting, "No, I'm not he. I haven't done anything. Let me go!" until his legs went soft. They had to pull him out, holding his shoulders as his legs dragged. Fernando heard shouts coming from the nearby office and the dry sound of the pizzle, then the shouting stopped. The young man never came back to the cell. After a few hours of wondering what had happened to his companion, Fernando finally fell asleep.

Three hours later, two new guards came to the cell door to escort Fernando to another office, where Don Miguel waited in an armchair with a cigar in his hand. He instantly noticed that Fernando's lips were swollen and that he looked broken and torn. "Are you okay?"

Fernando nodded. A guard handed Fernando his belt, shoelaces, driver's license, and an empty billfold.

Don Miguel drove Fernando home. It was a bright and beautiful day.

"They called me early this morning and asked if you worked for me," Don Miguel explained. "I told them you did, and that you were with me around five o'clock. I know a bomb exploded, because Georgina told me. I don't think they believed me, but they couldn't prove otherwise. Fernando, they told me you're involved with the rebel groups in the hills."

"I'm not, Don Miguel. You know me very well."

The old man frowned, knowing he was right. "I don't think you're safe here. I'm sending you back to the farm."

Fernando nodded. Georgina was not worth a night at the *Castillito,* as the G2 prison was called. He had better girls to see in San Joaquin.

. . .

THE NEXT MORNING, Don Miguel took Fernando to the bus station and sent him back to Ciego de Ávila. Before boarding the bus, Fernando bought a copy of the *Prensa Libre*. Half an hour into the trip, he pulled out the newspaper, scanned a few pages and froze. He stared in disbelief at a photograph of the young mulatto with whom he had been imprisoned the day before. He was clad in the same *guayabera*, now torn and bloody. The newspaper reported that, according to official sources, a bomb had exploded in his hands and killed him.

After leaving the bus station, Don Miguel drove to a gas station to find a working public phone and called Dr. Comillas, who sounded upset, sleepy, and spoke in strangely vague sentences. He would meet him at the minister's beach house. He would be on time—no later than one o'clock.

Don Miguel felt uneasy as he drove through the tunnel under the bay and onto the Via Blanca. The road was empty, for it was late for the heavy traffic. He had left Havana behind, and the unspoiled white beaches started to appear on the left. The salty air that rushed through the open car windows reminded him of childhood trips to Varadero Beach. The sea was blue and brilliant. It was a windless day, and the ocean looked like a gigantic placid lake. He left behind the housing developments of Tarara and Celimar, passed a few family cars loaded with children, and eventually slowed down as he approached the town of Guanabo. The low hills to the right softened and opened into a narrow valley that enclosed the tortuous meanderings of the Guanabo River. The small Victorian seaside town was named after the river, and the river named after an Indian, now lost from recorded history. Small stores that sold souvenirs, cold sodas, beer, and hamburgers flanked the beach. Hawkers rented black tire tubes to swimmers. A small navy boat with sunburned sailors kept the tubers from drifting into the Gulf current. Entire families held hands as they waded knee deep into the ocean and jumped over the waves. Behind them, upbeat music blared from the food stands. Men showed their bare chests and tried to impress the women by rippling their muscles. Children made sand castles, and then watched them toppled by the incoming waves.

Don Miguel turned left at the end of the highway, before it crossed the river. He found the white two-story house he had been looking for, and parked behind a tan Oldsmobile. He saw the minister's bodyguards, looking bored and lethargic as they sat slumped in their cars. The youngest bodyguard stepped out to meet him.

"Buenos días, Don Miguel. *El Ministro* is waiting for you."

Don Miguel handed the bodyguard his car keys and followed him to the back of the house, where the minister sat under the shade of a large mango tree, sipping coffee from a delicate white porcelain cup.

"Miguelito! I thought you weren't going to make it. Comillas called, said he was running late. I think he has a young one. He sounded tired." Don Miguel chuckled, and his friend continued, "Well, I'm so happy you're here. You have to enjoy life a little more. *El Doctor* told me that he pleads with you to come to Havana more often, not only when you have to deal with me. Here, let me hang your hat. You and I are the only ones that still need them. These young guys are never in the sun."

He signaled the maid to bring Don Miguel a cup of coffee. "I have a special blend. The beans are handpicked and roasted just for me. At least, that's what they tell me. You can never believe a courtesan. They'll say anything to make you feel that you owe them a favor." He turned to the maid. "I'll also have another cup." He smiled at Don Miguel, patted him on the back, and then led him to the covered porch.

"Let's play dominoes and forget about all the problems you think you have to solve. I'll have Lieutenant San Pietro join us. He just returned from training in the States." He stopped abruptly, remembering something. "But excuse me, I'm not a very good host. If my wife were here, she'd kill me. Would you like something to eat?

"Not now, but thank you," Don Miguel said.

Half an hour passed before Comillas appeared with a grin on his face and a cigarette in his holder. The four sat at a square wooden table on the porch, surrounded by the sounds of birds, waves, and dominoes spilling and sliding against the wood.

The friends swapped old stories. The minister switched from coffee to Scotch, and Don Miguel and Comillas joined him. By this point it was close to two o'clock. Don Miguel decided it was time to discuss a troublesome, delicate subject.

"Yesterday, a small bomb exploded in the park near my house," he began. "It happened around sundown. Thank God no one was hurt. The G2 arrested my driver. You know him, the big black man who shows my bulls. They held him all night and roughed him up before someone finally called my home to verify that he worked for me. I went to the G2 at the Castillito—you know the one on 23rd Street. Well, in the end, they released him to me. But they should have called me earlier. He's a good and loyal employee. He was scared to death. This morning I sent him back to the farm, because I want him to be safe."

The minister took a long sip of his Scotch. "Well, they make mistakes, but we do have to stop the bombings. It affects our economy, and it hurts innocent people. If you read about these bombings, would you come to Havana to gamble?" He sighed, realizing that Don Miguel was still not satisfied. "They place a bomb and run away. They're mostly students. We don't have a problem with the communists, since they're too old and tired. And we know it's not organized labor, since they've never been more powerful than with our president."

"Are you certain that it's the students?" Don Miguel asked.

"Who else would have the time? They aren't going to the university. We have great employment. New casinos are opening, bigger hotels! We have the best rates of tourism we ever had. That is where they want to hurt us. They want the *Americanos* to think that it's unsafe to go to the Sans-Souci or Tropicana. It's just a small, very small group of people," the minister said. At last he did offer a form of apology. "You should have called me. I would have sent Lieutenant San Pietro to go to the G2 with you. Are you sure that your man wasn't behaving suspiciously?"

"No, Fernando did nothing wrong," Don Miguel affirmed stoutly. "He's a good, loyal man. Hardworking. He shouldn't have been punished."

THE NEXT MORNING, Don Miguel was having breakfast on the terrace and reading the editorial in *El Diario de la Marina* when Estrella interrupted. "Don Miguel, Mike is calling you long-distance." He got up and hurried to the library.

"*Alo, alo.* Mike, is that you? Is everything okay?"

"Yes, everything is fine. I saw Fernando this morning, and he told me what happened. I'm calling because I'm worried about you alone in Havana without a driver."

"I don't need a driver. I never had one in Havana. I can take care of myself. Thanks for asking, but how do you think I've lived for the last five years?"

"Dad, you work too hard. I was afraid that you might decide to drive at night when you're tired and may have been out with your friends. I wanted to know that you're all right."

"Well, I'm having a great time. I've met with the minister and with Dr. Comillas. I've played dominoes, and Estrella feeds me too much. I'm well, thank you."

Mike gave him a short report on the farm. Everything was running smoothly.

"Wonderful news, Son. Wonderful! I'm doing well, too. Actually, I'm having lunch with your sisters today. I'll tell them that you miss them. Good-bye, Son. I love you, and keep me posted."

Adelaida arrived first, not surprisingly. She was always punctual, organized, but today she was worried. Georgina answered the door. She had set the table with the best china and made sure that she wore her least tight uniform.

"*Buenas tardes,* Señora Adelaida. I'll tell your father that you've arrived. He's in the library on the telephone."

Adelaida barely acknowledged Georgina. "*Gracias.* Tell Father that I'll be on the terrace."

Rather than heading to the terrace, though, she walked slowly through the house, checking it for cleanliness. Adelaida found the house in good order, then went to the terrace, sat on an iron chair, and surveyed the garden. In the yard, a big Flamboyant tree competed with a more restrained acacia, the fruit trees were in flower, and soon the mango, orange, and grapefruit trees would have fruit. The gardener still kept her mother's roses in beautiful condition. Adelaida's mother had personally selected and planted them. The terrace was full of pots containing geraniums of various colors. Her mother had had Felix Ramos paint the riotous colors of her garden, and the painting now hung in the library.

Estrella interrupted her reminiscences. "Adelaidita, do you want something to drink? Your father, like always, is on the telephone. You know how he is. He just finished talking to Mike. Did you hear about Fernando? It was awful."

Adelaida got up, not wanting to chat with Estrella. "No, thanks, I think I might need to call Lourdes. I hope she didn't forget about lunch with Father."

Just then Lourdes arrived, her arms hung with glossy shopping bags. She greeted Adelaida, then immediately started to complain about the heat, about how her Mercedes was in the shop, about how her chauffeur was off that day, and about how she had to take a taxi to go shopping downtown.

Adelaida pressed her lips into a small, tight smile. "Things can't be that bad in the stock market. You shop and he plays golf. Well, well . . ."

Lourdes was accustomed to her sister's barbs, and she dropped her bags on the floor and continued, "You know I had to a buy few small things. It's so difficult to be well dressed these days. My dressmaker has become less reliable. She's lost her flair and can't copy a dress as well as before. It's so difficult to coordinate."

"Yes, yes, I know." The two sisters walked to the terrace.

Don Miguel finished his latest conversation with Lustre. "I'll call you after I have lunch with the girls. By the way, how are they doing? Are they living within their income?"

Lustre was used to this difficult question. "Well, Lourdes has a tendency to be overdrawn once in a while. I cover her overdrafts, and she promptly makes a deposit on her account. It seems to be a problem of timing. She's very generous. She calls almost every month to see if she can give money to another cause. They're all good causes. One day it's *La Liga contra El Cancer*, the next month it's *Pro Arte Musical*. The other day she wanted me to write a check from your account to the Hungarian refugees. I always tell her that who you give to and how much is your decision, that I don't control it. She told me that she couldn't talk to you, that you're a hermit and that they need the money now. She is so persistent. She's inherited that from you."

Don Miguel smiled. Lourdes was his favorite daughter, and as obstinate as he.

He hung up with Lustre and went to join the girls. Georgina appeared with fried green plantains as he poured a Scotch and water. Lourdes mockingly frowned.

"Papi, are you still following the doctor's advice—one drink before each meal? It's the only one piece of advice you always follow."

He laughed, for he enjoyed joking with his daughters. He would have preferred that they had married men interested in farming, but at least they married well. The girls asked about Mike, a bit hurt that he hadn't stopped to visit them. Their father tried to mollify them.

"He thought I was very sick, so he came straight to the country. It sounds like Lustre misled him."

"What did Lustre tell him, Daddy?" Both girls asked him almost at the same time.

"That I was sick."

"Are you? When was the last time you saw a doctor?" Adelaida asked.

"You have to see Dr. Castillo," Lourdes said. "He could take good care of you."

Don Miguel smiled, touched. Yes, he was sick, but his sickness had to do more with absence than with the status of his heart or lungs. Time would cure everything, though. At least he could take comfort in the fact that his children loved him.

11

Mike and Rita

AFTER THE PHONE CALL, Mike had one problem to take care of, one he had not revealed to his father. He drove to the warehouse and asked for Mulato, who approached Mike ready to serve.

"What do you need today, Mike?" he smiled.

"I don't have a list. I came here to tell you that you can only extend credit to farm employees if *I* approve it," Mike said curtly, then left.

Mike stopped by the saddle shop to see if Ricardo's new *domadora* saddle was ready. Then he visited the electrical shop owned by Kato, the Japanese, to see the new set of batteries for the electric plant. After he bought the last *Bohemia* from the newsstand, he returned to see Rita at the telephone company. He sat at one of the booths and called her. "I have to go back to the farm soon, but I have time for lunch. Would you join me at the Oriental?"

Rita wondered if it would be better to find an excuse and say she couldn't go. Would Mike think she was too easy, or if she made herself a little more difficult, would Mike be more attracted to her? But she had already taken it upon herself to visit Mike. What did she have to lose?

"Mike, it will be a pleasure, at what time?"

"One o'clock?"

"Sure, I'll be there."

Mike walked over to the small café that had no more than twenty white marble-topped tables. On one side, there was a bar with a mirror behind it, a large complex espresso machine, and an ornate cash register. Behind a glass enclosure was a station for preparing sandwiches; it was filled with long loaves of bread and legs of ham hanging from the ceiling. The waiter barely acknowledged Mike's presence when he took him to the table. When Rita appeared ten minutes later, the waiter suddenly became obsequious. He was faster than Mike in pulling back a chair for Rita, and he immediately asked Rita about her mother, and how hot it was, and told her how beautiful she looked that day, while cleaning the marble tabletop with great force.

"Thank you, Roberto, you're always so nice."

She remembered that Mike had been quiet during their afternoon together. This time she vowed to remain calm until Mike broke the silence.

"It's going to be a hot day," he said, taking a self-deprecating stab at his impatience for small talk. Then he added with a broad smile, "You look very pretty."

They finally ordered their drinks and lunch. The waiter served Rita first; then almost dropped the plate in front of Mike. Another few minutes passed while Rita sipped her drink, but she did not look up. She continued to look at the tabletop.

"Rita, it was so nice of you to come to the farm the other day. I was a poor host. I promise that I can be better."

Rita spoke quietly, "You're special to me, Mike."

Mike reached toward her hand under the table and then thought better of it. "You're also special to me, Rita, but I don't know how long I'll be at the farm this time. I might have to go back to Havana. Father may need me. That was the reason for the call. What are your plans?"

"Mother is out of town and will be back tomorrow, but I may have to go to Camagüey for a short stay after she comes back. They want me to train on a new switchboard. When do you leave?"

"Maybe while you're gone. I don't know yet. It all depends on Father."

Rita smiled, "I don't know, either, when I have to go to Camagüey. It's so odd, we don't control things or events, they just happen."

"Maybe," Mike said, "but there are things that we do control. We're capable of making decisions, creating events. Some may occur because of luck, but others we cause. You must know what I mean."

Rita did not want to admit that she understood, so she played with her food and just smiled. They made more small talk as the café filled up. When the waiter brought the check, Mike quickly assessed the total and gave the waiter a good tip.

Rita fumbled in her purse. "I'm running late. I have to go."

Mike apologized, "I'm sorry that we didn't talk more. I'd like to know you better. You—"

"You're so nice. I'd like to talk to you some more, too."

"What time will you be free tonight?"

"Maybe around eight o'clock," Rita said as she smiled.

That night, Mike sped to the *pueblo*, arriving at Rita's house exactly at eight o'clock. She answered the door.

"Hi, welcome!" She gave Mike a lingering hug. "I know you must be thirsty. Please come in! What can I get you to drink? As I told you at lunch, Mother isn't here today. She's visiting her sister in Ciego de Ávila."

Mike was wearing his best linen *guayabera* and carefully pressed slacks, while Rita had on one of her tight silk dresses, more appropriate for a dinner party than receiving a beau. The small living room had few pieces of furniture, Mike noticed. A large sofa, covered in a heavy pink damask, held court in the middle of the room. Rita's mother had covered the furniture with heavy plastic to protect it, and the lampshades still had their store cellophane covers.

"Please sit down. Let me open the windows, it's always so hot in here. What would you like? I have Coca-Cola, Bacardi, Domecq, and beer, but no Scotch." Rita flitted around the living room, opened windows, fluffed pillows, and started the fan. "Please, make yourself at home," she said and went to the kitchen.

"I'll have rum. Thanks so much."

Mike wandered around the room, looking at photographs of Rita at different stages of her life. He paused at a picture of her kneeling in a white communion dress with a rosary in her hand, lit as if she were a Hollywood star. Rita returned with a tray of cheese wedges and saltine crackers.

"Last Saturday was such a nice day," she said. "I didn't expect you to spend so much time with me."

Mike swirled the ice in his drink, but didn't reply. She tried to enliven the conversation, but Mike answered with monosyllables. They were perched on the sofa, tense, waiting. He reached for another saltine cracker; she reached for one at the same time. Their hands touched, and Mike felt as if a strong current had gone through his body. He instinctively picked up her hand, lifted it to his mouth, and gently kissed it. First, it was one small kiss, then a longer one. She held his other hand against her chest. He started kissing her face gently, first her eyelashes, and then her lips. Mike shifted closer to Rita, and in the process, accidentally tilted the coffee table, sending the plate with cheese and crackers crashing to the floor. The room fell silent except for the gentle sound of the oscillating fan in the corner of the room. They started kissing with passion, as if there would never be a tomorrow. Suddenly laughter floated in through an open window, and a voice said, "Boy, this is better than the movies!" Rita pulled away and jumped up to shut the windows. "Those stupid brats," she cried.

Mike stood up as well and collected the pieces of cracker and cheese from the floor. As Rita closed the last window, he approached her and touched her back. When she leaned toward him, he dropped his hand and started to unbutton her dress. She laughed. "We're like a little boy and girl."

"It's not your first time?" he asked cautiously.

"No," she said.

They slowly moved to her bedroom, where small votive candles in a corner lit a small shrine of painted wooden statues of the Virgin de la Caridad and Santa Barbara. They made love, and then loved again. Tightly embraced, they slept together illuminated by the flickering lights in front of the Virgin and Santa Barbara.

THE SKY WAS full of deep oranges and reds, a painterly backdrop for the twin windmills turning rhythmically with the breeze, pulling water for the *batey's* tank. It was late afternoon when Ricardo rode his white mare to the *batey*. Two water bottles wrapped in burlap hung on the pommel of his *domadora* saddle. The heat from the bulldozer's engine and the dust stirred up by the clearing activity had caked his face, and it looked dark and mean. He was ready for a hot shower and a quick dinner accompanied by the CMQ radio station from Havana. An old cow had been butchered, and he knew that Cuca had prepared beef jerky with tomato sauce. It was not Ricardo's favorite meat dish, but it was meat, and he believed that if he did not eat meat every day, he would compromise his strength and virility.

Ricardo unsaddled, washed the back of his mount, and let her loose in the milk cow pasture. As he walked back to the house, he noticed that Mike's jeep wasn't parked in front. It was odd for Mike to be out. Ricardo entered the house and asked Paulino where Mike was.

Paulino answered with a snippet from a song:

> *"Amor, amor.*
>> Love, love.
> *Nació de ti,*
>> It was born of you,
> *Nació de mí,*
>> It was born of me,
> *De la esperanza.*
>> From hope."

Ricardo nodded at Cuca and went to take his shower.

CHIRRA HAD WORKED all day. His tongue was as dry as paste. He had been drinking a lot, and his hangover was with him, on him, in him, around him. During the day, every time Paulino saw Chirra, he tried to collect for the beers that he had drunk at the baseball game. The third time Paulino asked, Chirra stood and shouted, "I worked my ass off! Beers were part of my pay. I didn't get a penny." His head was pounding as he went on. "You want to profit from me after I helped you so much. You're disgraceful. I'll never work for you or under you for the rest of my life!"

Paulino stood speechless.

NANDITO HAD GONE to the *batey* in the morning, looking for more work from Mike. He had to spend the entire morning waiting. When Mike saw Nandito, he reminded the pitcher that he had agreed to weed Don Miguel's garden. Now, after working the whole afternoon around the big house, Nandito would return home with no pay, and to a trifling dinner of cornmeal and small pieces of pork. Cuca saw how dejected Nandito was. In seconds she handed Nandito a canteen with leftover black beans, jerky, and rice, lifting his spirits.

The night descended. The dreams and frustrations of a monotonous life were forgotten in the sleep of exhausted bodies.

EARLY THE NEXT morning, Mike was driving back from Rita's house in the dark when he noticed a man walking down the center of the farm road. Mike stopped. It was Paulino. He was dressed in a white *guayabera*, a pair of perfectly pressed blue slacks, and a pair of black leather shoes so polished that they shone in the light of jeep. Paulino was so filled with joy, he felt as if he were walking on clouds.

Mike opened the door of the jeep. "Do you want a ride back?"

"Yes, thanks," Paulino replied and jumped in.

Each, afraid the other might ask questions, made the rest of the trip in silence.

12

The Family Reunion

PAULINO HANDED MIKE a telegram: "Make a reservation on the Pullman from Ciego de Ávila. Call when made. Family reunion. Dad."

He read it again. He had to go, he understood that much. Normally, he would have looked forward to visiting his sisters, nephews, and friends in Havana, but that was before Rita. He had spent the last three nights with her, since her mother was still out of town. He could not get her out of his mind. Every time he passed through the living room, he remembered her dozing on the couch, her blonde hair covering her eyes. He recalled the demure way she sashayed with her parasol and their trip on the gig. Mike envisioned her on the bank of the river, her soft hands when he held them. He could hear her gentle laughter and smell her sweet perfume.

Yet Mike was nervous about their relationship. He felt chained to the family's expectations and traditions. Rita didn't have a university education, nor did she know the nuances of society life. Yet she was bright, observant, ambitious, and had a great sense of humor. She loved to read books, and she had, once their relationship had begun, induced him to spend more time talking than loving. She surprised him with her discussions about books she had read. In addition, she was a great listener. She understood what he said. She comforted him, and she made him feel good. There had been others before him, he knew, but he forgot his prejudices about what makes a woman "decent" and an acceptable candidate for a "proper" relationship.

Mike reread the telegram, stuffed it in his pocket, and hurriedly left the room. He had to be alone.

Paulino noticed Mike's hasty departure and knew that something was wrong. Paulino was perplexed by his reaction. He had read the telegram before handing it over. Paulino was left alone in the living room, so he went to the kitchen, where Cuca was preparing lunch. Leaning against the table, he said, "Mike is going back to Havana." Cuca continued to peel potatoes. Paulino noted her indifference, and knowing that Cuca was not going to give him the time of day, he left to straighten up Mike's room.

It was late afternoon when Mike left the farm. At the exchange he picked up a telephone. Rita answered, and his conversation with her was a short one.

"Father wants me in Havana, so I'm leaving tomorrow. I don't know for how long. I'll write you and I'll miss you," Mike softly whispered in order to avoid being overheard.

Rita did not answer at first. She moved restlessly in her chair and tried to control her anxiety and fear. Havana was full of elegant women. She asked herself, "Why? Why did I go to bed with him so soon?" Yet she calmly answered, "Don't worry, my *bébé*, I'll be waiting for you. Be careful. Call me."

Mike had her connect him with his father. Don Miguel wasn't mushy in the slightest. He snapped, "You didn't have to call. Just get on the train."

The next day, Fernando drove Mike to Ciego de Ávila. The Pullman car he boarded had seen better days. Once he got into the bed, the clacking of the train put him to sleep, and he slept until the train entered the Havana station. It was a long trip across the city, and as soon as the taxi left the port area with its narrow cobblestone streets, they entered the Malecon. The sky was a cloudless deep blue, and the waves could be heard breaking against the concrete seawall as car horns blared on the avenue. The noise and the smell of the sea brought back memories of childhood trips to the port with his mother and grandmother to watch ships arrive from faraway places. The old chauffeur drove them with preternatural care, as if he had a delicate cargo of crystal in the backseat.

Georgina answered the door and greeted Mike, then shouted for Estrella. The cook came running from the kitchen with arms wide open. She threw her arms around Mike and kissed him. Her words came out in a ceaseless torrent.

"*Malagradecido*, why didn't you stop here first? What have we done to you? I've cooked your favorite dishes. We're going to have *arroz con pollo* and just for you, ham croquettes. You look famished—isn't Cuca feeding you at all? You must be tired. Let me tell your father that you're here. He's in the library."

His father was in the library with Lustre when he heard Mike's voice in the kitchen. Don Miguel went into the kitchen, offered Mike a perfunctory embrace and kiss, and then announced, "We're meeting with Lustre after lunch."

Mike went with his father to say hello to the accountant, and he left them in the library while he went to his room to clean up.

A few hours later, the rest of the family arrived: Jose Maria and Adelaida, as always, on time; Lourdes and Julio, as usual, late.

Don Miguel huffed. "You two are going to be late to your own funerals!"

Lourdes appeased her father with small kisses. "Silly Papa. I'm not going to die anytime soon."

At lunch, Jose Maria started out tentatively, alert to Don Miguel's sensibilities.

"It's so nice to be all together. It's been a long time since we last convened. Mike, it's nice to see you back in your own country. Don Miguel, what do you want to discuss?"

Don Miguel answered, "Well, I thought you and Julio knew, because you called for this meeting."

Julio coughed and said, "We feel it's important to see each other in private and discuss things rather that at the country club or at El Carmelo. I have ideas that I'd like to explore with the family, but especially with you, and you're difficult to reach. I know you trust Lustre, but he can't make a decision for you."

Don Miguel interrupted, "Yes, I know that you want me to diversify. The problem is I already diversified back in the twenties. I was making more money in the stock market than you can imagine. I was on margin. I knew all the answers. Then the '29 crash came, and I was lucky to be able to pay the margin calls and barely escaped with my skin. From then on, I made a decision. I want bearer bonds that pay in dollars in the States. I want to continue to improve the farm. The farm is in full production. Our purebred cattle are in Colombia, Venezuela, Costa Rica, and El Salvador. We've sold all the bulls we want to, to the Dominican Republic, to their president and other cattlemen. We're making money."

"Yes, we know," Julio said, while thinking that none of that cash flowed from the farm to Lourdes."

Don Miguel continued, "The girls and Mike have their rental properties. All of you have a comfortable life. If we stand together and invest together, we'll make more money. We are an example of how a family can prosper without quarrels and divisions that sap growth. I don't want or like or approve of fights or quarrels. United we can prosper, and but if we divide and fight, we'll only be left with the name of a family who once had money and power."

Jose Maria added, "We have to thank you, but at the same time, we need to meet more often."

Don Miguel agreed with a nod of his head and continued, "Do you want your children to be poor? Or do you prefer to keep doing what we are doing, and do it well—or, do you think that I don't know how to invest?"

Julio said, "Well, I don't expect you to change your way of doing business. You're successful, and you also have very definite ideas." His voice slipped into a smoother gear as he brought up a new complication. "Yet in truth, I'm nervous about the stories I'm hearing about the rebels. Have you read *Time* magazine? Herbert Matthews of the *New York Times* is writing about Castro all the time. Many of your friends, Don Miguel, are investing in the United States. The American market gives you liquidity, but if you prefer good quality bonds, I can buy them for you and when you—"

Don Miguel was patient. He knew what Julio was driving at. Comillas had just opened a numbered account at First National Bank in Miami. Lustre was nervous about him pouring money back into the farm. Don Miguel did not agree. He had fought too hard to convince the government to authorize purebred cattle exports, but if they had a very dry season and the meat supply for the market dwindled, the uproar of the press would make it impossible to export cattle. He turned to Mike.

"What do you think?"

The girls looked askance at Mike. To them, he was just their baby brother. They wondered why their father had asked for Mike's opinion and not for the opinions of their husbands. Mike looked around the table. He took a sip of water and answered unhesitatingly.

"It is your money. We have our own. You should diversify. We can spend your lifetime, my lifetime, and our children's lifetimes working and improving the farm, and the process will never be complete. There's always something you can perfect, a new piece of machinery that you can buy, a new bull that has a better pedigree. But Julio is right—you should have American stocks. Xerox and IBM are the future."

What Don Miguel really wanted to ask was, "Mike, what do you want to do? Do you want to stay? Do you want to see the grass planted, the cattle fatten?" Yet he knew it was not the right time. Instead he turned to his children.

"Well, you've had your say. I respect your opinions. Let's hear what Lustre has to say. Remember, numbers don't lie, but liars make up numbers."

They left the table and went to the library to meet with Lustre, whom Estrella had ushered in during dessert. The meeting was brief. Lustre had brought the profit and loss statements for the apartment houses, the sugar plantation, and the farm. He also had the bond portfolio. Mike was the only one who asked questions; Jose Maria and Julio remained silent. They knew Don Miguel was going to do whatever he wanted to do with his money. Mike was the key to all of their questions.

13

Mike in Havana

MIKE HAD HIS daily routine: In the morning he read *El Diario de la Marina* and glanced at the society pages for pictures of his friends and himself. He fought the traffic in El Malecon to go to his father's office in Old Havana. He worked with Lustre on the numbers, analyzed the business, and tried to create a model with separate profit centers. At eleven o'clock, he took a coffee break with Lustre, and later had lunch with his father and his friends at one of their favorite restaurants, El Carmelo de 23, La Floridita, or El Centro Vasco. He attended meetings with his father at the associations of sugarcane growers and cattlemen, and accompanied his father to meet with politicians and lawyers on the drafting of governmental decrees. In the late afternoons, he drove to the Habana Yacht Club to exercise and play squash.

Two weeks after he arrived, he went to the yacht club to play tennis with Jose Maria. The locker room was located on the fifth floor and he stood on the balcony, listening to the wooden sandals flapping on the hard tile floor, the white and green domino tiles slapping the wooden tables. The small beach in front of the club was surrounded and protected by its two white concrete brick piers, the beach of Náutico y Militar, and the public beach, La Concha, with its Moorish buildings.

Jose Maria arrived dressed in tennis whites. They took the elevator to the first floor, and walked past the bar with the Massaguer caricatures to the tennis courts, occupied by foursomes. Jose Maria had reserved a court, but they had to wait until the previous match ended. It was mixed doubles, and Mike knew three of the players. The men had gone to school with Mike. He knew one of the girls, and the other looked familiar, but he couldn't place her. He kept finding himself watching her. She moved with grace and agility on the court, and she had an infectious laugh. She was tall, dark-haired, with a tanned, well-built, athletic body. Where had he met her before?

The foursome finished the game and approached Jose Maria and Mike to greet them. Mike gave an effusive hello and hugged his old friends. They promptly introduced him to the beautiful woman who had caught his eye, Maria Alicia. He suddenly remembered. She was the youngest daughter of Maria, Mike's mother's best friend. They invited Mike and Jose Maria to join them after their game for drinks by the pool.

The pool area was crowded when Mike arrived later. Both the business-men from the city and some students from the Catholic University of Santo Tomas de Villanueva had convened there. The tennis players sat at three round tables. They were drinking daiquiris and gin and tonics. There was a seat open next to Maria Alicia, and Mike took it.

"May I sit here?" he asked.

"Sure, please, sit down."

"Thanks. I know that I've met you several times before. But it's been a long time. How are you doing?"

"Great, very busy. It's my last year at Villanueva, so I've been concentrating on my studies. I haven't been coming to the club as often as before. And you? I haven't seen you lately, either."

"I've been working on my master's in economics at University of Illinois, Urbana, near Chicago. For the past few weeks, I've been at my father's farm in Camagüey. What are you studying?"

"Business, with a minor in economics," Maria Alicia answered.

Mike was surprised. "You're serious? I don't know many women who are studying business and economics. Most of the girls I know are taking interior design."

"My father wants me to help him with his business."

This was very curious indeed. "That's interesting. Do you have any brothers?"

"No, only two sisters. They didn't want to go to college. They preferred to be the perfect housewives. French, cooking classes, needlepoint, and children."

"So you're breaking the mold! You're going to be different," Mike said.

"Well, things are changing," she said with a slight shrug. "More women are getting an education and working now." She took a sip of her gin and tonic, and then turned to Mike with a smile. "So, how's your tennis game? Do you play often?"

Mike gave a self-deprecating grin. "No, I'm trying to start again. I spend most of my time working with my father at our farm. It's about five hundred kilometers away. We don't have tennis courts there," he laughed.

"Let's play one day," she suggested cheerfully, with a note in her voice that she was about to leave. "Look, it's been nice talking with you, but I have to go." She stood up and extended her hand. "Good luck." Mike watched her walk away and gulped the rest of his cocktail.

The campaign organized by his sisters was effective, and Mike became an active participant in Havana's social scene. The telephone was busy: A friend of Lourdes or Adelaida would want Mike to meet another girl. Why not go to Tarara for a Saturday swim and later a *quateque* or lunch at the Biltmore or a "small sandwich" at El Carmelo after the movies? Chaperones were always present, always discreet, trying to fulfill their duty to encourage, without quashing, the flow of feelings between young people. Every Friday night, Mike went with his group of friends to nightclubs to see shows with international stars like Maurice Chevalier, Nat King Cole, and Mario Vargas, who, along with the rumba dancers, roulette wheels, baccarat, blackjack, and craps tables, made Havana the center of the Caribbean's nightlife.

Mike was also a popular guest at the parties hosted for the younger generation. At one of the debutante parties at the country club, he met a friend from school, Laureano, who had stayed in Cuba to study and work. Laureano embraced Mike and jokingly offered to buy him a Chivas Regal and soda. They sat at a small table far away from the orchestra's blare. The friends were eager to catch up.

"I haven't seen you for a while!" Laureano began. "How do you like it up there?"

"It's great!" Mike answered. "It's been a lot of work, but a lot of fun. The weather is a pain to deal with, though. I've finished my B.A., and now I'm working on my master's. You?"

Laureano shook his head. "Phew! Like you, working all the time. I'm finishing up my law degree at the Universidad de La Habana, if and when we have classes. Meanwhile, I'm also working at my father's bank. I don't have much time for parties like this anymore."

The friends relaxed into their chairs to enjoy their cocktails, the music, and the beautiful young women who filled the club's ballroom. Laureano turned to Mike and said, "Hey! Look at Juanita. She's become a gorgeous girl! Do you remember how she looked at her debut?"

Mike turned to see the girl. "Wow! Back then she hardly fit in her dress. Is she with Marcelino?"

"Yes, he's become such a snob. Get this, he's apparently forgotten his Spanish," Laureano said. Mike rolled his eyes. Laureano continued, "And guess what? Now he has an English accent." The pair broke out in laughter. "It's so obviously fake," Laureano added. "Who does he think he's kidding? Four years in Boston, and he's more British than the Prince of Wales! Talk to him later, you'll enjoy the spectacle."

Just then a young man bumped into their table and nearly fell on top of it. As he struggled to straighten up, he kept one hand on the table to hold him steady, but continued to sway as he looked alternately at Mike and Laureano.

"Hey! Why does it look like you guys are holding hands!" he said thickly. "Hey, Mike, *cabrón*, you don't even get up to say hello to your friend? *Que te ha pasado?*" With that, he collapsed into a chair next to the two friends. Mike recognized Julian, with whom he had played baseball when he was a small child.

Laureano and Mike quickly lifted him up. They took him to the locker room, undressed him, and threw him into a shower stall. Later, with a more sober friend in tow, the three joined the other men at the bar and continued drinking, talking, and laughing at the stories of their friends' supposed sexual conquests.

Mike eyed many beautiful women that night, but his eyes locked when he saw Maria Alicia sitting at a table near the bar. She was wearing a soft white off-the-shoulder dress that showed off her glowing tanned skin.

When Mike approached, she said, "I didn't know that you were a doctor!

It was very nice of you and Laureano to treat that drunk. What a failure of a man! Why do you waste your time with people like that?"

Mike was surprised by her acerbic tone. "I didn't know you felt that way about Julian. I've known him all my life. We played together when we were kids."

"Yes, well, I was engaged to him."

The reason for her bitterness became more apparent. "I didn't know. But given his condition tonight, perhaps the breakup was for the best." The two shared a knowing look. "May I dance with you?" Mike asked as he extended his hand.

She smiled and placed her hand in his. "Sure, I'm not good at fast dances, but this is my favorite bolero."

They ended up dancing all night.

The next morning, he ran over his memories of the night before. The way he had touched her hands, the way she smiled, the way her hair softly fell over her eyes. He shook his head to remove her image from his mind. He sat at his desk and played with a pencil, doodling Rs and MAs on a yellow pad.

Finally, feeling disloyal, he made his weekly call to Rita from his desk. She asked the same tentative questions over and over again, about his health, his work, and when he would be back. He told her about what he was doing, mostly about his work with Lustre, and not about his social life. She had heard about Fernando's trouble, and thought that Don Miguel now wanted to keep Mike around for company, as well as for his private chauffeur. The weeks had passed, and their conversations became almost a rote exercise. She worried that every word that Mike had ever said to her was untrue and unfelt. Maybe he had only used her as entertainment during his lonely nights at the farm. Mike noticed a change in her voice. He wasn't sure if his absence or her decision to hide their relationship from her coworkers caused the coldness he heard.

LAUREANO CHECKED THE provisions for his night salon: glasses, J&B, Chivas Regal, Jack Daniel's, Smirnoff vodka, and Bacardi, an ice bucket full of ice, silver tongs, and white linen napkins. Once he had approved the setup, he dismissed his mother's uniformed Spanish servant, who left after opening the French doors to the small side garden.

Laureano never knew how many guests would show up. His parents let him use the left wing of their house for his weekly meetings. If Laureano enjoyed someone's company, if they participated and contributed to the discussions, he invited the guest back. If the guest had novel ideas, or argued, using violent words and occasional foul language, or drank too much whiskey, or had an overpowering personality and vehemently imposed opinions, the person was labeled a "character" and invited back. Above all, Laureano expected his Sunday night guests to express their ideas with clarity. Graham Greene, who was in Havana in search of material, was expected that night. The prior week's guest of honor had been an Italian author who bored the group with a long monologue in Italian about his past novel. The group included an economics professor, a writer for the Communist paper *HOY*, two or three "democratic candidates," and a poet from Matanzas who supplemented his income by working as a tutor for rich children. Laureano also invited a brooding follower of Jacques Maritain, and the son of a Puerto Rican patriot with the sadness of his island inscribed in his face. A medical doctor who had spent most of his professional life in exile completed the nucleus of the Sunday salon. Each week the meeting began promptly at eight, and sometimes it didn't end until the early morning hours at a Chinese restaurant in Zanja Street. The members talked, argued, and discussed the books and magazines they had read, borrowed, and loaned.

Laureano served as the moderator. The themes were varied, and he guided the flow of the discussions between the political, social, and economic themes of that week: Are we having elections? What is better, to become a revolutionary and disappear into the hills, or try to bring democracy using the popular vote in free elections? Can we have an honest election? Can we cause a change in our society? Is poetry important? Why do we use "okay" in our language? What is the true relationship between Cuba and the United States? Do we hate the Spaniards? Should we speak as a Spaniard or should we create our own language? What is the destiny of Cuba? Should we read and practice the encyclicals of the Pope? Do we believe in Pitaluga's theory that Cuba will be the center of a zone of influence in the Caribbean? Was the *Report on Cuba* by the International Bank of Reconstruction and Finance accurate? If a guest was spending too much time on a certain subject matter, he asked for a clarification, or diverted the discussion to another group member. Laureano, always with patience and care, brought new issues to be discussed.

Mike wandered onto the terrace at eight-thirty and found himself in the midst of an intense argument. The young communist newspaperman was preaching absolute nihilism. "Only the burning of all the icons of our society will make us free!" He gesticulated with his left arm, while his right hand held tight to a Baccarat tumbler full of Scotch.

Laureano acknowledged Mike's presence with a nod and pointed out an open seat. At the same time, he used Mike's arrival as an excuse to interrupt the diatribe. He introduced Mike to the group, most of whom he already knew. Yet Laureano's attempted diversion failed, and the preaching continued.

"Revolutions have never created a viable society. New symbols, new icons, and new gods will substitute for symbols that we destroy, and the new icons may be less attractive!"

The poet, who relished showing off his knowledge of the classics, reminded the group of a fable: Frogs that lived in a swamp had demanded from the gods a better king than their current one, a mere log. So the gods send them a crane. "Let's be sure that we don't have this happen to us," he warned.

Mike enjoyed the exchange. The sentiments of young people seemed different in Cuba than in the United States. Here, there was a more intense coalescing flame. Mike's friends used phrases like "we can do," "we can create," "we are the ones who *know*."

Graham Greene appeared late, escorted by two young men who were showing him Havana nightlife. No particular words of wisdom came from his mouth. After his second drink, he left with his companions. Shortly afterward, the group dispersed. Mike was ready to leave, but Laureano asked him to wait until he could count all the glasses to be sure that no one had walked out with a piece of Baccarat in his hand. Finally, when the count was completed, they left the house.

It was too late to go to the better cafés, and they didn't feel like Chinese food that night. They were hungry, so they drove in Laureano's car to El Cortijo, a dump in Old Havana that doubled as a Spanish nightclub with its Flamenco dancers, Rioja wines, Gypsy palm readers, and a marvelous potato and onion Spanish omelet. They found a table far away from the dance floor.

Laureano asked, "What did you think of the group?

"I loved the discussions. They were refreshing and interesting, and I felt that I had come back home. In the States we never have this type of meeting. But," Mike pointed out, "no one seems to agree on anything significant."

"That's why we have a great nucleus, and we need more discussions like the ones we had tonight. We have to define the problems and find political solutions. The government is holding a farcical election, so Batista and his group can end their term on a positive note. I know, from good sources, that the American ambassador wants to have an honest election and get Batista out of the country. They say that Batista wants to leave on good terms so he can keep his fortune in Cuba. He needs a new government friendly to him." Laureano shook his head at this chicanery. "I don't know why he wants to keep what he has in Cuba when with the money he has in Switzerland, he could live anywhere in zillionaire splendor, thanks to years of corruption at our expense. They say, though, he didn't like his first exile in Daytona Beach. But now he has plenty of money to live the kind of life he's used to." He sounded discouraged by the corruption and he abruptly changed the subject. "You and I have friends that believe in and support Fidel Castro's group. Do you remember Cayo Confites?"

"What a disaster," Mike answered. "Castro even took the cooks who worked at his Belen. Fidel is crazy. Although the left-wingers love him in the States."

Laureano agreed. "We've had too many *caudillos*—Menocal, Machado, Batista, and now the possibility of Castro. Please. If he ends up in control, forget democracy. It won't survive. I feel like the priest telling the altar boy: 'Put out all the candles and let's get out of here!'" He frowned, thinking of the prospect of another dictator. "We don't have much time. We need change, and we have to achieve it soon. Our group and those who think like us can't blow it! We may not have another chance. What do you think?"

Mike was hesitant. He trusted Laureano, but he had not seen him for a while. Nevertheless, he did not think that he was an *agent provocateur*. Laureano did not need the money, and his family, like most of the good families in Havana, was related by blood or marriage to Mike's family.

Still feeling ambivalent, he answered, "Maybe we have to take an active role in the political process. Our families never believed in it. Our class thinks that they can solve all problems with money and bribes and that we shouldn't worry about the problems of other people or the country. We know that most of the politicians, labor leaders, army officers, and tax collectors are for sale, and we buy them. It's how we do things. Let's be honest, we're selfish." He stopped to catch his breath, and then introduced an idea he'd also thought about for a long time. "We always look to the States for answers. Back in the thirties, you know, we had our own ideas and desired to be different. We wanted to live according to our own customs. Now we just try to follow the Americans. The *Americanos* do this and the *Americanos* do that. The *Americanos* like to gamble, so we give them gambling casinos. The Americans like to see *Superman,* and we show him naked, all doped up, with an extremely large penis, and we give the tourists this sexual freak show."

"What do you think we should do?" Laureano asked.

"We have to have our own ideas. Create our own way of thinking. Adapt the best of those cultures that we're familiar with. France, Spain, and the US are different, but we can use what they've learned, take the best, and make it ours."

Mike was surprised after he finished. He meant what he had said, but he had never expressed his thoughts so concisely.

Mike and Laureano talked into the early morning until the manager asked them to leave. The effects of their earlier drinking were gone. Now they were revved by their enthusiasm. They drove on the Malecon toward Laureano's house. The streetlights still glowed, and the dawn had started to cast its rose colors. Mike thanked Laureano and went back to his house.

A few weeks later, one Wednesday afternoon, Laureano picked Mike up at his office, and they drove off in Laureano's sports car. They drove for twenty minutes, seemingly arbitrarily changing lanes and directions. Mike did not ask why, and after a few minutes, he didn't have to. They arrived at a garage in El Cerro close to the baseball stadium. Laureano parked his car and motioned for Mike to follow him. They walked several blocks and knocked on the door of a medium-size house. Elvira, a close friend of Laureano's, opened the door. She escorted them to a small room with drawn window shades. Laureano knew three of the four men, Candido, Manolete, and Eloy. Mike had met Eloy and Candido years earlier. Manolete, whom he had never met, was from Cienfuegos and active in the Catholic student movement. Neither Mike nor Laureano had ever seen the fourth man.

The smoke from their cigarettes created a dense haze in the room. Manolete thanked Laureano for coming and asked who Mike was. Laureano explained that Mike had just returned from the United States and shared their ideas and was willing to work for the cause. Eloy vouched for Mike's integrity.

The fourth man spoke without a preamble. "I just arrived from the Escambray Mountains. We've started a Third Front. We have the support of the *guajiros*. The people in Trinidad are helping us with money and supplies. Manolete and Eloy are willing to help us at the university and tell the students and professors that we're opposed to Batista. We need to contact the foreign press and let them know that we're fighting against Batista, that Castro is not the only one who is in the hills. We want a democratic form of government, and to be ruled only by *La Constitucion del 40*. We welcome everyone who's willing to fight."

Manolete took over, speaking to Laureano. "You can help. You have contact with money. There are sugar mills in our area of operation. If the administrations of the mills help us, we can use their resources to move equipment and people. Their company stores will 'sell' goods to our people, who'll deliver them to our places in the hills. We need good boots. We can always use canned food. You have to explain our views to your group. You have writers, newspapermen, and professors. They can always write and speak. How do you feel about all of this?"

Laureano hesitated. "Yes, another front is needed. I need to think about how I can help."

They continued to smoke. The coffee cups were emptied, and the ashtrays overflowed with filter tips and half-smoked cigarettes. Two empty soda bottles stood against the wall.

Laureano added, "I don't believe in violence. I share your displeasure with Batista. But before I agree to work with you, I need to know more about who you are, where you're going. I need to know more from you than how you feel about Batista."

Each one explained his position at length. When it was time to leave, Manolete left with the *guajiro*. He had to deliver him to a safe house. Mike and Laureano waited another fifteen minutes to avoid suspicion by neighbors that a small group had gathered at the house.

By that time, Mike had missed dinner with his father. Don Miguel was watching television in the library when Mike passed. While he kept his eyes fixed on the late night news, he called out, "Be careful, Son. Long meetings never bring results."

The next morning, Mike phoned Rita. "When are you coming back, my *bébé*? It's been too long. Don't you miss me?" she whispered.

Mike felt at once flattered and annoyed. "Yes, I do. You're always on my mind. But I don't know when I'll return. Father is working me very hard. I have a lot of work at the office. I miss you very much." Even to him the statements seemed perfunctory, not filled with any enthusiasm at all.

After he had finished his unsatisfactory conversation with Rita, he had a vivid image of the last time he had danced with Maria Alicia, the warmth of her body and the cautious smile on her face. He was about to call her, but the phone rang before he dialed. It was his sister, Adelaida.

"*Hermanito*, what are you doing? I want to invite you to have lunch with us at the Habana Yacht Club. If you have plans, break them."

"No, I was going to stay home and organize my room."

"Forget it. You can do it later. Meet us at Santa Rita for the noon Mass. I'm taking the children. You have to set an example for them, so be early to Mass."

As it turned out, he arrived late for noon Mass at the Church of Santa Rita, so he quietly stepped to the rear of the church where he joined other men. Father Spirali was in the middle of his usual injunction, "No coins in this collection plate." Adelaida sat in a middle pew with her children, while Jose Maria stood in the back with the other husbands. Craning her neck, Adelaida glanced back to see if Mike had arrived, and seeing him, pointed to Maria Alicia, who was next to her. Mike smiled, pleased at this surprise, and nodded.

At the end of Mass, the main entrance of the church became the site of a social gathering. Everyone had to say hello, kiss, and update each other. Chauffeur-driven cars waited, double-parked, on a side street. Husbands left to fetch cars, and women compared dresses to determine whose dressmaker had copied which French designer. Among the crowd was Father Spirali, his white Augustinian habit draped loosely over his short, heavy body. A perennial smile was pasted on his face and a cigar hung on his lips as he worked the people like a political boss.

Mike waited for Adelaida, who emerged from the throng with Maria Alicia in tow. "Look who I found! I invited her to have lunch with us. That way you and Jose Maria can talk business, and Maria Alicia and I can gossip."

Maria Alicia stood behind Adelaida with eyes downcast and a slight smile on her face. Mike escorted them and the children to his sister's car. She then asked Mike to drive the children to the club, since her car was not big enough for six.

Jose Miguel and Lalin were delighted to ride in Mike's new car. "Pass them, pass them! Your car is faster than Papa's. Boy, I like the red and black seats. Let's see what's playing on the radio." Jose Miguel spun the controls of the radio frantically from station to station. When they arrived, the parking lot at the yacht club was full. Mike gave his car to an attendant, who tore off in a trail of smoke, leaving Mike with an image of his new car mangled in a heap.

Jose Maria, Adelaida, and Maria Alicia waited at the door, and together with the spirited children, they entered the dining room. Jose Maria held his son's hand to keep him under control, and Lalin, who had, in the short trip from Santa Rita, developed a strong affinity for Mike, clutched his left hand. Mike was conscious of the interest stirred among the society matrons by the sight of him pulling out Maria Alicia's chair. That night, gossip would spread about the "new couple." Would Mike be Maria Alicia's new beau? Why had she broken her prior engagement?

Maria Alicia was shy at the start, but by the end of the luncheon, she was the center of attention, whispering saucy tidbits of gossip while the others leaned in, laughing. Adelaida looked at Mike and Maria Alicia, and congratulated herself for making such a good match for her brother. When lunch was over, Mike could scarcely believe it was past three o'clock. Lalin and Jose Miguel were tired from having spent all their energy behaving well, and began to tease each other.

Mike noticed that Jose Maria was eager to leave, so motioned to the waiter for the check. But Jose Maria said, "This is my party. We're happy that you could make it. Adelaida, it's time to go."

Adelaida looked annoyed. "Jose Maria, I can't leave Maria Alicia with Mike. What will her mother think of us? You take the children and Mike will drop me off later."

The dining room was now full of busboys and waiters clearing tables, and the threesome moved outside to a table next to the pool. Adelaida took it upon herself to tell stories about Mike's childhood. Maria Alicia laughed as Mike squirmed, red-faced. After a few failed attempts, Mike finally managed to redirect the topic. He asked Maria Alicia about herself. He wanted to know about her likes and dislikes. Purposefully, Adelaida excused herself to greet a friend who had arrived with her children.

Maria Alicia spoke to Mike in a soft, low voice. "Yes, I like music. Mother wants me to go to Pro Arte Musical, but I like to hear the older *sones*. They're so romantic, don't you think? Do you think that the old *criollos* were different than we are, or do you think they were just more poetic in expressing their feelings? It seems that a man could not court a woman if he weren't a poet or a songwriter."

"I think those were more romantic times. But popular music today is more vibrant, happy, and salacious," Mike said, thinking of all the night-clubs he had frequented lately. "We don't have the great romantic song-writers, but we've seen an evolution in music, which is exciting. Now we have cha-chas and the mambo."

Maria Alicia nodded. "I think Lecuona was able to capture the essence of our music. Do you consider him a classic, or do you prefer the more modern Latin feeling of Villa-lobos?"

"I like Lecuona, and I like Bach. I also enjoy jazz."

Maria Alicia smiled. "You have such broad interests." She suddenly laughed. "Aren't you glad Adelaida told so many funny stories about you? Sometimes sisters can be so annoying. Mine try to control everything I do."

"Well, sometimes," Mike allowed. "But I love Adelaida. Since Mother died, she has filled in beautifully as the family matriarch."

She smiled, liking that answer. "Do you like ballet? Have you seen Alicia Alonso in *Giselle*?"

"She's our national treasure! Yes, I've seen her several times."

"My mother wanted me to be a ballerina," she told him. "I actually took lessons with Alicia years ago, but we didn't get along. I was too willful, too tall, and maybe a little too heavy." Her face twisted downward, remembering another part of that experience. "I was also embarrassed when I went to the classes. Most of the girls took the *guagua*. I arrived in a car driven by my father's chauffeur, who waited until the lesson was finished. I wasn't very talented, either. So I quit, but I do enjoy dancing."

It was getting late, and Adelaida had to return to take care of the children. She continued to watch her brother and Maria Alicia from afar, however, and thought of her mother as she watched the pair laughing and telling stories. She thought how laughter often dissipates with age and added responsibility. Her children laughed all the time. She had laughed when she was a child, and she had once found Jose Maria very funny. At one time, they danced and laughed all night, and shared intensely romantic moments. But now what had happened to them? He thought only of his work, of how to place and sell another piece of machinery to another sugar mill, she of what dress to wear, what party to attend, if she would have a *merienda* or a tea. But laughter, laughter was gone.

She got up and approached Mike's table. "Okay, it's time to go home. It's almost five o'clock. Mike, please order the car so we can take Maria Alicia home. Jose Maria will be ready to explode, if he hasn't already done so. He's alone with the children and the help is off today."

Maria Alicia watched Mike exit the pool area. Her relationship with Julian had left her wary of men. At least Mike was serious about his studies, but she was not sure if she could imagine spending the rest of her life in either the confines of a university in the frigid north married to a professor or a farm located in a sparsely-populated countryside with no one to talk to outside of the help. She also had her own ideas about working for her father.

Then she caught herself up short. After all, it was just lunch. She had to admire Adelaida's adroitness in arranging the date. Mike did not seem too serious or too pious, and he certainly was better than Julian. At least he could control his drinking.

14

The Tractor

PAULINO HAD HUGE amounts of free time, which he filled with thoughts of his beloved Elena. With Don Miguel and Mike gone, there was little work to do around the house, so he had time to concentrate on his writing. He wanted to write poetry to read to his beloved, but was afraid that she might think he wasn't macho. He was trying to understand her. He had never dated a woman who ran her own business. So he concentrated on reading the classics borrowed from Mike's room, and continued to write short stories under his nom de plume. He still had contact with a group of young writers in Havana. It was difficult to know what they were thinking, because in their letters to him, they never talked about what was happening at the university, or what they thought about the present political situation, which Paulino thought was getting worse. The absence of Mike and Don Miguel was fortuitous in another way. His nightly forays to Elena's house were taking a toll on his body. His siesta, combined with his new interest in reading and writing, barely left time for him to help Cuca set the table in the employees' dining room.

One Wednesday morning, an excited Nandito drove his worn-out truck to the *batey*. His spirits were sky high. That weekend his baseball team was scheduled to play against a team from the Central Florida sugar mill, twenty minutes beyond San Joaquin. His friends from the *pueblo* would come and see him pitch. Unaware of this development, Paulino strolled up to Nandito's truck to chat. But Nandito was only interested in talking about the upcoming game. Paulino quickly grew bored and put an end to the discussion. He left to work on a business plan for the next game. This time he would sell drinks and hamburgers. But he knew he could not sell, cook, and serve all by himself; he needed an employee. Chirra had drunk more than he sold. Fernando was honest and sober, but he was an unlikely candidate for the job since he already had a profitable businesses driving a taxi and pandering *putas* for the Joaquineros. Anyway, Fernando was playing that week. He considered his other options. Ernesto was Nandito's catcher. Manuel was too stuck up. Arturo only knew how to milk cows. So who? He thought. What about a girl? A girl could help! She had to be attractive, smile once in a while, and smart enough to give the correct change—or err in favor of the house.

By happenstance, Paulino caught sight of Chirra leading a show mare to the wash rack. "Hey, Chirra, I need to talk to you! I have an idea."

Chirra glared at him, but Paulino shouted, undeterred, "Man, I'm telling you, I have a proposition, one that could improve the finances of your family. Obviously, that's not something you're interested in!"

Chirra, who was proud but not foolish, replied, "Well, I know you're trying to ask me to forgive you for what you did to me. You know that I worked very hard. So what if I tasted a few beers as part of the job! Since you're now sorry, I could give you my undivided attention."

Just then the mare shook herself dry, splashing Paulino with sudsy, cold water. Paulino hated horses, but he brushed soapsuds off his clothes and told Chirra, "We have to talk business. You know that the team is going to play the Central Florida team next Sunday. I need an attractive person to help me. I was considering—"

Chirra interrupted. "You mean you want to use my service? Well, I don't know. I'll have to see if I have a previous engagement."

"No, no, no, Chirra," Paulino said. "I need to get in touch with your daughter to see if she wants to work for me."

Chirra replied by turning his back to Paulino, letting the hose slip, and drenching him with cold water.

That afternoon, just after four, Ricardo popped up on the porch, lighting a cigar with his Zippo lighter. He was planning to call Mike to report on Manolo, the *mayoral*, who was disregarding Mike's orders. Paulino caught him and asked, "Ricardo, where are you going? You're all dressed up. Are you partying tonight?"

Ricardo replied curtly, "I have to make a telephone call, but I'm waiting for Manuel to give me a list of animals for the next show."

"Can I ride with you to the *pueblo*?" Paulino asked. "I have to stop at the warehouse, and I need to mail some letters to friends in Havana. Give me five minutes. Wait for me."

During the trip, Paulino yammered as Ricardo looked blankly ahead. He was pensive and gave scant thought to Paulino's incessant questions. "I need to get transportation. I am tired of walking so much. I am not the *Andarin Carvajal*. What do you recommend—a used car? Where should I go to get one? Do you think I have to go to Camagüey to get the best deal? Do you think that the boss will sell me the jeep? I can pay for it in installments. Where can I learn to drive? Is it difficult? Can you help me?"

Ricardo limited his answers to nods, grunts, and coughs. Finally, fed up with Paulino's bombardment, Ricardo snapped, "Learn to ride a horse. They're available, they only eat grass, and you don't have to change the oil or fix them."

Paulino was silent for the rest of the trip.

At the *almacen*, Paulino looked for Mulato. "Hey, we need to do serious business."

Mulato walked slowly toward him and extended his hand. "Well, what do you want today? Do you want to buy out the store?"

"Here," and he gave Mulato a roll of cash. "I'm paying you what I owe. I need a receipt, and mark it paid. I don't want you to bill Don Miguel or the farm again for my provisions." Mulato counted the money as Paulino continued, "Now, I need to place an order. This time charge it to my account."

In the meantime, Ricardo went to the telephone exchange. Rita was at her station when Ricardo asked her to call Don Miguel's office in Havana. In a few seconds, Mike came on the line. Ricardo was brief and spoke quietly. He did not like to rat out a coworker, he felt it unmanly, but his loyalties were with the family, not with Manolo.

Mike understood his reluctance. "Ricardo, I'll talk to Father. I should come back. I've got work to do here, but it can wait. I'll send you a telegram telling you when I'm coming."

Rita took a moment to slip out of her post to talk to Ricardo. She looked at him with inquisitive eyes. "What's going on?"

He simply said, "He's coming," and quickly left.

He would have liked to visit his favorite bar, but instead, he just picked up Paulino and his batch of provisions, and then went to the post office.

During the ride back, they casually glanced at the passing scenery, varying shades of green in the sugarcane fields, small *bohíos* hugging the road, white egrets feeding amongst the cow, and the placid Camagüey savanna. Paulino was silent, thinking of his next move.

The next morning, Paulino went to the machinery shed. In a corner was a forgotten old Farmall H tractor covered with dust, its brilliant fire red color muted by the tropical sun, the dusty seat raised in the up position. He studied it from the side. He moved slowly around it, as if studying a foe. He touched the gear lever, looked at the clutch pedal and the two brake pedals, one for each wheel. There was no key. He found the starter; it was in the center near the transmission box. The choke was a black pull, the accelerator a simple lever on the left. He tentatively raised his right foot and climbed in front of the raised seat and tipped it down.

He let his mind wander. He was driving a new Cadillac. It was red, the seats made of soft red leather. The radio was on. It drowned the sounds of the road with bolero, the sexy voice of the female singer urging her lover to come closer.

> *Ven, ven aquí, sé mío.*
> Come, come here, and be mine.
> *No tenemos tanto tiempo.*
> We do not have much time.
> *Sólo quiero besar tu boca,*
> I just want to kiss your mouth.
> *Sentir tu abrazo.*
> Feel your arms around me.
> *Una vez más.*
> One more time.

He saw Elena standing next to him, looking like a celestial apparition wearing a flowing, delicate white dress. He leaned over and extended his hand to touch her—a sudden, sharp bark jolted him back. The dog Mitzi had followed him into the shed. Reminded of why he had come, he sat erect on the seat and pressed the starter. The engine fired at the third try. Now what? He moved the accelerator lever. The engine increased its revolutions. He felt for the pedals and pushed two down, one with each foot. He put his right hand on the transmission stick and moved it.

Suddenly, the tractor backed out of the shed faster than he expected. Mitzi ran, barking after Paulino as he held the steering wheel with both hands, twisting his body around in the seat, praying out loud as the tractor raced toward the milking shed. Fernando saw the racing tractor and Paulino bobbing on its seat, floundering for a way to stop it.

"Cut it back, cut it back! You're going to hit the shed!" Fernando shouted as he ran to help Paulino.

"How, how?"

"The accelerator, you idiot, move it toward you!"

Paulino was afraid to take a hand off the wheel, but the milking shed was getting closer, and with a trembling left hand, he yanked the lever toward him. The tractor shuddered and almost stopped. Fernando ran up to the tractor, leaped onto its seat, and turned the wheel just before it hit the shed.

Manuel and Chirra came running from the barn to see what had happened. Fernando shut the tractor off and began to laugh uncontrollably. Chirra joined in. Manuel, shaking with anger, snapped, "Paulino, what the hell are you doing on my tractor? Get down! You could have caused serious damage."

Paulino, still trembling, meekly obeyed. Chirra climbed into the driver's seat and with extreme care, guided the tractor back into the machinery shed.

Manuel looked at Paulino, Fernando, and the tractor. He knew he should report it to Mike, but it would be tricky, since Paulino was Don Miguel's favorite. The tractor had not been damaged. Paulino was visibly shaken, and Fernando was not going to go to Havana, especially after his last trip. So, who was left, Chirra?

Fernando was still trying to catch his breath after laughing so hard. "I tell you what," he said, "you have to be in love to be doing something so idiotic. What were you thinking? Replace Ricardo on the tractors? Or do you want to cut the pastures like Nandito or Martinito?"

Paulino just shook his head and walked back to the house. Fernando followed him. "Look, Paulino, if you want to learn to drive, talk to me. I can help you."

Paulino was too humiliated to respond.

That night at the employees' table they joked about the tractor ride, even as Paulino passed plates overflowing with rice, beans, and beef. Ricardo laughingly called him the new *Fangio*. Only Manuel, who sat at the head of the table, did not join the ribbing. When Paulino spilled the coffee he had just brewed, Manuel asked Paulino why he was in such a hurry. He muttered, "I want to see Elena."

"Don't worry. I can drive the jeep. We'll go together."

MANUEL'S CAREFULLY COMBED hair reeked of lilac tonic, and he had shaving nicks on his face. He wore a white western shirt, stiff with starch, and highly polished black western dress boots. Paulino sat next to him in the red jeep, clad in a long-sleeved pale blue shirt that hung loosely from his shoulders and his old tennis shoes. The grass in the pastures shone in the light of a descending sun, the cattle had formed into small groups, and the land exuded the laziness of late afternoon with its muted colors, soft tones, and birds flying back to their roost.

Paulino kept up a brisk monologue as they drove down the Central Highway toward the Gomez sisters' plantation.

A bed of well-kept elephant ears flanked by a pair of large *tinajones* with green *malangas* overflowing from their wide mouths greeted them at the gate. Well-kept potted geraniums surrounded the porch. The flower-beds proudly displayed roses and camellias. Lime, grapefruit, and papaya trees grew against the side of the house. A mutt barked as Manuel pulled the jeep to the edge of the driveway. Julieta heard the commotion and opened the door. When she saw Manuel and Paulino, she hurriedly called Elena and Cristina.

Paulino was the first to get out of the car. "Oh, hello, ladies, Manuel wanted to drive me here. Hope you don't mind."

"Of course not. Welcome. Come in!" Julieta answered. The sitting room furniture was rich and simple, mahogany with yellow cane backs. Elena excused herself to brew coffee. On the walls hung colored photographs of the sisters' parents. In one corner of the room was a small altar with a statue of the Virgin of El Cobre. Manuel held his Stetson in his hand, which he nervously spun. Cristina ushered them in and showed Manuel and Paulino to their seats as the four waited for Elena. Julieta, having observed Paulino smirking at Manuel's discomfort, turned to Manuel and asked him about his job. He looked around and shifted his position on the love seat until his shoulders were square, like a military cadet at mess hall.

"I'm in charge of all the purebred operations at the farm. I select the show animals, and I decide which bulls we breed to which cows. I price calves and heifers for the exportation market. I break colts and train them for the show string . . ."

As Manuel recited a litany of duties and responsibilities, Paulino became increasingly astonished. Did Don Miguel and Manolo not exist in this version? As he talked, Manuel relaxed his shoulders and crossed his legs, holding a boot with his hand. As he elaborated further, he began to vary his previous monotone. He made eye contact with Julieta, who encouraged him with a smile.

Paulino stood up when Elena entered the room with demitasse cups of coffee and a small porcelain sugar bowl on a tray. Manuel tried to stand, but fumbled and lost his balance. He bumped into a table covered with porcelain figurines, sending two of the pieces crashing to the floor. Paulino and Elena struggled to control their laughter. Cristina knelt to pick up the pieces of the broken figurines as Julieta helped Manuel straighten up. Julieta then turned to Paulino and gave him a deadly look.

"I'm . . . I'm sorry. I'll replace them . . ." Manuel stammered.

"Don't worry. They're just small figurines. This house is full of them. Don't worry," Julieta assured him in a convincingly unconcerned manner. Then she cast another surreptitious glare in Paulino's direction.

As time passed, Paulino grew quieter and Manuel bolder. His accounts of his importance to the farm grew grander. He could see that the sisters enjoyed his stories. Paulino finally swallowed what was left of his coffee and summoned up his energy. He interrupted Manuel and described his friend in elaborate terms, as a modern knight undaunted by harrowing tasks like pacifying even the most vicious, recalcitrant bull. Manuel knew Paulino had to be up to something. Manuel became quiet and nervous, starting to spin his hat again.

Having achieved his objective, Paulino began to talk about his business plans for the next baseball game. The sisters promised to attend and were excited about another outing. Julieta asked Manuel if he planned to go. Manuel coughed and said he wasn't sure. "I have so much work to do. I'm always needed at the *batey.*"

Paulino shot a threatening look at Manuel.

Julieta pleaded in a sweet tone, "Don Manuel, I know you're a very busy man, but you have to take some time off. I know if you wanted to be at the game, you could. Would you try this time?"

Manuel could not turn down an invitation like this. He bowed his head. "Your wish is my command. I'll go to the game."

Paulino tried to steer Elena onto the porch to sneak a kiss and an embrace, but she knew what he wanted and resisted being alone with him. At the end of the visit, everyone shook hands at the door, promising future visits. Paulino tried to kiss Elena on her cheek, but she turned her face sharply.

On the trip back, Paulino turned to Manuel and said, "What kind of a friend are you? You made me feel like a no one in there, while you portrayed yourself as the farm's big honcho. I don't even know if *El Viejo* exists in that story you spun. You were something else."

Manuel muttered, "I don't think I told a lie."

"I tell you, you made me feel like a nobody. It was just I, I, and I—I wish Mike or *El Viejo* could have heard you."

"You shouldn't have laughed at me," Manuel said.

"Well, you fell on the floor holding your boot. It was funny, you idiot!"

"I'm clumsy. I'm afraid I made a fool of myself in front of Julieta. She's so pretty."

"She's a very attractive girl," Paulino allowed. "She got pissed at me because I laughed at you. I've never seen a look like the one she gave me tonight. Phew!"

"Don't worry. The ladies are very nice. I know that Elena likes you very much."

Manuel's attempt to placate him did not hit the mark. "Unfortunately, I spent most of my night watching you make a fool of yourself and not much time with her."

"You will," Manuel assured him.

Paulino nodded. "Yes, and you know why? I don't make a fool of myself."

15

Back to the Farm

MIKE OPENED THE door to the library and found his father sitting in his leather chair, reading the *Prensa Libre*, his favorite tabloid.

"Father, I have to talk to you."

"How was your day at the office? What did Lustre think about our meeting?"

"He was happy that we had it, because his job will be easier. But I came in to talk to you about another matter. Ricardo called. He told me that Manolo hasn't followed my orders. I left a memo to all the employees, so there would be no confusion or misunderstanding. For instance, Manolo pulled Ricardo out of the *Ceiba* pasture and told him not to buy the Guinea grass seed you told him to order."

Don Miguel was very displeased about this news. "What do you want to do?"

"I want to go back and check on what's happening there."

"Do you think that Ricardo told you the truth?"

Mike didn't hesitate. "Yes, I believe him."

"Do you think he has an ulterior motive?"

Mike paused. He had grown up with Ricardo, and he knew his short-comings. He seemed more like a distant uncle or cousin, though, and if he couldn't believe in him, whom could he trust?

"No, I believe Ricardo. Manolo is out of line. If we give an order, it has to be followed."

"So, are you ready to go back and tell Manolo he has to follow your orders?"

"Yes."

"Well, before you go I need to know your long-range plans."

"What plans? I like working with you, but I still have do go back and complete all my work on my degree."

"I need to know if you're going to stay." Don Miguel shifted forward in his chair. "I want to tell you something. I didn't want to bring you back here. I don't want you to work at the farm unless you love it. I won't allow it. The truth is Lustre was nervous about my health and my behavior. He'd never seen me as I was, and frankly, he panicked. He thought that I'd withdrawn so much since the death of your mother that my mental well-being and the farm's future were at risk."

"Yes, Father, I know how much Mother . . . how much she meant to you," Mike gently replied.

His father nodded. "Of course, I'm fine now and the farm will survive, but the truth is life in Havana became empty for me. Life is easier on the farm. I don't have to laugh if I don't feel like it, or dress up, or even shave. Your sisters were worried, too. They wanted me to go out in society after the first anniversary of your mother's death. They tried hard, but I just couldn't do it. I didn't want to. Of course, all of you adored her. But your sisters, well, they have their families. You went to the US to study, which was the right thing to do. I was left alone."

Mike had never heard his father speak so frankly. He moved restlessly in his chair, and after a few silent moments, his father asked, "Were you as angry as I was? Did you look at God and ask him, '*Why her?*' Why someone so good? Then I thought, perhaps, that was the reason. Maybe she was just too good for this world. The Church tried to help me. I prayed, but I remained angry. Lustre worried that I was becoming mean and absent-minded, that I had abandoned my friends and family. He was scared and brought you back on his own."

"Why?" Mike asked. "Did you need me? Do you need me now?"

Don Miguel answered nervously, "Yes, maybe."

"You've always told me how important a good education is."

"Yes, it's true, especially these days! I don't want to interrupt your studies. In my time, things were different. Your grandfather trained me his way. I didn't go to college. I worked at his bank. Maybe I wanted to do the same with you. I was jealous of the American professors who teach you. I felt that you went away, hiding from us, abandoning your family, your country, to learn another culture, another way of life."

"That's *not* true! I've missed you, my family, and my country. But I wanted this education and I couldn't get it here."

"I worried that you would pick up values that are different from ours. I worried that you would return as a stranger to your homeland."

Mike felt a deep sadness sweep over him. He wondered if he had changed. If so, how much? Was change so wrong?

"I see things from a new perspective, but I'm the same," Mike said hesitantly.

"Well, maybe you want to teach at your university, or get a job in a business firm on Wall Street, and not return. Learning business and economics is not the same as running your own business. You need experience. I will always help you if you stay. Running a business takes time, and you make mistakes, and you need ability and luck to survive them. I will allow you to make the small mistakes. That's how you learn. That's how your grandfather trained me."

"Thanks, I know you want the best for me. I love working at the farm. I just don't know if I'm ready now, or if I start, if I can do it forever."

"Farm life isn't easy. The nightlights of Havana don't shine in the middle of a pasture."

"I can handle that."

"I don't want you to be a *Floridita* rancher, dress like a rich Texano, and go to the bar and talk about how many head you sold last week. I've worked very hard for what we have."

"I know that very well, Father."

"If you aren't ready to spend the time and make the sacrifices it takes to run the farm, then go back to the States. I'll go back and fix the problem with Manolo. Then we, with your sisters, will decide what to do with the farm."

"But, Father—"

"I know I'm getting older, but I'm not retiring. I'm too young for that. I see friends who've retired, who play dominoes and keep young girls. They think they're loved! I don't want that life. I never have."

"Father, you are not that old!"

"Bah, that's your opinion. Look, Son, you have to decide which life is best for you. It's your decision." He walked to the bar and mixed himself another drink.

"I do like Havana, but the farm is more important to me," Mike said. "I've had enough formal education to run the farm. I can do it, and do it well. But I need the authority to change things. I'll consult with you, consider your advice, but I must have the final say. It's the only way."

His father nodded, very pleased with his son's decision. "I know we'll work together well. Now, how are you going to handle Manolo?"

They talked for hours. They became exhausted but too excited to sleep. Just before sunrise, father and son shook hands, embraced, and retired into their rooms.

That morning, Mike called Maria Alicia and arranged to meet her at eight that night at her home. They went to the softly lit patio and sat close together, surrounded by the delicate rustling of trees in a gentle breeze. Maria Alicia quietly nodded as Mike revealed his new life plans. She listened patiently and, at times, held his hand. Mike was relieved to have made up his mind. At eleven o'clock, they heard Maria Alicia's mother calling for her. She kept quiet, held onto Mike's hand, and leaned forward. Her hair brushed his face, his lips touched her cheeks, her mouth found his. The tropical night engulfed them.

BEFORE MIKE LEFT for the farm, Estrella handed him a box filled with sandwiches.

"Don't stop at any of those roadside stands," she urged. "I've packed good food for you."

Mike patiently placed the box on the backseat, next to his new *guayaberas*. As he pulled out of the driveway, he recalled when, as a child, they left Havana to visit the farm. Their old chauffeur drove below the speed limit and often made stops so that his sisters could relieve themselves, making believe that they were searching for wildflowers, as their mother nervously watched the road for upcoming vehicles.

Gigantic trees lined the long, monotonous road, forming an arch that often looked to Mike like the nave of a leafy church. He loved the silence and ease of the road trip, and before reaching Matanzas, he drove past a hill shaped like a sleeping woman, a Taino girl waiting for her lover to come and wake her. The land was rich with sugarcane plants on both sides of the road. Two hours later, the plains started and the vegetation was poorer. Sugarcane fields changed into pastures, and then he drove through another set of hills until he reached Santi Spiritus. His goal was to drive to the farm without stopping. He didn't mind making the six-hour trip during the heat of the day if that meant he could arrive at the farm just before sundown. On long stretches of road, he could drive more than eighty-five kilometers per hour, sometimes a little faster. After Ciego de Ávila, it was a straight road to the entrance to the farm. The drive was so boring as to be dangerous.

He slowed down when he turned onto the dirt road to the *batey*. He had made the trip more times than he could remember, but now it was different. The farm was his future as the new steward, the torchbearer for his family's way of life. As Mike pulled up at the entrance to the house, Mitzi, who was napping under the jeep, came out barking. Mike stepped out of the car, and she sidled close to his legs, waiting to be petted. Paulino appeared in the driveway with a bewildered expression on his face.

"Hey, man, you didn't send a telegram. We didn't know you were coming!" Then his face changed. "Man, that is a nice car!"

The screen door on the porch slammed shut. Mike looked up and saw Cuca standing there, squinting past the light of the setting sun.

"Hi! How's Don Miguel?" she asked.

"He's feeling better. Thanks for asking." Mike went inside, carrying his suitcase and new *guayaberas* as Mitzi trailed him.

"Well, *Doctor*, what would you like for dinner?" Paulino joked.

"Just corn flakes and a banana. Please tell Ricardo that I have to talk to him."

Mike took a shower to wash off the road dust and went to the kitchen, where Ricardo was talking to Cuca. "Come with me," Mike said.

Mike and Ricardo talked for a long time in Don Miguel's office. Paulino found an unusual amount of work to do right outside the room. He cleaned trophies, dusted the piano, reorganized, straightened, swept, and mopped. Yet every time Paulino drew close enough to hear, Mike and Ricardo halted the conversation. Finally, tired and frustrated, he left. Mike and Ricardo continued the meeting past ten o'clock.

Mike woke up early, had his coffee, and then sent Monito to fetch his father.

Manolo showed up at the *batey* at nine o'clock. By that point Mike and Manuel were deciding which calves to take to the Santi Spiritus cattle show. Manolo arrived on his horse and tied it at the corral. He wore a clean *guayabera*, and his neatly-laced boots were covered with dried mud.

"Good morning, Mike. My son told me that you had to see me."

"Yes, thanks for coming. Let me finish with Manuel and we'll take a ride to check out the pastures."

They drove in the jeep and stopped at the first gate of the alley. A windmill rhythmically moved its pump; the water flowed into the holding tank in spurts. Mike took a long look at Manolo, who bit harder on his cigar. A bull watched the car and seemed to stare at them before moving on. Finally, Manolo got out of the jeep and opened the gate, and as Manolo closed the gate after them, Mike said, "Manolo, I want us to understand each other well. Father told Ricardo to buy Guinea seeds to plant in the *Ceiba* pasture. You told Ricardo that they weren't needed, and didn't allow the purchase." He went on, listing another strike against him. "I gave written instructions of what pastures needed to be cleared. You changed the order." Mike paused a beat to emphasize that this couldn't be tolerated. "You may have a better idea, and may know how do to something better, but you have to talk to me before you change an order I give to you or to the employees."

Manolo continued munching on his unlit cigar.

"I'm the one who's responsible for the operations of the farm. I'm in charge now. You need to talk to me."

Manolo looked at Mike with a mixture of pity and disdain. "Your father has always left me alone to do what I thought was best. The farm has operated well for many years. He was happy with my work."

"Well, that's my father. I'm who I am. I don't want to have a misunderstanding with you. I respect you. You need to tell me if you have a problem with what I've said. I'll hear you out. With the information you give me, and with what I find out, I'll make the decision. We should work well together." They continued the drive around the pastures, not talking to each other.

The next morning Manolo arrived at the *batey* at six o'clock. Mike was talking to Arturo at the milking shed. He approached them and nodded slightly at his boss. "Mike, we need to talk," he said. They left for the office. He sat across Mike's desk and took off his hat, revealing a bronze forehead, a milky white scalp, and thin hair. He took the cigar he was smoking out of his mouth and looked Mike in the eye. "Mike, I've worked for your father for many years. He respects my judgment. You don't. I can't work with you. We think too differently."

"It's true that you and I differ. I also disagree with my father in some areas," Mike responded.

"It seems to me that you find my methods outdated. I don't like tractors, herbicides, or fertilizers. I know how to take care of the cattle and how to make people work. I'm not going to change the way I do things, because what I do works. I don't like the changes you plan to make. I'm going to present my resignation to your father."

"I'm sorry to hear this. Is that really the way you feel? I thought we could work together."

"No, I don't think so. I'm going to move to my small farm near Trinidad. I believe that Monito will stay for a time."

Seeing that his foreman had made up his mind, Mike rose to his feet and shook Manolo's hand. "Thanks for your time. I'll talk to my father. When are you leaving?"

"Soon."

"We're going to miss you and all the great work you've done for us."

In truth, though, Mike was relieved. Manolo had been a good *mayoral*, but it was easier for Mike to take the helm without him. Mike walked to the show barn and ran into Chirra, who was cleaning a horse stall. Chirra wasted no time filling Mike in on the farm gossip: How Paulino and Manuel were going every night to see the Gomez girls; how Paulino was selling beers and fried hamburgers at the baseball games; how Fernando had become a successful *chulo*. Mike nodded as they walked, but still kept his eye on the animals, assessing them.

The next day, Mike went to the *pueblo*, picked up provisions at the warehouse, and walked over to the telephone company. Rita was not at her usual station. Adela waved at Mike.

"Hi, Adela! How are you doing?"

"Great! Is your father back?"

"No, but I'm back for a while."

"Please tell him I said hello."

"I will."

Mike quickly made his business calls, and then tried to sound casual as he asked about Rita.

"She has the late shift. She'll be here in about three hours. Do you want to leave a message?"

"No, thanks."

Mike was torn. Would he feel differently about Rita after being in Havana? He stayed in town and killed time. He ran errands, bought the paper, walked to the bank, even though he knew it had closed at three, and had his boots polished. He finally drove to Rita's house and knocked on the door. Rita's mother answered.

"Hi Mike, Rita's taking a nap. She works tonight. Please come in, come in. I'll brew some coffee. Please, please sit down."

He sat on the same sofa where they had kissed. Mike glanced at her photos. The portraits were colored in pastels that muted the beauty of her face and the golden color of her hair. Rita's mother returned after a few minutes. "Please stay. She's getting dressed. Poor thing, she always works late now. The hours are horrible. You know, she's the youngest of the group and she gets the worst shifts. I'm positive that they're jealous of her. She's so intelligent and works so hard."

Mike nodded. He should have known he would be in for this onslaught.

Her mother continued. "Please tell me what's happening in Havana. I've seen your pictures in the newspapers at all those fancy parties. Are the women as pretty as they seem?"

"Some are very pretty," he said.

"How long will you be here? Oh my! I forgot all about your coffee. The water should be boiling by now. I'll be right back." She leapt up and dashed off toward the kitchen.

Rita appeared fifteen minutes later with a carefully made-up face. Mike rose to greet her. She advanced slowly, nervously waiting for his reaction. He felt awkward and didn't know if he should kiss her, so he stood, waiting for a sign from her.

"Hello, Mike. It's good to see you looking so well. Please, sit down. It's so good to see you."

Rita's mother brought in a cup of coffee and left immediately, saying, "I need to start supper."

Rita extended her hand, which Mike promptly took. They awkwardly shook hands and sat silent for a moment.

Mike cleared his throat and spoke first. "I was in Havana and didn't expect to come back so soon. Yesterday, my father and I decided on the spot that I should make this trip. I didn't call you beforehand because I wasn't sure what time I was going to arrive."

"You could have called. You always did before," Rita said.

"I'm going to be spending a lot of time at the farm," he informed her. "I'm moving back after I make a trip back to the United States."

Rita smiled broadly and her posture suddenly straightened. "I understand, *bébé*! It's just that if you had called first, I could have made arrangements at work so that I could spend time with you. I'm going to have to leave for work soon." She stopped, aware that she was babbling in her happiness. "Well, at least you remembered where I live," she laughed.

Mike was thankful that Rita's mother did not hear her call him "*bébé*."

"Well, I'm sorry too. Do you want me to take you? I have my car. I'd be happy to do it."

Rita cheerfully accepted. "Sure, why not? It's too hot and humid to walk. I'll meet you outside."

Rita left for the kitchen to say good-bye to her mother, who chided Rita, "Why don't you eat dinner first? You don't eat enough. Why are you leaving so early?"

Rita quickly kissed her mother's cheek and hurried outside, where Mike was waiting with the passenger door of his car open. Rita sat in the front seat, admiring its luxury. "Mike, you didn't tell me that you have a new car. It's beautiful."

"Yes, Father ordered it and gave it to me as a present. It was a surprise."

"Does your father want another daughter? I could use a car like this one. I love the color. White is such a good color for our climate. It doesn't get too hot," Rita said while stroking the seat, as if caressing a newborn puppy. When Mike didn't respond, she pulled back, uncertain all over again where she stood with him. "You didn't call for a long time, Mike, far longer than any time before. You used to call me every day. What has happened? What's going on? Then you suddenly appear at my house today with a big smile on your face, as if nothing had changed."

Mike smelled the faint scent of her jasmine perfume, appreciated the sensual contours of her body. Yet the sad expression in her eyes made him lose the nerve to tell her that it was over, that he had had a great time, but that was all. At that moment, he intensely desired her. She was close, so beautiful, so soft, and so vulnerable.

"I'm sorry, Rita. I'm not clear about what I want," he told her. "I had to spend this time in Havana. I feel bad that I didn't call you. I'm sorry."

Rita searched his eyes, but they told her nothing.

"I have to make a trip to the Unites States to close up my apartment," Mike said.

"Yes, you told me already," Rita replied.

Mike immediately regretted not telling her the truth. The truth ultimately would be so much easier for both of them. He thought, "Okay, Rita, here's the truth. I have another woman in my life. I'm having too much fun with this girl, and I don't have time for a beautiful guajira I hardly got to know, who lives in a small town in the middle of the countryside." Instead he said, "I'm sorry. Maybe I was too busy. I was worried about my work at the office. I'm also going out with different girls."

Rita crossed her arms and looked through the passenger window at the people walking on the street. After a few minutes, she turned to Mike. "Well, I'm sorry too, but I don't want to be your second choice. I thought we had something very special." Her voice became insistent. "I don't do things halfway. You're the only man in my life, you know. I haven't even looked at another man. I love you, *bébé*."

She was angry with Mike, and knew she had gone too far. Her desire for him had betrayed her judgment. She longed to feel the burning passion when their naked bodies touched, the security of his arms around her, the soothing sensation of his hands gently rubbing her back, and the tenderness of his whispers caressing her ear. Yes, perhaps she had said too much, but she still wanted to say more. She wished she had the courage to say, "You know that I am yours. Unconditionally. I will have your children. I'm not afraid to work long hours, scrub your floors, cook your meals, ride your horses, and sweat with you in the corrals. You know it. You might be afraid. I am not."

Rita could not bring herself to say another word, though. She moved closer to Mike and tenderly looked into his face. Mike didn't respond, and in his stony face she learned everything she needed to know.

Mike stopped in front of the telephone company's office. He got out of the car and opened the passenger door. He took Rita's hand and tried to caress her fingers, but she ripped her hand away. As tears rose to her eyes, she turned and hurried into the exchange.

Mike slowly drove back to the farm, feeling terrible. When he arrived, the sky was flooded with the setting sun. Paulino stood in the doorway, ready to unload Mike's packages. Cuca, who was smoking a cigarette on the porch, asked Mike what he wanted to eat for dinner. "Just cereal," he answered dully. Mike had lost his appetite.

Later, he went to the employees' dining room, where he saw Manuel and Ricardo sitting at the table. Manuel wore a clean, pressed white shirt and black boots polished to a high gloss. Mike pretended surprise. "Manuel! Where's the party? Or is it a wake? This can't be your Sunday best, since you never go to Mass!"

Manuel blushed. "Well, Mike, you know, I've started to see Julieta Gomez. I was waiting for you to arrive. I'd like permission to use the jeep tonight."

Mike sat on one of the *taburetes* and turned to Paulino. "And you, are you going with Manuel?"

Paulino coughed. "Well, I'm through with my work for today. Manuel and I are visiting the Gomez sisters."

Mike smiled at his admission. Paulino had changed. He remembered the lanky student who was afraid of his own shadow, reciting poetry and telling jokes in the café as he bantered with all the customers. Now he was muscular and stood steady and confident, though his eyes still darted about as if they were trying to discover something new or find an unreachable answer.

Mike's hands slapped the table and said crisply, "Okay, this time you can use the jeep. But in the future you need to check with Ricardo. He's in charge of the equipment. I can tell you that I don't like the idea of farm property being used for personal reasons. Please, understand this is a privilege, and don't abuse it." Turning to Ricardo, Mike said, "We have work to do. Let's leave these *enamorados* searching for their Dulcineas."

Manuel and Paulino left, but Paulino didn't like the tone of Mike's voice. Mike had never spoken to him that way, as a servant. He thought that they were friends. Why did he act that way? It was not like Mike. Was Mike nervous about his new responsibility? Was he afraid to be a boss?

Manuel drove, but he was worried for his own reasons. So, Ricardo was the new *mayoral*. How was he going to be able to see Julieta every night if he had to get Ricardo's permission to use the jeep? What would happen if Ricardo decided to use it? He remembered the advice Ricardo had given Paulino one day: "Get a horse."

After the meeting to discuss farm business with Ricardo, Mike walked into the garden and smoked a cigarette. He slowly walked along the gravel paths, thinking of both Maria Alicia and Rita, and then he returned to his office to write a letter.

> *Dear Maria Alicia,*
>
> *It was a long trip. I'm still thinking about you. I still hear your laughter, see the twinkle in your eyes. I would like to close my eyes and when I open them, find you here, next to me.*
>
> *I have a lot of work to do. It's not going to be easy. Manolo, the old* mayoral, *has resigned. He was too set in his ways. He knew me as a kid, and didn't like the changes that I'm making. My uncle, Antolin, brought up Ricardo, the new* mayoral, *so he is like family. I have known him all my life. He and Fernando are the only employees we trust to drive the family.*
>
> *The house is empty. Mitzi, the dog I mentioned to you, is sleeping under my desk as I write. Paulino, whom I met at the university and who works for us as a* canchanchán, *is in love! Maybe it's the hot weather or maybe its' just time. It seems we are all falling in love.*

I'll go to the post office tomorrow, so hopefully this letter will
be placed on the next train to Havana.
Let me hear from you.
Love,
Mike

Mike spent the next day in Ciego de Ávila running errands and didn't
return to the farm until nightfall. He was driving on the dirt road leading
to the house, and as he passed the creaky old wooden bridge, he caught
sight of a brilliant glow from behind the *bohíos* of San Joaquin. He stopped
and focused on the light. He saw great flares of fire jumping into the sky.
A sugar field had caught fire. Mike knew it had to be on or near the
Gomez sisters' plantation.

He began to honk his horn to alert everyone in the *bohíos* next to the
road. The closest fire-fighting equipment was about fifteen kilometers
away. He sped toward his farm's *batey*. Nandito had already driven his red
truck to the *batey* to get people and load what fire-fighting apparatus they
had. Manuel nervously stood next to the red jeep, urging the *vaqueros* to
get in the vehicles. Paulino and Arturo were running back from the warehouse to get machetes. Cuca was handing out red bandannas taken from
the farm's saddle room. Ricardo unlocked the liquor cabinet at the big
house and removed two bottles of white rum. Cuca worried that the
thatched palm roof of the big house might catch on fire, started soaking it
with a water hose.

Manuel, agitated, cried, "Let's go! We're not doing anything here. Let's
go. Who's coming with me?" Paulino took a seat with Manuel in the front
of Nandito's truck, while Martinito and Arturo jumped into the backseat
of the jeep. Nandito's truck bed was filled with volunteers. Mike headed
out in the jeep with Ricardo at his side.

Ricardo opened a rum bottle, took a swig out of it, and passed it to
Mike. "You'd better have a drink. You're going to need it. You have to fight
fire with fire." He also gave him a bandanna. "Use it around your mouth.
The smoke can kill you. You follow me. I've been in fires before."

Mike took two swigs out of the bottle and passed it back to Ricardo.

He welcomed the feel of the rum in his throat. He needed all the courage he could get.

The fire was close to one of the farm pastures. The men wore long-sleeved shirts and bandannas over their noses and mouths, carrying machetes or scabbards in their hands. It was the season's first sugarcane fire. In the fields, red and yellow flames jumped against the dark of the night, softened by the beams radiating from the full moon. When Mike's farm group arrived at the Gomez plantation, they found that the sisters had already mobilized their cutters, joined by a large group of the neighbors from San Joaquin. The light wind allowed the workers to quickly create a firebreak by cutting a wide swath next to the burning field. When a spark flared or a piece of burning cane shot off, a worker quickly snuffed it out with a jute sack. The intense heat created random explosions, propelling sparks and bits of burning cane into the air. Next to the burning field, standing on the bed of their truck, stood the three Gomez sisters, holding back tears, their eyes reflecting the kaleidoscopic blaze of colors. Julieta accepted Manuel's tender embrace, and said, "Manuel, go with your group to the end of that field and start cutting another break."

Manuel took Paulino, Martinito, and Arturo, and with their machetes, they started cutting a new lane. Mike and Ricardo went to the truck to get their own instructions from the sisters. "Mike and Ricardo, we thank you so much. You go and help Manuel."

Just then they heard a shout from the field—a spark had just started another fire in a different area. Ricardo and Mike shifted direction and started to work their way through several rows of the sugarcane, cutting the leaves and the stalks with their machetes, to reach the new, incipient fire. It was spreading quickly and generated unbearable heat. The beating of the sacks against the flames made a concerted noise of whacks and fizzles.

The efforts of the firefighters continued throughout the night, and after ten hours, they finally had it under control. The cane had turned black, and its green colors ended abruptly at the firebreaks cut to contain the burnt fields. The exhausted volunteers slogged through the field with bleary eyes. The sun rose on the horizon, and a few birds flew over. Mike could still hear faint sounds from the burnt cane stalks as they cracked and popped.

Soot and sweat covered the faces of the volunteers as they retreated to their trucks, where they drank water and took swigs from rum bottles that were passed around.

Suddenly, their job accomplished, they disappeared as if by magic. They left as fast as they had arrived the night before to help a neighbor in need. Before Mike left, he caught a glimpse of Paulino. His white shirt was blackened; his always clean face was almost unidentifiable under a thick layer of soot. His right arm could hardly hold up his machete as he staggered forward, because he could no longer walk. He collapsed from exhaustion next to the truck, gripping his machete like a priest holding a sacred cross, ready to give benediction.

Mike did not feel or look any better himself. His eyes were red, his muscles sore, and his back aching. He waited for all of his workers to climb on Nandito's truck and into the jeep. He passed what was left of the rum, and they slowly took turns. For once they had more thirst for water than for rum. He went to Paulino's side and helped him get into the jeep. It was time to go back to the house, have a hot shower, and go to sleep. Their work was done.

The sugarcane, now dark and scorched, would have to be cut, and taken soon to the sugar mill. New stalks would then shoot out, full of life—a symbol of Cuba that would always come back, vibrant and sweet.

16

El Norte

MIKE PACKED LIGHTLY since he had left his sweaters, overcoat, and heavy winter clothing at his college apartment. The Cubana Airlines plane carried the usual mix of ladies on shopping trips to Miami, businessmen, and hungover tourists. Mike moved quickly through US Customs and stopped to have a hamburger and French fries, followed by a cup of American coffee. His connection left on time, and a few hours later, he landed in Chicago. He went to the Blackstone Hotel, his father's favorite, ordered room service, and went to sleep. He woke up to a crisp morning. After the farm, the life and energy of the city seemed especially alive. He walked in the Loop, gazing into the storefronts. He sat for a few minutes at a Merrill Lynch office watching the stock boys chalk the stock trades on the blackboard as he checked the stocks bought with his mother's inheritance. He returned to the hotel just in time to check out. He caught his train to the university.

Mike sat by a window and watched the tranquil countryside as the train raced through. The Plains were in full splendor. The farmland was planted with corn and wheat. White-faced Herefords were bunched in feedlots. Occasionally, a pristine white clapboard house with a small garden in the back and a pickup truck in the front rolled into view and broke the monotonous rhythm of the well-kept fields. He had seen this landscape many times, and understood the care those fields had received for at least two generations of farmers. They came as immigrants; now this was their home and their life.

The taxi dropped Mike in front of his apartment building. It had the tired beauty of worn barracks, and the smell of carpets and floors cleaned many times. His landlady had neatly piled his junk mail on his small dinette table. The door of the unplugged refrigerator was open and his cupboards were bare. Dirty towels hung in the bathroom, and a page of an incomplete term paper remained rolled in his typewriter. He opened the windows to let out the musty air. Mike was exhausted. He dropped onto his bed and promptly fell asleep. Waking up in the middle of the night, he walked out to a nearby convenience store to buy food for breakfast. It was close to final exam time on campus, and even at this hour, he saw the glow of study lights from windows. Mike, free of deadline worries, was soon asleep again. He woke up at ten, ate breakfast, and walked to the university campus. Mike remembered his first day there and reflected on how much he had learned and changed. The weather was crisp. He enjoyed the coolness of the early morning. Some students were already reading their books, sitting on the well-kept lawn. He remembered the contrast between slovenly dressed professors and finely attired classmates, as if the way they dressed could gain the approval of their teachers, who mispronounced their names. At first he had found it strange to sit next to a woman in a classroom, never having attended school with female students before. Mike walked past the Gothic nondenominational chapel toward the economics and social sciences building, where he had spent much of the last two years. His advisor's office was on the second floor. The professor's loyal secretary was his gatekeeper, and shielded him from student demands to give him time to write books and prepare lectures. Mike opened the door and said, "Good morning, Ms. Smith. You look as lovely as ever."

She smiled. "Come in, Mike. I haven't seen you for such a long time!"

"I went home for a while. Is Professor Samuels available?

"He's on a long-distance call right now, but I'll let him know you're here."

Five minutes later, the professor emerged from his office, with his old cardigan sweater unbuttoned, an unlit pipe in his mouth, and a business magazine in his hand.

"Mike, you disappeared. Mary told me you had to go back to take care of your father, but I didn't expect you to be gone for such a long time."

"I'm sorry, things got really complicated. I wasn't sure until last week when I could return. I should've sent you a note. Mary told me that she had talked to you and given you my last paper."

The professor smiled and waved Mike into his office. "Come, come. I have a lecture soon, but we can talk for a few minutes. Do you have time?"

"Sure," Mike said, and followed the professor into his office.

Books covered the floor in neat piles; a Dictaphone machine and an old Royal typewriter sat on a small table near his desk. The two comfortable chairs offered a view of the large rectangular green located at the center of the campus. The sound of students' voices could be heard from the large, open windows. "First, how's your father? How sick is he? I was worried about you. You still have some unfinished business here, and I never heard anything else from you, other than the note you gave Mary for me."

"It was a short-term scare. Father is doing a lot better. But he wants me down there. He wants me to take over the management of our ranch."

"Well, you have a lot of thinking to do. We can talk about it later if you want, but tell me, do you see change happening there? I hear these are more prosperous times for the people of Cuba. That's all I read, new casinos, new hotels, and more tourists."

"Yes, we have lots of new buildings and real estate developments. Yet the windfall is all going to Batista and his cronies."

"Well, that's endemic in your country. It all depends on who's in power," the professor said.

"I'd like to hear more, but I have to go." He stood up, took off his cardigan and draped it over the back of his chair. "Please stay. We'll have lunch later at the club." Professor Samuels grabbed a blazer from a coat rack.

"Thanks. I'll wait here, then meet you at the club at twelve, if that's all right."

"Make yourself at home," the professor said, and then left.

Mike roamed around the room and ran his fingers over the familiar books in the bookcases. Some he had learned to love, others reminded him of long, frustrating hours of work. He lit a cigarette and watched its smoke playfully rise to the ceiling and out of the window. Mike was not ready for what was sure to be a philosophical discussion with his advisor during lunch. He did not want to think about the politics in Cuba. His mind was on taking over the family farm, Rita, and Maria Alicia. But he had to, and he felt the same as he had when he worked on a term paper late into the night—multiple cups of coffee altering his heartbeat, his eyes focused on the typewriter, ideas flowing faster than his ability to type words. What was happening on the island? He knew that some of his father's friends gave money to Castro, and they laughed about it, saying they liked to buy insurance.

He closed his eyes and dozed off; when he woke up, it was close to noon, time to leave the placidity of the armchair. The club occupied an old house deeded by an alumnus to the university. It had tried, without much success, to copy the décor and ambiance of a private club. The bar had the mahogany austerity of a Victorian drinking parlor. The walls were cluttered with grim portraits of the past club presidents, and all the cocktail tables had peanut bowls. Mike sat at the bar watching the parade of new and old faces full of self-importance in that small academic pond.

Professor Samuels arrived fifteen minutes late. They sat at a small table in a corner of the restaurant that commanded a view of the entire dining room. The waiter promptly brought two menus and two rectangular chits on which to mark food selections. They ordered, and then Samuels stared at Mike for a long moment with an inquisitive frown. "Mike, you look so serious. What's going on with you? Have I hit a nerve?"

"Yes, you have, actually. I feel as if I'm too close to Cuba to get a clear view of it. Sometimes it's better to leave, to step back, and see things from afar. The irony is that when I was attending your classes, I was isolated from what was happening in my country. I thought I knew what was going on, but I didn't. Now I have a better picture. It's worse than I thought."

Professor Samuels responded, "Of the players you mentioned, Castro is the one to watch. Our media, especially *The New York Times*, but also *Time* magazine and even *Look*, has adopted him. Talk to your fellow students. They're all for him, even your Cuban *compadres* and friends. However, Castro will use everyone and anyone, and he'll make deals to achieve his goal. Castro behaves like a Jesuit—he had good teachers."

Mike replied, "Yes, he went to Belen. He was a leader even then, but he never achieved anything after that, either in politics or in his law practice. Father says that we've had revolutions before. After a few months everything went back to normal."

"That's the thinking of your social economic group, you and your rich friends and their families, those who I, as a good liberal, call the oligarchy.

You're accustomed to buying the politicians of the ruling party and pretending that you're opposed to them. The way you're acting now. The last time you all took a real position was in the thirties. You all were against Batista. He's not forgotten that, nor will he ever forget that you won't let him join the Habana Yacht Club because of his mulatto blood. But don't be so sure that you can control what may happen. Times are different. Castro has charisma, and he has the American press and some of the American bureaucrats rooting for him. Batista has made many enemies in the States. The government doesn't like his contacts with the Mafia, but they don't want to say it out loud."

Mike frowned. "Maybe, but my generation thinks differently. We want to do something. We want change. We'll work for it. We're tired of not being heard."

They ordered coffee, and Mike lit another of his Pall Malls and asked how to go about extending his leave of absence. The professor dropped the subject of Cuba, gave him advice, and they exchanged goodbyes at the door of the club.

Mike walked to the student union to check his mailbox and empty his locker. While he was busy sorting through abandoned papers, rulers, half-used pencils, and overdue books, he felt a nudge on his back.

His friend Mary smiled. "Mikito, I thought you had died and gone to hell. You didn't even write a postcard! Is that the way you treat your best friend?" Mary was tall and athletic, her blonde hair was held back in a ponytail, she wore a black sweater and a nicely cut gray wool skirt. Her skin glowed, even though she wore no makeup.

Mike hugged her, responding to her infectious smile and said, "I missed you! I was really busy with Father. He's doing better now."

Mary laughed, "I thought you had done something crazy, like gone to the hills and grown a beard and joined all those people with rosaries around their necks." They went to the cafeteria, where they talked for a long while.

Mike was delighted to see her. Their bond was more friendship than romantic. They had an understanding and a respect for each other's intellect. Late at night, tired of reading the same texts and working on the same problems, they had gone for walks, each baring their souls to the other.

Mary updated Mike on campus gossip: who still attended the university, who had left, who had a teaching job, who fooled around with whom, who had left the Greeks, and which girls were still trying to find husbands. She briefed him on school politics: who had become an assistant professor and who was drinking too much. Mary invited him to go to a party, hosted by Terry, a common friend. They made plans to meet up later, embraced, and parted ways.

Mike carried his books to the library to pay his fines, and then walked to his apartment carrying the junk that had been stored in his locker. Suddenly, Mike felt uneasy. Although he thought he knew his Cuba's situation, other people might see it differently. Where he saw a chance for political change, others thought that a revolution was the answer. What worried him were not their divergent opinions, but that his reading could be wrong. How would a revolution affect his family's future? Would he ever live in a democratic country? Mike had time for a quick shower and changed into his collegiate uniform: a button-down blue Oxford shirt, his favorite pair of brown mocassin shoes, and a comfortable pair of khaki slacks. He slung a sweater around his neck just as Mary knocked. She gave him a quick kiss and they headed out.

Terry's apartment was in another barracklike complex, but farther away from the university. The party was in full swing when they arrived—young people talking, flirting, and arguing at the top of their voices. A record player was in the small living room with a stash of records of all different types of music. Ashtrays were scattered all over the area, and the room was so packed that they could hardly move. Mary and Mike went to look for Terry. Long-necked beer bottles cooled in a tub of ice on the patio, and the air was dense with cigarette smoke. Seeing them, Terry left a blonde girl in a black beret and came to hug Mike and to kiss Mary.

"I thought we'd lost you. Welcome back to the rat race."

"It's good to see you again. Wow, what a party!" Mike answered.

"Come, have a beer," Terry said while steering them toward the cooler.

The party stayed lively well past midnight, when neighbors finally complained, dampening the mood and thinning out the crowd. At the end, a handful of close friends remained: Mike and Mary, the girl in the black beret, and an adjunct professor who had a crush on Mary. Terry had switched from beer to Jack Daniel's, which he kept for "medicinal purposes." Mike, exhausted, sat in one of the patio chairs, sipping a beer. Mary sat next to him with her eyes closed, trying to follow the lyrics of a ballad. The girl with the beret, Camille, Terry's latest undergraduate conquest, leaned in toward Mike. "Terry told me that you're Cuban. Do you know Fidel Castro?"

Mike tiredly nodded. "Yes, I know of him. We went to the same school. His father is a sugarcane grower, the same as my father."

"I'm so excited about him. He's our freedom fighter. Tell me, how I can help in the battle against the oppression of your countrymen?"

Her question jolted Mike, and he looked at the girl with disbelief. "Have you ever been to Cuba?"

"No," she replied, "but I know all about it. There's poverty, corruption, prostitution on the streets, and the workers have miserable wages. Cuba is the worst American colony."

Mike glanced at Mary and Terry, both of whom had been his guests in Havana.

"Well," Mike answered in a low, controlled voice, "we have poverty and prostitution. You have those in any country—just go to the other side of the tracks in any city in this country and you'll find them. Yes, Cuba has problems, and we're trying hard to solve them, but we also have very strong labor legislation, and our workers share, by law, in any increase in the price of sugar."

Camille shrugged, "So?"

"You don't know anything about my country."

"So everything is perfect in your paradise—palm trees, sandy beaches, moonlight blanketing the sea, romantic nights, guitars playing in the background?"

"No, but we have strong laws that protect the workers—"

Camille shrugged. "How can the rule of law be said to exist in a dictatorship?"

"Well, *some* rules exist. We have a large amount of government intervention in our economy. Have you read Professor Samuels' book? Our system is based on a market economy with a great degree of government intervention, which in the end makes us—from the work legislation standpoint—almost a socialist government."

"So?"

"I don't know Dr. Castro, but I know some of his followers. He's not the only one who wants change on the island."

Camille looked disdainfully over Mike's shoulder as he spoke and then said, "I think you've sold your soul to the company store. You're another capitalistic pig. I don't know how you can be here, drinking beer, when you should be fighting in the hills against Batista!"

Mike felt a wave of fury well up inside. "What the hell! Do you know me? Do you know what I do? How I think? You believe that the only way of helping Cuba is going to the hills? What about believing in free elections? How about bringing our constitution back in full?"

Camille raised her eyebrows. "You're not serious about what you're saying." She examined Mike's Rolex and glared, "You're another plutocrat living from the sweat of the working people."

"Yes, I have people working for me, but dammed if I don't work as hard as they do."

Terry intervened, "Camille, you don't know what you're talking about."

Camille stood up, saying, "You've both sold your lives to the system. Terry, I'm so sorry, I thought I knew you better." She swept out with the hauteur of a lady making a grand exit, a woman offended.

Terry apologized to Mike, and Mary, noticing his annoyance, feigned tiredness and asked him to take her home. They exchanged pleasantries and left the party.

The trip back home was quiet. Mary drove carefully while Mike sat slumped in his seat in silence. Finally, she said to him, "I don't understand why you're so upset. Camille is just a student playing her best Sartre communist shit. But you seemed livid. You never used to overreact like this before. Why?"

"I'm tired of fighting clichés. They're so easily said and so difficult to refute," he complained. "I'm worried. I don't know if I know what's happening or what's going to happen. Everyone has a different idea. I know that Batista has to go. But how and when, and what happens afterward?" He closed his eyes, exhausted. He knew that reason should prevail and define the outcome of Batista's dictatorship in his country. "Aren't we reasonable people?" he asked himself.

Despite his many thoughts and worries, he could only muster a few words. "It's been a long day. I don't feel like talking anymore. It's hard to explain what's going on." Mike extended his hand. Mary took it, and she continued driving with his hand in hers.

A week later, Mike left for Havana.

— 17 —

La Roca

MIKE WOKE UP as the plane landed at Rancho Boyeros Airport. The customs agent took his time searching Mike's bag and handled the two cartons of Pall Malls that he had brought as if they were poison.

At the house, Estrella gave him a big hug. "I thought you were never coming back. I have chicken croquettes for you. You never called your poor father, but girls have been calling you almost every day! I told them I didn't even know where you were. A Maria Alicia called the most times." She turned to Georgina. "Well don't just stand there! Help take Mike's luggage to his room."

He joined his father in the library, who offered him a drink, and asked, "Are you happy to come home? You know you can go back. I want to be sure that this is your decision. You have to do it for *you*."

Mike had made up his mind. "I thought it would be easier. The peace of academic life is attractive." He remembered something and added, "Oh, Mary sends regards. She says that you'll have to wait for her to finish her master's degree before you get married! She doesn't think that you're too old."

Don Miguel laughed. "I've always had better luck with young and beautiful women who are intelligent and nice."

Mike continued in a more serious tone. "My professor Samuels is worried about our political situation. The *barbudos* are very popular in the States. Batista is hated." He became more annoyed as he went on. "The American press seems to be one-sided. They only think of Castro. For them, the rest of the opposition against Batista doesn't exist."

His father played with his drink. "Yes, there's a flight of money to the

United States and Switzerland. But I don't believe in taking my marbles out of our own country."

Michael glanced at him with concern. "Father, maybe a little?"

"No, Son, if you're not involved in politics, if you work, keep a low profile, and treat your people right, you should never worry. I remember when Batista replaced Machado. The rabble had their day as they sacked the houses of the Machadistas. The riffraff now mingle with the known people, and they're entertained at homes they once sacked. Our countrymen are too few to harbor resentments," he said as he got up to add water to his glass. As he poured in the water, he changed the topic. "Oh, by the way, I'm going to Varadero. I've accepted your sisters' invitation to spend part of the summer with them, and since I'm paying the rent on the house, they'll be my guests. Now, you can join us. You won't even have to feel guilty about taking advantage of your poor sisters and their poorer husbands."

Mike liked that proposal very much. "It'll be fun. I love Varadero. It has so many memories of us being there. Mother loved the beach."

While they were eating lunch, Estrella peeked in several times to see if Mike had enough to eat, as if he were a growing boy of twelve in need of supervision. As he conversed idly with his father about the trip to Varadero, his mind ricocheted between Rita and Maria Alicia. He could understand the preoccupation with Rita—she embodied his sexual fantasy—but why Maria Alicia? The answer wasn't long in coming. She was sensual, too, in a way, mysteriously seductive. After dinner, he called Maria Alicia and made a date for dinner the next day.

Late that night, Mike had coffee with Laureano at a small café on the Havana side of the river Almendares. Laureano was interested in Mike's report on the political situation in the United States. They joked that Eisenhower was only interested in playing golf and that the person to watch was Kennedy. They talked until one o'clock in the morning. Laureano disagreed with Mike's assessment of Americans' attitudes toward Cuba, and argued that Mike had just returned from a college environment. Laureano thought that the ideas in Washington were more nuanced.

The next morning, Don Miguel and Mike met with Lustre, who was concerned about the political instability and recommended moving the family's surplus funds to a Miami bank.

Dr. Comillas called Don Miguel, excited to say that the minister had agreed to present to the president a copy of the decree they had drafted. They should celebrate, he suggested. "How about lunch at La Roca?"

Don Miguel arrived on time. The headwaiter led him to a table near a big boulder with a small waterfall, the trademark of the restaurant. A waiter came to tell him that Dr. Comillas had called and left a message that he was shopping but would arrive shortly. Don Miguel, frustrated, ordered a drink, promising himself that he would only wait fifteen minutes.

Comillas showed up just under the wire, escorted by two women. His face was red, his speech slightly slurred, and he held a cigarette holder in his left hand. His right hand held the shoulder of the younger woman as he tried to keep his balance

"Miguelito, you rascal. You work too hard. Look at the jewels I have brought. Would you believe it? This is Esmeralda. She's a teacher, and this lady," he said, pointing to the younger one, "this is Patricia, and she is *quite* a beauty in a small package. And you know—she's also smart! I had Esmeralda invite her. Patricia didn't want to accept my invitation to lunch because she had not been introduced to me—*moi!* So I asked Esmeralda to call her and come as her chaperone! Now we have a respectable table of four." By this point Don Miguel had stood up to greet the guests.

Comillas continued, "We have to make serious decisions. You are the guest of honor. You are the oldest." He got sidetracked by that thought and asked, "How old are you, anyway? Don't tell me. I don't want to know. But you are a player. Ha, ha, ha." He indicated the women with a grand sweep of his hand. "What do you want to play with, emeralds or dreams? Let's see . . . I'll sit Patricia on your right and Esmeralda on your left."

Don Miguel pulled out a chair for Patricia as his host continued, "What should we drink? Waiter, waiter, what are you doing, staring at us? Bring us something to drink. For Esmeralda, a stinger—the green of the drink goes well with her name. As for Patricia, what do you think she likes to have? Champagne? Daiquiri? Or maybe a Hatuey beer?" She didn't have a chance to tell him, because he quickly shifted to himself. "For me, just the best—I want brandy, a Napoleon, with ice."

The waiter left with the order, and Comillas rambled on, "I know it can be considered a sacrilege to have a great cognac drunk with ice! But this is Cuba, and we are hot, our climate is hot, and I can buy the best the French can offer, and I'll have it with ice if I please! Do the French care? Yes, they may care, but they don't live here!"

Drinks were brought and they ate, and more drinks were brought. Comillas told bad jokes and Esmeralda laughed at them. Don Miguel felt uneasy about the mood of the lunch, noticing that Patricia reacted badly to Comillas's jokes. He tried to make her feel at ease and kept changing the topics of the conversation. When it was past three o'clock, Don Miguel looked nervously at his watch.

Comillas noticed it, and squeezing Esmeralda's knee, ordered another drink. "Whoa, Miguelito! Aren't you enjoying the company of your talented friend? Are you getting bored glancing at Patricia's beautiful face? You're checking your watch like you have an important meeting to go to." He wagged a finger in Don Miguel's face. "No, my friend, this afternoon you are mine. I know your schedule. I have more surprises. So let's retire to a more private place, where we can relax, enjoy, and see the coming of another day."

Comillas wiped his mouth with his napkin and made signs to the waiter to bring the check, which he signed with a flourish. Esmeralda stood next to him with a complicit smile on her face. Patricia stood up, but she gazed at the floor and played nervously with her small purse.

Dr. Comillas's black Mercedes waited at the curb, and they drove to the underground parking garage of his building. The foyer of Comillas's penthouse opened into a big living room featuring large windows and sliding glass doors that opened onto an open terrace facing the grounds of the Hotel Nacional and the full curvature of the Malecon. The furniture was simple and elegant, the art colorful. Amelia Pelaez's oils hung next to the more traditional pieces by Francisco Ramos. In the dining room, a small collection of Ponces subdued the riot of color created by the Pelaez. Comillas went to his small bar and Esmeralda, who evidently knew the penthouse, brought out glasses.

Comillas stepped out onto the terrace and surveyed the city. "Havana is my first mistress. I love her. Every time I leave, I dream of her—of her cobblestone streets, of the waves breaking against the seawall, of the smell of the flowers, of the feel of the breeze." He turned to the young women. "When I was exiled during the Machado dictatorship, I went to Rio de Janeiro because it was the closest to her. I still missed Havana. I cried every night. I couldn't walk her streets or see the blue of her sky and her bluest of seas."

He took Esmeralda by the waist. "Enjoy a view that is unique in the world."

Comillas stood there for long moments in deep communion with the city that he loved. Don Miguel and Patricia followed them to the terrace, and Comillas said to them, "This is your house, too. Esmeralda is joining me in my siesta. I am getting too maudlin for my own taste. Imagine, me a romantic. *Hasta luego.* Make yourselves at home." He threw a kiss in the air and left, Esmeralda on his arm.

Don Miguel and Patricia went to the living room and found a leather sofa that commanded a great view of the Malecon. He remarked, "I'm sorry about today. I just met you. Please don't be nervous. Dr. Comillas is a very good man and my best friend." She began to relax, and he continued that process by asking her to talk about herself. "Please, I've not heard what you like or dislike. Do you like living in Havana?"

Over the next few hours, Patricia told him about growing up in Pinar del Rio. Her father grew tobacco. She had liked to go horseback riding in the hills, and she was anxious about coming to Havana. Her sister worked long hours as a seamstress, she told him, and had designed the dress she was wearing. She had started to study engineering at the university in Havana and was now studying computers. She admitted that she had been nervous about accepting Comillas's invitation. Don Miguel sat calmly, asking questions as she told the story of her life. He was so patient, Patricia told him, that he reminded her of her first father confessor at her First Communion: She was dressed in white and wore a long veil that touched behind her knees, and carried a candle in one hand and in the other, a white lily.

The sun started to set in the horizon. The sky changed colors from the blues to the pinks and reds, and now the red and white lights of the cars driven along the Malecon formed a swift procession that melted into a stream of light. Don Miguel stood up from the sofa and took Patricia's hand. "The sky is clear tonight. I've always liked to watch the sun set. Maybe we can catch the green ray. My wife used to say that if you see the green ray and make a wish, it will be granted."

The moment indeed came, for a brief instant, and he smiled. He turned to Patricia. "Did you see it? Did you?"

"I don't know. I may have. I saw a change, a light that flickered and disappeared. Is that it? But I didn't have time to make my wish. Did you make yours?"

"Yes, I did." He turned to face her. "I think it's time to go. I would be very happy to take you home, if you don't mind. My car is parked near the restaurant. It's a nice evening, so we can walk. I'll leave a note for Dr. Comillas."

A FEW DAYS later, the two old friends sat on the porch of Dr. Comillas's farmhouse. The rocking chairs creaked in harmony with noises from the farm menagerie— bells on cows' necks, hens cackling, the random bark of a dog protecting his territory—and the rustling of bamboo in the gentle breeze.

"I'm surprised at you. You've forgotten your manners," he said, teasing. "You left with Patricia without even saying good-bye. You could have knocked at my door. Your mother taught you better. By the way, how did you like her? I thought she was perfect for you."

"She is a nice, intelligent young lady. I agree."

He smiled at his scheming to hook up his friend with a female escort. "Esmeralda knows Patricia's sister, and convinced her to come to lunch by telling her that a nice gentleman was joining us. You are a very respectable old man! I must have a very unsavory reputation to have young, intelligent girls think so badly of me—well, at least this one *seems* intelligent."

Comillas got up from the rocking chair and poured another drink. It was past five o'clock, but the sun was still high on the horizon. Don Miguel shifted uneasily on the rocking chair. Patricia was younger than his youngest daughter. She was pretty. He liked the way her eyes were set, their color, how she smiled, how her lips fell slightly open as she listened, how she seemed to be inside herself, unsure, vulnerable. Was she lonely like him?

Comillas returned with a small plate. "I just prepared these mojitos with handpicked mint from my herb garden. You have to understand, I am a connoisseur. I demand the best." He frowned at his old friend. "That's what I don't understand about you. You can have anything that this island has to offer. But what do you do? You become a hermit. You work, work, and work."

"I work because I like to work," Miguel replied.

"Worst, you eat whatever that old lady you call a cook serves you."

"Come on, she's a very good cook."

Comillas continued, "You worry about how successful your children are, and try to eliminate the normal pressures of life for them, and then you complain."

"I don't. I'm happy with what God gave me," said Don Miguel.

Comillas knew better than to believe that. "No, I know you complain, about what? About being alone? Of not having enough friends, when you abandoned them by hiding at your farm? Or not having a warm body next to you in bed? Why did God create a woman? So we both have pleasure. Is it bad? Some priest may have put that in your mind. Oh, 'It's going to be a mortal sin, a venial sin. It's Friday. I have to eat fish.' *Carajo!* You are older and wiser than that."

Don Miguel just rocked, looking at the view. He would not be provoked into replying to this inanity.

"Please," Comillas continued, "I'm your friend. You may not approve of the way I live. Many do not approve. So what! Do they pay my bills? Do they come to see me when I feel down or when I'm sick? When I need the solace of a true friendship? No, I know you're my friend. Why do I know it? You don't need anything that I have and give me more than I give you." He chewed a mint leaf in his mouth. "Have another drink, reconsider your attitude, and call Patricia. See her, go out with her, and if you feel like a sinner tomorrow morning, I'll absolve you today."

Don Miguel remained silent for a while and then he got up and said, "The evening is beautiful, but I have things to do back home. Could your chauffeur drive me home?" He paused and said in a low tone, "By the way, I disagree with what you said, but don't worry. That's why friends are so important."

18

Santi Spiritus

THE BELLS TOLLED, inviting parishioners to come to seven o'clock Mass. Mike and Don Miguel's hotel in Santi Spiritus faced the church from across the square, and the sound woke Mike. He sleepily ambled to the bathroom. His father had finished taking a shower and had a towel wrapped around his waist.

"Good morning, Father."

"Good morning, Son," his father replied briskly. "You slept late, so we'll have coffee at the fairgrounds. I'll see you downstairs. You can take your shower later."

Mike joined him in the lobby.

The fairground setup was simple and practical with a large open arena with wooden bleachers on two sides, a white fence around the back, and a series of large thatched-roof barns that were used as stables for the animals. Vendors roamed the grounds peddling soft drinks, ice cream, *pirulis*, and roasted peanuts. Loudspeakers on every light pole blared with announcements, competing with the voices and guitars of troubadours, who improvised *décimas* for unwilling listeners and then demanded tips.

Don Miguel, smoking his first cigar, went to see his cattle. Manuel, with three of his helpers, was in the middle of their preparation. The horns of the cattle, sanded at the farm, were now finished with a finer sanding paper and coated with a greasy substance, then buffed to a lustrous shine. Mike followed his father and closely inspected each animal to be shown that the morning. Manuel wore his work clothes, but soon they would all change into the farm's show uniform of white shirt, red bandanna tied around the neck, white straw Western hat, white jeans, and a red-and-white leather chap that showed the farm brand on its wings.

The first class was to start in thirty minutes, and the farmhands' activity was at a high pitch. Mike put on the farm's leather chaps so that he could show a heifer in the first class. The breeders' children now handled the farm animals in the ring. As with other customs copied from North American breeders, the cattlemen's children and their employees showed their animals. The animals received the final touches—one more time their coats were brushed and toweled. Each handler pinned his animal's number to the back of his shirt. In his right hand, he held a stick to make the animal stand perfectly in front of the judge with neck high, four legs to form a perfect square, back straight.

The judge was a tall, lanky professor from a Texas agricultural and mechanical college. He had two assistants; one was his interpreter. The judge was quick to evaluate the lineup. He promptly eliminated the animals that did not meet his standards of conformation or were not in perfect show condition. The culled handlers left the ring, downtrodden, many to face the anger of their parents or owners, who would accuse them of handling their stock poorly.

Manuel's heifer won first place, while Mike placed third. For Mike it was, at best, a bittersweet success. Mike had not selected *his* heifer. Manuel had just handed him a lead rope. He would have liked to win, but he understood. They both wanted the farm to win, and since Mike had not shown an animal in the ring for some years, it would have been a risk to give him the best animal. Other classes followed. Mike and Manuel showed in every class, and the farm continued to place with its animals.

The contest stopped at noon to give the judge and the handlers a lunch break. Mike joined his father, now surrounded by a group of friends, in a special area of a restaurant reserved for the show patrons and exhibitors. The food was simple: a thin steak surrounded by French fried potatoes, chicken and noodle soup, and a fruit salad directly from a Del Monte can. Don Miguel was having his usual Scotch and water. A breeder joked with Mike that the reason the farm had won so many ribbons was because he was able to speak English to the judge. Mike laughed, but he understood the implication. The patrons soon left the restaurant to watch the showing of their cattle. Finally, the championship class was to be judged. Manuel showed the bull that had won the two-year class, while Mike showed a bullock. But another breeder, who had just imported his bull from Texas, won the championship. The farm won the Reserve Champion, and Mike's two-year old bullock won the Junior Champion trophy. Don Miguel was less than delighted with the outcome—the farm had not made its usual sweep of the trophies—but there were other judges and shows, and he joined the other exhibitors to celebrate their wins of the day in the patron area of the restaurant.

Another celebration was going on: Manuel had invited his crew to a small bar near the stables. They drank beer, and as the evening progressed, they changed to brandy and ginger ale. Employees from other farms joined in, and they had spirited arguments, mixed with hearty laughter and jokes, about how their bosses made them dress to show their cattle. They were caricatures of Tom Mix or Hopalong Cassidy with fancy chaps, bandannas tied around their necks, and oversized cowboy hats.

The exhibitors had a dance that night at the Yayabo Riding Club, housed in a modest building near the fairgrounds with a thatched palm roof and a red-painted cement floor. On one side stood a long bar; opposite was a bandstand, where a large band played *chachachas, sones,* and *guaguancos,* and when it went on break, a colorful Wurlitzer with a collection of American top-ten tunes provided music. Cattlemen, exhibitors, club members, and guests occupied wooden tables around the dance floor. Others stood at the long bar to watch the dancers. Don Miguel and Mike sat at a table close to the orchestra with Gordo Zayas, who was the announcer for the show, and other exhibitors. Bottles of Fundador, Bacardi, and Cutty Sark were lined along the length of the table with empty bottles of ginger ale, Coca-Cola, and tonic water. An ice bucket held Hatuey beer, and dishes full of potato chips and olives completed the spread.

IN A CANTINA on the fairgrounds, Manuel sat with a group of employees at the end of the bar. His group had split up, as the more adventurous had left for the city to find *putas* with whom to spend the night, while others stayed nursing their beers. Manuel looked at his companions and realized that he had achieved more than they had. Don Miguel respected him, and he increasingly asked for his advice. He had saved a lot of money, because of his frugality and his free room and board. He could go anywhere and say, "I know how to train horses. I have my own saddle." In Manuel's view, he thought that he should be the administrator of the farm and Ricardo should answer to him. He should only have to answer to Don Miguel.

Mike's arrival had spoiled his dreams. Mike would never put him in charge. He preferred Ricardo. Why not him? He had saved more money than his compadres, but not enough if he wanted to marry Julieta. If he were the farm administrator, at least he would feel equal to her. The farm was at least thirty times bigger than the sisters' plantation, and its sugar quota at the sugar mill was larger than theirs. He could manage the whole farm. He knew he was capable of doing it. "Why did Mike have to return?" He lamented. He talked more to *El Viejo* than Mike ever had.

A friendly slap on his back brought Manuel out of his ruminations. He turned around and saw Paulino with Fernando and the three sisters behind them. Julieta put her arm around Manuel's shoulder and said, "So you thought you could come and party with your compadres without me? At least I found you without a woman." Manuel was so surprised that he didn't know what to say. "Is this the way you receive someone who has driven hours just to see you?" she asked.

He got up and gave Julieta a small embrace and shook hands with the two other sisters, who were still laughing at his bewilderment.

Paulino took over. "Manuel, we haven't had anything to eat." Manuel took the group to a larger table and called for a waiter. The group was in a party mood. Fernando excused himself and went to find the other employees of the farm.

Manuel sat next to Julieta and, feeling more composed, held her hand. "I'm very surprised to see you tonight. You should have told me. I would have taken you to a better place." He leaned toward her and said more softly, "I've been doing a lot of thinking. Maybe we can talk tonight. Can we have time by ourselves?"

Manuel hurried them through dinner. When the check came, Paulino made a feeble effort to pay it, but Manuel, feeling important, grabbed it from him and, throwing a twenty pesos bill on the table, invited the group to come back to the stables to see the trophies and ribbons that they had won. At the stables, he gave a short speech about the mistake the judge made by not pinning the farm's older bull as the great champion. Paulino, who wanted to go to the amusement rides, left with Cristina and Elena. Julieta hung back, holding Manuel's hand. It was the first time they had been alone.

Manuel closed the door of the box. Four directors chairs with red canvas backs, an army cot, and the two saddle boxes filled the space. Manuel dusted a chair off and asked Julieta to sit. He pulled another chair close to it. He picked up her hands and, looking into her eyes, tried to think of the right words. He wanted to say how much he loved her; how bad he felt when she was not near him; that his thoughts were always with her; that he did not know if he deserved her; that he was honest and hardworking; that he wanted a family; that he would work hard and that if they wanted, he could work with them in helping them manage their plantation. He looked at her eyes and he forgot everything he was about to say. She was still smiling, holding his hands. Manuel just blurted, "I love you."

Julieta moved in closer and kissed him. "I do, too, Manuel."

19

Kawama

AN EARLY BREAKFAST had been served. Don Miguel was in the library reading the newspapers when Estrella entered with Georgina. "Do you know when Mike is coming back from the farm?" Estrella asked. "Lourdes told me that you're going to spend the summer with them at Kawama. Now, if Mike isn't returning soon, I won't have anything to do." She briefly paused and then divulged the real reason she was asking. "I'd like to spend time with my sister in Santa Isabel de las Lajas. I think Georgina can take care of the house."

"Well," Don Miguel responded, turning to Georgina, "you're going to be here all alone. You have to promise me that no one, *no one*, will enter these doors. You'll clean the house, water the plants, answer the phone, and record in writing who called, when he called, his phone number, and what he wanted from me. If you do so, you can stay and Estrella can leave. Do you understand?"

"Yes, Don Miguel, I'll do everything you want me to do," she said eagerly. "Estrella can visit her sister. You'll be pleased."

"Okay, Estrella. I'm going to Varadero for at least three or four weeks."

"Thank you, Don Miguel. I'll send a telegram to my sister and find out what will be convenient for her." They hurried away, leaving him feeling not like a tough old grouch, but a kind, benevolent master.

Adelaida was the first to arrive at the rental house in Varadero, and she opened all the windows to let in the sun and sea air. The house had enough bedrooms for the entire family. They didn't have a swimming pool, but the house faced the beach, which extended for kilometers in both directions with white powdery sand and clear blue water. Lalin and Jose Miguel immediately tore through the house, unleashing energy they had stored up during the two-hour car trip.

Lourdes arrived an hour later in a station wagon packed with her three children and two maids. The sisters embraced as if they had not seen each other for years. Lourdes' children ran to meet their cousins, and the house became filled with laughter and shouts. Soon they could hear the cousins arguing over who would get which beds.

The house was located within walking distance to the Club Kawama, a semiprivate club that also served as a hotel. Adelaida and Lourdes chose the room farthest away from the children's wing for their father, as well as a room opening onto the garden for Mike.

Lourdes and Adelaida then called a meeting of the children. They struggled to keep still as their mothers instructed them on the house rules: No going to the beach alone. No talking to strangers. Each must have a buddy to go into the water. They must have breakfast in the morning. They could play in the sand and swim from eight to eleven. They must take a nap in the afternoon, dinner at seven, everyone in bed by nine. And they must have permission to visit a friend's house. The bikes had to be ridden against the traffic. The children readily agreed, not because they would comply, but because they wanted to avoid a fight with their mothers.

Lourdes had two boys, Julio and Manuel, and a daughter named after herself. The cousins were roughly the same age and liked each other. As soon as the meeting was over, the maids took the luggage to the rooms. Within minutes, the children had changed into swimsuits and ran to the beach to catch the last waves of a glorious afternoon.

Lourdes dropped languorously on a porch chair to watch them play in the shimmering clear water. Adelaida fixed a pair of Cuba Libres and then joined her. The two sisters were a study in contrasts. Lourdes was blonde and petite with short hair, showing the effects of the summer sun. Adelaida was tall, tanned, and dark-haired with long, beautiful legs. The one physical feature that united them was the structure of their faces: highly sculpted and beautifully proportioned with an aura of refinement.

"I've never felt more tired! I don't remember the drive being so long," Lourdes said, leaning back into her chair and propping her feet on a small coffee table. She took a long sip of her Cuba Libre. "You should have seen them go wild when they saw the water—you know, when you drive over that beautiful bridge? They wouldn't stop jumping and shouting! I had to stop the car to calm them down." She cocked a thumb toward the inside the house. "Eulalia wasn't much help. She slept most of the time. I guess she stayed up most of the night with her boyfriend."

"That's the problem with young maids," Adelaida said.

"I don't know how they find the energy to stay up most of the night. I tell you, when Julio comes home, I'm ready to go to bed and sleep."

"Well, things change. You think it'll never happen to you. Then, a little at a time, while we're caught up in our lives, everything we know is fundamentally shifting, like the sand over there." Adelaida squinted at the shore. She quickly tallied the number of heads to make sure all the children were accounted for. The sisters listened for a moment to the sounds of frolicking children, whose shouts and laughter were muffled by the sea breeze and breaking waves.

Lourdes continued, "I hope Julio and I can get reacquainted here. It seems as if it's been years since we had sex." Her sister turned sharply, and she quickly added, "That's not really the case, but it's been a long time. Are we so old?"

Adelaida took a sip. "Yes, we are, but that shouldn't matter. Men sometimes get very busy." Adelaida softly touched her gold necklace. "There was a time when I was worried sick by Jose Maria's constant travel. Now I can see how much he enjoys being with the children and me. After a long trip to one of the sugar mills, he loves to spend time around the house. He's still thoughtful and considerate."

"Sometimes, I'd like Julio to take a trip or two and relax. He's always coming and going to meetings," Lourdes said. She suddenly brightened and asked, "What have you heard from Maria Alicia? Is she coming to Varadero with her parents?"

Adelaida slyly smiled. "Yes, she'll be here soon. Her father just bought a Prowler at the Miami boat show. He's bringing it down, navigating it all by himself. Maria Alicia promised to take us fishing in it!"

Lourdes said, "I thought she and Mike had fallen for each other, but he's so reserved. It's hard to know what he's thinking. Maybe we should give a cocktail party—how about Saturday? He and Maria Alicia make such a cute pair. I wish Mother could see them!"

Adelaida turned her attention to the beach and called out, "Boys and girls, time to come in! It's getting late. We have to dress for dinner. It's time to come inside."

That night the boys had a pillow fight. Lourdes had to go upstairs twice to calm them down. In another room, Lalin and the younger Lourdes whispered secrets to each other. By ten o'clock, Lourdes was ready to go to bed, but before going to her room, she called home. No one answered. A few minutes later, Adelaida got a call from Jose Maria asking how she and the children were, and for details about the trip.

Early the next morning, Lourdes wandered into the kitchen. She was ready for a cup of coffee, but the cook had just begun to boil water. Julio had not called her the night before, and while she waited for her cup, she sat on the porch, facing the sea. The breeze had not started. The ocean was placid and only timid waves disturbed the white sand. She watched the birds chasing a school of sardines and remembered the first time Mike had learned to use the cast net. He brought back a pail full of small, thrashing, glistening bodies to be fried by Estrella and eaten with a squirt of lime. She closed her eyes. "How things have changed!" Their last time in Varadero, her mother was alive. She had met Julio here twelve summers ago. He was tall, muscular, with a smile that exuded confidence, and those eyes! He crewed for the Biltmore, and his crew had lost the race at the annual rowing regatta. She noticed him after the regatta on the beach in front of the Club Náutico de Varadero: tanned, shirtless, and sporting tight wet woolen crew shorts and sun-bleached hair. They met that evening at a party at the International Hotel and danced until two. The next morning, he showed up at their beach house and asked permission from her mother to take her out. Smiling, he claimed that since he was in training, he had to be a perfect gentleman: no drinking. "Just like a monk," he said with a laugh. Her mother allowed Lourdes to go, but with Adelaida as their chaperone. Jose Maria, who was already Adelaida's fiancé, met them at the cabaret, where Julio, true to his word, contented himself with water while the other three enjoyed Veuve Cliquot. That night when he said good night, Julio stole a kiss from her.

Adelaida's footsteps startled Lourdes from her daydream. "Did you rest well?"

Lourdes smiled absently. Adelaida rambled on as she pulled up a chair and tried to find a small side table for her coffee. "I couldn't sleep! I missed the sound of the air-conditioning unit in my bedroom. The sound of the waves is soothing, but it seems I have to have the whirring noise of that damned air-conditioner. Father's right. It's better to use a mosquito net and an electric fan."

She had barely drawn a breath when she was on to her next topic. "Well, we better start making phone calls! I want to be sure that ours is the first big party of the season. Who do you think has arrived?"

They sat down, each one with their address books, and started to create a list. The sisters' cocktail party was for everyone who was anyone in Varadero's society. It was set for six-thirty and they knew how to do it right. The evening of the party, Lourdes and Adelaida mingled with the guests, while seeing to it that the maids passed trays full of croquettes and small sandwiches. Two bartenders from the Kawama Club served gin and tonics, whiskey sours, Cuba Libres, mojitos, Scotch and waters, daiquiris, and Dubonnets. The partygoers clustered under the shadow of the porch. The men wore Lacoste polos or *guayaberas* with white slacks; the women, silk beach pants. This scene was repeated every Friday and Saturday during the summer at different homes. The guests included the same group of friends who had known each other since primary school, who went to the same clubs, dated among themselves, prayed in the same churches, married within their circle, and gossiped about each other. The men discussed politics, the price of sugar, and when alone, their latest conquest or the newest crop of girls at the Conga Club.

When the party started, Don Miguel stood alone in a corner, looking out toward the sea. Before long, friends joined him to engage in small talk, finding or feigning interest in the most inconsequential or wearisome of topics, like the weather, the rate of growth in Varadero, their new apartment in Florida, the latest business deal, the failing health of an older friend, their last fishing trip, or a golf round at the small DuPont golf course. Don Miguel realized that the only people he now truly enjoyed spending time with was his family. The pressure to say the right things at the right time, to pay attention to the description of a friend's pursuit of a business venture, his last purchase, or exploit was exhausting. He just didn't care.

At that moment he realized he wanted to see Patricia again. Being with her was different. He was excited when he talked to her. She intrigued him because she didn't have airs. She was interested in what he said, not as a social exercise, but really interested. She asked questions and smiled when he admitted that he didn't have an answer to her question. How delicate she had been as she extended her hand to thank him for the night, slowly closing the door, keeping her eyes on him as he turned away.

Mike's arrival jolted Don Miguel's musing. He briskly greeted his father with a kiss, briefed him about the trip, and then excused himself to go to talk with Laureano, who was talking to Julio. Laureano was talking about the absence of honest political figures in the present political environment, while Julio's position was that it really didn't matter, because in Cuba a free political environment had never existed, so there could not be good political figures. Soon Mike found himself engrossed by Laureano's discourse. He was startled as a smiling Maria Alicia tapped him on the shoulder. She wore a white linen dress, stunning in its simplicity.

"Hi, Mike," she said. "You look tanned. Are you sure you haven't been playing tennis every day instead of cow punching?" Her hair was cleanly pulled back, and she wore a simple silver necklace, but no makeup besides a swipe of vivid red lipstick. Her eyes glimmered with mischief.

"You . . . you look so beautiful," Mike stammered. He noticed the way her white dress contrasted with her tanned skin and how her smile seemed to offer a world full of joy and sophistication. Adelaida stood next to Maria Alicia with a wide smile. His sister gave Mike a quick kiss. "Welcome back, *hermanito,*" and quickly left to greet other guests.

Mike asked Maria Alicia if she wanted her drink refreshed. "Sure, why not?" she said, and they walked to the bar. Then Mike noticed his father had been left standing alone. "Have you met my father?" he asked her.

"Yes, I have. I met your parents years ago at a party at my house. I'd love to say hello to him."

They retraced their steps. "Father, this is Maria Alicia Suarez y Garcia."

Don Miguel stood erect and waited for Maria Alicia to extend her hand in greeting.

"My father knows you well," she said to him. "He's always said that you have the best horses. It's a pity that he doesn't ride, but prefers boats. My parents will be coming later. I'm sure they'll be happy to see you."

"I grew up with your father, *El Gordo.* We went to the same school.

Even then he was interested in boats and fishing. How's your mother? She, like you, is a gorgeous lady. She was a very good friend of Adelaida's."

Don Miguel offered Maria Alicia a seat and proceeded to do most of the talking. Mike looked on, surprised by his father's sudden energy. After a while Laureano, tired of preaching in the desert, joined them, while Maria Alicia continued to laugh at Don Miguel's jokes and stories.

El Gordo finally arrived with his wife and invited Mike's entire family to spend the next day on his new boat. The party wound up at nine o'clock, at which point the wives asked their husbands to take them to the International Hotel to dance and gamble. Mike invited Maria Alicia along, and she accepted after getting her mother's permission to go.

At the casino, Julio was lucky at blackjack, while Maria Alicia and Mike tried their luck at the roulette wheel. They danced and drank, and when the casino closed at two o'clock in the morning, they reluctantly left and slowly drove back to their homes.

Mike escorted Maria Alicia to her house. The walls were of the limestone prevalent in the nearby hills, giving the house a clean, textured exterior, a reminder that at one time the whole area was part of the sea. In front, a large blue-tiled swimming pool was bordered by a great veranda. Maria Alicia's father, who had sugar mills and plantations, had built the house after the end of World War II, when the island floated on money, and the traditional way to spend it, after buying jewelry for your wife and mistress, was to lavish it on a home.

Maria Alicia asked Mike to sit with her by the pool. It was a moonless night with a gentle breeze; the only sound was the soft, rhythmic beat of the waves. They spoke in hushed voices about everything and nothing, and after an hour, they walked to the beach, barefoot, letting the waves wash over their feet. She spoke about her sisters, about the excitement in her father's eyes when he described his new boat. Mike talked about the land, about animals, horses, and Mitzi sleeping under his bed and following him around, about the sound of the drums during the night, the simple life of the *guajiros*, his studies, his sometimes feeling out of place in the north, how he missed the tropical sun, the flowers, the smell of the newly-cut pastures, the sound of the wind rustling through the cane fields. She talked about her studies, how she wanted to be independent and able to decide what she wanted to be, and about her disagreements with her mother, who accused her of not caring about housekeeping, cooking, or French lessons at the Alliance Française. They laughed at how their parents would like to shape and control their lives. They walked until the morning light colored the water.

Maria Alicia challenged Mike to a race back to her house and took off. As Mike raced after her, he stumbled in the sand. Maria Alicia laughed, seeing him covered with sand, his blue *guayabera* wet all over and his hair falling over his eyes. She wet her hand and cleaned the sand from his face, moved his hair away from his eyes, and slowly gave him a small, gentle kiss. They quietly walked hand in hand back to the house.

By eight o'clock, *El Gordo* Suarez had his yacht ready, the ice chest full of soft drinks and beer. He waited at the dock, smoking his first cigar. Maria Alicia and Maria, her mother, arrived with two hampers full of sandwiches. Don Miguel's group arrived a little bit later. "Welcome aboard," *El Gordo* said. "It's great that you could come. It was a fantastic party you girls hosted last night. You know how to throw one!" He indicated the boat as he instructed them, "You know the rules—Unless you have rubber soles, the shoes go in the basket. We'll be leaving in a few minutes. The weather report calls for a gorgeous day."

Maria went inside the galley as Maria Alicia and Mike headed for the bow and sat with their backs against the windshield. Julio climbed to the flying bridge to stand next to *El Gordo*, who revved the engines and gave Rigoberto orders to cast off. Rigoberto was their family gardener who doubled as a deckhand. Fifteen minutes later, the yacht was out at sea, and the color of the water became a deeper blue, indicating a clean and fast Gulf current, flowing at full force in the middle of the ocean. Flocks of seagulls and other birds flew in scattered directions, and occasionally one dove into the water. *El Gordo* slowed the boat, and Rigoberto prepared the tools for Gulf Stream deep-sea fishing, attaching the rigged ballyhoos to the lines. Rigoberto extended the outriggers and dropped a red and white teaser in the water. When the lines were out, Rigoberto shouted to *El Gordo* that they were ready to fish. *El Gordo*, a mild person during the week, transformed himself into a Latin version of Captain Bligh. Julio, who had spent the first part of the trip selling himself to Maria Alicia's father as a great stockbroker, abandoned the would-be client for a fighting chair. Don Miguel went to the bridge and took a seat next to *El Gordo*.

By ten o'clock they still had not gotten a bite. The bright sun and the cloudless sky made the day blazingly hot. The girls sunned on the foredeck. The water was placid; no white caps disturbed the slowly rolling waves. *El Gordo* looked for signs of fish as Rigoberto stood on the bow of the boat, looking for birds or the bill of a sailfish or a marlin.

El Gordo turned to Don Miguel. "You know, this is the life. I work all week and worry. I worry about this. I worry about that. I worry about everything. How I am doing on my sugar contracts? Should I sell short? Should I borrow money and buy more land? Can I buy a plantation for its quota? Will it be better to replant the sugarcane? Yet when I set foot on my boat, my anxieties disappear."

Don Miguel agreed with a smile. "Well said. Just as you have your boat, I have my horses. When I ride, I'm in control. The horse turns and moves just because he senses that I've slightly changed and moved my body. When we go deep into the farm and I don't hear the sound of a motor, only the singing of birds or a cow calling for its calf, and the sun is shining on my face and I feel the gentle breeze, that's when I'm fully alive."

El Gordo nodded as he continued to scout the sea, looking for birds. "I feel my tension draining away when I'm getting ready to leave the office for the boathouse. I'm a different man. If I want to fish, I fish! If want to go to the Keys, in a few hours I can be at Cayo Sal. Best of all, I forget. I forget that I lack control and I'm subject to other persons' wishes and commands. They say, 'Don't do this, don't do that. The law says—Be careful, Lobo is shorting the market. The unions will not allow you to use herbicides. Get dressed. We have a black tie affair tonight. Be nice to him. He's a friend of your mother's.'" By this point the two men were smiling together. "Here, it's different. It's just Rigoberto, the sea, and me. I love it!"

"I can't afford a boat, they cost too much. But I do love the sea." Don Miguel laughed. "That's why I have friends with boats!"

They both laughed. "Miguelito, you can buy me and sell me three times over, and you would never know the difference. I was talking to your son-in-law Julio and he—"

Suddenly one of the lines tore from the clip of the outrigger, and

Rigoberto ran aft. "One hit on the port line!" The line started to run at a high speed from the reel. Rigoberto took the rod in his hand and gave it a strong pull. The rod twisted as he hooked the fish. Julio took the rod as Rigoberto strapped the leather fighting-belt on him. The sailfish jumped in the distance, and the fight began.

"Easy, take it easy. The boat will help you. You don't have to do all the work," *El Gordo* said as he followed the direction of the line and backed the boat in so that Julio could retrieve more line. Rigoberto told him to increase the brake pressure on the reel so the sailfish would have more resistance. Julio pulled back on the rod, helped with his back, and as the rod went down, he reeled in line. Julio's strong arms were capable of handling the work of pulling the rod back and forth. Lourdes stood behind him, cheering him on.

"Julio, you have a good one. Bring it in!"

In the meantime, Rigoberto asked Mike to help him bring in the other lines to avoid any entanglement.

Julio's face showed the fight's exertion and he swore at the fish under his breath, "I'm going to get you. I'm going to get you." His arms began to tire. The sailfish flew one more time; the beauty of its blue, white, and silver colors glistened above the deep blue water. As the fish was brought nearer to the boat, the group saw its bill breaking the surface. Rigoberto took the end of the steel leader and pulled the fish up, and with the bat, hit it on the head. The fish flipped and convulsed, its wide mouth open, gasping for water, and before it died, the colors of its skin shone most brilliantly. Rigoberto lifted the sailfish by its bill and dropped it in the starboard cooler, then cleaned the blood off the deck with buckets of salt water. *El Gordo* was jubilant as they raised a sailfish flag on the port outrigger.

Half an hour later, Rigoberto noticed a spot where birds were diving into the water, calling it to *El Gordo's* attention. He immediately increased speed. In a few minutes, the boat edged into the area where the birds fed. Rigoberto changed the leaders on the lines and used silver spoons instead of bait. *El Gordo*, who wanted some action, turned the controls over to Don Miguel and told Rigoberto to trade places with him. Huffing and puffing, he joined the rest of the men on the fishing deck.

In seconds, the first fish hit, and suddenly all of the four lines were whirring. The air filled with the sounds of the crickets and the excited voices of the men reeling medium-size bonitos and albacores on board. As soon as one was caught, the spoon went back into the water to catch another. The activity started to acquire a frenzied state, and smiles filled every face. There were repeated shouts of joy: "I got another one!" "Man, this one is bigger." "I bet you I'll catch ten in less than eight minutes."

Maria Alicia, noticing that Don Miguel was alone on the bridge, went up to sit next to him. "This is great fun. We have to share that sailfish, so I'll make sure that Mother invites you. She has a great recipe for *escabeche*. It takes such a long time, but it's worth the wait. Do you like it?"

"Oh, I love it," Don Miguel said.

After the frenzied fishing, Maria felt hot and tired and asked her husband to head back to Varadero. *El Gordo* was exhausted, too, and Maria Alicia took the helm. In less than half an hour, they saw the outlines of the International Hotel and the small DuPont castle. Maria Alicia loved the privacy of the beach east of the DuPont estate, so when she saw the tower of the DuPont's estate, she steered in a northeasterly direction to find a deserted area of beach. The wind had picked up and she went as near to the shore as they could. Rigoberto dropped anchor and set a ladder on the lee side of the boat.

Maria Alicia was the first one to jump into the water, and Mike followed. They were both powerful swimmers and reached the beach at the same time, only to find they had to wait for the others.

The older people stayed in the boat. Rigoberto swam the short distance with one hand held above the water, carrying a hamper full of sandwiches. On a second trip, he brought beer and soft drinks. Mike's sisters and their husbands followed, and the young couples had a picnic in a shaded grove.

After they ate, Mike and Maria Alicia started looking for *hicacos*, which grew there in abundance. She didn't have a container, so Mike took off his wet polo shirt and used it to carry the fruit. She teased Mike about the color of his chest and arms. "Look at you. You're a *guajiro*. Your belly is white, your chest is white, and you can see the outline of your shirt, while your face and arms are really tanned. We have to do something about it!" Mike laughed heartily in response.

Maria Alicia knew that she was in love. She sensed Mike's generosity and how attentive he was to her needs. Mike felt the same magnetic attraction. He carried the fruit like a faithful servant as Maria Alicia continued her search. He had never met anyone like her before. She could discuss art, and at the same time, navigate a boat. She was extraordinarily feminine and strong, she teased and laughed, yet was serious and sensitive. At one time he had thought he was in love with Rita—but how could one ever *know* about these things?

He had talked about her with Laureano, who had never met Rita, but he had said to Mike, "There are other fish in the sea. Forget it. It won't work. You're now like a dog that has found a bitch in heat. You're not thinking with your head." Mike was offended, but now he wondered if Laureano was right. He was at the beach, sunburned, with a girl he could unreservedly love.

Their harvesting over, Mike and Maria Alicia swam back to the boat. He carried the hicacos bundled in his shirt, his hand held up high above the water. Yes, just like a servant.

They arrived at the dock around six o'clock. The last half hour everyone had dozed except Rigoberto, who handled the boat. After a full day together, the good-byes were short. *El Gordo* stayed to supervise Rigoberto as he cut, cleaned, and packaged the fish. Mike offered Maria Alicia a ride, which she declined, as she had come with her mother. Mike persisted, asking to see her that night, and Maria Alicia smiled and said, "OK, I hope you're not too tired. I'll wait for you. Eight-thirty?"

As they drove home, Maria queried her daughter about Mike. Maria was not unhappy, for she knew Don Miguel's family, but she wanted to be sure.

The next Sunday was the annual President's Cup rowing regatta. The crews had been training for four months, and during the training, the club's boathouses had been transformed into convents of a sort: no smoking, no drinking, and no partying. The coaches were stricter than the mother superior of Poor Clare novices. The coaches told the rowers: no masturbation, no going out with *putas*. "There'll be enough sex after the season. You can then pick and choose." Every morning they toiled on the rowing machines and lifted weights. In the late afternoon they rowed escorted by the club's motor launch. Four men and a coxswain waited for the moment of glory, their payoff after months of grueling training, hard work, and an unaccustomed ascetic life.

The regatta was held in the morning, when the sea was as calm as a lake. Varadero Beach had been decked out as if it were a fairground. The official regatta boat flew nautical flags, and the judges, umpires, and representatives of the clubs looked grave—with their captains' caps, blue blazers, white pants, gold braids in their caps, and the insignia of the club on their jacket pocket. The verandas surrounding the Club Náutico de Varadero's old Victorian gingerbread clubhouse were full of members and guests. All types of boats, yachts, powerboats, sailboats, and skiffs sailed in front of the clubhouse, jockeying for anchoring positions with good sight lines. A small lonely motorboat of the Cuban navy policed the area, as if order could be imposed.

Maria Alicia, Mike, Lourdes, Adelaida, and Jose Maria with their children had gone to Mass at the small brick church across from the clubhouse. At the Mass, the Club Nautico's crew stood at attention in the center aisle, praying for victory.

El Gordo's boat, packed with friends, flew the burgee of the Habana Yacht Club. Rigoberto, in his best whites, stood on the foredeck, and *El Gordo*, to be close to his guests, sat at the controls in the main cabin. They anchored next to the finish line. Their penance for their efficiency and speed would be to wait under a hot sun until the race started.

Vendors with flags and balloons of all colors walked the beach. The *piruleros* with their multicolored cone candies wrapped in brown paper moved with the grace of dancers in a conga line. Vendors sold hot peanuts in greasy brown paper sacks, while others sold tamales, *con pica* or *sin pica*. Some spectators rented floats and black inner tubes to watch the regatta while floating in the water. People had come from all over the region, from Cardenas, Matanzas, even from Havana. Young and old, they stood on the beach in front of the Club Nautico. The club members themselves observed the crowded beach from their shaded haven, drinks in hand.

Adelaida and Jose Maria herded their children among the crowd in front of the club. The kids were attracted to the birds and small figurines made of seashells, the pennants, and straw hats for sale. At every turn,

Lalin tried to convince her mother to buy her the latest shell figurine she had fallen in love with until Adelaida felt the only word she had said for hours was "no." Eventually, she located a suitable spot, spread the beach towels, and sat on the sand, enjoying a few minutes of peace in the midst of the bedlam, surrounded by a sea of strangers.

The race had three false starts. When it finally started, the Club Nautico scull pulled out in front with a spurt of power, but by the midpoint the scull of the Habana Yacht Club started to catch up. As the boats were nearing the finish line, the crowd became excited and loud, muffling the rhythmic sound of the oars hitting the water. Club Nautico won by at least two lengths, followed by the Biltmore and the Yacht Club sculls. The celebratory mood of the crowd swelled, and the Club Nautico's fans ran to the their crew and surrounded them as the other crews took off their shirts and gave them to the winners' crew, who strung them around their necks, like trophies won in an Aztec battle. President Batista presented the silver cup to the commodore of the Club Náutico de Varadero.

The friends on *El Gordo*'s boat had a great time. There were enough members from the favored clubs, and a full-scale celebration started in the middle of the race. Even so, Maria Alicia noticed a change in Mike's demeanor. He was pleasant to her but appeared worried.

That night Jose Maria, Adelaida, and Mike went to Maria Alicia's house on the way to the hotel nightclub. A tired Rigoberto opened the door and announced their arrival. Maria made Mike promise her that he was going to take good care of her daughter, since the family would be breakfasting early at a friend's house in DuPont. Maria Alicia showed up wearing Mike's favorite outfit, the white linen dress that accentuated her tan and the beauty of her black hair.

The nightclub at the hotel was jammed. Every few minutes a new table was brought in for a heavy-tipping patron, adding to the congestion on the dance floor, but no one cared. It was the place to be seen, to flaunt the fact that you had enough money, contacts, or influence to sit near the dance floor on the biggest night of the summer season at Varadero. Mike and Maria Alicia tried to dance, but they could hardly move. The air-conditioner was overwhelmed because of the packed room, and the heat became oppressive, so they moved to a table near the pool bar where they could talk.

Maria Alicia clasped Mike's hand. "What's worrying you? You're not here tonight. Your mind seems very far away."

Mike hesitated. "I had a call from Ricardo, our new *mayoral*. I'm having personnel problems. Manuel, one of our best employees, is playing power games in my absence. I haven't talked to my father yet, but I should leave tomorrow."

Maria Alicia was silent for a moment. "Is that all? What else worries you?"

Mike got up and lit a cigarette. "Yes, I'm worried. I hate to leave you. I've only been with you a short time, but I feel that I've known you forever, and I want us to be together all the time." He flicked his fingers, scratching the surface of their small table. "Worst of all, I know that I can't offer you everything you'd like in your life."

Maria Alicia pulled back sharply. "Mike, please . . . that's not true. I'll miss you, too, but how do you know what I want? Do you know how I feel about you? Don't you sense it? I love to be with you. I love to hear your stories, and I like it when you touch me. But I'm worried, too. What happens to you when we're together and you become silent and unreachable?"

He looked up, startled. He hadn't thought of it that way. "I'm sorry, sometimes I'm moody. I like to think, to meditate—"

"But how do you think I feel when you go into your shell, even if you're sitting next to me?"

"I don't know," he said quietly.

"You don't ask. Have you asked me if I love you? Have you asked if I want to be with you? You have to know that I'll miss you, too."

Encouraged, Mike moved close to her. "I'm sorry . . . I don't express myself well."

"*Bobo*, you know I love you. Maybe I should have said more. I don't want you to go." She picked up both his hands and held them.

"I just want to give you the best of everything. I love you."

"I love you, too," she replied in a low clear voice.

Now that they had declared themselves, they walked to the beach. The sand was packed and hard, and Maria Alicia held her shoes in her hand. They stopped several times to look longingly at each other. They could hear the band playing romantic music, *boleros*, and old songs. Finally, after half an hour of walking, they joined their group at the cabaret. Adelaida saw Maria Alicia's tender face and understood immediately that something had changed. Adelaida asked them if they wanted to leave at once and forget about the breakfast party. It did not take much persuasion in the packed room to get people to agree to go.

At Maria Alicia's house, the lovers sat near the pool and Mike said, "I never thought I was going to say this. I've never felt like this before. I'm in love with you. I want to marry you."

Maria Alicia looked into his eyes. "I love you, too," she said, and kissed him slowly and softly.

Mike was elated and relieved "I didn't know what to do. I wanted to say it, but I was afraid. I'm still afraid that you won't want to share my life at the farm."

"But I'll be with you," Maria Alicia said.

"I don't want you to sacrifice your dreams for me. I love you and I'll always love you."

They reached out and fell into each other's arms. Mike continued, "The only thing that's important to me is your happiness. If I sound like an idiot, forgive me. Sometimes I can't express myself well. I only know that I love you." He picked up her hand again, and held it as if he would never let it go.

They embraced for a long while, merging as one, until finally Maria Alicia pulled away. "You have a long drive ahead of you. Be careful. I'll be waiting for you. Come back as soon as you can. I need you now more than ever." They slowly walked through the garden and kissed one more time before saying good night.

Early the next morning, activities started at the beach house. The children had their breakfast while Adelaida and Lourdes, still in their robes, supervised the maids, who brought out cereals, fruits, and milk. Don Miguel appeared, kissed the grandchildren and his daughters, and got a cup of coffee. Mike came from his room, dressed and ready to leave. Lourdes and Adelaida wanted to know more about Maria Alicia, but before they had a chance, Mike asked his father for a few moments alone.

"Dad, I spoke with Ricardo yesterday. He called me. I'm going back to the farm."

"What's going on?"

"Ricardo is having problems with Manuel. He wants to spend more money than we've budgeted. Hire more help, prepare more animals for the shows."

His father lit his first cigar. "Do you want me to go with you?"

"No, I can handle it."

Don Miguel assented. "You're running the farm. Be careful with Manuel, though. You can't fire him for what he's trying to do. He's a good man, but jealous of Ricardo and you. He's valuable to us." Don Miguel waved the tip of his cigar to cement his point. "Ricardo is right, but don't get in the middle of their quarrel. You have to be above it."

Mike agreed, and then softened his tone. "I have something else to tell you. I proposed to Maria Alicia, and she accepted."

His father reared back in surprise. "Have you thought it over carefully? Both of you are very young. Give it time."

"Yes, I've thought about it. I love her."

Don Miguel couldn't have been happier. He embraced Mike warmly. "She's the right girl. I've known her family for years."

"I haven't formally asked her parents, but I'll do so when I come back. Please don't tell the girls until I talk to them."

"*El Gordo* is a great friend of mine. At one time, when we were young, we were very close. Maria was a good friend of your mother." Don Miguel was beaming. "I love Maria Alicia. But you better talk to them now."

Mike realized that it would be impossible to keep the secret for so long. "Thanks, Father. I'll do that."

20

Manuel

MIKE DROVE SLOWLY, stopping often to refuel with coffee, and arrived at the *batey* at six o'clock that evening. Mitzi trotted out to greet him, followed by Ricardo, Cuca, and Paulino. Paulino said, "Welcome to paradise! It's nice of you to remember that we, poor peons, still exist in the middle of this great republic." He eyed Mike's deep tan. "Did you get tired of sunning yourself? I knew you had taste, but I never thought you'd go to such extremes to be like me. Your color is almost as dark as Fernando's!" He lowered his voice, and with a firm handshake added, "Welcome back. I know you had to return."

"I was about ready to come back." Mike shrugged, hiding the real reason. "It's good to see you all again! How's your love life? Are you still visiting the plantation?"

"Yes, but not every night. I have to work, you know. Cuca likes to keep me busy," said Paulino with a laugh.

Mike turned to her. "I'll have a small dinner, because I'm not too hungry. When you plan to have it ready, call me, but I'm in no hurry. I'll be in the office."

As the group walked toward the house, Mike sidled up next to Ricardo. "Thanks for calling me. You did the right thing. I talked to Father. He's in agreement, but he wants to be sure that Manuel understands. Where is he? At the Gomez plantation?"

Mike and Ricardo left for the office, while Paulino took the small amount of luggage that Mike had brought.

"Ricardo, what do you think Manuel is thinking? Has anybody he's hired worked for more than thirty days?"

"I don't know. I think he may want to test you to find how much you'll let him do without your direct approval. He's not talking too much to me. I believe he resents that I'm above him and you give me instructions, and I'm the one who talks to you instead of him."

They settled on a good time for Mike to speak with Manuel to resolve the issue. Before they parted, Ricardo said, "Oh, and Mike, I saw Rita at the telephone office. You need to talk to her. She's not a happy girl." Mike nodded, but that was not a topic he wanted to discuss any further.

Mike planned to call his father after gathering more information from other employees. He had to confirm without a doubt that Ricardo's version of events was true. He drove the jeep to the back pastures to see Martinito, met with Arturo, and visited Alfred, who asked for permission to poison the wild dogs that were killing his sheep.

That evening, before the employees sat down for their dinner, Mike called Manuel to his office. He did not want Ricardo to be present at the meeting, as he would tell Ricardo later. Manuel came all dressed up, since he was going to go to the Gomez plantation after dinner, and sat across the desk from Mike.

"Mike, Ricardo told me you wanted to talk to me tonight. Did you have a good trip? How is your father feeling? Is he better?"

"Yes, he is doing very well. We were all together at Varadero beach," Mike said, smiling. "Listen, I need to talk to you. It's important to have a clear line of communication. I won't be able to be here all the time. I have to spend time in Havana, and other places, and I want you to understand that when I'm not here, Ricardo is in charge. I gave him strict orders not to hire any more personnel." Manuel's face had turned sullen, but Mike pressed on. "I know you talked with him, and he told you so, but after that talk, you hired two more people to help you at the show barn. I want them to be fired tomorrow." Manuel looked shocked, but Mike was in no mood for arguments. "Also, I'll decide, with your recommendation, what animals we bring to be part of the show string. I have to be able to control our costs. I don't want to spend more money on the show string. We have enough show animals. If we sell one, we can replace it." Mike was not done, however. "Manuel, you have to talk to me about these things. If something is bothering you, you can write me a letter or, better yet, call me long-distance. I'll answer you. Do you understand?"

Manuel was surprised at the severity of Mike's tone. He had in his mind an image of a little boy that liked to ride ponies, not this young man who sat across him and gave orders. His first reaction was of anger. Manuel thought, "Who does this pip-squeak think he is?" He did not care for Ricardo as a *mayoral*. He should have been given that position. Then he realized that it was not worth a fight. Manuel glanced at the floor and said, "Yes, sir. I'll talk to you in the morning. I'm happy that your father is feeling better. When is your father coming back? When you talk to him, give him my regards." He quickly left the room, and Mike let him go without saying a word, as there never was a nice way to reprimand an older man. The painful task was over.

Mike knew he also had to see Rita, and he knew what to say. He did not want to wait. He went to the kitchen and told Cuca, "I have to run an errand in the *pueblo*. I'm not too hungry. Leave food in the fridge." He drove to Rita's house, and as he drove through the streets he heard the familiar theme song of a soap opera that had a fanatical following, *The Right to Be Born* by the Cuban novelist Felix B. Caignet.

When he knocked, Rita's mother opened the door greeting him with a big smile. "Mike! How nice to see you. You've been like a lost soul. I saw your picture several times in the rotogravure of the *El Diario de la Marina*. You're having a great time. Did you come to see Rita?"

"Yes, ma'am."

"I'm so sorry, you should have called. It would have saved you the trip. She's out tonight. Do you remember that nice young man Facundo Martinez y Garcia? They just made him the new assistant manager at the Royal Bank of Nova Scotia. He's such a good, honest, hardworking man."

Mike was elated to hear this news. "Yes, I bank with him."

"Well, don't just stand there. Come in! Rita will be so disappointed that she missed you!"

"I'm sorry, too," Mike said. "Well, I—"

"She'll be back tomorrow," her mother continued. "She went with Facundito to Camagüey. He is going to meet the bank's manager from Havana. They have some sort of bank meeting, followed by a dinner at the

Gran Hotel. She has to be in early tomorrow morning to work at that telephone exchange." She pursed her lips. "They really abuse her, the hours!"

"Yes, she always has the tougher shifts. Well, tell her I—"

"Please, Mike, the program has just started. Do you want to watch it? The grandfather is very sick. He can hardly talk. You see, he had a stroke, and he has something very important to say to his granddaughter. It's about the young doctor she's dating. Come, come, and sit with me."

Mike, half dazed, felt as if he had fallen into a whirlpool. He hesitated, and then entered the living room and sat on the sofa. For thirty long minutes, he watched the soap with Rita's mother, and with each passing moment, he became more upset. How did he allow himself to be caught up in such a tawdry affair? Yet he could not excuse himself until after the last commercial. Finally, Mike rose to his feet. "I'm sorry. I can't stay any longer. I have to be home for supper."

"I understand. Thank you for such wonderful company." Rita's mother followed Mike to the front door. "Wasn't that quite a show? The grandfather hasn't talked yet! We don't know who her father really is. The tension frazzles my nerves sometimes!"

"It was a pleasure to watch it with you," Mike said. "The script and the actors are quite good."

"Oh, what talent!" she gushed.

"Please, do tell Rita that I came by to see how she was doing. I'm glad to know she's well." Mike waved back to Rita's mother, who was standing at the front door.

"Please call again. I'll tell her that you dropped by," she said, gently closing the door behind her.

21

Dinner at La Zaragozana

DON MIGUEL SPOKE to Patricia in a tentative voice. "My son Mike is back in Havana. I'd like you to meet him and his fiancée, Maria Alicia Suarez. Would you join us for dinner this Friday night?"

"Yes, of course, I'd love to meet them. It would be nice to meet your son. At what time?"

"I'll pick you up around seven-thirty."

Mike wanted to meet Patricia, and Friday morning he spoke on the phone with his sisters and Maria Alicia about the dinner. Meanwhile, his father was in excellent spirits; he had even jokingly asked Georgina about her boyfriends.

Mike and his father arrived at Maria Alicia's house early and paid respects to her mother, who was polite but chilly. She had been one of Adelaida's closest friends, and to see her widower going out with a girl as young as her daughter! *El Gordo* invited them to stay for a drink, but they declined. In his view, his friend should have set up this young hussy as his mistress and avoid all the gossip. Yet he admired Don Miguel. He had principles and he was setting a good example to his son: A true gentleman does not keep a mistress. Amid the strained politeness Maria Alicia appeared, and after the usual flurry of kisses and goodbyes, they left to pick up Patricia.

Patricia, nervous because Miguel was now late, waited at the street corner below her apartment. The wind had disrupted her careful hairdo, which upset her because she wanted to look perfect before his family. Don Miguel got out of the car, followed by Mike, and introduced her first to him and then to Maria Alicia, who nodded her head. They headed to La

Zaragozana, where they ordered paella and beer. At the table, Maria Alicia and Patricia carefully examined each other. Maria Alicia noticed that Patricia's dress was made of expensive fabric and very well cut, but she did not wear expensive jewelry. Her earrings and necklace blended well with the color of her dress. Maria Alicia could now tell her mother that Miguel's date at least knew how to dress. Patricia's delicate features and graceful manner surprised both Maria Alicia and Mike.

Patricia also analyzed Maria Alicia: She had the physical assurance of a person who had never lacked for anything, even though she wore a simple dress. Her only possible affectation was a necklace of perfect pearls, not too big in diameter, which she wore with the ease of someone born to it.

Mike and his father talked about baseball and about the price of sugar and cattle, the minister, and Comillas. His father carefully watched Maria Alicia's reaction. Eventually, the women started to make small talk and later they left together to powder their noses.

Don Miguel leapt at the opportunity. "What do you think?"

"She seems shy," Mike commented neutrally. "She's very pretty, though, has class, and knows how to behave, but she seems so young, younger than me, I'd guess." He gave his father a probing look. "What do you know about her? Her family? How she feels about you? What do you plan to do?"

Before his father could answer, the two women returned to the table, laughing.

When Maria Alicia returned home later that evening, her mother was waiting in the living room.

"What do you think of the girl? Is she a tramp?"

Maria Alicia was shocked at the question. "She's very attractive, but she told me she's surprised that Don Miguel is calling on her. Right now, she's studying computers, and then she'd like to work at a bank." She saw her mother's face start to relax. "She got along with Mike and me, and I liked her, too. I don't think they're lovers. I may invite her one night to have dinner with us, if you don't object."

"But what kind of girl—?" her mother interjected.

"Report concluded. I'm going to bed now. I have the feeling that you're going to be very busy tomorrow morning, or maybe tonight, calling all your friends and giving them a detailed account of this conversation.

Please, be gentle. She's a very nice girl. I love you. Good night." With that, she stood up and gave her mother a kiss on the cheek and left the room.

Patricia felt that Don Miguel was nervous that night, and when he kissed her at the door, he was more aggressive, more forward than any other time before. He held her in a tighter embrace. He was not the shy man she had met before. She did not reject his advances. She enjoyed them, because they showed his interest in her. She might even want to be closer with him.

She went into the bathroom, brushed her teeth, and wrapped herself in her favorite old robe. She found herself reflecting about Maria Alicia and Mike. She felt at ease with Maria Alicia. She thought that they could confide in each other, or at least it seemed that way when they were together in the ladies room. Maria Alicia seemed so open, or maybe that was the way those girls talked. "Let's get together. I'd like you to meet my friends." Was this just all talk?

Mike, she couldn't read. He was so reserved with her, but open with his father. They acted liked equals, laughed the same way, loved the same cigars, but there was a certain reticence. She had so much to consider.

She opened the windows of her room to let the breeze in and heard the reassuring sound of the waves hitting the Malecon and the honking of the cars: sounds of the night, the sounds of her Havana. She had planned to study that night, but her sister knocked, and they ended up talking until the soft light of a new morning illuminated her room.

Lourdes called Mike at seven-thirty in the morning. She was not pleased by his abrupt answers to her anxious questions. In desperation, Mike said, "Well, why don't you ask Father what his plans are? I don't think he knows. I don't think she knows, either."

Lourdes hung up the phone and immediately dialed Adelaida. Mike had just enough time to go to the kitchen to ask Estrella for his first cup of coffee when the phone rang again; it was Adelaida this time. "Lourdes just called me. She says that you approve of our father seeing and going out with this girl! How can you do that? You don't know her family. You don't know where she comes from, her background."

"Hold on, you're going too fast. I just met her for the first time last night."

"Lourdes also told me that she is very young, younger than Maria Alicia! No more than twenty-one years old!"

"Yes, she's young. She's also beautiful and seems to have a gentle disposition."

"I don't care. Father should not be dating such a young girl. And you're approving of his behavior. You men!"

"I just met her. I haven't talked to Father about her. It's his life."

"Have you gone crazy? Are you sick? Is that what you learned at your American university? Mother would be offended by your behavior."

Mike got irritated. "Look, I haven't approved or disapproved of my father's dating, if that's what you want to call it. If you want to call her by her name, her name is Patricia. Yes, Patricia Menendez. She's getting an education, which is better than what a lot of your friends have done with their lives." He paused to let that sink in a moment. "Please, leave Father alone. He seems to be in very good spirits. You should have seen him at the farm. Both of you should meet her, and then make up your minds after that." He knew what his sister's continued silence meant: disapproval. "I have to go to the office now. I leave for the farm tomorrow. Don't worry. It's not that bad. And I love you. Bye."

After he hung up, Estrella poured his cup of coffee, and she asked him, "Well, you met the young lady. What do you think?"

"She's fine," he said curtly and left for the office, leaving his coffee untouched. Why wouldn't these women leave his father in peace?

Maria Alicia got calls from her future sisters-in-law. Maria Alicia's mother called her friends, and her friends called their friends. That afternoon some of the ladies who played Canasta voiced their belief, based on excellent sources, that Don Miguel had eloped with a stewardess of Cubana Airlines, or that he was engaged to the daughter of a tobacco grower from Vuelta Abajo, or a that he was leaving the country and moving to Paris with a fifteen-year-old girl.

Mike, now at his office, had a phone conversation with Maria Alicia about his sisters' reactions. He was disappointed with his sisters and the way they had condemned Patricia without even meeting her. Maria Alicia was conciliatory. "Mike, it's difficult for them to see your point of view. My mother is upset as well. They're imagining all sorts of horrible consequences. Your father is not gaga. He knows what he's doing. I think we're all creating a *fait accompli* where one doesn't exist. Patricia hasn't made a decision to either marry or not marry your father. He hasn't even asked her! Everyone is causing a big uproar about a situation that's not what it seems to be. You know how much I love Adelaida, and yet she was almost rude to me on the phone. She was so upset. She's just worried about taking care of your father, about making sure he's not taken for a ride."

Mike looked forward to the farm, where he couldn't be reached. He now understood his father's phone policy. "I want to thank you. I know this isn't easy for you. Well, now you know my family better. I'm leaving first thing in the morning. The sugar harvest is now in full swing, and I have to be there. I understand that your father has already left for his plantations. Give my regards to your mother. I love you." Maria Alicia invited him to have an early dinner at her home, and he accepted.

Lustre entered his office with a copy of a morning paper. He pointed to the headlines. "It's not getting any better," he said as he dropped the paper on Mike's desk.

22

The Girls Meet

AROUND SEVEN THAT evening, Mike joined Maria Alicia and her mother for dinner at their home. Maria asked him about his father's health, and then launched into a discourse on how beautiful, kind, intelligent, and generous Mike's mother had been: a model of Catholic piety, dedicated to her children, loyal to her friends. She recalled that they had made their debut the same year at Sarra's home; how Adelaida had worn a gown from Worth in Paris; how they had played mah-jong with their mothers. Adelaida, according to Maria, excelled at the game. Shifting directions, she looked at Mike and asked, "Is your father going out with someone? That's what I hear."

Mike smiled before answering, and Maria Alicia quickly interjected, "Mother!"

Mike casually answered. "Oh yes. Don't you remember? Maria Alicia and I had dinner with her and Father last night. Her name is Patricia Menendez. She's from Pinar del Rio, and her father is a tobacco farmer. Let's see, and also my father has gone out with her several times. She's around Maria Alicia's age and is a lovely girl. That's all that I know."

Maria listened carefully but kept quiet, hoping Mike would say more. Mike smoothly moved to another topic. "About Father's health, he's actually in good shape. He's working hard and plans to stay in Havana for a while. As for me, I'm returning to the farm. As you know, the *zafra* calls."

"Are you nervous about the *alzados*? They aren't near any of our plantations or the sugar mill. Is anything happening at your farm?" Maria asked politely, now resigned to not hearing more about Don Miguel's young date.

"No, not at all. Everything's very quiet at the farm. Nothing is happening there," Mike said, pleased that he had successfully navigated away from the shoals. "I've heard that the situation is more serious around Sierra Maestra and Trinidad, but not in Camagüey. I wish we had a few hills. It's so flat there. The land is only good for sugar, rice, and cattle, not for revolutionaries," he joked.

"Be careful," Maria Alicia said.

Mike then explained his future plans for the farm. Maria, a skilled socialite, feigned curiosity, asking questions, even though she had no interest in Mike's details of running a farm. After dinner, Maria Alicia and Mike retired to the terrace and sat side by side on a bench. "I'm sorry about Mother. I didn't expect her to react this way. Your poor father! Everyone is trying to run his life, including me." She told him about the conversation she had had with Patricia and her plans to have her meet his sisters for lunch the next Friday.

Mike laughed and put his arm around Maria Alicia. "Do you know what you're getting into? You're fearless. You're not afraid of anything or anyone!"

"What's there to be afraid of?" Maria Alicia asked, and then leaned on him. "There's no reason why we shouldn't meet, for your father's sake especially."

Mike kissed her cheek. "I know you want to do what's best. That's why I love you so much."

Patricia was surprised that Maria Alicia invited her to have lunch. Maria Alicia, knowing that Lourdes, inevitably, was going to be late, told her to meet at twelve, Adelaida, twelve-thirty, and Patricia at one o'clock. On Friday afternoon, Maria Alicia was the first one to arrive at Kasalta restaurant. She selected a table for four in the corner of the terrace, near the street. She executed her plan like a general, strategically placing his divisions to confront a frontal attack by the enemy. Adelaida arrived on time and immediately noticed the table setting for four.

"Who else is coming?" Adelaida asked.

Maria Alicia smiled blandly. "It's a pleasant surprise. Let's wait for Lourdes, and then we can talk about it." Lourdes arrived just before one in a frenzy of activity; she gave a quick kiss to Maria Alicia and excused herself to go to the bathroom. She returned with a new application of powder and lipstick. "I'm sorry I'm late. Some last-minute things came up. I had to take care of them right away." Then she looked around at the table. "Who else is coming?"

Maria Alicia smiled again, and in a sweet voice said, "I thought you'd like to meet a new friend. You've asked so many questions about her. She may be able to answer them personally."

As if on cue, Patricia walked in. She wore the same simple dress she had worn when she first met Don Miguel, along with her small alligator bag. She approached Maria Alicia and kissed her on her cheek.

"Ladies, this is Patricia Menendez," Maria Alicia said. Turning to Patricia, she said, "You met Mike the other night. These are his sisters, Lourdes and Adelaida. I know you'll love them," she said warmly.

Patricia couldn't help but smile. "Yes, of course! How nice to meet you. Your father has said lovely things about you."

"It's nice to meet you," Adelaida replied warmly and extended her hand to Patricia. "How wonderful of you to join us. Please, sit down!"

Adelaida was taken aback by Patricia's appearance. She was more than surprised, she was intrigued. She had imagined a cheap-looking young woman in a tight dress with bad makeup, kewpie-red lips, blue mascara, large ass barely enclosed by her skirt, reeking of imitation French perfume.

Lourdes shifted nervously on her seat and glanced around the room. The restaurant was full of people she knew, and on her way in, she had greeted Julio's best client at a nearby table with a group of his friends. She bit her lips, played with her napkin, and took small sips from her glass of water. She defiantly looked at Maria Alicia, but determined not to make a scene as she played the role of an aggrieved matron. She was going to show this Maria Alicia that she had manners, more savoir faire, better breeding, and a worldlier demeanor than Maria Alicia and Patricia put together. That Patricia girl was sucking her father dry, she was sure of it. Still, Lourdes eked out a tight smile, a slight nod, and a stilted "Hi."

Maria Alicia understood the nuances of the situation and hastily asked for the menu. The more quickly they engaged in mundane chatter, the better. The captain knew the sisters and stopped at the table. He asked Adelaida about her daughter, and she reported how she was doing in school. The captain left and the waiter stepped in. Lourdes broke her near silence and ordered stone crabs, Patricia ordered a chef's salad, and Maria Alicia, the perfect hostess, ordered the same. At the beginning, there was very little talk. Patricia didn't want to say something that could be misinterpreted, and watched Maria Alicia for cues. Maria Alicia started chitchatting to lighten the silence suffocating the table. She addressed Lourdes, "How are the children doing now that they're back in school? They behaved so well in Varadero. I was so impressed by Lourdes. She has so much poise for a girl of her age!"

Lourdes answered in curt sentences. "Fine. They always like school. Yes. Yes, they're good. She's a very pious girl."

Maria Alicia tried again, but this time with Adelaida. "How is Jose Maria? Is he in town? We should play tennis when Mike returns. It won't be so hot then."

Adelaida, more relaxed, joined the conversation. "Oh, he's fine, he's back from the interior! I'm so glad. This is his busiest season. Now that he's sold all that machinery to the sugar mills, he worries about it working properly." She paused to glance at Patricia, and found her paying rapt attention. She turned back to Maria Alicia. "We'd love to play tennis with you and Mike. But you're far better than I, plus I'm a bit out of practice!" Then to Maria Alicia's surprise, she turned to Patricia. "Do you play tennis?"

"No, I don't, but I'd love to learn. Miguel says he plays tennis, too, but not in a long time. For myself, I enjoy horseback riding."

Lourdes looked at her with visible contempt. "Father is an excellent tennis player. He taught all of us how to play. He just doesn't do it anymore because he feels he's too *old* to play."

Maria Alicia burst in, "Oh, your father isn't old. My father still plays tennis with me." She focused on Patricia. "We should play doubles. It's such good exercise. I'd love to play with him." She included the sisters in her gaze. "Maybe we all can go to the club and have a round-robin. Wouldn't that be fun?"

Lourdes was seething at the thought of Patricia calling her father "Miguel." How dare such a nymphet address a man of her father's stature in such a familiar way!

They all played at eating. Adelaida, feeling sympathy for Maria Alicia, tried again to engage Patricia. "How long have you lived in the city?" she asked. Patricia paused for a very short moment, and in that fleeting pause, decided she had nothing to fear. She was who she was. She described her life, speaking sincerely and without apprehension. The rest of the lunch passed in a three-way conversation among Patricia, Maria Alicia, and Adelaida.

Lourdes focused on extracting every possible scrap of flesh from her crab claws. Promptly after she finished her meal, Lourdes excused herself, saying she had to be home before her children returned from school. She left without kissing or shaking hands. A few minutes after Lourdes left, Adelaida told Patricia that she was happy to have met her, shook her hand, and left.

Maria Alicia and Patricia stayed for a few more minutes, staring at their empty demitasse cups. Maria Alicia spoke softly, "I'm sorry, I didn't know what to expect. I apologize for Lourdes. She's so strong-willed. How do you feel?"

Patricia answered, "I don't know what to think of all this."

"What do you mean?"

"All this attention from you. I'm not Miguel's girlfriend or lover. I do like him very much. He's such a fine gentleman. I believe they may have the wrong impression."

Maria Alicia wondered if she had read too much into the relationship as well. She felt foolish and annoyed with the results of the luncheon.

"I'm going to Old Havana. I need to stop at El Encanto. Why don't you come along and I'll drop you off wherever you want?"

"Thanks, you can drop me home. It's on your way."

Once Patricia said goodbye, she walked slowly to her door. It had been only two months since she had met Miguel at La Roca. During that time she felt that she had lost control of her life. Had she told Maria Alicia the truth? *Was* she his girlfriend? She had accepted his fumbling embraces and kisses. She fell into her bed; she needed time to think. A little while later, Carmen knocked and entered her room. "Miguel has called several times this afternoon. What's going on?"

"I don't know! I'm confused. Maria Alicia is acting as if Miguel and I were engaged, and she introduced me to his daughters before he did! I don't know what Miguel has told them. His daughters think that there's something going on. I don't know what I'm doing. He calls, I answer. Maybe I should tell him that I can't talk to him, see him, or go out with him, that I have lots of work to do."

Carmen hugged Patricia as if she were a small child. "I know it's not easy for you. Look, sweetie, life's difficult enough, don't make it even more so! Look at me. Pepe is a good man. He's honest, hardworking, snores, and likes to eat his breakfast in his underwear. He loves his t-shirts more than he loves me, and he's a lovely slob. Do I love him? Yes. Would I change him today for someone else? Frankly, yes, I would. My life is hard, but Mother warned me. She wanted me to finish at the university. I wanted to become a dress designer. Pepe, he was so good-looking and such a sweet talker back then. What happened? I compromised and exchanged my dreams for a man who was good, honest, but couldn't afford to give me my dream. Oh yes, my dream: Paris, Madrid, Dior, and Balenciaga. Now, here I am in Havana making dresses at a cut rate for those that can't afford Dior, Balenciaga, or Bernabeau. I make believe that this is my atelier." Patricia sat upright in her bed, listening to her sister. "Now you're my dream. I see it every time you go out wearing something I've created for you. You're my model. You go to a nice restaurant and I'm there. You go to a dinner party at his house and my dream is alive. I know that you aren't impressed by money, position, or status, but, my little sister, you can have it all! Why? Because someone may be in love with you! Do you feel revolted when he holds your hand? No. Is he nice, and good to you? Yes. How does he treat you? Do you want to be in his arms? Do you want him to kiss and possess you?"

Patricia didn't know what to say. Carmen continued, "Have you felt jealous if he goes with someone else? How about Esmeralda? Don't you think she would steal Miguel from you if she could? Don't let the age difference bother you. A fifty-plus-year-old man is not old. Look at our parents. How old was Papi when he married Mami? What happened next? You're the last of the bunch. Think about it. When Miguel calls back, why don't you tell him that you had lunch with his daughters and Maria Alicia?"

Patricia had tears in her eyes and couldn't answer her sister.

Carmen gave Patricia a big kiss. "Okay, if he calls again, I'll tell him that you went to the laboratory to work on programming. You can call him when you're ready."

Patricia embraced her sister and lay on her bed, gazing at the ceiling.

THE NEXT DAY, Estrella prepared lunch for the girls. Don Miguel ordered that he wanted to eat at one o'clock. Adelaida arrived on time, but Lourdes was more than forty minutes late. She said, "Sorry, I had so many things to do. The help is horrible these days. My maid lost the belt for my dress and she couldn't find the right purse. They just don't have pride in what they do anymore."

As they sat down, Don Miguel addressed them all. "I understand that Maria Alicia, you, and my friend, Patricia, had lunch at Kasalta yesterday. Pepe told me that he saw all of you. Apparently, it wasn't a very friendly lunch, because he's a good reader of body language." He put both of his hands down on the table. "I don't know whose idea it was to convene all of you girls in one of my favorite restaurants, one owned by one of my good friends, no less. Plus, I'm upset that I had to hear it from a friend. Patricia called me, upset about your misunderstanding of our friendship." He peered in mock curiosity at all of them. "What do you need to know?"

"Dad, she's so young!" Lourdes protested. "She's almost Maria Alicia's age. She's not like us. She looks sweet, a little shy, and perfectly nice, really, but she's so *young!*"

Don Miguel smiled at this dig at his age. "What do you mean she's so *young?* What age do you think your grandmother Lola was when she married your grandfather? How old do you think he was?"

"Papi, I didn't say she was too young to get married, I just think she's too young for you."

"Adelaida, you're sitting there, not saying a word. You haven't asked me how I feel or what type of relationship I have with Patricia. Now, what are your thoughts?" He laughed. "Your mother would have loved to see this, how her daughters react to their father's feeling alive once again."

But before he could utter another word, Adelaida said, "Papi, she *is* very young. You haven't met her family. If you had one of your friends in this situation, what advice would you give him?" Seeing that hit home with him, she went on calmly, "I don't know what to say. I've talked to Mike and

Jose Maria, and they both said it's none of my business, you aren't gaga, and we should leave you alone." She leaned forward slightly to make her next point. "We love you. We want the best for you. I know you loved Mami. She was always so happy with you and she loved you so much. But Mami has been gone now for a long time. Patricia seems to be a nice girl, and maybe she can make you happy. I know that Maria Alicia thought it was a good idea, but I was very nervous meeting Patricia."

Don Miguel gave Lourdes a scolding look. "Well, let me tell you something. First, we are not engaged. Second, we aren't even lovers. I met her through a good friend. I had lunch with them, and since then I've taken her out several times. She's been to this house once. I repeat, once." Ever voluble, he decided he would let them know exactly where he stood. "I feel good when I'm with her. She's young and attractive, obviously, very intelligent and easy to talk to. She's a decent, honorable girl. Sure, she's not like us, but let me ask you, who are we? We all came from the interior. I didn't, but my father and my mother did. Are we nobility? No, we've worked hard all our lives. We're just another *criollo* family, and as much as we know, with Spanish blood. Her family has the same background as ours. Her father works the land. I work the land. They live together in a big house. We all used to live together in a big house. You think we're sophisticated because we're Habaneros, while she and her family are *guajiros* from the interior? We were *all guajiros* at one time, and regarding what people think . . ." He made a face, feeling annoyed all over again. "Bah! Who cares! I don't even know that she would accept me if I proposed to her. She has her whole life ahead of her. Aside from that, I don't feel old anymore! I have many, many years ahead of me, too! Do you understand?"

The sisters glanced at each other with dropped jaws, then answered in unison, "Yes, Father."

Adelaida sipped her coffee and stood up. "I have to run. I'm sorry. I have to go to the dressmaker's. I'll call you tonight. Bye, love, kisses, bye." She left briskly, without even nodding goodbye to Georgina as she opened the door.

Lourdes stared at her father. "I want to understand you, but you've changed. After Mami died, you only wanted to work. You didn't seem to realize it, but you lost interest in life. You disappeared in the *manigua* and spent all that time with your animals, your horses, dogs, bulls, and cows. You became unsociable."

"Well, I suppose this is what happens when one becomes alive again!" he smiled.

"I don't like the girl, it's true, but it's also true that you've changed for the better," Lourdes said. She stood up and walked over to embrace her father. "Father, I'm just so glad you're out in the world again. You are as I remember you. In the long run, I don't think she'll be good for you. I think she is too young, doesn't share our same friends, or knows how to run a household. You don't have shared experiences. *Mami* always told me that was important. If you decide to marry Patricia, I'll accept her as your wife, but not as a friend."

"You don't know her. You'll like her when you get to know her," Don Miguel assured his daughter.

"I'm sorry, I just can't do that yet. It's awkward knowing that my step-mother will be younger than I. But, Father, I love you, no matter what." Lourdes kissed his cheek and left.

23

La Zafra

TIME DOES NOT pass in the countryside; it stands still until the sugar harvest, which was in full swing. The roads were full of loaded trucks carrying the green stalks of sugarcane to the mills. The railroads owned by the sugar mills had their trains rolling. The old rhyme used to teach children how to roll the Spanish *r* was alive: *"R con R cigarro, R con R carril, rápidos corren los carros cargados de azúcar por el ferrocarril."* (R with R is cigar, R with R is track, and the trains loaded with sugar run fast on the railroad tracks.)

The *vallas* were packed with people shouting and gambling as cocks died in pools of blood. The bordellos were full every Saturday night, and the churches rang their bells, waiting for the faithful to pray for the best weather and higher sugar prices in the London market. Everyone was employed. Fernando worked his taxi every night. After driving the farm's truck, heavily loaded with sugarcane, to the Florida sugar mill, he had enough energy to hustle customers for his girlfriends, who worked the slummiest part of the *pueblo* with its badly paved streets and all-night bars, operating under the protection of the Guardia Rural.

Mike drove his new car on the Central Highway and watched how the sugarcane was being cut. Night descended and the moon climbed, the road cleared, and he began to think of Maria Alicia and the last days they had spent together. This time he had not been ready to leave Havana. Now everything was different. He had to think of the future, of how he was going to balance his life between his two loves: Maria Alicia and the farm.

The next morning, Paulino woke Mike up with a cup of coffee in hand. "You don't look so tired. Have you been taking some powerful vitamins?"

"No, I just live a clean life," Mike said dryly as he took the cup from Paulino, who walked to the bedroom window and drew back the curtains, allowing the sun's first rays to enter.

"Just two weeks at the best sin spot of the world and here you are—relaxed, with a *guajiro* tan. Why didn't you wake us up last night when you came in? You're becoming civilized," Paulino gently chided.

"I didn't want you to be too tired, because now you're going to have to work."

"Come on, I always work."

"Ha, we'll see—"

"The world wants to talk to you. I don't want to talk. I just want action. I want a significant raise. I should talk to your Papa, who is the gentleman who hired me. You recommended me, I want to believe that we are friends, and I know it's very difficult for you to show your friendship to me, because you may be now in charge, and you don't have the money to afford my incomparable and sophisticated services as the manservant of a great estate. I have to formalize my relationship with an angel, and the only way I can progress with her is to spend *guano*, that mighty piece of paper you call a dollar. No money, no girl. So as soon as you're fully awake with full command of your senses, your wit, and the creative juices of incomparable intellect again start to flow, we have to discuss what is vital to me—money, and more money."

Mike, half asleep, sauntered into the bathroom. "Paulino, please, you hardly work. You spend as much time writing your stories as cleaning around the house. I know your shenanigans. I know you very well, please don't make me get serious with you," Mike relieved himself. "I appreciate your humor. I just don't need a buffoon. I'm satisfied with my level of enjoyment. Please, find Ricardo. I have to talk to him."

Paulino had gambled and lost. He knew that pursuing his request further would be counterproductive, and left, crafting his next plan.

Mike dressed and walked around the *batey*. No more groups of unemployed workers milling around the show barn. Mike now saw the *batey* through the eyes of Maria Alicia. He thought how she would fit and feel in this male-created environment. His mother's last visit had been around six years ago. The big house needed a new paint job. The rocking chairs on the big porch looked tired, and the garden, what garden? The flower beds had started to show weeds; the roses, still flowering, needed pruning. The lime, grapefruit, mango, and avocado trees were in excellent shape. The garden was devoid of color and needed flowers. Everything was so green, so organized, and so drab. What about color?

Mike met Ricardo at the office. Cuca peeked in to ask about Don Miguel's health and when he would return. Mike said, "Cuca, rest assured, he's doing quite well. He's very busy right now. He may come back to pick out the show string for next season. I'll tell him that you miss him," and then "Cuca, we need flowers in this house. Here, take twenty pesos and buy some potted geraniums. I think they would improve the portal."

"Sure, if Ricardo ever takes me to town, I'll buy them for you."

Mike turned to Ricardo, "When?"

"Maybe tomorrow."

Cuca said, "How long are you going to stay? I don't think we have enough of the food you like."

"I'll stay around three weeks, but don't bother to get any special food for me. I'll eat whatever you cook for Ricardo," Mike answered.

"I still need to buy more groceries. I could go with Ricardo to the store, but today I should send Paulino, because there's a lot to do here, but I don't trust him to pick out the geraniums. Are you sure you don't you want anything special?"

"No, thanks, anything you decide to cook will be fine with me," he said, and returned to his meeting with Ricardo.

Paulino was glad that Cuca had trusted him to pick up the groceries from the store. That way, he could stop on his way back and see his girlfriend. For the last three weeks, the sisters had been so busy with the sugar harvest that his nocturnal visits to their plantation were shorter every evening. His leisurely visits had been whittled down to mere minutes, a brief "How are you?," a small peck on the cheek, and good-bye. Paulino honked the horn of the jeep as he passed a busy Manuel, waved at Arturo, and passed Nandito and his truck loaded with cane on his way to the sugar mill. Paulino was happy, full of life, driving a vehicle once forbidden to him.

In the *pueblo*, he found a spot in front of the main door of the warehouse, and in his excitement to see Mulato and tell him that he now was driving the jeep, he opened the front door in a hurry and hit the old army sergeant, who was walking on the sidewalk. The force sent him and the groceries he was carrying tumbling to the ground. Mulato, who saw the accident, came running out of the warehouse. The sergeant lost his composure as he struggled on all fours to get up. Mulato moved quickly to help him, as Paulino, kneeling on the ground, tried to repack the dispersed groceries. A group of nearby children laughed, further raising the sergeant's ire. He stood up, and with all his might, kicked Paulino in the head. "No, no!" Mulato stopped the sergeant from kicking him again.

Paulino toppled over as he tried to hold the groceries he was packing. Despite his pain, Paulino was controlling his laughter as he replayed the scene of the sergeant's pratfall in his mind. But the danger of laughing in his face was too great. Just get through this, he thought. "I'm sorry that I opened the door so fast. I didn't intend to bump a member of La Guardia Rural. Please accept my apology."

The sergeant huffed and stared down at Paulino with disdain. He brushed off his khaki uniform, grabbing his wide-brimmed cavalry hat from Mulato. The sergeant marched to his old army jeep, parked by a fire hydrant, and left in a hurry.

Paulino's neck stiffened with fear. The encounter had spoiled his good mood. Still, he was consoled knowing that after he bought the provisions, he was going to see his girlfriend. Mulato filled the order, and they put the bags in the front seat of the jeep.

On his way out of the *pueblo*, just before he entered the Central Highway, Paulino had to stop at a military roadblock, now a common scene in the *pueblo*. The Guardia Rural was checking the vehicles' registration papers and the drivers' licenses. The rebel activity had increased both in the Sierra del Escambray and in Oriente province, and the army wanted Camagüey to remain isolated from the fight. Paulino stopped the jeep at the roadblock, and a Guardia Rural, whom Paulino had known for several years, asked him to step out of the cab. Paulino complied with a questioning smile. He was ordered to stand spread-eagled with his arms touching the front fender of the jeep. Paulino jerked his head back with surprise. He started to worry: What are they doing? Why? He managed to keep a calm, steady voice. "Hey, what's going on?"

Suddenly, he was hit on the back of his head, then on his back by the flat of a machete.

"*Hijo de puta*, this will teach you how to open a door!" a man shouted. Paulino slowly turned and saw the sergeant standing over him, his machete drawn back.

"Get up! Arms back on the fender!" the sergeant yelled.

Paulino moved to the fender and grabbed it. He was dealt more blows. The machete cut through Paulino's shirt and blood started to flow. "*Cabrón*, this will teach you not to go out with nice white ladies!" the sergeant shouted. "You don't belong here, you're just a mulatto maricón!" The Guardia Rural, whom Paulino knew as a friend, kicked him in his legs. Paulino collapsed to the ground.

The Guardias Rurales picked him from the ground and shoved Paulino back into the front seat of the jeep and left him barely conscious, surrounded by a mess of broken grocery packages. Suddenly the roadblock was lifted. Sobbing, bleeding, and hurt, Paulino carefully positioned himself behind the wheel and drove back to the *batey*. His manhood was sullied, his head hurt, and his back was bleeding. He stopped the jeep outside the kitchen entrance, his body slumped against the steering wheel, and he repeatedly sounded the horn. Manuel and Arturo came running and surrounded the jeep. Ricardo and Mike dashed out of the office. Paulino became unconscious. Manuel and Arturo pulled Paulino out of the jeep, took him to the employees' dining room, and laid him on the table. Cuca quickly cut away what was left of his shirt and began to clean the cuts with soap and water. Ricardo ran to get the car for a trip into town to see Dr. Paco.

Paulino moaned and trembled as Mike spoke calmly into his ear. "You're home. You're among friends. We're going to take care of you. You're going to be okay," Mike whispered as Paulino went in and out of consciousness. "What happened, Paulino? Who did this to you?"

Paulino initially offered no answer. Finally, he said, "I had a fight. I don't know how to choose a good opponent." Paulino turned his head away from Mike as Cuca continued to clean his wounds. Welts began to swell on his back.

Mike told Ricardo to take Paulino to Dr. Paco in Ciego de Ávila. Mike jumped into his car to go to the *pueblo* and find out what had happened. He first stopped at the warehouse. Mulato saw Mike and took him to the private office.

"What happened to Paulino?" Mike asked. "He was beaten up badly."

Mulato paused, and then shook his head with clenched jaws. "Paulino was in a hurry and hit the sergeant with the jeep's door. I heard that he was beaten at a roadblock."

The men look at each other for a few moments without a exchanging a word.

"Those bastards! They can't abuse people like this."

"Mike, be careful," Mulato finally said. "They're out of control."

"I know what I have to do. Thank you," Mike said, and immediately drove to the sergeant's barrack.

A guard stopped Mike at the front entrance. "What do you want?"

"I want to see Lieutenant Pozo. It's urgent. Tell him that Mike Rodriguez is here. He knows who I am."

As Mike waited, he saw the sergeant entering an office. He tried to follow him, but was forcibly stopped. Moments later, Lieutenant Pozo came out of his office.

"Mike, welcome back, how can I help you?"

Mike had met the lieutenant years earlier when his father had Mike deliver bottles of Scotch to him, not as a bribe, but rather as a Christmas present. "So he doesn't forget me," his father explained. Mike spoke firmly, "One of my employees, Paulino Rodriguez, was badly beaten by men under your command. He's a very decent man, and my father and I absolutely trust him. He's our employee, but he's also my friend. I know he made a mistake, but he apologized and he's sorry. It wasn't his intention to harm your sergeant."

The lieutenant invited Mike to his office and offered him a chair in front of a steel desk. "Do you care for a cup of coffee?"

"No, thanks, I have to return soon," Mike replied.

The men watched each other for a few seconds. The Lieutenant looked down and admired his highly polished shoes. He was tired of his tour of duty in this forgotten village in the middle of the island, whose claims to fame were having a sculpture of a rooster named after it and a good-sized sugar mill. He missed Havana; he could have had a better service post. However, he had to placate Mike. He could be moved to a worse post. He could have duty in the Oriente province. He did not want to chase guerrillas up and down the hills or be subject to ambushes while on patrol.

"I don't know what happened. I've been out all morning. When did this happen?" the Lieutenant asked.

"About eleven o'clock. It happened at a roadblock the Guardia Rural had set up before you hit the Central Highway on the West side of the town."

"Did you see it?"

"No, but I saw how badly beaten my employee is. He's in bad shape."

"What did he tell you?"

"Nothing, only that he had made a mistake . . . but I got a report from a good source who saw the accident and heard his apology to the sergeant."

"Well, did anyone see him at the checkpoint?"

An edge entered Mike's voice, "I don't know who saw it. But he was beaten."

"I'll thoroughly investigate. My people respect honorable citizens."

"I want answers. You can't go around beating up innocent people."

"It's a sad situation. I know you're upset. I'll find out the whole story. If my men were out of line, they'll be held accountable. Be assured, I'll personally conduct this inquiry."

Mike said, "I appreciate it. Paulino is an exemplary citizen. I trust that his rights won't be trampled again."

"Of course, we're only after the bad guys. We have to be very careful. There are a lot of undesirables roaming around." The lieutenant decided to change the subject, lighten up the mood. "Now tell me, how is your father? I haven't spoken with him in some time."

"He's in Havana. I'm running the farm now," Mike said.

"We should have a drink. You may not enjoy this provincial atmosphere, but at least you don't have to worry about bombs exploding near you. We have the situation under absolute control. That's why I've instituted searches and the checkpoints. You have to be prepared, always prepared."

Mike was not going to let him off the hook. "Lieutenant, thank you for your time. I have to return to see how Paulino is doing. I know that you'll investigate this case to the fullest."

"Yes, I will, be assured. Please give my regards to your father. Tell him that we need more men like him."

"I will, thanks."

The lieutenant escorted Mike to the door. They shook hands. Mike was not satisfied, but he hoped that from now on his employees would be left alone.

PAULINO LAY IN the backseat of the car, too proud to cry in front of Ricardo. His body hurt most when he breathed. He felt like he was wearing a tight corset with spines and hooks piercing his body. Paulino felt every bump of the road, every turn. When they reached the clinic, Ricardo carried Paulino in his arms, as if he was a small child. The nurse in the admitting office knew Ricardo, and when she saw Paulino openly bleeding, she rushed them to an examining room. Two nurses came to undress him, and wash and clean his wounds again.

Dr. Paco arrived and quickly examined Paulino. He instructed the nurses on the immediate measures that needed to be taken and ordered them to give him painkillers. He then motioned Ricardo to the side. "How did it happen?"

Ricardo explained and Dr. Paco nodded. To be safe, he ordered Paulino to be x-rayed. After analyzing the results, Paulino was admitted. Yet in the admission papers, Dr. Paco noted that the patient had fallen off a horse and had broken some ribs.

"I want him to stay for a few days. There's nothing else to do. The ribs will have to mend by themselves. I'm giving him penicillin to fight any infection plus a tetanus shot. He can rest here. We'll put him in a private room."

"I'll tell Mike and Paulino's girlfriend," Ricardo said.

"He won't be dancing for a while. It'll hurt too much," warned the doctor. "Give Mike my regards."

Ricardo drove home slowly, lost in thought. The sunset was especially beautiful that evening, yet he was clutched in the grip of trepidation. He had been very young the last time the army was so active on the island, during the last days of Machado. In those days, he had sensed the fear felt by the members of his family about the army and the police, even by his own father. Now he understood.

Ricardo drove up to the *batey* and found Mike waiting for him on the front porch of the big house. He walked up to the car as Ricardo slowed to a stop.

"How is he?" Mike asked.

"He's going to be okay. He has several broken ribs, and he's badly bruised and swollen. He has a small concussion in his head. The cuts will heal, but Dr. Paco put him on antibiotics to fight against infection and gave him a painkiller. He says it'll be a slow recovery."

They went inside to update Cuca. Seeing Manuel lingering in the employees' dining room, Mike asked him to go to the sisters' plantation and tell them what had happened. Bad news traveled fast, but worse news traveled faster, and Mike did not want them to get incorrect information.

Mike returned to his office and closed the door, exhausted. He sat at his desk, leaned back into the leather chair, and closed his eyes. He knew this situation could not continue. He was now more aware than ever of the differences between the States and Cuba. He had lived in a place, not perfect, but where one felt free, and you didn't have to worry about being beaten or arrested for a crime you didn't commit. If you wanted to be involved in politics, you could, and if you didn't, no one cared. He thought about Laureano and his friends, their meetings, about the rebels in the hills, and the growing political opposition in the cities. Where did he fit? What could he do? Was he going to be a spectator who watched his world crumbling around him? Was he going to accept Paulino's beating and the experience with Fernando as normal occurrences? How about his encounter with the sergeant?

Mike glanced at the stack of mail that Paulino had picked up at the post office earlier. A blue envelope with well-rounded script caught his eye. He carefully slid it out of the pile. It was from Maria Alicia. He smelled the envelope and lightly touched the heavy blue paper, as if touching it would make her appear before him. He opened the envelope and read:

Havana
September 15, 1958

Dearest,

I thought I could never feel like I'm feeling now. Do you know how much I miss you? How I want to be close to you, touch your hands and slowly kiss them and walk, walk on the beach and feel like we never, never had to leave, just stay there forever. I feel sad, dejected, abandoned, even though you never promised that you were not going to leave me. I so desperately want to see you and hear your voice.

There is something else that is causing me sadness. I made a terrible mistake. The luncheon I arranged with Patricia and your sisters at Kasalta was a disaster. Instead of helping, I created a mess. Adelaida was the better of the two, and in the end, she actually talked to Patricia, but Lourdes is another story. I had never seen her act that way. She even called my mother to say I was crazy, and she thought I had been brought up better than to invite her father's mistress to have lunch with her!

And when I drove Patricia to her home, she told me that she and your father are only friends, and that we seem to be making too much of their relationship! She did say she liked him very much, that he is a true gentleman. I've only met Patricia twice, but I feel that she and I could be friends. I just wanted to let you know, as you may well be hearing from Lourdes about this.

I have to finish a paper now. It is the beginning of the term. I miss you. How I want this time apart to end so that we can always be together. Mother, who just came into the room, sends you her love. Dad is still in the interior, at his plantation, like you. He will be coming soon.

I love you. Write, and write, so that I can taste each of your words.

Yours,
Maria Alicia

At least he had one ray of sunshine in his life. But he was still upset, and he went out to the paddock where the black stallion was let out for the night. He put one foot on the fence and looked at him. The stallion came toward Mike and placed his head over the fence. Mike caressed his neck. "Yes, Lucumi, everything will be fine," he whispered, while he stroked the horse behind its ears. "Everything will be fine."

The next day, Mike went with Fernando to Ciego de Ávila to see Paulino. The patient was in his private room surrounded by the three sisters. Mike was amused when he saw how Paulino reveled in their attention and showed bravado by insisting that Dr. Paco had unnecessarily admitted him into the clinic. The sisters said how worried they were about Paulino's "accident." They had, of course, heard about it even before Manuel arrived at their plantation with the news. Mike visited briefly and left Paulino to be fussed over and doted on. Fernando stood outside the room, while Mike searched for Dr. Paco.

"Mike, I didn't see you for years, and now almost every other day you visit me. Do you want to know about Paulino?"

"Yes, Doctor. How is he?"

"He was lucky. No piercing of his lungs, three broken ribs, lacerations on the skin, and a mild concussion. The ribs will mend, but he'll be in pain for at least three or four weeks. No lifting, no heavy work." He shook his head. "What's happening to our country?"

"I know. How long should he stay here?"

"Not too long. He can leave now really. But I thought he would be safer if he stayed for a few days."

"That's fine. I don't need him at the *batey*. Thanks for taking good care of him."

"Mike, be careful—"

"Yes, I understand. I have to go back. I hope the next time I see you is for a happier event."

On the way back to the farm, Mike noticed that Fernando was especially quiet.

"What's bothering you?" Mike asked.

Fernando kept his eyes on the road. Finally, he said, "I don't feel safe in this environment. If it weren't for your father, I would be rotting in a G2 cell in Havana. Paulino is lucky he survived his beating. You were, too! What's happening? Really. You're not political, nor I. I don't care who the next president is or who my senator will be. They're all the same. Just promises. They get rich and they forget about us. I don't even care about that anymore. I just want to be left alone."

"I understand the way you feel. I'm worried, about all of us. There is no letup in this fight, and things have to change. I still don't know how." He placed a hand on Fernando's shoulder. "I know you're a hard worker. You only want to have a better life, make more money, play a little, and what happens to you? They arrest you, they interrogate you, and they didn't even give you a chance to call my father. You were only in a shitty park when a petard exploded. That sergeant hit me because I wore ratty clothes. That's all wrong," Mike said.

"It's even worse for those of us who don't count. We have no money or power. Imagine what could happen to me! Today, tomorrow, anywhere and anytime, and suddenly life would be so different. We aren't free! We live through every day as if everything is the same, but it's not! Does no one else see it this way?" Fernando had a haunted look in his eyes. "When I was locked in that cell, there was a young man with me. He was afraid of being there. He was taken out, and he didn't return. Later, I saw his picture in the newspaper. He was murdered. I could have been him," Fernando mumbled, remembering that awful time. He didn't talk for the rest of the drive to the *batey*.

PAULINO RETURNED FROM the clinic a week later, leaving behind his private room with a courtyard view, especially attentive nurses, and the Gomez sisters' daily visit with care packages in hand. Back at the farm, he couldn't resume his usual routine. His ribs were mending, but he still had problems breathing, moving, and laughing. No lifting or cleaning. The Gomez sisters made trips to the big house at the *batey* to visit. At least that was an improvement, Mike noted wryly. The employees' dining room became a social center. Manuel had never dressed better, and Cuca played the role of the perfect hostess.

Paulino started to talk about marriage. Yet his Elena wanted to wait until her sister Julieta, who was the oldest, married Manuel. Paulino worried that Manuel would get cold feet. He soon would have more immediate worries.

That Saturday night, Fernando was feeling good. He had a lot of money in his pocket. He'd had a busy week and business was excellent. He had twice driven the truck loaded with sugarcane to the sugar mill. At nights, he worked nonstop with his taxi service. Tonight was special. He had taken a group of the San Joaquin young studs to the various bars at the *pueblo*. He felt good, really good. He was laughing, shaking hands, slapping backs, and buying drinks.

At the last stop, where the prettiest girls sat, not at the bar but at small tables, waiting for customers to buy them watered-down drinks, Fernando met up with the sergeant, in uniform and drunk, accompanying two old, bored *putas*. The sergeant on occasion ordered another drink for his group and looked around with glassy eyes to see if there was someone with whom to pick a fight. He was too drunk to stand, and when he saw Fernando, he shouted, "Hey, *negro*, come here. I want to talk to you. Don't you work at the Rodriguez farm? Yes, I know you. You and that little *mulatito maricón* own that dilapidated Chevrolet you use for your *puterias*. Yep, I know you, and I know your little boss. Tell him that he doesn't have to cry to anyone. I'm the one he has to talk to. I knew him when he was in diapers. I'm not going to touch him. I know his papa. Yes, I know Don Miguel real well. But tell your friend and partner, that little mulato maricón, that he's not man enough to have Elena Gomez as a girlfriend and that he's not welcome in this *pueblo*. I don't want to see him in my *pueblo*, and next time, he won't be able to tell a tale and go back to cry on your boss's shoulders. Here, you're big enough. You, be a man, buy my ladies another drink. I won't drink with you, but I'll let them drink what you buy them." He called the bar girl, "Hey, you, come here. The law is calling you. Shit, I'm the law. I order you to come here, now."

The girl, accustomed to the sergeant's drunken behavior, moved lasciviously from behind the bar and put one of her arms on the sergeant's back. "Tell me, my little lion, what do you desire?"

"I don't want anything. I want this man to be a gentleman and buy drinks for my women. Yes, a good drink, no beer, a good brandy."

Fernando was angry, but he knew that if he showed it, nothing would be accomplished. "Sergeant, I'm more than honored to be able to share a drink with you and these nice ladies. Now, Carmelita," he addressed the barmaid, "you know me well enough. When have I been cheap? Now, give the ladies a Felipe II. I'll have one with ginger ale. It's a pleasure to see you!" Fernando patted the sergeant on the back. "Now, if you allow me, I'd like to go be with my friends. We're also thirsty and the night is young. We still have a lot of dancing to do."

Fernando took a roll of notes out of his pocket and gave Carmelita a ten-peso note. "Keep the change. I'll have my drink at that table with my friends. Excuse me, it's always a pleasure," and he left the sergeant with his two *putas* waiting for their fresh drinks.

Yet for Fernando, the charm of the night was lost. He didn't want to leave early, because the sergeant might think he was afraid of him. He sat at a table with his customers, sipping his drink, hearing the music that blared from the Wurlitzer. His customers, friends for the night, started dancing with the girls. Later, the angst from the incident dissipated with the heat of moving bodies. They all had come to forget who they were, if only for a moment, in fleeting embraces inside dimly lit rooms at the back of the bar.

The next morning, Fernando told Cuca he had to talk to the boss. Mike heard Fernando's voice and came to the door. Fernando told him of his conversation with the sergeant. Mike knew he couldn't go back to see the lieutenant. Then and there, he decided to take Paulino back to Havana under the guise of wanting another doctor to check his wounds. He went into the kitchen, where Paulino was watching Cuca prepare his breakfast.

"Paulino, I need to talk to you," Mike said.

A few minutes later, Paulino returned from his room with his luggage, a small cardboard box with his classic books, and envelopes with rough drafts of his new stories. "I'm ready to go."

24

Time to Leave

DR. COMILLAS HAD had three Scotches. Rubio, the bartender at the American Club, knew that Comillas was in a bad mood, so he had fled to the opposite side of the bar. Don Miguel showed up, summoned by a cryptic call, unusual since Andres usually couldn't stop talking. When Don Miguel entered the bar, Comillas gave him a long embrace.

"Miguelito, you're my friend. Come, let's sit down. I've got to talk to you." Comillas motioned to the table farthest from the bartender. "Excuse me, what a terrible host I am." Comillas turned back and waved to the bartender. "Rubio! A drink for Don Miguel, please."

"A Pinch," said Don Miguel.

The friends, with their drinks in hand, walked to the table. After they sat, Comillas, leaning forward, somberly said, "You're the first and only one to know. I'm leaving. I'm going to Mexico tomorrow. I haven't talked to the minister about this, and Esmeralda does not know." He lowered his voice even further. "I'll have to figure out a story, but I know they're checking on me. My phones are tapped, not only the one at my office, but also the ones at my penthouse and the farm. I know that if I mentioned it to the minister, he would try to put an end to it, but he doesn't have the power. I tell you, they all are out of their minds."

"You don't have to leave. It's probably a mistake. The minister knows that you're working with him on important issues."

Don Miguel had never seen him this way. His friend, who typically did not care what people thought, the cheerful bon vivant, was afraid, suspicious of everyone around him. He repeatedly scanned the bar for any signs, even though the American Club was virtually empty.

"It started a week ago. Esmeralda showed up at the farmhouse with two young men. They said they wanted my advice because I had been an active revolutionary against Machado back in the thirties. I was flattered," he admitted. "I wanted to look important in front of her. Lately, we haven't been doing very well together. She's kind of distant and not always ready to come when I call." He straightened up, and a look of discomfiture came over his face. "Well, that's a different subject. We talked for a long time—about the rebels, the political parties, having a free press, and freedom of speech. I tell you, it felt great to talk openly about political issues, to think again. I felt young and full of fire, like I used to be a long time ago." He scratched his forehead, thinking. "I don't know when I quit caring. After talking with them, I realized that I've only been interested in what affects me—my business, my money, my *finquita,* my cows, my dogs, and my rabbits. You know, Miguelito, talking with those young people, I was ashamed." He glanced around again before saying, "They asked me for money and I gave them some, not much. When they left, I took Esmeralda to the penthouse. We had wonderful, fantastic sex. Then, less than two days later, funny things started to happen to my telephone lines."

"Yes, I've noticed that all your lines have a little bit of an echo."

"So, you don't think I'm crazy."

"No, I think you're anxious, but not crazy."

"Yesterday, I got a call from Esmeralda and she was really nervous. One of the young men has disappeared. She believes that Captain Velasco arrested him." Comillas gave the table a slight thump. "I'm leaving for Mexico on the morning plane. I bought the ticket directly from the airline. I'm taking a lot of traveler's checks and a letter of credit from my bank. I'll be in good shape for a while. I'll wait until the elections are over and see what happens, and then I may be back. I'm traveling alone. I don't have a family to worry about, and Esmeralda, well, she's young, and I don't think that she'll miss me too much."

Don Miguel watched the ice melt in his drink. "Aren't you overreacting? What is going to happen to your business, and to your clients? It's fine for you to go to Europe in the summer, as you always do, but this is the busiest season of the year! Deals are made and your clients need you. You're not going to write contracts in Mexico. Are you sure?"

"Yes, I have to go. But why don't you come and visit me? You may bring that little Patricia. I know she hasn't traveled much and both of you may enjoy it." He could tell from his friend's dour expression that that wasn't going to happen. "If not, I want to celebrate our last night in Havana in style. Let's start at Monsignor, we can drink champagne and hear the violins. Pity that when I leave my country, I want to drink champagne in a *faux* French place. After that, let's go explore our real Havana. Let's go to La Playa, have a *frita*, look at the sunrise from the pier of the yacht club. I'll be your guest." He got up, signed the bill, and gave the bartender a large cash tip. "I'll be back tomorrow. Be sure you have my Scotch."

"Wait a minute, let me call Estrella. She was expecting me for dinner."

"Aren't you nice! Hurry, I don't have too much time."

Don Miguel made a phone call, and then followed his friend to his chauffeur-driven Mercedes, which waited at the club entrance.

The next day, Don Miguel woke up in his bed with no recollection of how he got there. He looked around the room, remembered he had been with Comillas the night before, and then fumbled for his bedside clock. It was past one o'clock in the afternoon. His mouth tasted a multitude of opposing flavors, none of them agreeable. He saw his *guayabera* thrown on the floor, and he looked for his roll of money, which he always kept on the nightstand. It was notably diminished. He slowly walked to the bathroom and threw water on his face. He looked at himself in the mirror. If he had had a worse night before, he couldn't remember it. He brushed his teeth and his tongue, and groped for the bottle of Listerine and gargled until he felt its sharpness in his throat. He slowly tottered to the toilet. He dropped himself against the wall and held his body with an extended arm while he urinated. He began to remember. He still had his car at a parking lot near the American Club. He and Comillas had stopped at Floridita for a last daiquiri. The last one, Comillas had said, "is the best." They moved to the Zombie Club, just for another cocktail. Then Monsignor, for champagne, and there, he wanted to call "his girls."

"Join me, just for the night. You're a widower, but you aren't old," Comillas had said. Don Miguel remembered declining the invitation. Comillas called another girl, not Esmeralda. Now, Esmeralda was afraid to be in his company, Comillas explained. A young lady met them at

Monsignor's restaurant. They drank champagne and heard the violins, and then went to see the action in the nightclubs at La Concha. The driver took them from spot to spot. Comillas drank so much whiskey that he could hardly dance with his young partner. They walked across the Quinta Avenida and to the beach at La Concha. The yacht club was closed. They all sat in the sand. Comillas touched the wet sand and threw flat shells into the calm water of the inlet. When the sun rose, Comillas took his shoes and walked to the edge of the sea. He threw another few shells into the clear blue water.

"This is in honor of Yemaya. I know she'll protect me," Comillas declared.

The young lady laughed at the two old farts, playing like kids on the beach, and soon joined them in the water. Finally, Don Miguel carried Comillas back to his car, as the chauffeur held open the door. They dropped off the young woman at her apartment. Don Miguel handed her some money. "Please, have your dress cleaned."

When Comillas arrived at his penthouse, he picked up a briefcase and a small bag, and they left immediately for the Rancho Boyeros airport to catch his flight to Mexico City. During the trip to the airport, they hardly talked. Don Miguel waited until his friend had passed through the controls at the airport before the chauffeur drove him back home. He went directly to bed, but despite all the drinks he'd had, he couldn't avoid the one thought he had tried all night to forget. He knew that he had lost his good friend.

Don Miguel took a very hot shower and luxuriated under the stream of water. He scrubbed and scrubbed his body until his skin turned red. He tried to remove the smell of alcohol and tobacco that had permeated his skin. He had to talk to Patricia. Last night at the beach, he had carried her image with him. When he was dancing with the girl, he pretended she was Patricia. Then it occurred to him that he had never danced with her. He realized he had not been living. He was a robot that worked, slept, and ate. No time for fun or to do what he wanted to do. He remembered his youth, the lists he made, and his promise to himself: to search for the best. He thought of his horses, his personally-bred cattle, and the battles he had fought. He went to the kitchen, opened the door of the refrigerator, poured himself a glass of milk, and drank it slowly. Estrella came from the garden with fresh-cut flowers.

"Would you like some coffee? It looks like you need some."

"Yes, I'll be in the library." As he left the glass on the kitchen table, he knew what he wanted to do. He would call Patricia at six o'clock.

PAULINO WAS SILENT. The pain pills made him drowsy. Mike was in a hurry to get to Havana. He had stopped for gas, and they hastily ate an empanada in Colon. They arrived at the house around six, and as he opened the front door, he heard his father talking on the phone. Estrella and Georgina came to greet him. His father's conversation abruptly ended. Paulino stood in the rear, holding his packages and a small suitcase.

Estrella noticed that Paulino was battered.

"Mother of God, what happened to you?" she said. "Georgina, get his things. I'll make some chicken soup." Estrella looked wide-eyed at Mike and Don Miguel. "Why didn't anybody tell us about this?" She shook her head, and before leaving for the kitchen, ordered, "Come, Paulino, come."

Embarrassed, Paulino followed Estrella to the kitchen while greeting Don Miguel with a nod and a soft "hello" as he walked by.

Don Miguel turned to Mike, "What's going on?"

"Let's go into the library," Mike suggested. There, he explained to his father what had happened. Don Miguel was shocked and outraged.

"Let me call my friends. I'll take care of it."

Mike calmed him down. "Dad, I don't know that a phone call is going to help us anymore. The army rank and file isn't taking orders from the top anymore. There's no order in the army. None. They're after money for themselves now." He lowered his voice so only his father could hear. "I don't believe that Paulino is safe at the farm. The sergeant wants to kill him. The lieutenant doesn't have control over the garrison. He's even worse than the sergeant."

Don Miguel was baffled that such a thing could have come to pass. "I don't know what's happening. This morning I lost a friend, he left for Mexico, and before that, we had the problem with Fernando, and now Paulino. . . . I don't think you should return to the farm. Things are out of control."

"Maybe not, but when the situation calms down, Ricardo will let us know, and we'll bring Paulino back. But for now, he should stay here."

Don Miguel sat silently for a minute. "Well, I want you to stay as well. We have a lot of work to do. Wait until after the New Year, and then everything should be back to normal. It always happens during the sugar harvest. The worst comes out. Now, let's decide what we're going to do with Paulino. Do you think another doctor should see him?" Don Miguel felt his hangover coming back to bite him. He was worried about the political situation. Too many things had happened. His whole world seemed to be out of control.

Suddenly he was panicked: Could anything happen to Mike? He was young. Could he be mistaken? Then what? Whom do you call after your son is killed? Can you bring him back? He should have stayed in college and finished his master's. Lustre had made an error, and now it was too late.

25

Patricia and Laureano

PATRICIA PASSED HER last test. She was exhilarated, for she had reached her goal. She was a certified IBM computer operator and programmer. Her instructors were delighted with her performance, and told her she was intelligent, and hardworking, with an especially good facility for computer languages. Her difficult new journey had started. The tuition at the academy had drained her savings, and she did not want to go back to Pinar del Rio and ask for more money from her father. Even though she was more than welcome at her sister's house, she hated to extend her stay.

She nervously knocked at the door of the director's office for her exit interview. "Good morning, Director," she said in a low voice. The director, who was absently looking at papers, raised his head, and without standing up from his chair, motioned her to sit down. "Patricia, welcome. I'm very pleased that you finished our program with such good grades. You show a lot of promise. What are your plans now?"

Patricia was taken aback. Plans, what plans can you have when you finish school, are broke, and need money for food? "Well, I need to work. I understand you know people who can use my computer skills. I would like your help on where to apply."

The director sat back and considered the young woman. "Yes, I have friends who are always looking for someone like you. Everyone likes you here. Would you be interested in working for us part-time as an instructor? I'd like you to work in the lab. The hours would be flexible. However, if you want to work full-time, I'll give you two names. I'll call them to set up an interview. I assure you, you'll be well received."

This was just what she was hoping he'd say. "I'm so grateful and honored that you've offered me work here. I know I'd love it. But the truth is, I need to work full-time."

The director wrote the names, phone numbers, and addresses of two men who managed computer-programming departments. One was at the Banco Nacional de Cuba; the second, at the Trust Company of Cuba, which was the largest Cuban-owned bank. Patricia thanked him, nervously took the slip of paper, and almost bowed as she exited his office.

Two days later, full of confidence, she sat in the reception room of the personnel department of the Trust Company. She had carefully picked her most conservative dress, over the objections of her sister, who wanted her to wear something a little more provocative. She had already spent part of the morning filling out an employment questionnaire. Miguel was the only person she knew well whom she did not use as a reference; however, she had named Dr. Comillas. Why? She didn't really know; she just thought at least she could mention someone who was well-known. They had already tested her skills. Patricia had to keypunch data and write a basic computer program. When it came time for the interview, she was surprised to see a rather young man call her into his office and then sit next to her rather than behind his desk. The office was small and Spartan, there was no rug, no window, and only a calendar published by the bank. The desk was of steel, and on its top sat a pen and pencil set in a faux marble holder. Patricia waited for him to speak after she gave him her resume, diploma, and letters of recommendation. He sensed her anxiety as he took her papers, asked her to be comfortable, and moved behind his desk to read her application.

"Let me see," he said as he slowly examined the file. He grunted, made notes on the side of her application, stared at her several times, and finally spoke. "I think we can use you. You don't have experience working at a bank, so we're going to give you a ninety-day trial period. Your salary will be eighty pesos a month, and it's a good starting salary, above minimum wage. After that period, we'll see. You can start this Monday. Do you want to work with us?"

Patricia exhaled. "Yes! I'm so delighted. Thank you!"

"Let's go to another office. You have more paperwork to fill out." The manager stood up and headed toward the door as Patricia awkwardly reached out to shake his hand. He caught a side glimpse of her extended hand and shook it.

Around six o'clock, Don Miguel called Patricia. "How was your day?"

"It was great. We have a lot to talk about."

"Will you tell me?

"Not on the phone. It's a surprise."

"Well, when may I see you? Are you free tonight?"

"Yes, I am."

"I'll pick you up at seven."

"You're going to love my news!"

"I've never heard you sound so happy!"

"Wait and see." A joyous Patricia hung up the phone.

Patricia saw Don Miguel driving up to her apartment building and ran to meet him. The moment he pulled to a stop, she opened the front passenger door and jumped in, giddy with excitement.

"I was hired! I got a job. I start Monday! I'm so excited!" She put her arms around his neck and gave him a kiss on the cheek. "I'm going to work at the Trust Company of Cuba. They hired me as a computer trainee. Isn't it fabulous! I have a job!"

Don Miguel was taken aback. He had never considered the possibility of his wife working. In his world, a working wife meant the husband could not provide for his family, and then who would supervise the home to make sure he was taken care of? How would she have time to be attractive and well dressed? Even worse, a working wife would be subject to sexual pressures and desires outside the home!

Patricia sensed he was upset. "What's wrong?"

Don Miguel drove, staring straight ahead. "I've never dated someone who works."

Patricia thought, "I've never dated an older man, either," but before she said it, Don Miguel feigned a smile and said, "Well, we should celebrate! Where do you want to go? It's your lucky day!"

Patricia became ebullient. "Oh, Miguel, let's go dancing. I want to be happy tonight! I want to be alive. I want to dance, shout, scream, say funny things, and be careless and free. Can you imagine what this means to me?

I can have my own apartment. I can invite you and your friends for dinner. I'm a good cook, you know. Thank you for all the encouragement you gave me! I'm so happy! Thank you! Thank you!" She threw her arms around him and gave him another kiss.

The couple went to the nightclub at the Hotel Nacional, where they danced, drank champagne, played roulette, saw the second show, and danced again. Suddenly, Patricia was transformed into a new person, deeply happy and sure of herself. Her joy infected Don Miguel, who, putting aside his feelings about her job and Andres's departure, began to enjoy the night. During the orchestra's break, they sat down at their small table near the dance floor. After they ordered another bottle of champagne, he looked into Patricia's eyes and held her hand.

"I don't know if this is the time, but I have to tell you. I love you. I'm complete with you. I haven't felt like this for a long time. I close my eyes, and I see you. I want to be with you. I'm not young, but I feel young and strong when I'm with you. I have many years to live, and I want them with you. Please be my wife. Marry me."

Patricia had known he cared, but marriage and *today*? When she was starting a new, independent life? "You know how I feel about you. But this is a serious step. I have to think about it." She saw his disappointment and rushed to add, "I'm happy when I'm with you. I just don't want to rush. Plus, your family may never accept me. And how about your friends?" She searched his eyes and couldn't tell how he was feeling. She held his hand tighter and smiled. She was happier than ever before.

"You don't have to say yes. I want you to think about it. You know how much I respect and care for you."

"Let's dance. It is a beautiful night. It's a perfect night!" she said.

HAVANA WAS A small town. Everyone knew what everyone else was doing. Who was in town, who was traveling, who had money, and who was having a difficult time. So when Mike received a phone call from Laureano, he wasn't surprised.

"Welcome back. Do you have any plans for lunch? I need to talk to you. Let's meet at El Carmelo. I'll be there around, say, twelve-thirty?"

Mike was worried by the tone of Laureano's voice. He sounded tired, and lacking the fiery energy that he normally exuded. Mike left at noon and found El Carmelo crowded. He searched for Laureano, but didn't find him, so he sat at a small table near the sidewalk, and then went to the magazine counter to buy a *U.S. News & World Report*, which covered in detail the Nixon and Kennedy campaigns. Mike was absorbed in the magazine when Laureano, showing a two-day stubble, tapped his shoulder.

"Sorry I'm late," Laureano said with a smile, though his face looked drawn. "We need to talk, but we can't do it here—too many ears." They ordered sandwiches and while they were waiting for them to be prepared, they exchanged small talk. Laureano asked Mike about Maria Alicia, and Mike asked about Laureano's many brothers and his sister. They left in Mike's car and headed to the Malecon. Using the tunnel under the bay, they left the city behind. Laureano regained his composure once they were in the Via Blanca.

"I've spent the last years trying to fight the regime. It doesn't work. I can't fight against a tank with a pen. Our compatriots don't read. They couldn't care less about reasoned arguments or the law. We've always been against violence. I thought that if we educated the people, they would react against what's happening. I was wrong. It looks like force can only be fought with a stronger force. Gandhi's ideas won't work in our country." His laments kept pouring out in a rush. "I've wasted my time, yours, and my friends'. I made fools of you and everyone who attended meetings at my home. I'm responsible for giving all of us the idea that if we discussed, talked, wrote, used sophisticated arguments, we would recreate a democratic Cuba."

Mike tried to stop him. "But, Laureano, you did create something. We were able to discuss things that I feel are important."

Laureano shook his head in dissent and continued, "No, it didn't work. But meanwhile, those who care only for themselves laughed at us, at our pretensions, at our unsophistication, our romantic and impractical ideas. They knew we could accomplish *nada, nada*—so many meetings, so many articles, and so much money. They tolerated us and made fools of us. Why? Because they knew that we weren't going to change anything," he cried. "We were ineffectual. We played into their hands. We were their loyal opposition. We wrote great articles. 'See,' they said, 'there is freedom of press.'

We met and discussed the philosophy of government. 'See,' they said, 'there is freedom to meet.'" He was disgusted at how naïve he had been. "What I did, what we did, didn't count. It didn't stop them from torturing us, jailing us, killing us, persecuting us. We were romantic, absurd, poetic, and ridiculous. We were more existentialist than Sartre, more Christian than Maritain, and more poetic than Marti." He paused, and Mike sensed that he was reaching a conclusion. "We need to change. We are slowly asphyxiating in this corruption. That's why I wanted to talk to you, because we're the same."

"You're too hard on yourself. What you did is important. You wrote, and you wrote what you believed in. You broadcast our conscience, our ideas. Yes, they may be ineffectual today, but the writings exist for someone to read. Maybe someone has read the articles, joined our discussions, and reached a decision to fight, to do more than what he was doing. Remember, silence is the best ally of a dictatorship."

"Thanks, but you're too generous," Laureano said. "Look, I'm leaving Havana. I'm becoming an *alzado*. I'm joining a group of our friends who are ready to open another front in the western part of the island. I'm not going to tell you where, but you can help us." He looked at Mike searchingly. "We're going to need medicines, boots, and more money. We're also going to need safe houses. We have the arms. We have money to bribe the soldiers in the area. We're going to need more to buy supplies from the people that live in the hills. I think they'll cooperate with us, but if we have money, it'll be easier." As he waxed on, his voice gained its usual fervor. "I don't think we'll be there for a long time. The army is concentrating on the eastern and central parts of the island, around the Escambray Mountains." His lips twisted and he broached a new topic. "I need a favor from you. I hope I'll come back, but if something happens to me, I've named you my executor. Here, this is my will. I also want you to keep my papers in a safe place. If I die, I want them published."

"You honor me. Thanks, my friend, but you aren't going to die."

"Just in case, I left enough money in my will for you to publish my papers. I still want to preach after I'm dead."

Mike still thought he was being maudlin, but he merely said, "Don't worry. Your wishes will be carried out."

"The balance of my assets will go to my family, even though they don't need it. Our inheritance law is so ridiculous. One day we'll change it!" He clasped Mike on the knee. "You're my best friend. I wish we could have spent more time together."

"That's all right. You can count on me."

"Mike, I know that you and Maria Alicia are a great couple. I plan to dance at your wedding."

"But when will I dance at yours?"

The serious moment was broken by the friends' laughter.

Back in the city, Laureano gave him a box with his papers. They parted with a strong embrace, and Laureano walked away.

26

Cienfuegos

PAULINO HELPED ESTRELLA in the kitchen washing dishes. He polished Don Miguel's and Mike's shoes, and cleaned the car. When he felt better, he started to call his university friends, and one of them, Llaca, a published poet and an habitué of Laureano's meetings, invited Paulino to a reading of his poems at the house of the editor of a poetry magazine.

Paulino asked Don Miguel if he had work for him that night. Don Miguel, astonished, looked at Paulino. "When have you ever worked at night for us? We have Georgina to serve at the table, and Estrella cooks. I don't have any work for you here, so do whatever you want to do."

Paulino thanked him, and full of excitement, went to Llaca's reading. The apartment was on the second floor of an old building that faced Prado Avenue. The large living room, where the reading was held, had a high ceiling with large open windows that brought in a healthy breeze together with the sounds of cars and the conversations of people walking on the street. The sounds mingled with the conversations of the guests at the reading. It was not a big group, and Paulino knew many of them from his university years. He felt energized. He moved around, shaking hands, slapping backs, hugging acquaintances as if they were his oldest friends. Finally, Llaca read his poems that had a similar rococo feeling of a Lizama poem without the simplicity of Guillen. Paulino recognized Lizama Lima and Cabrera Infante in the audience.

After the reading was over, he stayed for a short while, mostly going from group to group to listen in to their conversations and reintroduce himself as a *guajiro* that was living and writing in the middle of a big savanna near a nowhere village in Camagüey. He felt exiled from a civilization where he wanted to belong. He did not live in Havana. Would he come back? Was he happy with his sexless love life with Elena? After this taste of what he could be part of, could he be happy working for Mike at the farm?

The next morning Paulino was in the kitchen when Mike came to order his breakfast. Paulino said, excitedly, "Mike, I saw Cabrera Infante last night at Llaca's reading. He remembered me from when we went to Laureano's home. He asked if I was writing. I told him yes! I'm going to show him my last short story. Isn't it great?"

Mike was encouraging. "That is great. He has great taste. He's an excellent writer. Are you feeling better now that I brought you to Havana?"

"Yes, I'm so happy. I want to read my story one more time. Would you like to read it?"

"You know I'm not good at editing. I'm a numbers man, but I'll read it. Maybe you can have it published in a magazine."

"Thanks for the encouragement." He twisted his torso, showing Michael his freedom of movement. "I feel better. I walk without pain. I'm sleeping better, but I miss Elena. Have you heard from Ricardo about the sergeant?"

"No, haven't. He'll be calling soon. I'll ask him." He remembered what he had talked about with Laureano, and he made a plea. "Paulino, you have a gift. You can write. Don't blow it. I know that times are difficult for you, but Father and I like you, and you can work for us and still have time to write. I wanted to be sure you weren't going to be attacked and hurt again at the *pueblo*."

"Thanks for taking care of me, but I have to make my own decisions. I'm not doing any real work here. There's nothing for me to do. Any help I contribute can be done in a few hours."

"Well, then, write, or I'll create new tasks for you," Mike said, joking. "Look, I hope you can return soon to the farm. Let's wait and see what Ricardo says."

Mike went to the terrace and joined his father, who was having his breakfast. Paulino returned to his room in the garage. Late that afternoon he walked to the park and sat on a bench under a ficus tree. He thought about what he wanted to do, but soon grew tired of thinking and took a bus to visit his old café. He said hello to his old boss, who barely recognized him, Paulino having changed so much. He was happy to see Paulino and asked him if he was looking for a job. "No, not at this time," he replied. He saw Eloy as he was leaving the café, whom he had met at one of the political committees at the university. Paulino ran after him. Eloy stopped and they embraced, and after an exchange of pleasantries, Eloy asked Paulino to walk with him for a little bit. They finally sat on a bench.

"Paulino, you look great. Where have you been hiding? I haven't seen you for at least two years. How are things going?" asked Eloy.

Paulino filled him in on all the salient facts of his life. "After I had a problem with the G2 here in Havana, I started to work for Mike Rodriguez's father at their farm. It's easy work. I'm biding my time. I'm writing a lot. I'm dating a beautiful lady who's one of the owners of a small nearby plantation. I always have bad luck with soldiers and policeman. I just got a horrible beating from a local sergeant of the Guardia Rural. Mike brought me back here, and I'm staying at their home. And you?"

"I'm not going to the university, as you know, we're still on strike. I'm working at my father's business. Not too much to do. I have a lot of time on my hands. I'm waiting until I can return to the university. I read a lot, write a little, and meet with friends." He was running on and on, and he stopped himself. "Do you remember our meetings, organizing strikes and painting banners? You were so active and so full of ideas—and now?"

"Yes, we had fun. I was so full of energy," he said, remembering that busy time. "I don't know how long I can stay in Havana. Mike doesn't want me to go back to the farm right now. He's nervous about what might happen to me. But I have to go. I'm in love with this wonderful lady. I know I'll miss all that Havana offers, but I'm trying to make some money. I have a taxi and a small *timberiche*, and I sell food and drinks at the baseball games. I make small change. I'm saving money."

"You're making lemonade out of lemons," Eloy said, laughing.

"Yes, I am, but I miss the excitement."

"Hey, do you want to meet me tomorrow night at the café? At seven? I'm meeting some friends you'd like to know."

"Sure, I don't have to work tomorrow night."

As planned, Paulino met Eloy, and they walked to Eloy's friend's apartment. The windows were closed in the small room where the meeting was held. The smoke was so dense that Paulino could barely breathe. Eloy introduced him around, and immediately the conversation turned to how they could help the Second Front, in the Escambray Mountains near Trinidad. They discussed bringing arms and ammunition, but it would be difficult and dangerous. Someone recommended sending work boots. They agreed. But how many could they buy without raising suspicion? Others, more practical, said let's send them money. They could buy food and boots. Paulino was excited. He was ready to volunteer his services, but before he had a chance to speak, Eloy said:

"Manolete is living with his family in Cienfuegos. You all know him. I know he has contacts with the Second Front. Last time I saw him was here in Havana a few months ago. Why we don't have someone bring him some money, and he'll know the best way to use it."

They all decided it was the best solution. Then silence fell over the group. Who would do it? Paulino raised his hand. "My mother lives in Cienfuegos. I have to return to my job on a farm in Camagüey. I can deliver it."

The next day he went to talk to Don Miguel and Mike when they were having their coffee in the library.

"Don Miguel, Mike, I'm sorry to intrude. I have to go back. I feel I'm in a prison. It doesn't have bars, but I can't stand it anymore. I'd prefer to die than to hide."

"You aren't hiding, you're only recuperating from your wounds," Mike replied.

"No, I have to return. I got a letter from Fernando, and things are quiet at the *pueblo*. I need to be next to my loved one. The sergeant is not going to rule my life. With your permission, I'd like to leave as soon as possible."

Don Miguel said, "Paulino, son, I understand. I know that you're in love, and when that happens, there is no logic, no prudence . . . only impulsivity. Give it some thought, we're worried about you."

"Thanks, Don Miguel, but I have to go."

After a long ride, Paulino woke up when the bus reached Cienfuegos. He had left it eight years ago for the attractions of Havana—eight years since he had met with his father at his *bodega*. He hadn't contacted him since. He had seldom seen his mother, but at least he had spoken to her on the phone on important occasions like Christmas, on her saint's day, and Mother's day. His mother regularly penciled him long letters on paper torn from a school tablet with wide margins and thick lines, and he dutifully answered them, telling her about his dreams, about Cuca and Ricardo, his short stories, and that he still read books. She worked for the same family in Punta Gorda.

He started walking, carrying a box of sandwiches, his books, and his new suitcase, the money for Manolete hidden in his sock, but he was nervous about calling too much attention to himself, so he went to a taxi stand and negotiated a fare to the house in Punta Gorda. The driver looked at him, wondering why this guy wanted to go that neighborhood, and without saying a word, put his suitcase in the trunk. Paulino couldn't sit still, for each block brought back memories. He entered the Punta Gorda peninsula, passed the Palacio del Valle with its Moorish overtones, built during one of the periods when sugar was valuable in the world market, and stopped in front of the house where he was raised. It seemed smaller, and the shade trees surrounding it had grown taller. The small front lawn looked inviting, but he remembered the house as being better kept. The taxi driver dropped his suitcase on the sidewalk and handed him his books and the box of sandwiches. Paulino stood in a trance, looking at the house, the garden, the bushes that he had planted with the gardener when he was a little boy under the constant supervision of the lady, who did not trust either to do a good job. He walked to the back door and rang the bell. He heard a familiar voice: "We haven't ordered anything from *la bodega*. Who could be calling at this hour?"

The door opened; it was his mother in a white uniform, her head showing wisps of white hair. When she realized it was her son, she started to cry, "My baby, is this my baby! My son, you look so good. Come here. Come here. Why didn't you call me? I would have prepared a special dinner for us. Come, come into the house."

Paulino followed his mother and then, mildly embarrassed, kissed her on both cheeks and let her hold him tightly. Suddenly, his embarrassment drained away and tears pricked his eyes. He wished he had never left home. Soon the other maids came into the kitchen, surrounding them, all asking questions at the same time without giving him time to answer the first one. His mother finally took control. "Please, sit down, here, let me make you coffee. Where did you come from? Camagüey?"

"No, Mother, I came from Havana," Paulino answered as he sat and placed his suitcase on the floor.

"What's happening? You haven't answered my last few letters."

Luisa, the owner of the house, an older patrician lady, entered the kitchen. "What's going on?" she asked. Paulino scarcely recognized her; she had aged so much. After a moment's hesitation he stood up. "Doña Luisa, it's so good to see you. You look so pretty."

"Paulino, my son, I thought you had abandoned us. Your mother worries about you all the time. What are you doing here? What are your plans?"

"I wanted to visit all of you on my way back to my job at the farm."

Luisa took Paulino and his mother to the salon, where oil pictures of her parents commanded the most important wall. Paulino answered her questions while his mother sat next to him, looking at her son, so grown-up, speaking so beautifully with such command of the language, and looking so strong. Oh, she was so proud of him.

Paulino woke up very early the next morning in the garage that was used by the chauffeur. The night before, he and his mother had talked until he could no longer keep his eyes open. His inner alarm clock had woken him at five-thirty to go to the kitchen and start boiling the water for the first morning brew. He glanced at the small mirror in the bathroom. Wake up, he said to himself. You're here. You have a few days left. You'll never be able to do this again. They're not waiting for you at the *batey*. Well, maybe Elena is, but nobody else. He looked at himself one more time. His beard was sparse and his eyes were sunken with exhaustion. He shaved, brushed his teeth, dressed, and wore his new *guayabera*.

His mother was preparing breakfast for the lady of the house, who always had her morning meal on a silver tray with two newspapers to read in her room. He crept up behind his mother to surprise her. She turned around and almost dropped the coffee cup she was putting on the tray. "Jesus, I didn't recognize you! Since when have you become a gentleman? That's a beautiful *guayabera*. Let me look at you. Boy, oh my boy! You look so handsome! Are you sure you aren't hiding a girl in Cienfuegos?"

Paulino laughed. "No, I just felt like wearing it. I bought it at the same store where my boss buys his, only this one isn't made to order. Let me tell you something. I want to do something special for you and *la Señora*. Please tell her that I'll buy your lunch today. I'll be back around twelve-thirty. I'll pick the place. It'll be a surprise. I have to go, but before I do, let me have a taste of your coffee. It smells so good."

Paulino knew were Manolete lived, because he had called him the night before. He only said that he was Eloy's friend. He walked to Manolete's house, but stopped next to a tree and checked around. No parked cars with people in them, and no one walking on the sidewalks. He walked fast and rang the doorbell. When Manolete opened the door, Paulino remembered his face. He handed over the envelope and shook hands, and hastily departed.

Half an hour later, he arrived at his father's *bodega*, and as he entered, he noticed a modern cash register and an abundance of packaged goods with gaudy colors, some of their titles written in English, instead of the old barrels full of potatoes, rice, and beans of all types. A young employee stood behind the counter and smiled. "What can I do for you? Do you need something? We have the freshest vegetables and fruits."

"I came to see the owner. Is he in?" Paulino replied.

"Oh yes, he's in the back. May I tell him who wants to see him?"

"Sure, tell him it is his son, Paulino, just back from Havana."

The young man did a double take and ran to the back. A few minutes later his father showed up. His hair was sparse, he was heavier, and his once healthy face color was pale, as if his red blood was now watered-down milk.

"What are you doing here?" he said, "Come around to the back. I don't want to talk to you up front."

Paulino followed him deep into the building, to a part that opened onto a small courtyard. His father pulled out a taburete.

"Sit down. What do you want?" he asked, as he remained standing.

"I came to say hello. I'm with my mother, and I decided to visit you and see how you're doing."

His father was suspicious. "I'm fine, you said hello, and now you can say good-bye."

Paulino smiled at the familiar gruffness. He felt good about coming. His father's anxiety at seeing him was worth the trip. This was the man responsible for both his conception and abandonment. Now, the one who thought he was so much better than his mother was nervous with sweat beading on his forehead.

"No, Father. I don't need a thing from you. I'm getting married. She's a very nice, hardworking girl. She and her sisters own a plantation. I came to tell you. You may have grandchildren—isn't that exciting?" His father looked anything but excited. "I'm happy to see that you still know me. Don't worry. I'm doing well. I don't need you. Good-bye," and then Paulino turned toward the door without even reaching to shake his father's hand.

By the time he returned, it was almost noon, and Paulino's mother, wearing her best dress, was waiting in the kitchen. She had used a little bit of lipstick and held one of the La Señora's old purses close to her chest. Paulino nodded to her. It was her moment. "Are you ladies ready?" he asked.

"Yes, we are," she said, and went to find the lady of the house.

Luisa gave him the keys to her car and sat in the backseat. Paulino's mother sat up front next to him. He drove down to the end of the boulevard. There, built on piers over Cienfuegos Bay, stood the town's best restaurant, La Covadonga. The sides were open to the elements, but the customers were protected from the sun by a well-built roof. Paulino stopped the car at the front entrance, opened the doors, parked the car, and guided his mother and Doña Luisa to his reserved table next to the water. Paulino felt the stares of the other patrons. He sat erect and touched his mother's hands.

"What would you ladies like to drink? Beer? A soft drink?"

"Beer will be great," said Luisa, while his mother's eyes sparkled with pride.

Paulino ordered beers and a paella for the table, while his mother sat erectly next to her son, who wore his white linen *guayabera*, and with her employer of so many years, surrounded by the best of Cienfuegos' society.

When they returned to the house afterward, Luisa thanked Paulino. She had not been out in a while, and she thought that her outing would spark enough gossip to last a few days. She enjoyed her lunch, and it was time for her siesta. The beer had made her sleepy. Paulino stood next to his mother, who was bursting with pride.

"Mother, I wish I could stay longer. I have to go. I miss Elena. You'll meet her and will love her. I'd like to marry her soon."

His mother kissed him. "You're a good son. Write. I always love to read your letters and your stories. But be careful. The world is full of hate and bad people. I'll pray to the *Virgencita* to take care of you."

"I'll be careful. I'll write. Tell *La Señora* that I had to leave. Thank her again for allowing me to stay here when I was a little kid. Tell her I didn't forget."

Fernando was waiting at the bus station in Ciego de Ávila. Paulino was the last one out. He was relieved to see Fernando, who gave him a strong embrace.

Paulino squirmed, "Hey, if I didn't know you, I'd think you want to send me back to the hospital. Be careful, *hermano*, that hug hurt."

Fernando laughed. "You spend a little time in Havana, and suddenly, you're a delicate child? You need to get back to real life in the country." Fernando patted Paulino on the back, grabbed his suitcase, and led him to their car.

On the way to the farm, Paulino asked about Elena, and Fernando said, "She's great. I don't know how you got so lucky! She came to the farm to talk to Ricardo several times. She drove the plantation's big truck. She's something else. She wanted to know about you. She suspected that Manuel was not giving her the real news and that he was holding back on his reports about you."

"That sounds like Manuel, all right." Paulino said, hiding how good he felt that Elena had come to find out about him. Fernando brought Paulino up-to-date on the whereabouts of the sergeant; that Ricardo was making everyone work harder than Manolo; how busy he was now that the *zafra* was in full swing. After a few minutes of silence, Fernando commented, "Yeah, Elena really loves you. Man, she was pissed at Manuel because he wasn't giving her enough news about you."

"I've missed her. I wrote her a letter every day. Thank God she doesn't have a phone at the plantation. I'd have gone broke calling her long-distance."

"Do you know when Mike is returning?" Fernando asked.

Paulino laughed. "I tell you—they're both in *love*. You should see the old man! He's getting all dressed up and going out with a real cute girl. Younger than his daughters! Can you imagine that? The old rooster wants to crow!"

Both laughed out loud. As they entered the *batey*, Fernando sounded the horn. Cuca came out from the kitchen entrance, wiping her hands on her white apron. Manuel, who was trimming the hooves of the black stallion, looked up and smiled, and Ricardo hurried out of the office. Paulino felt welcomed home, the best home he'd ever had, as his friends surrounded him, talking at the same time, asking for news about the family and city life. Cuca prepared coffee, and after hurriedly downing the small cup, Paulino left in his car and drove to see his love. Paulino felt his ribs, but the excitement of driving his car and seeing Elena made the pain manageable.

The sisters greeted him with incessant questions: "What did you do in Havana? How was it? Cienfuegos?" Paulino wanted to be alone with his love rather than answering such questions, and answered monosyllabically. As soon as he could, he embraced Elena and they kissed. The other sisters, giggling, disappeared on the pretext that they had to prepare supper. Holding hands, the pair walked to the back garden to kiss again. Paulino wanted more than simple kisses and touched Elena's hip, but she stopped him. "Not here, not yet. I also want to, but not now. Just because I haven't seen you in a long time—"

Paulino, who was frustrated, said, "Baby, it's been so long. We're all alone. No one can see us. Please—"

"No, no, and no. I love you, but no."

"You know that I love you. I want to marry you."

"Yes, I know. That's why I won't!"

Elena was his girlfriend. He knew it, she knew it, and everyone else knew it. Then, among the mango and banana trees, at the beginning of a gorgeous tropical night, Paulino dropped to his knees.

"Elena, will you marry me?"

She pulled him up and kissed him one more time on the lips. "Yes, my fool. My *bobito*. I love you, too. Come, let's go and tell my sisters. They were wondering when you were going to have the courage to ask me."

By the next morning, everyone knew. Ricardo was the first to congratulate Paulino as Cuca teased him, "Hey, now you're not even going to say hello to us. You're moving out to your own house!"

"No, way. I would never do that!"

27

The Apartment

JULIO WAS TAKING a shower to wash the sweat from his body. The air-conditioning unit in the small apartment scarcely cooled the bedroom, which was so small it could hardly contain the king-size bed where Esmeralda lay naked, curled into fetal position, rubbing her puffy eyes. They had had a violent argument when she had asked Julio for money to go Miami. She tried without success to persuade him with her tears, and now her face was swollen and wet. Julio resisted her, even though her tanned, well-formed body, contrasting with the soft, white sheets, cast a powerful allure.

"Papi, *everyone* is leaving," she whined over the rattle of the air-conditioner and the splattering of the water in the tub. "I just want to go to Miami, yes, only Miami, only for a few days. I need to go. Papi, please. Do you hear me?"

Julio did not answer. He hated arguments and hadn't expected this development. He had thought they had a clear understanding. We have sex; I give you gifts. Well, it wasn't working. If he gave her money this time, the demands would never stop. He would have to keep her, but what purpose would that serve if she was in Miami and no longer close at hand for their occasional lunch-hour assignations? An older man, who had left the island, had kept her. She felt that responsibility for her well-being should be his. The old bastard, whoever he was, should have taken her. Julio gave himself an especially thorough scrubbing, closed his eyes as the hot water fell over his body as he tried to forget this annoying complication.

Esmeralda, naked, entered the bathroom and firmly said, "You have to help me. I don't want to cause problems, but if I have to, I will. You never told me that you're married. Who's the blonde lady and who are those children in the pictures in your wallet—niece and nephews? Come on, I'm not a fool. Look, give me money for the plane ticket and two weeks at the Fontainebleau. It's only a thousand dollars. You can come and visit me, things will calm down. I can't stay in the city anymore." She stepped into the bathtub, reached down and touched him.

"Papi, come on, Papi. You have it. Just give it to me," she whispered into his ear.

Esmeralda attentively dried Julio's body and helped him get dressed. "I have to go to the bank," he said. "I don't carry that much cash with me. Let's meet here tomorrow at the same time."

She came closer to him and purred, "Thank you, my love. You'll not regret it. We'll continue to see each other. I'd never want this to end. I thought you would never stop. You're quite a man! My Papi, I already miss you. Promise me, please, that you'll come to Miami to be with me, at least for a few days in the middle of each week. We'll never leave the room— just room service. Tomorrow we'll make love over and over again."

Julio ran late the next day. He had a client who talked forever about what to do with the Cuban treasury bonds he owned. Julio was worried that his line was tapped. He had recently started to hear the echo of his voice, so he was reluctant to discuss his opinion about holding Cuban paper, lest it be considered an opinion contrary to the government's interests. In the end, he agreed to meet the client at La Floridita for a drink. At least there, he could talk without fear of being heard. Besides, it was good for his reputation to be seen with such a wealthy man. He then walked to his bank and got the money, ten crisp hundred-dollar bills. He placed them in an envelope and carefully put it in the inner pocket of his jacket. He was so proud of this jacket; it had been custom-made by Pepe, his Spanish tailor at Mieres & Co., of very light English wool. He got into his car, carefully draped his jacket on the seat. It was a scorching day, and the steering wheel was so hot that he had to use his handkerchief to hold it, and the leather seat was hotter. As he drove slowly to his garçonier, he resolved that his next car would have an air-conditioner. Esmeralda was waiting, and she was going to be fantastic. He had reached a moment where his whole life was under his absolute control. He had spoken to his manager about opening an office in Miami to take care of the clients that were moving money to the United States. He could fly over, spend two to three days with Esmeralda, and then fly back. It was so easy, less than thirty minutes. He could take care of his clients outside of the government's watch. Also, he did like an occasional American girl, usually the tall, athletic blondes, but Esmeralda was even better. Everything was so easy, so convenient, and to have so many choices would be ideal!

He grandly flung open the door to the apartment, the gate to his private castle. He was struck by the silence—Esmeralda did not deliver her usual greeting. She must have a special plan for their last day. He spoke in a low voice, "Dear, my *cuchi, cuchi*, where are you? I have the gift I promised you. Are you hiding? Shall I try to find you?"

Julio opened the door to the bedroom to find, sitting in his armchair, calmly smoking a cigarette, Captain Velasco of the National Police, the man who was in charge of security for the city.

"Welcome, Julito," Velasco said. "I've being waiting for you. You're running twenty minutes late. I was about to give up on you. I'm sorry I must report I'm not as pretty or as talented as Esmeralda. She's not able to join you today, or tomorrow, or maybe for a long time. I'm sorry to bear bad news, but she's mine." His voice was firm and sarcastic. He crushed his cigarette on the floor with a highly polished brown shoe.

Julio was shaken. "I don't understand what you're doing here. This is my apartment."

"I know, and you've been using it for activities and meetings against the government. Your so-called friend Esmeralda Martinez is an operative of the 26 of July Movement, which raises money for Fidel Castro's rebel cause. Señorita Martinez is in my custody. I understand you have money for her. I don't know yet if you are worth my time, but I'm soon going to find out," he said with true menace in his voice. "There are ways you can help me, and if you don't want to help, I invite you to come with me and sit in a prison cell next to your lovely friend. Oh, I forgot to tell you a little bit of news. Señorita Martinez was not going to Miami. She doesn't have a passport. What are your plans now, Julito, my dear friend?"

Two plainclothesmen entered the room and blocked the door. Julio leaned against the small dresser for support. "Now, you know who I am.

I'm not political. I like to have a good time, and that's what I was having with this girl. I've never conspired against the president, whom I hold in great regard." The captain did not seemed moved by this profession. "So what are my plans? Well, for one, I expect you, Captain, to understand the situation, shake hands, and leave. As a gentleman, I can assure you that everything that I have told you is true. Yes, I have a sum of money with me. Exactly one thousand dollars, it's my money. It's mine to use as I please, and indeed I was going to give it to Esmeralda so she could go to Miami. That part of your story is correct. This apartment is simply where I entertain. I'm sure you understand, because you're a gentleman. So, Captain, please, I would like to consider this an unhappy misunderstanding. I would like to escort you and these officers to the front door."

The captain calmly regarded the crushed cigarette. "I appreciate your sangfroid, but I'm not playing games. It's better if you come with us. Maybe you'll be able to remember a bit more." He motioned to the plain-clothesmen, who grabbed Julio by the elbow and marched him out of the apartment and into an unmarked car.

Captain Velasco's station was in El Vedado, very close by. The officers walked him past the prison cells full of men and women. Esmeralda was in the last one, alone and sobbing. When she saw Julio being escorted past her cell, she covered her bruised and swollen face with her hands and re-fused to meet his eyes. They took Julio to a small office and relieved him of his black crocodile belt, wallet, money clip, watch, gold cigarette lighter, and cigarettes. They put everything in a big manila envelope, scribbled his name on the corner, and sealed it. They transferred him into a small cell with a light bulb and a small pot, but no windows, no chair, no table, and then closed the door.

Julio couldn't keep track of the time. He started to worry about his children and wife. He felt assaulted and violated. He hadn't participated in activities against the government, other than the usual bar jokes. He didn't care about politics; he just wanted to make money and have sex with beautiful women. How could he explain this to Lourdes? He was hardly the only man in Havana to have something on the side, but truly, the way Velasco was handling him was uncalled for. He would make phone calls when he left. Velasco would be sorry!

After hours without anything happening, he banged on the door. "I have to make a phone call. I'm late for an important meeting. People, very important people, are waiting for me." For fifteen minutes he kicked the door and banged it with his fists, but nothing happened. Exhausted, he crept to the corner of the room and, holding tight to his knees, panicked.

When the door opened six hours later, Julio was relieved. The stench in the room from his piss and excrement was offensive, he was terribly hungry, and the heat of the room and the lack of water had dehydrated him. Two men blocked the small door as two others grabbed his arms and took him to an office with a small desk and two steel chairs. They pushed him down on one.

"Hey, be careful. You know who I am!" Julio snapped, glaring defiantly at the two policemen. "I'm sure you're aware you're making a big mistake. I'm ready to leave. Please call Captain Velasco."

Just then, he appeared at the door and sat in the chair opposite Julio. The clock on the wall of the office read nine p.m.

"Well, Julito, how do you feel being a traitor to your country and your class? What games do you like to play? Don't you know that I know what's going on? Do you think we're stupid? We can do it two ways, my way or my way. I know you've given money before to this young lady. She told me. You thought you were very generous, but she thought you were cheap, very cheap, and what you gave her was more than what the best puta could charge you for sexual favors. No one has to pay so much for a puta, unless you are a maricón who wants to change. Are you a maricón? No, I don't think so. I would have known. Now, tell me, I've not hurt you, not yet. Do you want to smoke a cigarette? Here, have one of mine. They're fresh from the States, special delivery last night. I'll light it for you." Julio took the lit cigarette. "Now, you see, I'm your friend. I haven't hurt you. I treat you better than you deserve."

"You're making a mistake," Julio said.

The captain laughed, "Who do you think you are? You're making all this money while I do all the dirty work to keep this society churning along. You, and the others like you, who play revolution as if it were a mental exercise, and think it's chic to believe in existentialism, free love, and liberty for all, and all that garbage! You'll just be eaten alive by the monster, if the monster succeeds. See what happened in Russia. You don't believe me?"

"But, Captain, we're so close to the United States."

"Just wait. We'll win, but you're not helping. We know you and what you do."

"I haven't done a thing."

The captain continued undisturbed, "Playing hero, giving money, thinking you have the ticket for a new world. No, it won't happen. Not this time, my friend. We're tired of holding your society together, taking care of the crap, while you and your friends make money and joke about us."

Julio moved restlessly in his chair. He crossed and recrossed his legs as the captain added, "Now, let's get this over with. Who else is with you? Who of your friends give money to the rebels, so they can kill innocent children? Who?"

Julio tried to get up and was pushed down by one of the agents. His face was red with anger. He had never thought that he would be subjected to this type of interrogation. "I don't know. I'm not helping Castro. I was having a good time. She doesn't mean anything to me. I don't believe in a revolution or in Castro, or in the *Segundo Frente*. I work hard at what I do—all I do is manage money—I sell stocks and bonds. I don't need to change things. I'm doing very well, and I don't have anything to do with this Esmeralda, just sex."

Velasco spat on the floor, threw his chair down and, without making any further eye contact with Julio, left the room. He signaled one of his subordinates who stood in front of Julio. He sat erect in the chair, smoking his cigarette. The agent took hold of the handkerchief pocket of Julio's sport coat lying on the table and ripped it off, and threw it on the dirty floor.

Julio was shaken. "Hey, what are you doing, this is my best jacket!"

The man looked at Julio, picked it up from the floor, and ripped off the right front pocket.

"Hey, what's going on? Please, this jacket is custom-made!" Julio said as the agent forcefully took his mangled jacket, and began to rip it into strips in front of his eyes.

"No, no, no," whispered Julio, but it was too late. His life would never be the same.

They returned him to the same cell and left him in total darkness. He felt his way to a corner and huddled against a cell wall, then slid against it to the bare floor. He shivered and sobbed, "Oh my God, my God!" He slept, exhausted by his impotence.

Five hours later, the door to the cell opened, and two men entered to haul Julio out. He was taken to Captain Velasco's office, where the captain was sitting in front of his desk. It was early in the morning.

"I hope you had a chance to refresh your memory. I don't play games here. I know you're part of a big, influential group. Here, this is a piece of paper and a pencil. I need names, names of your friends who give money to the rebels."

Julio froze. He couldn't think of any names to write. In fact, he couldn't think of anyone's name at all.

The captain waited for ten minutes before he turned around to his henchmen. "Okay, let's give him another chance to stew. Take him back to his suite. I'll be back."

A pair of men easily hoisted Julio, as if he were a sack of potatoes, and dumped him in the dark cell.

Around seven in the morning, Don Miguel received a call from the lieutenant who served as the minister's military attaché. He had gone to bed rather late after having celebrated his engagement to Patricia with her family. The ringing of the phone startled him from his sleep, and he rushed to answer, worried about the kind of news that comes so early in the morning.

"Don Miguel? It's Lieutenant Sampietro, the minister's aide. The minister needs to speak with you urgently. This cannot be done on the phone. Be assured that it's urgent. That's all I can say."

Don Miguel quickly dressed and drove directly to the ministry.

"Miguelito," the minister began, "I have bad news for you. Captain Velasco has your son-in-law, Julio Consuengra, at his station. He was arrested yesterday afternoon. Don't worry. He's safe. Nothing has happened to him. But he was caught in very bad company."

"What sort of company?" Don Miguel asked.

"A young girl, whom you may have met, because she was seen with Andres. Her name is Esmeralda Martinez. She is an operative for the

26 of July Movement. She went out with rich men to raise money for the *hijos de putas* who are fighting against us. Your son-in-law admitted that on several occasions he gave her money. She confirmed it. He was going to hand her a large amount of money when he was arrested in his garçonier. We can not condone his behavior."

"Of course not," Don Miguel said in a soft, assuring voice, trying to appear collected.

"I know. I vouched personally for you to the president," the minister continued, "that you didn't know of his involvement. If I thought you knew, you wouldn't be here now. This young girl, Esmeralda, is extremely dangerous. We thought that the best way to handle this is to give Julio to you and have him leave the country until he comes back to his senses. We don't want to file charges against him. It would be embarrassing for your daughter and your families. But what he did has serious repercussions. I want you to know that our president is aware of the situation and is unlikely to forget it. He's the one who has asked me, because of your friendship with us, to handle it this way. He knows how hard you work with me."

"Thank you," Don Miguel said. "I appreciate the leniency."

"Now, we need to arrange for his departure. Lieutenant Sampietro will escort you both to the airport. He can take an afternoon flight to Miami. We're keeping the money he was going to give to her as evidence. It was a thousand dollars. We expect Julio to give you his word of honor that he won't be involved further in antigovernment activities. One day he may return and everything may be forgotten. However, if he gets involved again, we'll know, and his future treatment will be different and severe."

"I understand," Don Miguel said.

The minister continued, "We're being generous with him only for your sake. Be assured that we're not going to tolerate such behavior, and he'll be watched very closely wherever he is, especially if he returns to Cuba. The young ones can't play revolutionaries and think that they'll not get caught. We have a very effective intelligence service. Do you agree?"

"You know what I think. I deliver on my promises," he assured the minister. "I'm deeply sorry that this has happened. I'll make certain that he understands. Please give the president my personal thanks for protecting my family. Be assured that this will not be forgotten. When can I see Julio?"

"Soon," the minister replied, as he got up from his chair and the two briefly embraced. "You can pick him up at ten at Velasco's station. My attaché will be there. Then you can take him to the airport. You'll be escorted." He clapped Don Miguel on the back. "They never learn, the young. She has to be a great fuck for people to risk so much. That's the one good thing about being older. We don't fall for such traps anymore." The lieutenant escorted Don Miguel to the elevator door. "I'll see you at ten o'clock at the station."

Don Miguel called Mike at the office and asked him to go to Lourdes' house. He waited for Mike in front of her door. When they knocked, Lourdes opened it, still in her robe. "Papi, Mike, what's happened? You all look terrible! Is it about Julio?" She cried, "He's dead! Oh my God, he's dead, that's why he didn't come home last night. He had an accident. Please tell me it isn't true!"

"He's not dead or hurt, but something very serious has happened." Don Miguel put one arm around his daughter and wiped her tears. "Come, let's talk in your room." While Mike waited in the foyer, her father took her into the bedroom and told her in a low voice, "Julio is okay—that is, he's alive and well. But he's in the custody of the *Policia Nacional* at Captain Velasco's station." He sat her on the bed. "I just talked to the minister. Julio made a mistake, but the government is being lenient and will allow him to leave the country today. He has to go into exile immediately."

"Into exile?" she gasped. "Now? Right now? What happened!" she cried.

Don Miguel took Lourdes in his arms and explained as gently as he could that Julio had been accused of giving money to a dangerous revolutionary group, but assured her that the accusation was not true. Don Miguel told her that Julio was spared because of his connection to the minister and the president, but that they asked him to leave immediately. He said it was not clear when, and if, Julio could return again.

"Oh, Papi, oh, Papi!" she sobbed.

There was little time, so Don Miguel helped Lourdes up, told her she had to be strong, and had her collect Julio's passport, pack a small suitcase with essential clothes, and a clean set for him to change into at the station.

"What am I going to do?" Lourdes asked. "My children are in school now."

"I'm calling Adelaida to come over here, right away. Mike and I will pick up Julio at the station. Mike will call Julio's parents. You shouldn't go to the airport. I don't want a scene, and you belong here with the children. I might be able to bring him here. I'm not sure. He's alive and he'll be safe in Miami. For now, take care of yourself and the children." Don Miguel called in the maid and instructed her to remain with Lourdes until Adelaida arrived.

Mike helped Lourdes pack the bag. "Let's go," Don Miguel said, "we have work to do." They didn't speak. Don Miguel thought about Comillas, and how smart he was to leave when he did. Then a thought froze in his mind: He had met Patricia at La Roca with Comillas and Esmeralda. Could she be involved? And Mike? Was he involved in whatever this mess really was? Don Miguel chased the suspicions from his mind. There was too much else to do right now.

Lieutenant Sampietro waited for them at the entrance of Velasco's station and escorted them to his office, where Julio waited—stinking, unshaved, dirty, his hair matted, his customary cocky expression shattered. The captain briefly acknowledged Don Miguel and then looked at Julio and said, "You're leaving against my wishes. I wouldn't have let you go so easily. You're damn lucky." He made Lieutenant Sampietro sign the release papers. The captain collected them and told the lieutenant, "He's all yours."

Julio was too ashamed to talk. Don Miguel asked if Julio could change his clothes. The captain motioned to his private bathroom. Julio changed and came out, looking like a man who had a bad night on the town and smelling worse. The captain gave the lieutenant the sealed envelope containing Julio's personal belongings. From it, Julio retrieved his watch and his alligator belt; then promptly lit a cigarette with his gold lighter. They left Velasco's office and the lieutenant, Don Miguel, and Julio entered an unmarked police car. Mike followed in his car.

Julio smoked one cigarette after another. Don Miguel did not speak to him during the ride to the airport. When they arrived, they were showed into a small waiting room. Mike shook hands with Lieutenant Sampietro, and Don Miguel merely nodded. Escorted by the lieutenant, Julio walked slowly up the ladder to the Cubana Viscount's door, and then turned around to watch the small crowd that was always present for a plane's departure.

Mike took his father back to his car, and they drove to Lourdes' home. For a few minutes, Don Miguel didn't speak. Finally, he said to Mike, "I'm very disappointed in Julio. I'll never trust him again. I don't know how much to tell Lourdes." He shook his head at the disgraceful behavior. "I hope Julio has learned his lesson. It could have been worse. I owe the president and the minister one."

"Julio didn't use his head. What are we going to tell Lourdes?"

"I'll think of something for the time being, but not the whole truth."

When they entered Lourdes' home, they found a large group of friends consoling her. Julio's parents were there. Adelaida and Jose Maria had arrived, and Mike was surprised to see Maria Alicia. The maids were busy offering small cups of coffee and soft drinks. Lourdes, seeing her father, got up from the sofa to embrace him.

"Tell me, how is he?"

"He's fine, he wasn't hurt. He should be in Miami already. He'll be calling you soon. I reserved a room for him at the Everglades."

Don Miguel approached Julio's father, and they went to an empty room. A few minutes later, the two somber men returned to the group.

Jose Maria separated Mike from the women, but before they could speak in private, Maria Alicia came to hug and kiss Mike.

"How terrible! What's happened to Julio is just awful."

Mike squeezed her hand. "It could've been worse."

She understood immediately that Mike did not want to talk, so she went to console Lourdes.

"What happened?" Jose Maria asked. Mike told him what little he knew.

Jose Maria said, "It's going to get uglier. How much does Lourdes know?

Mike said, "Very little. Father is going to handle it."

Four hours later, Julio called from his hotel room and spoke with Lourdes. No one heard what he said, but Lourdes did not cry. Slowly, the group left. Adelaida stayed with Lourdes, and at around five, the children returned from playing with friends. Lourdes told them that their father had gone to Miami on a business trip. The children reacted with excitement. "Oh goody, he'll bring us a lot of gifts!"

THE NEXT MORNING, Julio woke up in his room at the Everglades Hotel in Miami. He had a vicious hangover. Every muscle hurt, and his head! He had not been able to go to sleep the night before. He had tossed and turned in his bed; finally, he got up and went to the hotel bar, where he drank until it closed. He still couldn't sleep; nightmares taunted him every time he dozed off. In one, he was in a small room. No lights. No windows. The walls were moving. He wanted to scream, to stop them from closing in on him. He could not. He had lost his voice. Esmeralda opened a door. Her face was cut. One eye hung out of its socket. Her front teeth were broken and her lips puffed. Her face was painted like a cheap whore's. "Papi, Papi!" she cried. She fell back, shrieking. The door closed soundlessly.

He woke, hoarsely whispering, "Help!" He got up for a drink of water, and then went back to bed. Again, the nightmares came. He was in a new room, this one large and fully lit with large windows on both sides. Through one of them, he saw Lourdes and his children. They all sat on black chairs, immobile, and unblinking. He went to the window and knocked on the pane. He waved his hand. They continued to look straight ahead; they didn't see him. He cried. He couldn't see them anymore. They had disappeared. Through the other window, he saw Esmeralda partially naked with blood all over her body, holding a bloodstained white sheet and sitting on a white rocking chair. He ran to the exit door on the other side of the room, but when he got near it, the door closed in his face. The floor moved. He lost his balance and fell flat on the floor. He woke up again, sweating. He looked around the room. It took a few moments for him to realize where he was, but he still couldn't believe what had happened. He took a cold shower, shaved, and went down to find some breakfast.

28

Maria Alicia's Engagement Party

IT WAS THE perfect night. The garden was illuminated by carefully placed soft lights. Iron tables were scattered on the lawn and off to one side, and behind a long bar stood four attentive bartenders. Maria Alicia was overwhelmed when she saw how many friends her mother had invited; her list had expanded exponentially. It had happened this way: Maria invited Gloriosa, who had been one of Adelaida's best friends, but Maria didn't know that Gloriosa had spoken with her current best friend, Amalia, who had also been a close friend of Adelaida's and who had married Don Miguel's best friend, Antonio Gonzalez, who had been the best man at Don Miguel and Adelaida's wedding. Maria found out while playing canasta with Amalia that she knew from Gloriosa that Mike and Maria Alicia were getting engaged, and Maria, afraid of not inviting her, because she had already invited Gloriosa, told her, "We're just having a small family party, why don't you come?" So after the game of canasta, Maria went home and added names to the list, and those names begat names, and those names begat more names until the party had swelled to two hundred of her closest friends.

The summer season had ended, according to the calendar. Although the seasons of the year are similar on a tropical island—there is rain or drought—Cubans followed European traditions. *Guayaberas* were relegated to the closet after the first day of September. Accordingly, the men wore lightweight, dark English wool suits, white shirts with French cuffs, gold cufflinks, colorful Italian ties, white pocket squares anointed with a dab of cologne, and black shoes. Mike tied his red silk tie in a Windsor knot and went down to the safe in the library to remove the engagement ring he had bought for Maria Alicia. As he opened the door, he found the safe open, and his father standing next to it.

"Mike, I have a surprise for you. I've been waiting for this day to give it to you. This was your mother's favorite solitaire diamond ring. I gave it to her after you were born. She wanted you to have it, so you could give it to the woman you loved. I'm sorry that she isn't here to give it to you herself. She would have loved Maria Alicia. She'll make you very happy. She's a superb girl."

Mike embraced his father silently, and slipped the small, worn leather box into his pocket.

"Thanks, Father, I know she'll love it. It brings back so many good memories." He gave his father a tight embrace.

Yet Mike felt awkward. He had already bought a ring, but he didn't want to hurt his father's feelings. Then he realized there was a solution. How lucky for Maria Alicia, he thought. She's starting her married life with two diamond rings.

Mike arrived early to be with Maria Alicia. "I have surprises for you. My father gave me this diamond ring. It was his present to my mother when I was born, and when Mother knew she was dying, she asked my father to give it to my future wife. He thought you would love it. My parents had a very happy marriage. My father wishes you to be as happy as my mother was."

Maria Alicia opened the small box and placed the ring on her finger. "Mike, it's so beautiful," and kissed him. "I have to thank your father so much. It's so touching. I love it. It means so much to me. I'm so touched by your mother's thoughts. Has your father arrived? I want to give him a big, big kiss."

"No, but he'll be here soon, he went to pick up Patricia, but I also have another surprise. This one is from me."

And he gave her the other ring.

"You . . . you're so special. You're spoiling me!" she said, as she kissed and hugged him again. "Let's show the rings to my mother and father. They'll love them. I'm so happy."

She ran to find her mother, who was putting the last touches on a floral arrangement. "Mami, look, look at this ring Mike gave me. It belonged to his mother . . . and this one he bought for me."

Maria held her daughter's fingers, admiring both rings. "Mike, they're absolutely gorgeous. You're spoiling my daughter. Let's find your father. They're fantastic!" Before Maria could find *El Gordo*, though, the doorbell rang, announcing the arrival of the first guests.

The party was in full swing around eight o'clock. By that point, Maria Alicia and Mike's cheeks ached from smiling for photographs. Though invited, Patricia was trying to be inconspicuous because she was nervous. She was careful about how much she drank. It was the first time she was in a large social group made up of friends of Don Miguel, and she wanted him to be proud of her. Meanwhile, Pepe and Carmen overtly enjoyed the party. Pepe, mindful of Patricia's request to control his drinking, nonetheless insisted on working his way through the garden with Carmen, introducing himself to every guest with a hearty "How do you do?"

"Beautiful night!"

"Maria Alicia and Maria look lovely."

"The weather is perfect."

"Yes, she's our sister."

"No, I don't know them well, but the name is familiar."

"Yes, I would really enjoy it."

The conversations moved gracefully—no politics, no religion, no baseball. Carmen was excited to see so many beautiful dresses, and to know what was "in." Not that she wasn't a great *modiste*, but in some trades, exposure to the habitat of your clients is everything. Around nine o'clock, the guests, sated by the food and happy from the champagne, made their way home.

Maria asked Mike's family to stay for a last glass of champagne. Don Miguel and Patricia joined Lourdes, Adelaida and Jose Maria, and Maria Alicia's sisters and their husbands in the living room as *El Gordo* opened another bottle. Maria Alicia and Mike entered holding hands. They were exhausted. Mike gave a big kiss to Maria. "Thank you. It was a beautiful party. I'll always love you as my mother. This was perfect. I've never seen so many of my mother's friends. You both were so generous, inviting all these people. Thank you, again."

El Gordo replied, "We want you to take good care of our daughter. I know you will."

"Yes, sir. I will."

El Gordo was getting ready to make a toast when Don Miguel interrupted.

"I don't know if this is the proper occasion. Our families are together, and I know that Maria Alicia and Mike will have a beautiful life. I loved his mother. You, Maria, and you, *Gordo*, knew her well. We were and are good friends." He was building up to his point, taking a careful route. "I have an announcement to make. Patricia and I are going to get married. I went to Pinar del Rio to ask for her hand from her father. He agreed. I didn't want to compete with these two lovebirds, but their marriage has been announced now, and there's nothing that will surpass it. Patricia and I will soon have an intimate church wedding in Pinar del Rio."

Adelaida and Maria Alicia ran to embrace Patricia, and *El Gordo* embraced Don Miguel, telling him in a low voice, "You bastard, she's beautiful."

The next day, Luis de la Posada's column at the *Diario de la Marina* had a complete description of the party and the guests. He took great care in describing the dresses worn by Maria Alicia and Maria; he also made a brief mention of Patricia, whose face appeared with Miguel's in several photos. The rotogravure section of the paper had plenty of photos of the party. Maria Alicia and Carmen both carefully clipped the section: Maria Alicia for her wedding album, Carmen for a special box she kept in her armoire. For both, it would be a night they would never forget.

29

Paulino's Turn

THE NOTARY PUBLIC'S office in the *pueblo* did not open until nine o'clock, with the arrival of the secretary and the clerk responsible for handwriting deeds and wills. Dr. Rico, the notary, usually came in after ten; he spent the early morning at his small sugar plantation. His job was not demanding, time-consuming, or well paid, since the jurisdiction his practice covered was not a busy one. Few people bought or sold houses, and the traffic in other land sales was nil; wills were few and far between and uncomplicated because of the testamentary provisions contained in the Civil Code. Dr. Rico wondered why he had spent so many years in law school and why had he bought the rights to this notary public office in the middle of nowhere. When he had such thoughts of regret, he considered what the life of a trial lawyer would have been like—long hours in a dimly lit, hot, and smelly courthouse arguing the merits of a client's claim before a magistrate or a judge. In that, he found consolation in his career, dull as it might be.

Paulino was exhausted. He forgot to set his alarm clock, and he was now in a hurry. He had, nonetheless, dressed carefully. He had never met Dr. Rico, but he wanted to look like a suitable groom for Elena. He pomaded his hair and brushed it hard to flatten it against his skull. As he left his room, wearing his white *guayabera* and blue slacks, Cuca shouted out, "Paulino, you look like a caricature out of Zig-Zag. What are you selling today, a new encyclopedia or guaranteed burial insurance?" Paulino snickered and waved good-bye.

Elena and Paulino had to wait for Dr. Rico, who had been detained by a very important piece of business: having a cup of coffee with Adela, the telephone operator, whom he was courting to no avail. He showed up wearing a crumpled linen coat and a tie, sharply clashing with Paulino's rigidly-pressed look.

"Elena, Elenita, how nice it is to see you, and you're all dressed up! You also look so well in your riding clothes." Dr. Rico was extremely effusive with her. The sisters had been excellent clients when he had settled their parents' estates. "And who is this fine gentleman?"

"This is my fiancé, Paulino Rodriguez. He works with Don Miguel Rodriguez at Las Guásimas."

Dr. Rico immediately said, "Welcome, welcome. You have to know how close I am to Elena and her family. She's like a sister to me, a little sister."

"That's very sweet of you to say," Elena said.

Paulino shook his hand. "Pleasure to meet you."

"I had the honor of being Elena's father's counselor. What a man! He was a titan! Unbelievable strength! And his mind! If he had played chess, he would've beaten Casablanca," Dr. Rico declared with exaggerated drama. "It's a pity that he died at such a young age. Imagine, he wasn't even sixty! I miss his humor and wit."

Nervous about what he was about to do, Paulino didn't utter a word.

"Sorry to keep you standing," Dr. Rico apologized without a hint of sincerity. "Well, you two look like a pair of doves. Come into my inner sanctum. Excuse me for the books and the dust. You know how hard it is to find good help. It's almost impossible, and it's so difficult to be kept abreast of what's happening in the world of law, every day a new decree. I've become a fervent connoisseur of *La Gaceta Oficial*. I'm obliged to read it every week. Well, well, Elena, it's true then that you're contemplating the institution of marriage? And if I'm not presumptuous in my logical deduction, this gentleman is the lucky man? Tell me, tell me."

Elena had to recover herself from Dr. Rico's whirlwind of superfluous chatter. She thought if she had not already known him for so long and had respect for his legal ability, she would have figured him for a babbling idiot. "Yes, Dr. Rico, Paulino is my fiancé, and I want to see if you could marry us. We've set a date next month on a Saturday—October 11th. I want to be sure that you're available. It will mean so much to me. We plan to have the ceremony at the plantation."

"Well, I have to see if I have a conflict on that date," he cautioned. He got up from behind his desk and moved to the door, talking at the same time, "Let me call my secretary and have her bring my appointment book, and if a conflict exists, I'm sure that for you, I can take care of it. Oh, it'll be a tremendous pleasure to perform such a lovely ceremony."

"We just want a simple ceremony at six o'clock in the evening," Paulino informed him.

"I'll be very pleased, let me see," he said, and shouted for his secretary. "Asuncion! Asuncion, please see if I have October 11th blocked out for anything?"

Asuncion played her role and promptly brought the empty appointment book out for him to see.

"Let me see . . ." He took his time, looking very carefully. "Yes, no, maybe, oomph, no, this can be moved . . ." After he handled each page with care, he, finally, after cleaning the lenses of his thick glasses, said, "Well, I can make minor changes to my schedule, and . . . Yes! I can do it!" he said, breaking the suspense only he believed had existed. "I'll be delighted to marry you. Now, let's discuss the details."

Half an hour later, Elena and Paulino left the office satisfied that Dr. Rico would perform the ceremony just as they wanted. Holding hands, they walked together to the warehouse store to order the liquor for the wedding party. A few customers were milling around, and Paulino recognized Mulato from behind. "Mulato, my good friend, come, come here. I'm back. Say hello to your best customer!"

Paulino held Elena's hand as she happily spoke to Mulato about the quantities of liquor she would need for her wedding. Elena asked about cider, she liked El Gaitero, but Mulato, the great salesman, told her that if she was having a bubbly, she should have champagne, and recommended Veuve Cliquot. Elena agreed, and before leaving, Paulino invited Mulato to the wedding. "Be sure you come early, so you have time to enjoy."

The sisters were thrilled. Elena told Julieta and Cristina how they had spent the day preparing for the ceremony and celebration, that Dr. Rico, the very busy notary public, was going to marry them, and that they were serving champagne. The invitations were printed and mailed. Elena went to the *pueblo* to call Paulino's mother, and invited her. In the portal that night, Paulino told Elena, "I'd like to help you with the wedding. What do you think if a group from San Joaquin plays so we can dance? If you like the idea, I'll arrange it."

Elena didn't hesitate. "It'll be fun! Remember, I was the one who asked you to dance. You were very bashful then." She nudged him with a coquettish grin. "You've lost it now."

The days passed, and neither Mike nor Don Miguel had returned to the farm, so Paulino had time to be with Elena. Together, they picked out their bedroom furniture set, including a new type of mattress that the salesman told them was the best. It was large, as wide as it was long. It was advertised as a "king size" mattress.

Mike arrived at the farm a week before Paulino's wedding, ending Paulino's extended time in Elena's company. Mike wanted to achieve certain goals, and one of them was for Paulino to do his job. Mike wanted to plan ahead for Maria Alicia's future visit, and made a detailed list of which rooms Paulino should clean, and ordered him to wear his uniform: black pants, shoes with socks, and a white Philippine shirt. Mike also had another task. Now that his father was going to marry Patricia, he was planning to live part-time at the farm. His father and he had not had an elaborate discussion of where each one was going to live. Mike's idea was for his father to use the big house, while he and Maria Alicia could move to a smaller house that he would build; or maybe, after his father's wedding and when he decided to move back to the farm, he and Maria Alicia could go to the States, and he would finish his master's, while Maria Alicia could take some elective courses in the business school. Mike thought that his father was going to be in great spirits and could now return to the farm. Dr. Paco's prescription for his father of finding the right person may have worked out for the best.

The morning of the wedding, Paulino woke up earlier than usual. He showered and carefully shaved the few whiskers he had. He had cut his hair very short and slicked it against his skull with pomade. He wore his white *guayabera* and a pair of white slacks. He looked like an oversized muscular *Santero*, ready to walk into the sea to offer flowers to *Yemaya*, the goddess of the sea.

Elena had chosen a white wedding dress. She had assiduously preserved her virginity for her future husband, and she wanted to make that clear.

Paulino's mother had made the trip from Cienfuegos and was staying at the *batey*'s big house, where Cuca entertained her like a long-lost friend. The wedding almost started on time. Elena waited for thirty minutes after the scheduled start time, anxious not to give the impression that she was in a hurry to get married. Her sisters added an additional ten minutes to the delay for good measure, but finally, everything fell into place, and the two sisters preceded Elena.

Elena walked alone. Paulino had Mike as his best man, and behind them stood Paulino's mother with a delirious smile on her face. The ceremony could have been short, but Dr. Rico felt obligated to exhibit his profound knowledge about the institution of matrimony, and declaimed in his deep, sonorous voice his trite and confusing thoughts about marriage as contract, commitment, and covenant. Mindful that the couple in front of him were nominally Catholic, he described with exemplary detail a linear history of marriage, its customs and traditions, commencing from the prebiblical, biblical, ancient Roman, and finally ending on the beautiful and sensitive parable of the wedding at Canaan in Galilee. Paulino stood next to Elena thinking of what a stupid, arrogant, pedantic idiot Dr. Rico was, while Elena stood enraptured, caught in his net of florid language. The guests became restless and the noise level increased. First, guests shifted in their seats, coughed, whispered, and finally, talked as they drowned out Dr. Rico's mellifluous voice. A guest left the group and returned with a bottle of rum tucked under his shirt, and passed it down. Dr. Rico, noticing guests hurriedly sipping the rum, focused on the task at hand and began the civil ceremony. The vows were made, the rings exchanged, the groom kissed the bride—in this instance, with perhaps more passion and at greater length than was strictly socially acceptable—and, under a shower of rice from Ceylon, the happy married couple walked among their friends, surrounded by a barrage of applause and laughter. The newlyweds stopped, as planned, in front of the multilayered bridal cake, which they hurriedly cut as they drank the champagne. Elena giggled when the effervescing bubbles tickled her nose.

Paulino's San Joaquin makeshift orchestra, a hastily assembled collection of guitars, flutes, drums, congas, and trumpets, enthusiastically played their version of a waltz. The newlyweds opened the dance, and shortly after, Manuel took Julieta by the hand and led her to the dance floor. Dr. Rico wanted to dance with Adela, the manager of the telephone company, but out of courtesy, asked Cristina first. Mike danced with Paulino's mother, who claimed to be tired after the first song and took a seat next to Cuca. As the celebration went on, champagne was abandoned for hard liquor. The band played new tunes and *guarachas*, congas, and *guaguancos*. A cha-cha ended up as a conga. The sound of the music and the excitement of the dance had melded disparate people into what felt to be one body—alive to the drums, all one in the semidarkness of the dance floor. Past midnight, the band began to play *boleros*, bringing couples close together. A few retired to the house to sit on rocking chairs to watch the flourishing of new romances. Mike saw Adela dancing with Dr. Rico. She had style, and that night she looked so pretty. Mike asked Dr. Rico if he could cut in and started to dance with her. Her dancing reminded him of Maria Alicia, and for a few seconds, with his eyes closed, he pretended that he had her in his arms.

The band took a break, and Mike led Adela to one of the small tables by the dance floor. Dr. Rico, with more liquor in his system than sense, confronted Mike. "Young man, I believe that you're spoiling our friendship. The lady you're dancing with tonight is a lady that I'm romantically interested in." With this, Dr. Rico made a small bow in Adela's direction, and she blushed. He turned to Mike again. "I understand that you have declared romantic interests elsewhere, and you're here tonight behaving in a manner not befitting a gentleman! Perhaps you're just passing the time with Miss Adela Martinez y Parraga! But this is a glorious example of a respectable Cuban beauty, and I would appreciate it if you would limit your interest in her to a strictly professional one. If you persist with your present conduct, then alas, I shall have to request that we meet as gentlemen in a field of honor!"

Adela giggled uncomfortably in a bid to cast the speech as hyperbole. Mike, who had had his share of liquor, began to laugh, and soon his laughter became uncontrollable. Ricardo and Fernando saw their boss bent double in laughter and made their way to him from across the floor. The more Mike laughed, the more Dr. Rico was affronted. "Young man! I'm talking to you! Have you not heard me?"

"Yes, I have—"and he continued to laugh.

Adela interceded, taking each by their elbows and guiding them toward a larger table. "Gentlemen, let's sit down and relax for a few minutes. It's such a great night and we're all having such a good time. Please, come, come—"

Ricardo and Fernando stood behind Mike, and seeing the muscular *vaqueros*, Dr. Rico thought that it would be more proper to follow Adela's advice. They sat down, and he opted to ignore Mike and continue his ardent pursuit of Adela. After a moment, Mike stood up and left.

Manuel had reluctantly danced the first waltz with Julieta, but as the night drew on, he was more relaxed and danced often and freely. Perhaps because he had drunk champagne followed by rum, or because he was in love, or because everyone was having a great time, he decided to make a toast and stood at the makeshift bandstand and asked the trumpeter to hush the crowd. The trumpeter hit a long, high note. The guests looked up and saw Manuel with hat in one hand and a half-filled champagne glass in the other.

"Ladies and gentlemen, I want to raise my glass to congratulate and wish happiness and prosperity to two people whose love for each other is evident and whose happiness has inspired those around them. They're great people, and I will soon have the privilege and the honor of becoming a part of their family when I marry my lovely Julieta. Now please join me in this toast—I wish Elena and Paulino happiness without boundaries, health without worries, and achievement of all of their desires, and to be rich, healthy, and happy."

The guests applauded, and then other members of the party made their toasts, some picaresque—at which Elena smiled and Paulino frowned. Finally, Paulino had had enough and led Elena outside. He anxiously waited outside by the car, which had been festooned with trailing cans and messages written in shaving cream. Elena went to her room and twenty minutes later, reappeared in a fitted blue silk dress. By then, the guests were standing outside, and the lovers departed to the ring of cheers and applause. Paulino drove as fast as he could, and he hit the Central Highway, oblivious to the raucous noise of cans sparking and banging at the back of his '52 Chevrolet.

30

Changes

A FEW DAYS later, Mike returned to Havana to find his father and Patricia busy in the preparations for their wedding. Patricia and Don Miguel had visited her family in Pinar del Rio several times, and the question was who should be invited to the wedding from Don Miguel's closest friends. They met the parish priest, and the notices were published on the doors of the church. Carmen was excited about designing a beautiful bridal dress for her little sister, and she also wanted to make the dresses for all the female members of her family, including her mother, her two other sisters, and her spinster aunt. She was going to be very busy. Don Miguel talked to Mike about his return to the farm. He felt comfortable with the idea. He would not be alone anymore. He had Patricia. The first conversation about how the newlyweds were going to live brought a serious discussion about Patricia continuing to work at the bank. She was not too happy about becoming the "housewife" of a rich man. She was not accustomed to a life of shopping trips, control of the household, card games with other ladies, *meriendas*, small dinner parties, and playing tennis. She enjoyed her independence. Don Miguel's world was one she knew about, but she had never thought to be a part of it. In the process of becoming Don Miguel's bride, she became closer to Maria Alicia, who did not fit the mold of a future society matron, either, because she wanted to work with her father, but at least she knew what was expected from a wife.

Mike started to have discussions with his father about what to do after he married Maria Alicia next June. Would he go back to the States to finish his master's? Meanwhile, he spent the balance of the winter season in Havana with Maria Alicia and his father. The national general election was about to take place, and political campaigns papered the countryside with cardboard announcements and posters of the candidates, sporting Madison Avenue toothpaste smiles. A story made the rounds that a television producer from Channel 4 was looking for the person who had told one candidate with a particularly dour disposition the joke that had made him smile for the camera. A comedian like that should be given a TV show of his own, he said.

Don Miguel was the only member of the family who was excited about the elections. He planned to vote, and pressured all his friends and acquaintances to do so. Indeed, elections came and went. The polls were open, but voters could have saved themselves the trip to cast their ballots. The elections were decided at the presidential palace and the military barracks of Columbia. The apparent support of the American government for the newly "elected" government dwindled to a trickle. The anti-Batista groups, composed mainly of the middle class and intelligentsia, were emboldened by the overt political corruption and the failure to have free elections, and launched a more powerful, and ultimately successful, propaganda war. The island was divided: On one side, there were the territories the rebels controlled, mostly in the Oriente province and in the mountains near Trinidad, while on the other side, on the eastern side, there was the kind of tranquility found in the eye of a hurricane. Life in Havana was difficult. Small bombs exploded throughout the city as a matter of routine now, and residents found it unsafe to leave their homes. The Friday and Saturday night visits to the nightclubs were abandoned. Families avoided crowded events. Everyone listened to the *Radio Rebelde*, which was broadcast from the mountains of Sierra Maestra, an area called "the free territory of Cuba."

In the middle of this tense situation, Don Miguel and Patricia got married. The ceremony was a tribute to Patricia's mother's sensitivity. The small church had a beautiful flower arrangement. The guest list was small; only their closest friends and family, and from Havana came all of Don Miguel's children with their spouses, except Julio, who was in Miami, and his grandchildren, and all of Maria Alicia's family. Ricardo and Cuca came, representing the farm employees. One exception to their rule was the minister, who came with his wife. Dr. Comillas sent a humorous telegram:

"You don't have to sin anymore. You are blessed. A big hug, Andres." The couple went to New York for a short honeymoon, and returned to Havana in the middle of November.

With the advent of the newly elected government, the new elected president would appoint new ministers. His friend Pepe approached Don Miguel to head the Ministry of Agriculture. He was honored, but was troubled, doubting he could be effective in the new government.

Patricia noticed he was distracted during dinner. "You look so serious. What's bothering you?"

"Pepe called, and I've been asked to serve as Minister of Agriculture. The problem is, I'm not sure I want to accept the position," Don Miguel answered. "Two representatives from the new government came by my office today and offered me the post."

Patricia paused a moment and then spoke guardedly, "It's certainly an honor to be offered a position like that."

"I told them that I was honored, that I want to help my country, but I need to think about it." Don Miguel tried to get a reaction from Patricia, but could not. "I wanted to discuss it with you first. If I took the position, it would affect our lives."

"Do you want to do it?"

"I don't know. I've never liked the idea of being too public or too political. I like my privacy."

"You'll lose your privacy," Patricia quickly replied. She stopped eating and leaned back into her chair. "Miguel, times are dangerous. I know you want the best for Cuba, but others may believe differently. They'll certainly wonder whether you want to use the office just to enrich yourself."

Don Miguel was slightly offended. "You know I'll be honest, Patricia."

"No one has been before you!"

"I'm an honest man, you know that!"

"I know! I know that without a doubt!" Patricia assured him. "But why be part of a possibly crooked government? What can you change? What good can you accomplish?"

"I have hope, I have ideas." He thought for a moment and then shook his head, "I just don't want to risk putting you or our families in danger."

"You're nervous about it, too, then."

"Of course. Our country is so divided. The rebels don't want the political process to succeed. They have their own goals, and besides that, even they're divided. We have Castro up in the hills, the university students in Havana, the old politicians who hate the corruption but are too afraid to stop it, and then there are those who are responsible for this 'crooked government,' as you say. All they want is power and to amass more wealth than they'll ever need."

They remained silent for a few minutes.

"Do you have to decide now?" Patricia finally asked.

"No, I told them I had to think it over."

"Good idea."

"How was it at the bank today?"

"The same, the same."

The next morning, Don Miguel called Patricia at the bank to tell her he had decided not to accept the position. Later, he called Pepe and declined the post.

31

The Letter

MIKE WAS IN his office in old Havana, adding the final touches to his business plan for 1959. His secretary came in to announce that a very shy young woman wanted to see him with a note from a close friend. Mike put on his jacket as he stepped into the small reception room. He recognized the girl, because he and Laureano had met at her home to discuss the group's plan to oust Batista.

"Good morning, Mike," she said quietly

"Good morning, Elvira. It's nice to see you. How may I help you?"

Elvira didn't reply, but kept gazing steadily at the floor. She looked different. She was wearing glasses, and her hair was a different color and was cut shorter.

"Would you like to speak in my private office?" Mike asked. Her eyes remained downcast as she nodded. Mike showed her in. He closed the office door behind them and raised the volume on his radio.

"I have a letter for you," she said. "It's from a common friend. He'd like to hear from you." She handed him sheets of airmail stationery, packed with Laureano's irregular, cramped handwriting:

Mexico

12 of December 1958

> *Amigo, I write you on the date of the* Guadalupana. *I hope you can decipher my horrible scribbles, as they will be the only way I can identify myself in this letter. First, I congratulate you! I have heard that you are marrying the perfect girl. You deserve a happy life with a good woman. With regard to this letter, you can trust*

the messenger. She is one of us. I know that my papers are resting in a safe place. I have left the hills of Cuba and am now trying to help our cause by raising money from the capital of Mexico. After I left the hills, I did not have the opportunity or the time to write until now. Now that I have arrived, I am sending letters, beseeching the aid of those who can help us.

As you know, I became an "ALZADO." I had to learn to live a different life altogether. First, I missed my daily shower; we had only cold streams to bathe in, but we didn't have access to them as often as needed. Our group started to have all sorts of facial hair, because none of us brought enough shaving blades. One by one, I started to eliminate from my daily rituals things that I had once thought were absolutely necessary, including shaving with my brush and my Yardley soap. I now understand St. Francis' poverty better. The first week was horrible. The mosquitoes swarmed around my face. I itched and was repelled by the smell of my own body. I cleaned my teeth with my fingers, rubbing them hard. We didn't have that much to eat. I developed a taste for canned tuna, bonito in tomato sauce, and canned sardines, especially those with olive oil. I now compare them favorably to the best Morro crabs at the El Carmelo de 23. I ate my first bread, real bread when I arrived in Honduras, but I'm getting ahead of myself. We walked during the night, and we slept part of the day under the cover of trees, and in those moments of solitude, away from the telephone, the radio, and the television, I had time to think. The air is very pure in the hills. We did not have alcohol, so when my mind soared, it did so for reasons other than Johnny Walker, Jim Beam, Jack Daniel's, Señor Cuervo, and Don Bacardi—all once good and trusted friends.

Our group was made up of men only, women were not allowed. We did not want to be responsible for their safety. They wanted to fight with us, but we thought they could help us better in the villages and cities rather than marching with us up and down the hills. We were different, yet had the same ideas and desires. We believed in freedom and felt desperate to be free. I never

fired a gun. We had a few firefights, and I believe we wounded a
few soldiers, but I was never a good shot, so they kept me in the
back, where I crafted many articles in my mind. As the time
passed, the articles became books, although they may never be published. Our group agreed on the important things. Despite our
differences, we were the same. We had the same ideals, dreams,
harbored the same fears, and believed in the same God. I met some
Christians in our group, not Catholics like us. I was ashamed that
with all our reading, our culture, and our knowledge of the classics—and I think that you are like me—we knew so little of the
Bible, just words we memorized during Sunday Mass. They were
a very small group. They came mostly from Havana and
Cardenas. They believed in Christ and wanted to help stop the in-
justices in our country.

Out here, I also had to learn how to deal with our less fortu-
nate members. I felt like Croesus, because they have worked hard
all their lives and have accumulated very little, and are risking
everything they have. I felt awkward when they asked me if I
had traveled. For them, travel meant taking a trip to Havana.
They wanted to learn, to know. They are very intelligent, but I
found that they resent the fact that we have been university students, while they struggled to learn how to read and write. We
have to change that. Our group was a mixture of students, some
professionals, some small businessmen, and a few guajiros that
were tired of the corruption and wanted a democratic Cuba. You
remember all of our meetings, our discussions, and our writings,
and that all that effort yielded us nothing. Here, I felt that, with
a rifle in my hand and the ability to fight for what we have always believed, I would be able to cause a real change in the way
my Cuba will be governed.

I'm sorry that this letter is so disjointed. You are the first person
I have written to. I wrote my father a note when I left for the
hills—the last he will hear from me. He was going to send me to
Europe to go to law school. I heard that he is furious and believes
that I'm lost forever. I received a package from Havana with

medications that were wrapped in newspapers. One of them had a picture of you and Maria Alicia with my parents. It's great that I have it. We rarely get our hands on papers. Initially, the government flew helicopters and small planes to spot us from overhead, but we were such a small group that we hid quite easily. The people who live in the hills were very generous to us. They helped us with transportation, food, and information. You know that they don't have that much to share.

Here's a strange story for you. My skin is too white for our sun. I grew a beard, wore a large hat, and I was still sunburned, so red that a member of our group who is a doctor ordered me to stay out of the sun! Crazy advice, of course, when one is living outdoors. He has a great sense of humor, but my skin got worse. In the end, on his advice, I was ordered to change from being a soldier to doing what I hate to do. I was told to go to Mexico and raise money for the cause. You and your friends, and your family, and the family of your friends, have it. My family is also included in that group. You all have money. I do what is best for the cause. I have to raise it. Call, plead, and beg. We need more money than we have. We have to be more effective than Castro and his 26 of July Movement. He has money, we don't. We have to get our message out and we are not succeeding yet. I shaved, looked like a guajiro, and one of our members drove me to Mariel. I was afraid I would meet someone I knew, but thank God, I did not. They took me to a safe house until they found a way to ship me out, so I left from the port in an empty lumber ship. I arrived in Honduras and was able to get my passport from my mother. She knew that I would be there. I have not written or called her. I'm afraid that they might intercept the message. So if you see her, tell her that I'm in good shape and missing her. I caught several rides in cars, trucks, and buses, and now I'm in Mexico D.F. doing what I do the worst, raising money, and what I do best, praying. I'm praying for you and M. A., and I'm also asking you to donate money to our cause. You can give it to our friend. I know you do not love money as much as you love the freedom of our country. Please take good care of E. She has risked so much and is not safe in Havana. I hope to see her in Mexico soon. One strong embrace, your friend and brother in Christ and in what we believe.

Elvira stood quietly in front of Mike's desk. After reading the letter Mike smiled at her and said, "Please sit down. You're safe. I'll be back in a few minutes. I want to give you something to take back." He went to Lustre's office and closed the door behind him. He wrote on a piece of paper and gave it to Lustre: "How much cash do we have in the safe?"

Lustre wrote back: "Five thousand dollars and ten thousand pesos."

Mike nodded and wrote: " Give me two thousand dollars. I'll pay you back."

Lustre opened the safe and counted out the cash. Mike went back to his office and gave Elvira an envelope with the dollars.

"Be careful. God bless you."

"Thank you," she said, and gave Mike a kiss on the cheek.

December

AFTER THE PRESIDENTIAL elections ended, the anti-Batista groups met in Miami and united against his rule. At the same time, the United States abandoned its support for the Batista regime. The CIA helped Castro with radio equipment to operate Radio Rebelde. The Red Cross International went to the war zone in the mountains of Oriente. The news from Havana and from the Sierra Maestra painted different and unreliable pictures.

By this time, Paulino had moved in at the Gomez plantation. Elena would be celebrating her first married Christmas, and nothing but a traditional Cuban *Noche Buena* supper would do. Julieta asked Elena to handle it, and she accepted. The menu was centered on the roasted pork, and the rest was easy: black beans and white rice, yams, yucca with *mojo*, fried plantains, and for dessert, *membrillo*, nougat, and coconut flan.

Elena picked the piglet in the pigpen, but now she had to have someone kill and clean it. Paulino, squeamish at the sight of blood, said he didn't have the correct knife or skill to do the job, and recommended Manuel, who accepted with pleasure, honored to be the man of the house. Elena asked Cristina whom to invite to the party, and to her surprise, it was Dr. Rico. The sisters always had exchanged gifts on the day of the Three Magi, the 6th of January, but Paulino wanted to exchange gifts on Christmas day, complete with a Santa Claus and a Christmas tree. He talked so much about Santa Claus, his red-and-white robe, his sleigh and reindeers—sorely out of place on the island—that to Julieta and Cristina, he became an absolute nuisance.

"In Havana we do this," "in Havana, we do that," he went on, day after day. Finally, they cornered Elena and pleaded, "You *have to do something about Paulino!*" Elena took him aside and lovingly reminded him, "*Querido,* you are not in Havana. You're now living on a plantation in the middle of nowhere. We know that our *Reyes Magos* will come on January 6th, but I have yet to see reindeer and a sleigh in Camagüey."

With such gentle coaching, Paulino bought a crèche and a Christmas tree and placed them in the living room, and forgot, at least for this year, Santa Claus and his red-nosed reindeer.

DURING A FAMILY dinner at Don Miguel's home, Adelaida asked where they were going to celebrate the coming of the New Year. In the past, the sisters had gone to the country club, while Mike went from party to party, but Don Miguel had not celebrated it since his wife's death.

"Papi, would Patricia and you join us this year at the country club?"

Before her father could answer, Jose Maria interceded, "Adelaida, Lourdes and her children are with Julio in Miami. Are you sure it's good for us to go out while he's in exile?"

Don Miguel said, "Why don't we celebrate at my house? Estrella will prepare the dinner, I'll hire a bartender, and Patricia will plan the menu. I have plenty of champagne and wine. Adelaida, bring your children, and if they get tired, they'll sleep in your old room. Maria Alicia, let's invite your parents, your sisters, and their husbands as well. Patricia, invite Carmen and Pepe. Jose Maria? What about your parents and your sisters? Do they have any plans? Invite them. Let's see whom else you may want to include. If half of the people accept, we'll have a great party."

New Year's Eve in Havana was a warm night. Carmen and Pepe were the first to arrive. Carmen wore her newest creation, a red dress copied from a Balenciaga design, and Pepe had a new Italian red tie to smarten up his old blue suit.

Patricia had supervised the table in the dining room. The silverware was polished, and the best crystal and dinnerware were laid out. The room felt festive with flowers, and the dining room table was set as a buffet with ham, turkey, sweet potatoes, vegetables, cheeses, and fruits, including the traditional grapes, all arranged on silver platters. Estrella had made *empanaditas*, ham croquettes, cheese balls, and boiled shrimp to pass around as *hors d'oeuvres*.

Patricia let herself into the kitchen. "Oh, Estrella, it's magnificent!"

"I haven't prepared this kind of feast in years," Estrella said. "I was worried I had forgotten how."

"I can't imagine a more beautiful table."

Estrella warmly smiled at her. "It's important for a family to celebrate together."

"Yes, I agree. I love it."

The white wine and the champagne were chilled, and rum, brandy, and the whiskey waited at the bar. The cocktail hour was prolonged. Some sipped champagne, and the group merrily laughed, forgetting their troubles for a moment, believing they could celebrate a New Year full of joy. The reality of what was happening in their country was set aside. They were nervous thinking about it. They believed that they had experienced similar situations before, but no one knew just how fast changes were occurring and their consequences. They were grateful that present events had not disastrously affected them as yet.

They ate and drank as Don Miguel served his best vintage wines. After dinner, Patricia played records, and they danced on the terrazzo floor of the back terrace as they waited for the New Year. They all had noisemakers and small funny hats, and a few minutes before midnight they rushed to the library to watch the countdown on the TV's Channel 4. Each had a handful of grapes to be eaten one at a time with each chime of the clock as it marked the arrival of the New Year. The help watched the TV from the hallway, and when 1959 arrived, Don Miguel kissed Patricia, and Maria Alicia kissed Mike, and even Maria, full of champagne, drew *El Gordo*'s face close and gave him a full kiss on his lips.

The streets of Havana were full of the sounds of celebration. Sirens blared along with the horns of the cars; buckets of dirty water were thrown out into the street to get rid of the bad things of the old year. At Don Miguel's party, the family and guests created their own cacophony for the New Year with their noisemakers, shouting:

Feliz año nuevo!
HAPPY NEW YEAR!

. . .

BEFORE MIDNIGHT, NOT too far away at Columbia's Cuban Army air-field, several army transport planes were prepared for departure. Their pi-lots had checked the weather for all the nearby islands and for the southern part of the United States. Finally, they left for Ciudad Trujillo in the Dominican Republic. The dictators had closed a deal. Batista carried enough dollars with him to please Trujillo.

The news of Batista's departure spread like wildfire among his closer followers. Some raced to the Columbia airfield to try to find a seat on a plane, others called their diplomat friends to ask for political asylum, while others, unaware of Batista's departure, were abandoned. Earlier that after-noon, a column of Castro's forces had entered Santa Clara led by an Argentinean doctor with a sparse beard and an asthmatic condition. He took control of an armored train, and after that, they only encountered light resistance. That night, Santa Clara became the first city occupied by the rebels.

DON MIGUEL GOT a phone call from Pepe around two o'clock. The party was going strong.

"Miguel, Batista has left the country."

"When?"

"A few hours ago. I have it from a very good source."

"Are you sure?"

"Yes, I am. He and his family, with some of his closest friends, boarded a plane at the Columbia airfield. I've heard a provisional government is being assembled. Che has taken over Santa Clara. Trinidad is now in con-trol of the Second Front of Escambray."

"Thanks for calling. Let's see what happens now."

Mike noticed that his father had a worried look after the short tele-phone conversation.

"Papa, what's the trouble?"

"Batista's left Cuba—" Don Miguel walked to the middle of the dance floor, raised his hands to stop the dancing.

"I heard from a trusted source, my good friend Pepe Torros, that Batista has left the country, and that a provisional government is been assembled until the newly elected president is inaugurated. That's all I know."

The group looked at each other with disbelief. Patricia stopped the music. Drinks were neglected. What had happened? They gathered in small groups. The men got together. No one was prepared for this outcome. They all knew about Castro, but his 26 of July group had not been able to call for a general strike, and they weren't the only group fighting against Batista. Who would take over control?

With so many unanswered questions, everyone decided that it was better to return to the safety of their homes. Mike offered to drive Maria Alicia, but after thanking him, she left with her parents.

Georgina, Estrella, and the bartender started the cleanup, and Mike, his father, and Patricia retreated to the relative quiet of the library. They could get no TV signal and Radio Reloj, the twenty-four-hour news radio, did not broadcast information about Batista's departure.

Mike suddenly became somber: What did this mean? What about Maria Alicia and him? He wished he had Laureano's phone number in Mexico to call him and give him the news.

His father was worried: What would happen to his friend, the minister? Would he be able to leave? Comillas, would he return? Esmeralda, where was she? Would she be released?

"My son, tomorrow is going to be a difficult day. We don't know what's happening nor how it will affect us. We have to be clearheaded tomorrow. We don't know how people will react."

Mike kissed his father good night and went to his room. Yet he couldn't sleep. He put on his robe, went to the library, and called Maria Alicia.

"I hope I didn't wake you up."

"Are you kidding? I couldn't go to sleep."

"Me neither . . ."

"How do you feel?"

"Anxious. I've never had this sort of unnerving experience before. Father remembers when Machado was deposed. Houses of the Machadistas were looted. Do you think it's going to happen this time?"

"I don't know. I'm happy that we're having a change, because we had to have it, but my father is worried. He's experienced upheavals before." Her voice changed as she considered what it meant to her. "This time it might be different. I feel optimistic. We needed the change."

"Let's pray we'll have a better group of leaders. Maybe everything will change for the better."

"You know what I think. Maybe all the talks we've had in the past, the meetings, the thinking, and the articles will create a better Cuba. I have to go back to the farm. Paulino and Fernando are going to be very happy. I don't know what's going to happen to our sergeant, though. As soon as he knows, he'll go into hiding, but where?"

"Father told Mother on the way back that this is the best thing that's happened to Cuba. He also wants to go back to his plantations and sugar mill. He hasn't heard anything from his managers."

"I haven't heard from Ricardo, either, but there's no phone at the farm. Maybe I'll get a telegram tomorrow."

"Mike, you should get some sleep. Tomorrow is going to be quite a day."

"Love you, good night."

"Love you, too," as she hung up the phone.

HAVANA SLOWLY FOUND out about Batista's departure. The G2 station where Fernando had been held was ransacked. The streets became filled with people, many who wore red shirts with black slacks or skirts. Young people drove in their cars, waving Cuban flags and shouting, "Batista is gone. *Viva Cuba Libre!*" The police disappeared. Neighbors congregated on the sidewalks in front of their houses as flags hung from their balconies.

Mike couldn't sleep. He wandered to the back terrace with a glass of milk in his hand, sat down, and took a sip. The moon faintly illuminated the grounds, outlining the mango and avocado trees in the backyard. He thought: We're starting a new era. Maybe Cuba will be democratic again. Maybe we'll have a good government. Maybe . . . but time will tell.

He slowly walked back to his room, and before he went to sleep, he said a short prayer to the Virgin of the Caridad del Cobre:

> *Little Virgin,*
> *You can talk to Him.*
> *He's your son.*

Please don't abandon us now.
We need you more than ever.
Have Him grant us what we need:
We need Peace,
We need Love,
We need Kindness,
Only you can intercede.
Without His help we are powerless,
Please don't forget us . . .
Amen.

Epilogue

MIKE AND MARIA Alicia married in 1959 and went to the United States after the final confiscation of the farm in 1961. Mike obtained his master's in Business Administration and accepted a position with a Wall Street firm. Maria Alicia became the mother of two boys, and worked in real estate, becoming a successful broker in Greenwich, Connecticut. She sold her business in the eighties. Mike retired. They have never returned to Cuba.

Don Miguel lived in Cuba until he suffered his first cattle and land confiscation in 1959. The government accused him of having been a counter-revolutionary. He was in Venezuela on a business trip, and hearing the charges, he remained. He worked in the purebred cattle business with former clients and died in 1980. Patricia left her position in the bank, also confiscated, and moved to Venezuela with Don Miguel, where she worked as a systems analyst for a series of banks. They never had children. After the death of Don Miguel, she retired and moved to Miami, where she now lives with her sister, Carmen, in Coral Gables.

Adelaida and Jose Maria left Cuba after the sugar mill confiscations of 1960. They moved to Jeanerette, Louisiana, where Jose Maria worked as a consulting engineer specializing in sugar mills. He is now semi-retired and works in Central America and Mexico, modernizing and taking care of sugar mill equipment. Adelaida makes frequent trips to Miami, where they have a small apartment. They have never returned to Cuba.

Lourdes and Julio were briefly reunited in Havana, but Julio continued as vice president in a stock investment house in Miami. Lourdes joined him there. They divorced three years later. Lourdes bought a condominium in Key Biscayne, and Julio lives in Coral Gables. Lourdes is very active helping the Cuban refugees in Miami. They have never returned to Cuba.

El Gordo and Maria remained in Havana, but after the passing of the Agrarian Reform, *El Gordo*, with Rigoberto, took his yacht to Miami and left it there. In 1960, after all his properties were confiscated, he moved with Maria to the Dominican Republic and became active in the sugar business. In 1974, they retired to Palm Beach. Both died without ever returning to Cuba.

Carmen and Pepe left Havana in 1963 and went to Miami. Pepe worked as an hourly construction worker, and later on, started repairing homes on his own. He died in 1982. Carmen worked as a seamstress and developed a large and profitable customer base of predominantly exiled society women. Carmen makes periodic visits to see her family in Pinar del Rio, bringing them money and clothing. Patricia and Carmen visited their parents in Cuba before they died. Patricia never returned to Cuba after the death of her parents. Carmen and Patricia now live together in Coral Gables.

Laureano returned to Cuba in 1959, and became active in politics and a member of the opposition to Castro. Because of his ideas, the Castro government considered him a counterrevolutionary, and he left for Miami in 1960, where he continued his relationship with Elvira. They married and had a child before he joined the training camps of the "2506 Brigade" in Guatemala. He never returned from the Bay of Pigs. Elvira lives in New York and in Madrid. Her son studied in the United States and now works in Geneva for an international bank.

Estrella and Georgina remained in the house in Havana. When Mike left, he left Estrella in charge. Mike provided her with a large sum of money. Estrella lived in the house with Georgina until it was confiscated, and she moved back to Santa Isabel de las Lajas, where she died. Georgina did not follow Estrella. She left for the United States, married, and lives in Miami.

Ricardo and Cuca moved to Venezuela when Don Miguel hired Ricardo to work with him there. After Don Miguel's death, Ricardo continued to work for the same cattleman until his retirement in 1985. Cuca made periodic visits to see her parents in Cuba. Ricardo never returned.

Paulino and Elena remained at the plantation. Paulino did not work for Don Miguel after March of 1959. He helped at the Gomez plantation, drove his taxi, and sold beverages and food at the baseball games played by the San Joaquin team. He had a fight with Manuel when he objected to the handling of Don Miguel's farm by the *Instituto Nacional de Reforma Agraria* (INRA). Thereafter, Paulino and Elena moved to Panama, and owned a small *bodega* in Panama City. Paulino continued to write. Some of his articles were published in Panamanian newspapers. He had a collection of short stories published in Mexico.

Manuel and Julieta married in 1959, and moved to the Gomez plantation. Manuel, to the consternation of Mike and Don Miguel, became an avid supporter of Castro, and after the first confiscation of their cattle, he began to work for the INRA, managing the breeding and selection of purebred cattle. After Ricardo left, he became the head of the large state farm that used Don Miguel's farm as its nucleus. Julieta kept the family plantation until the 1963 second agrarian reform. Julieta divorced Manuel in 1970 and now lives in Union City, New Jersey. They never had children.

Rita continued to work with the telephone company and married Facundo in 1960. His bank transferred him to a bank branch in El Salvador, where they retired.

Dr. Rico and Cristina were married in 1961. They moved to Union City, New Jersey.

Dr. Andres Comillas returned to Cuba in 1959 and stayed until the mid-1960s, when he left for Spain to practice law. When he returned to Cuba, he had contacted Esmeralda, who never called him back. He died in Madrid in 1975.

Esmeralda left jail on January 1, 1959. She continued to be active in the 26 of July Movement and was by hired the Education Ministry, but became disillusioned with the status of the reforms, and left for Mexico in 1966.

The Minister sought political asylum in the Peruvian embassy in January 1959, and went to the Canary Islands, where he died in 1976.

The Sergeant was captured by the rebel army and faced a summary trial in Havana. He was found guilty and shot by a firing squad.

ACKNOWLEDGMENTS

I WOULD LIKE to thank everyone who helped and encouraged me in writing this book. I have to start with John Guare, who, at a dinner one night more than ten years ago, told me to write, not to translate. Valerie Levy, read my first draft and encouraged me to finish it, while Patricia Arostegui de Cossutta read all the different versions. Phyllis Thompson Reid became my first editor, while she was teaching at Harvard, and Mary Alice Salinas made Mike talk. Juan Garcia de Oteyza advised me on the book while his wife Sofia encouraged me. My cousins, Enrique Falla, helped me write the Varadero fishing trip while Oscar Echevarria, reminded me of the Cuba we lived. John Payne's editing made it easier and faster to read, and Pauline Neuwirth is a pleasure to work with as my publisher and designer. The most important credit goes to my wife, Sondra Gilman, who forced me to focus and finish.